I0891589

BOTTLE Rocket

BOTTLE Rocket

KENNA KING

ANYA

Anya
An Imprint of Meredith Wild LLC

This is a work of fiction. Names, characters, places, and incidents either are the product of the author's imagination or are used fictitiously, and any resemblance to actual persons, living or dead, business establishments, events, or locales is entirely coincidental. The publisher does not assume any responsibility for third-party websites or their content.

The author acknowledges the trademarked status and trademark owners of various products referenced in this work, which have been used without permission. The publication/use of these trademarks is not authorized, associated with, or sponsored by the trademark owners.

Copyright © 2025 Kenna King
Cover Design by Anna Silka
Chapter Header Illustration by @art_of_azeem

All Rights Reserved.
No part of this book may be reproduced, scanned, or distributed in any printed or electronic format without permission. Please do not participate in or encourage piracy of copyrighted materials in violation of the author's rights. Purchase only authorized editions.

Paperback ISBN: 978-1-966300-03-8

DEDICATION

To: Cookie Dough Ice Cream

AUTHOR"S NOTE

This book may contain some deeply controversial opinions—namely, the unfounded slander of cookie dough ice cream, its flavor profile, and its glorious, chunky batter contents. I wish to make it perfectly clear that these misguided views belong solely to the fictional main character. They are hers, and hers alone.

As the author, I do not condone nor side with this heroine's heinous aversion to the frozen treat. In fact, I can only assume her opinions must be the result of fictional trauma, an unresolved dairy issue, or perhaps simply poor taste in dessert. (Tragic, really.)

Regardless, she is entitled to her wrongness. I, however, remain firmly and unapologetically committed to the belief that chunks of cookie dough swirling in vanilla are proof that the universe occasionally gets things right.

PLAYER POSITION & NUMBER

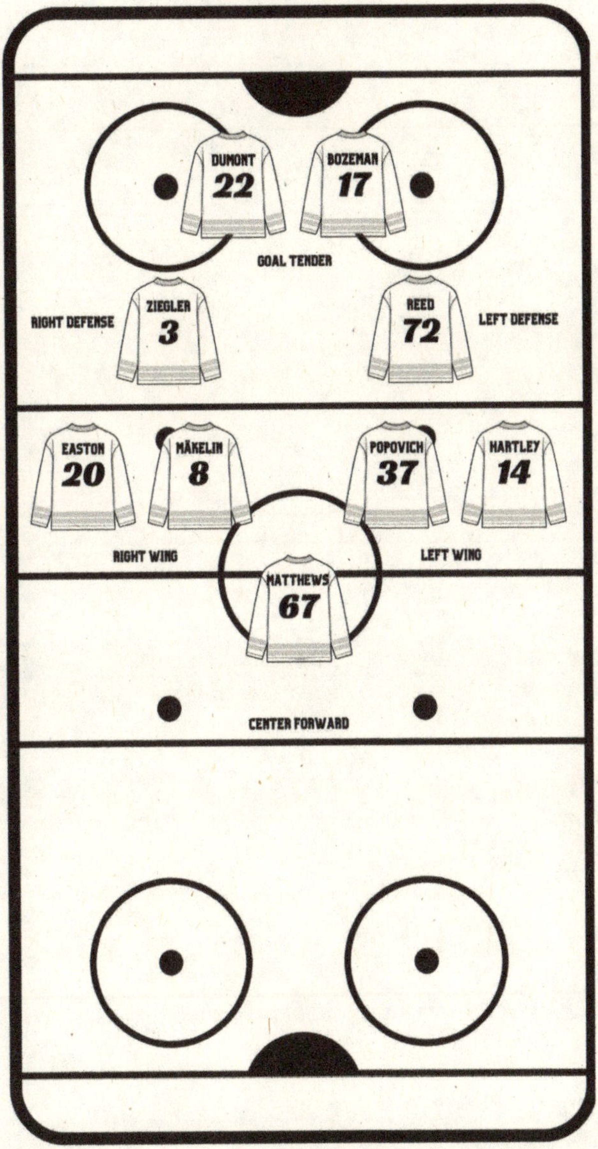

CHAPTER ONE

Vivi

Five minutes until I marry a man I don't love.

The bridal suite is decorated with expensive taste. My future mother-in-law's taste. Cream and blush roses climb the walls in elaborate arrangements, their floral perfume mixing with the smell of hairspray and anxiety. Crystal chandeliers throw rainbow prisms across the marble floor, and somewhere in the corner, champagne chills in a silver bucket, untouched.

And then there's me, trapped in a hundred-thousand-dollar dress that feels more like armor than silk. I run my unsure fingers down the corseted bodice, trying to ground myself in the sensation of cool fabric against my fingertips. My reflection stares back, honey-colored eyes wide with something that looks dangerously close to panic.

God—how did I get here? But I know exactly what got me here. From my own doing.

"You're a vision, Vivi," the wedding planner, Natasha, says while adjusting my train for the hundredth time. She's been my only ally in this entire planning process. Working behind the scenes to tame down Genevieve Holiday's "vision" for her firstborn's wedding. Keeping an eye on my reaction whenever my future mother-in-law suggested more flowers, dove releasing after our vows, a larger guest count. I'd just smile and nod her on. She needs this commission, and I'm the only one who knows why.

"Absolutely perfect," she tells me, knowing full well that Genevieve picked out this dress and not me.

Perfect.

The word everyone's been throwing at me since the engagement.

Perfect match. Perfect merger. Perfect optics.

The seven-carat ring catches the light, throwing sparkles across the wall like a disco ball of bad decisions. It's a Holiday family heirloom—fourth generation. Jameson didn't pick it. His mother did. Because God forbid her son's reputation-cleansing bride wear anything less than the price of a home in the Bellevue area.

"Five minutes!" The venue coordinator's voice carries through the heavy wooden door, making my heart stutter.

"Okay, thank you. We're almost ready in here," Natasha calls back and then smiles at me in the reflection of the mirror. "I'm going to head over to the groom's room and make sure they all file out before your cue so that Jameson doesn't catch a glimpse of you before you're walking down the aisle. Your father is standing at the double doors, greeting guests as they come through. He'll be ready to walk you down the aisle when you are."

Conrad Newport. My ex-stepfather but the only real father I've ever known. The man who fought to let me keep his name even after my mother left him—his third wife, though she should have seen that coming. Still, he gave me more stability than my birth father ever did. A man I've never met.

I turn back toward Natasha and grab her hand before she heads for the door. To be fair, this wedding has probably been a wedding from hell for her. With my future mother-in-law being the closest thing to a Bridezilla, Natasha has been running herself ragged trying to please Genevieve's every wish for her son's wedding. And Jameson has barely acknowledged Natasha's presence as if the wedding details are a bore and an inconvenience, keeping him from closing on a merger overseas for a cake tasting.

God help Jameson's other four siblings. They're next in line to be married off to whichever dynasty heir the Holidays pick to boost their influence among Seattle's elite. Not that I can judge. I'm marrying a Holiday for the same reason. My wedding is just as much a calculated transaction as theirs will be.

If Natasha nails this one, Mrs. Holiday promised her the rest of the siblings' weddings too. That means a massive commission—and a shot at making her firm the go-to wedding planner for the rich and famous.

A lot's riding on this. The red splotches climbing up Natasha's chest and her flushed ears say what her smile won't: She's barely holding it together.

"Just in case I don't get a chance to tell you this. I appreciate everything you've done. The wedding is gorgeous, and you're doing a terrific job today."

Her cheeks pinken, and her eyes begin to well with unshed tears. "Thank you for saying that. If I lose this account, my boss will probably fire me," she gives a nervous laugh. "But today is about you. Good luck out there."

"And good luck heading for the grooms' room. Don't pay Jameson any mind. He has a lot riding on a new merger he's working on. Don't take it personally," I tell her.

She squeezes my hand and then opens her mouth. There's a hesitation in her eyes. "I know I shouldn't be saying this ... but I can't help but feel that you're too nice for—" and then she stops, clamps her eyes shut, and shakes her head.

"Too nice for what?" Am I crazy to think she was about to say, "You're too nice for Jameson" or "for the Holiday family"? But neither are true in my case. I was raised for this lifestyle—these people—and my company will now have the capital to go public with the funds and influence that being married to a Holiday will bring me. I've let go of the dream of a white picket fence and married for love like my sister Isla has accomplished.

And I can't blame anyone for this decision. I've made it for my business, and the board members are ecstatic. It will all be worth it.

The moment she walks out the door, my stomach lurches.

Five minutes until I marry Seattle's most eligible bachelor. Five minutes until I secure my company's future. Five minutes until I prove to my father that I did it all without his precious Newport money.

Even if it means trading my dreams of a real family for a manufactured future.

Because who am I kidding? Jameson is handsome, wealthy, and from the outside, this looks like a fairytale. Only, there's no spark between us, no fire.

Six months of engagement have brought nothing but polite dinners, careful touches, and a gifted Bellevue mansion as a wedding gift from Genevieve—all part of the perfect image we're selling, though we're secretly in separate living situations. He moved into the Bellevue mansion, while I still sleep every night in my townhouse. We haven't even slept together yet, both of us too focused on maintaining the facade of a love match for his family's expectations.

I have no idea what he looks like without his shirt on, besides the old tabloid photos I've seen in the past of his yacht with one woman or another. The exact image of a Playboy billionaire that Genevieve is trying to rebrand with our union. I have no idea how he stores his toothbrush in his bathroom. I barely even know how he takes his coffee because his assistant is never far off to take care of it for him.

Our marriage is practical. It makes sense for both parties.

In the future, children will come, a requirement of the Holiday family, and maybe even love—or a version of fondness that makes sense considering our situation. I already have a lot of respect for Jameson and what he has done for the family—the deals he's closed—and the fact that he's willing to marry a stranger to keep his family trust growing. Not to mention that he's a fierce business negotiator and on paper ... Well, we're kind of a perfect match.

The door opens again, and Isla enters with Yvanne, my good-friend-from-college-turned-my-lawyer, both radiant in ice-blue silk. My sister's eyes scan my face with the knowing look she's had since our parents married in middle school. We couldn't look more different—her soft blonde beauty contrasting sharply with my dark hair and olive skin from my mother's Brazilian side. But we've never felt like "step" anything. She's just my sister, my rock, the one person who's always seen through my carefully constructed business-as-usual facade.

"You okay?" she asks softly, moving closer.

"Fine." The smile feels plastic on my face. "Just nervous."

"Vivi." She takes my hands, her blue eyes turn serious. "If you're having second thoughts, say the word. Kaenan can grab Berkeley and Oliver, and we'll be gone before anyone realizes. Just like that—poof, runaway bride."

The temptation hits so hard my knees actually shake. And my knees never shake. I'm Vivi Ann Newport, the woman who built a college nanny service into a nine-figure staffing empire. I don't do uncertainty.

"I promise, I'm fine." I lie, squeezing her hands. "I just need a minute."

She searches my face but nods, slipping out with Yvanne. Another knock comes immediately.

My heart jumps. Maybe it's Jameson. Maybe he feels this wrongness too. For the first time, I feel a sense of relief, but then my heart sinks when I see who comes through the door.

It's his mother.

"You look radiant, my dear." Genevieve Holiday's voice is smooth and precise. "The perfect bride for the perfect future that awaits us."

Us. Always us.

Never me. Never him.

"Mrs. Holiday," I start, "I need to see Jameson."

I just need to see him—talk this out. I know he'll rationalize all of this—make sense out of what we are doing and why this is a good idea. He's emotionally solid, confident, and seems to know all the right things to say when we're being interviewed by the media or when people ask him for business advice. He's exactly the kind of partner I need beside me. I would follow him into any boardroom, any negotiation without hesitation. But marriage?

I need to hear him say it.

I need to hear him say that this marriage is a good idea because then, I might believe it.

"Absolutely not." She adjusts my veil with careful hands. "We can't afford bad luck today. The press is already restless. I promise you, Jameson is just as anxious to get this wedding underway as we all are."

Why does that last comment not give me the reassurance I need? He's just as anxious as we all are? Not excited or relieved.

This wedding represents everything the Holidays have cultivated for generations. Power, influence, carefully arranged marriages that keep their dynasty growing. The trust is very specific about that part. Marry who your parents choose or lose everything.

And the pressure and responsibility land on Genevieve as the matriarch of the family to ensure the right matches.

"Right." I swallow hard. "Of course."

She nods with a confident smile. "Good girl. And besides, you'll have a long honeymoon to discuss anything you want with my son."

The traditional two-month Holiday newlywed trip. Essential since every Holiday marriage is arranged.

I guess they figure each couple needs time to get to know each other. Our honeymoon won't be like that though. Jameson's already arranged meetings with potential business partners throughout Europe. Even our honeymoon is a merger, designed after Holiday Industries purchased enough stocks to make them *the* major stock holder in Newport Staffing Solutions. With my board of directors having made sure to put our CFO as the interim CEO in place while I'm gone for two months, I might for once in my life get to enjoy this vacation.

Maybe.

The door closes behind her, and I'm alone again. My hands won't stop shaking as I stare at my reflection. How did I get here? But I know exactly how. One careful step at a time, each decision seemingly logical in isolation. But the biggest kicker was convincing Holiday Industries to buy a major stock option in the company, giving us the capital we need to make our next big jump. In return, Genevieve suggested a much bigger alliance: Marriage.

Her idea made a lot of sense, especially since most relationships I've had over the last decade have ended in shambles. Not a decent relationship in my thirty-two years of life.

I dated Demetri for almost a year right after college, but he broke up with me stating that I work too much. Then there was Aaron who lasted two years but accused my success of emasculating him. And I could never forget Robby, who was more than happy to spend my money on the side woman he lied to about being some big time CEO for a Fortune 500 company when he was a struggling comic who never booked many gigs.

The most attractive part of marrying Jameson is no more loser ex-boyfriends. None of that would happen with him. His family is worth billions, he works just as hard as I do within Holiday Industries, and he's looking for a partner, not a bank account.

Another knock, and this time it's my mother. Her dark hair is swept up elegantly, thinner than I remember but still beautiful. She's aged in the last fifteen years but, then again, I guess we all have. Her warm smile hits me like Brazilian sunshine, so different from the cold Newport wealth I've surrounded myself with.

"My baby girl." She reaches for me, eyes sparkling. "Look at you."

"Mommy." The childhood name slips out before I can stop it. Strange how I can run a multimillion-dollar company but still feel small around her.

"How do you feel?" She asks, that maternal intuition I've missed since she moved to Brazil after catching my father with the housekeeper—affair number three in six years of marriage.

"Like a bride," I lie, but my voice wavers.

"Well, you are the most beautiful thing I've ever seen." Her hands smooth down the silk material of my full skirt with beading all around. I look like a cupcake—a very expensive, high-fashion cupcake.

"Did you bring Javier?" I ask about her newest husband, though I already know the answer.

She's on marriage number four since leaving my father. Each one has taken her further from the single mom who used to braid my hair and tell me stories about growing up in Brazil and moving here with her family when she was four.

Back then, she was still the woman who loved me fiercely, even after my worthless college boyfriend of a father abandoned her the moment he found out she was pregnant with me.

I've never met the so-called "sperm donor," and I hope I never do.

"No, he said he couldn't make the trip. Work, you know how it is." She rolls her eyes. "But lucky for me, your father saved me a seat next to him after he walks you down the aisle." Her voice drips with sarcasm.

She still can't stand my father, but at least they always pretend to be civil in front of people they want to keep up appearances for. And that would include everyone one of the rich, famous, and powerful guests attending this wedding.

"You saw Dad?" I ask, though I already know he's waiting for me at the double doors to walk me down and give me away. He might be the one person who's more excited about this wedding than Genevieve.

The Newport and Holiday wedding. Two titan families, merging.

He sent seven dozen roses to my townhouse when he heard I was marrying a Holiday. After all my efforts to prove I could succeed without his money and connections, I'd ended up choosing exactly the kind of man he would have handpicked for me.

Ironic. Isn't it?

"I did, and I have never seen him happier." Her eyes narrow slightly. "He's thrilled with your marriage choice ... which is exactly why it has me concerned."

I suck in my lower lip, studying the intricate beading at the hem of my gown. Anything to avoid her knowing gaze.

"I know Dad's happy about it. But that should be a good sign."

She slides her finger under my chin, forcing me to meet her eyes. "You're marrying this Jamie guy because you want to, right? Not to please your father?"

The question lands like a slap. She knows about Isla's situation—she even flew in for Isla's wedding to Kaenan, one of her rare trips back. She saw firsthand how our father's attempt to control Isla's company and force her into a marriage of convenience almost destroyed their relationship.

"It's Jameson," I correct automatically. "And no ... this is for me."

But her words burrow deep, taking root where I've buried all my doubts. After everything I've done to prove myself worthy of the Newport name I wasn't born with—am I still that desperate little girl seeking daddy's approval?

And is right now really the best time to decide to unpack all of this?

"Two-minute warning!" The coordinator calls through the door.

My mother kisses my cheek, her familiar perfume bringing back memories of simpler times.

"Forget I said anything. I love you, baby girl. Enjoy your day. If anyone deserves happiness... it's you." She pauses at the door. "And remember...if this doesn't work out, there's always wedding number two."

The words echo as the door closes, as if divorcing my first husband is a given. As if first marriages are always doomed from the start. I guess in the world that my father and my mother live in, that's true, but it's not the fantasy I've had in my head. Not that anything about marrying Jameson is a fantasy.

My heart pounds against my ribs as reality crashes in. What am I doing?

Before I can think, I'm moving. Grabbing fistfuls of silk and yanking off Jameson's ring, leaving it on the coffee table. The feeling of an empty ring finger finally has me taking in a deep breath, filling my lungs with oxygen as I had been slowly suffocating before now.

I burst through the door. No time for my phone or the honeymoon bag waiting in the limo, prepared to take Jameson and me to the private airstrip after the reception. The EXIT sign's red glow beckons like salvation.

February air hits my bare shoulders like a wake-up slap. Seattle's downpour soaks into the dress and veil, making each step heavier as I run, my vision blurring with running mascara as I search the parking lot for my way out. Violin wedding music fades behind me, replaced by the click of my heels against wet pavement. Each step takes me further from "perfect" and closer to...what?

Panic rises when I realize I have no car, no escape plan.

I glance around frantically for anything. Anyone.

A conveniently timed public bus would do in the pinch I'm in.

Then I see it—an SUV idles at the exit. I sprint for it in five-inch heels.

Thank God I'm a veteran in stilettos.

"Stop!" I yell through the rain, struggling with yards of wet, heavy silk, ripping off my veil that's yanking against my hair.

For all I know, the driver is a serial killer, but with my heart beating in my throat, the only escape I care about right now is the one from my own wedding.

I yank the side passenger door wide open and immediately try to stuff myself inside.

I glance barely at the driver sitting in the driver's seat catty-corner from me. A look of pure confusion on his face.

Then I realize something...I know him.

Forest green eyes meet mine. Ex-military. Tatted up left winger for the Hawkeyes. My brother-in-law's assistant coach for the Little Hawks. Trey Hartley.

CHAPTER TWO

Vivi

Trey Hartley ...

The man who, despite barely exchanging more than pleasantries at family gatherings, makes my pulse race more in one look than Jameson has in six months of engagement. Six months of polite dinners and awkward kisses in front of the press. But one glimpse of those forest green eyes and suddenly I'm achingly aware of every inch of skin beneath this dress.

He blinks at me, confusion morphing into recognition. "Vivi?"

Before I can respond, he's out of the driver's seat, circling to my side of the SUV through the rain.

"What the hell are you doing?" he calls over the rain that's now coming down even harder.

I ignore him, still trying to wrestle a hundred thousand dollars' worth of tulle into his vehicle.

"Trying to get out of here. What does it look like?"

"You're going in the wrong direction. The wedding's that way."

Can he honestly not see that I'm making a run for it?

"I know, now shut up and help me in. I'll explain later." I say, my foot slipping on the underskirt of my gown as I try to hoist myself up onto the step railing of his newer black SUV.

"Where's your groom? Shouldn't he be with you?" he asks.

"If I had to guess, he's probably standing at the altar waiting for me to walk down the aisle," I say.

There's a slight pause as if I stunned him, and then I hear his voice again behind me.

"Did he hurt you?" he asks, his voice thick with concern.

"Did he what?" I ask.

"Did he hurt you, Vivi? Do I need to go back there and take care of it?" he asks. "I swear to God...if he laid a finger on you, I'll..."

He doesn't have to finish that sentence because from what I know about Trey's time as a Night Stalker for the US Army Special Operations Forces, I can only guess what he would do to Jameson.

Before I can get a word out, Trey pivots on his heel, the set of his shoulders promising he's about to storm back into that wedding venue like the Terminator and level Jameson's entire wedding party.

"No, Trey!" I grab his arm, my voice sharp with panic, fingers tightening into the tattooed flesh of his muscular bicep before he can take another step.

The image flashes in my mind—Trey going full special forces, hockey-enforcer mode on anyone who dared hurt me.

It's terrifying.

It's thrilling.

And it warms places in me I shouldn't admit out loud.

Jameson doesn't deserve it. He doesn't deserve any of this.

Trey turns back to me, his eyes locking on mine. The look is darker now, edged with something dangerous—protective instinct like a switch he can't turn off. That's when I notice it. The hearing aid in his left ear.

I've never asked, but Isla told me once about the helicopter crash overseas, how it almost killed him. The device should make him seem more human—vulnerable. But on Trey Hartley, it only underscores the truth I've come to know watching him play for the Hawkeyes.

He's invincible.

"He didn't hurt me. I swear. I just can't do it. I need to get out of here, please."

He lets out a heavy sigh. "I can't believe I'm helping you do this," he mutters, and then suddenly his hands are on my hips, lifting me effortlessly into the backseat. I yelp as he tosses the rest of my train in after me and slams the door.

The scent of leather seats and his cologne wraps around me—nothing like Jameson's carefully selected designer fragrance. Everything about Trey is raw, unpolished, and dangerous in a way that makes my skin tingle.

He climbs back into the driver's seat, and I check again to see if anyone is chasing after me, but the coast is still clear.

"Drive," I manage. "Please. Anywhere but here."

His jaw clenches as he slides behind the wheel, those massive hands gripping tight.

"Where do you want to go?" he asks.

Nothing instantly comes to mind. Everyone will be looking for me at my townhouse first so not there.

"I don't know," I say as I think through options.

"Where would you feel the safest?"

That question gives me an immediate answer.

"Isla's."

He nods once and pulls the car onto the main road. The wedding fades in the rearview mirror like a bad dream. Rain drums against the roof, windshield wipers keeping a steady rhythm as we drive in silence.

I notice the empty passenger seat with a girl's backpack lying on the floorboards. His niece's. "Where's Adeline?"

"Ballet. Dropped her before grabbing Kaenan's cufflinks that he forgot at his house." He checks his watch, the movement drawing attention to corded forearm muscles covered in ink. "I need to pick her up soon. I'll be a few minutes late, but I'll drop you off first."

I shake my head. "She shouldn't wait because of me. Let's get her first."

His eyes flick to mine in the rearview mirror, searching my face with an intensity that makes my skin heat.

"You sure?"

"Absolutely. I'm already ruining enough people's day."

The drive passes quietly except for the soft hum of the heater and the constant rhythmic drumming of the rain against the car's roof.

I catch him watching me when he thinks I'm not looking, each stolen glance making my heart skip in a way that no lingering eye contact with Jameson would have ever managed. I have to wonder if he regrets helping Kaenan now that he's stuck with a runaway bride in the back of his SUV.

"Sorry you got dragged into this," I say finally. "Especially when you were just doing Kaenan a favor."

He shrugs, the movement rippling through broad shoulders. "It's fine. Gave me an excuse to skip ballet anyway."

His comment has me curious.

"You don't like watching Adeline dance?"

"Of course I do." He runs a hand through his short dark hair, the gesture oddly vulnerable.

"But... It's just what? Too girly for a man like you?" I tease, trying to lighten the mood and distract myself from how aware I am of him in this enclosed space.

"No." His voice softens. "I like watching Adeline dance. She's a natural at everything she does, but the moms—it's a circus."

Right. Because when a tattooed, six-foot-five hockey player shows up at ballet class, the divorced mom brigade loses their ever-loving minds. I can't blame them, really. Even in profile, he's gorgeous in that dangerous way that makes good girls think bad thoughts. The kind of thoughts I definitely shouldn't be having right now.

"The moms are a problem? How exactly?" I press, partly to keep us both from dwelling on heavier topics, partly because I'm genuinely curious about what makes this powerful man uncomfortable.

Call it morbid curiosity.

"Me being there seems to cause a distraction, and I don't want anything taking away from her time to shine."

I can only imagine what it's like when women see him out in the wild. I'm sure he gets handed numbers daily, women flirting non-stop. He'd have his pick of anyone he wants. I've personally seen plenty of puck bunnies fawning over him at Oakley's and the times I've gone to a Hawkeyes game with Isla. His female fan base isn't small by any means.

Six-foot-five—an entire foot and three inches taller than me, of raw power, sharp edges, and tattoos—the kind of man I imagine the special forces deployed as a human battering ram.

He's the kind of man you'd want fighting for you, not with you. And I don't blame the ballet moms for wondering how that intensity would translate to the bedroom. I bet the sex is explosive—primal, in a way Jameson's careful touches could never be. The image of Trey pinning me against my bedroom wall, those massive hands exploring every inch of me ...

I squeeze my thighs together, mortified at where my mind has wandered. How can I possibly be thinking about sex with Trey while I'm still wearing my wedding dress for Jameson?

We pull into the dance studio lot just as class lets out.

"Stay here. I'll be right back." His voice is gruff, professional—a complete contrast to the heated looks he keeps trying to hide.

"Trust me. I won't be going anywhere." I gesture at my dress.

"Right..." he says, no amusement in his voice. He's impossible to read, but I bet that's what he was trained for.

What exactly was he thinking I'd do if he didn't tell me to stay put? Sashay into class in a rain-soaked designer wedding gown, dripping all over the floor, while every woman—poured into a push-up bra and wearing enough makeup to survive a hurricane—shot me death glares for daring to exist near Trey?

No thanks.

The last thing I need is someone tipping off the media that not only did I run away from my own wedding, but that I ran off with the Hawkeyes' left winger. As if this day could get any more complicated.

I watch him slide out of the SUV, closing the car door behind him and leaving the heat running.

He moves with athletic grace despite what I swear is a slight limp—so subtle I might be imagining it. I can't be sure if that limp is from the helicopter accident or hockey.

Alone in the heated car, I contemplate the ruins of my carefully planned life. Within minutes, the glass door opens, startling me. I dip down in my seat. After all, a woman in a wedding dress isn't exactly inconspicuous.

Barely peeking over the SUV's dashboard, I see Adeline emerge first, bundled in a large jacket with track pants over her leotard. Trey follows, her duffel bag in one hand and three women flanking him like perfectly coordinated satellites. All in tight yoga pants with their assets on full display. Of course they're glued to his side. A herd of horny dance moms circling a gorgeous hockey player, like a pack of hungry hyenas surrounding a water buffalo. It's a tale as old as time.

I smirk to myself, but when one of the women looks toward the SUV, I duck down so fast I nearly face-plant into the center console. The movement sends a ripple of tulle across my lap, and I have to bite back a hysterical laugh at the absurdity of my situation.

"Such a dedicated uncle," one coos as he loads Adeline's bag.

"Will we see you at Oakley's after the home game this week?" another asks.

"Probably not." His deep voice carries more easily now that the rain is a light mist. "Early bedtime for this one."

A chorus of "aww" fills the SUV, and I roll my eyes. Was that jealousy? It can't be. Or could it ...

Trey helps Adeline into the front seat. Her eyes widen when she spots me, but Trey gives her a warning look before he shuts her door. She giggles, and I wink.

"I thought you were marrying that Jameson guy?" she whispers while we are still alone in the SUV. "That's why Berkeley wasn't at ballet."

My heart twists at the mention of my niece. Another person I've disappointed today. I'll have to make it up to her too. I've really screwed this up.

"I was but..." I stall, the women's voices still floating through the car windows as Trey makes his way around the front of the car. How do I explain to a nine-year-old that our marriage was designed to be a business transaction? That Jameson and I were doing this for my company's future and his family's expectations—not love?

I'm not telling a young pre-teenage girl that I agreed to marry a man for...let's be honest, a boost to my business and social standing that would have launched my little college startup into something so much bigger than I ever imagined.

I'd die if Adeline or Berkeley thought that marrying for any other reason than for love was acceptable. In my case, I had given up on the idea of finding love... mostly.

Though I suppose if I had really given up on love, I would have accepted my fate and wouldn't have run.

Damn logic.

At the end of the day, I know why I agreed. Jameson would make for a good provider, and from my conversations with him, he agreed to be faithful and make this marriage work for the good of his family and mine. He would soon be the patriarch of his family and he seems like he's ready to take on that role. I know that marrying me—an arranged marriage—wasn't his first choice, but he was going to do it... for his family. And I was doing it for Newport Staffing Solutions, its clients, and the hundreds of employees who have put their blood, sweat, and tears into our company and deserve the best benefits and stock options we can offer them to support their families.

"Please tell me Uncle Trey stopped the wedding and now you're running away together!" Her eyes sparkle with romance. "This would be the best day ever. Can I be a flower girl?"

"What? Where did you get that idea?" I ask.

My pulse jumps at the scenario she's painted—Trey bursting into the church, those green eyes blazing...tossing me over his shoulder and hauling me out of the wedding venue in front of hundreds of guests. It's an odd fantasy to have all of a sudden. The idea of it is absurd.

Trey's never given me a reason to think he has any interest in me. Those heated, mysterious eyes seem to be his default setting. The man is practically being chased out to his car by a flock of man-hungry women who would be more than happy to keep him occupied. What motive would he have for breaking up my wedding when he clearly has his hands full of eligible women?

"Come on... You two would make the cutest couple," she says, her knee bouncing up and down. "And, oh my gosh, you could come live with us. My Uncle Trey just bought a house two blocks from Berkeley's house. It's perfect. Then Berkeley and I would be cousins. And the house has a pool."

Heat floods my cheeks. Married to Trey? What an image she's painting. "No, honey. Your uncle's just helping me. He's dropping me off at Berkeley's house after this. We're not getting married."

"Oh..." The disappointment in her eyes mirrors an ache I didn't even know I had. I chalk it up to wanting my own family... imagining my life in the suburbs like Isla, married to a man I love who's as obsessed with me as Kaenan is with her. That man loves her more than anything in this world...besides their kids, of course. That's why I started nannying for families in college to begin with. I love being a part of a family, and I've always wanted one of my own...a family with a groom I picked. Unfortunately, opportunities like the one I was offered with Jameson don't come around often. Genevieve Holiday made me a deal I would be an idiot to refuse, and now look at me.

Outside, the mom brigade continues their assault on Trey. I watch as they follow him from Adeline's passenger door to Trey's driver's side door.

"Such a bummer you missed today. Adeline was a superstar."

"Good luck with your home game this week."

"We should get the girls together for a play date sometime."

The words all meld together as they each talk over one another.

Finally, Trey seems to find a way to shake them off, giving a quick "see y'all next week" as politely but sternly as he can muster. His eyes lock on mine as he opens his door, and then he looks away quickly, but not before I see something flash in those forest green depths—interest? Or maybe that's the look of regret. I can't seem to read him at all.

He gets into the car and then puts it in reverse. We turn onto the main road, and reality starts creeping back in. By now, the wedding venue is probably in chaos. Phones ringing, social media exploding, my board of directors crafting damage control statements. And I have no cell phone to see any of it unraveling. Maybe that's for the best.

As I catch Trey's reflection one more time, those eyes meeting mine for just a heartbeat, I can't bring myself to regret running. For the first time in six months, I feel like I can breathe.

I just hope the oxygen doesn't run out when we reach Isla's house.

Trey

ADELINE'S GIGGLE breaks the spiral in my head. "You're such a great uncle..." she squeaks, mimicking one of the moms from the parking lot with terrifying accuracy, and then Adeline's eyes are on Vivi in the back.

I clear my throat. "I see you found the stowaway."

It comes out more gruff than I intended, but I can't help it. I'm not used to this kind of chaos now in my civilian life—beautiful women in ballgowns popping up in my back seat like we're in a rom-com.

Adeline lights up. "The wedding dress was hard to miss. Can we keep her? Please?"

"She's not a stray cat, Adeline," I say, trying to reason with her. "She's a woman. And she has her own home."

Even if she just ran from it like it was on fire.

"Boo...you're boring," Adeline groans, flopping dramatically in her seat.

Vivi laughs. That soft, breathless kind of laugh that makes something in my chest pull tight. I glance up, just in time to catch her looking at me in the mirror.

Her warm brown eyes rimmed with mascara just slightly smudged from the rain. But fuck, she's still gorgeous, and if it were up to me, Adeline would get her wish. We'd bring Vivi home. At least for a night or two until I can figure out what's going on with her and if she's in any real trouble, but that's not how this works. Vivi asked to go to Isla's, so that's where I'll take her.

I've barely had time to register what just happened over the last thirty minutes.

I take the turn slowly, getting us back on the road and heading for Isla and Kaenan's place. As far as I can tell, none of the ballet moms saw Vivi. The tinted windows in the back were dark enough to keep her shielded. My eyes flicker to the rearview mirror again.

She's still there. In the back seat. Wedding gown and all.

I could have sworn that I was hallucinating when I saw Vivi Ann Newport yank open the back passenger seat door to my SUV as I was pulling out of the wedding venue. But no, she's still sitting in my back seat ... in a damn wedding dress.

She didn't even see me when she climbed in. Just yanked the door open and jumped in like her life depended on it.

Would she have gotten in with anyone?

The thought leaves a lead weight in my gut. What if it hadn't been me? What if some jackass with bad intentions had pulled up instead?

Christ. She could've been hurt. Or worse.

She swears that Jameson didn't hurt her, but nothing else makes any sense for why she just ran away from a billionaire groom. The kind of guy that most women in Vivi's upper-crust social circles would have salivated over.

So why the hell is she in my car, headed to her sister's instead of to a life of luxury? It makes no sense unless something happened between Vivi and Jameson that made her run.

I'm not a guy who's okay with half-truths. She's not telling me something, and I need answers.

I shouldn't feel this pull to protect her. She's not mine. Not now. Not ever.

I've had a crush on Vivi since the first time I saw her—Oakley's, the night before the regular season started in August. She wore this pink dress that complemented her tanned skin, stealing every pair of eyes in that place, including mine.

I remember Isla introducing us while Kaenan hovered like a prison warden. Vivi smiled like she'd been raised on etiquette and champagne, and I stood there in my jeans with old habits from the Army still baked into my bones. Civilian life's been hard to adapt to.

I was barely a year out of the 160th Special Operations Aviation Regiment. Still waking up in the middle of the night, reaching for a weapon that wasn't there. Still sleeping on the floor down in the living room to keep my wits about me. Still hearing gunshots and the blade of my helicopter above my head. Still figuring out how to be an uncle to a grieving nine-year-old who'd just lost everything.

Dating wasn't just off the table—it was a foreign country for which I didn't have a passport.

Besides...the last time I had ever had anything that resembled a girlfriend... Well, I don't think I ever have. Growing up, we never stayed long enough for anyone to even remember my name, let alone meet a girl.

My parents lived like vagabonds, going from town to town, panhandling our way through life until the police or child services would start snooping around, then it was on to the next. No roots, no morals, just bouncing from one city to the next until we stayed long enough for people to catch on to my parents' hustle, and then we'd be gone again. And then high school came, but it wasn't about dating girls or partying with classmates. For me, high school was all about hockey and finding a way out of my parents' claws. That's where the Army came in.

And Vivi? She's basically royalty. Not just because of her name or her clothes or the way she carries herself, but because she's built of something rare. She has this...poise. Like the world bent to make room for her and she hates it, but still plays the part better than anyone.

Vivi grew up in a world I'd only seen from the outside looking in but never close enough to get my fingerprints on the glass.

And now here she is.

In my car.

In a wedding dress.

Her posture finally eases as if she isn't worried someone's about to catch her and rip her out of my vehicle. As if I'd let them get close enough to her anyway. Not a chance.

I steal one more glance in the mirror.

She's still looking at me.

And for a man who's spent fifteen years surviving off instinct, I know one thing for certain:

I'm already in trouble.

I hear her voice in the back. "I left my purse and phone at the venue. Do you mind texting Kaenan to ask Isla to grab them?"

"Yeah sure," he says. "Do you want me to tell them where you are?"

She thinks about it for a second. "They're probably worried sick. Yes, tell them I'll be at the house but not to tell anyone else except Yvanne."

I nod as we stop at a red light. I send off a voice-to-text

message and just after I send it, the light to turn into the gated community turns green.

The rain has mostly stopped by the time we reach our neighborhood, the same one in which Isla and Kaenan own a home. Big gates, pristine landscaping, a whole security team on rotation—not exactly the kind of neighborhood where threats linger in the shadows. It's one of the reasons I bought a house here too. Being close to Isla and Kaenan is the other reason. It gives Adeline a better sense of community here.

But it doesn't matter what the safety precautions are here. My brain doesn't register "safe" just because the HOA's tight.

I drive down the same streets I drive every day, but instead of going to our house, I hang a left just before—down a different street. Soon, we're pulling into Kaenan and Isla Altman's driveway, engine still rumbling low as I glance back at Vivi.

She hasn't said much since the joke about keeping her like a stray cat except for asking me to text Kaenan. She just sat there, quiet, hands in her lap like they don't know what to do anymore.

She looks so damn small right now, and my instinct to put the car in reverse and take her to my house instead is strong, but this isn't my decision, it's hers.

I shove open my door and circle around to hers before she can even reach for the handle. "Let me help you," I say.

She blinks up at me. "You don't have to—"

"Yeah," I cut in gently. "I do. You'll trip and face-plant in that dress trying to get out of here."

I reach in, careful not to touch her more than necessary, and ease her out. The dress is heavier than I remember but then again, adrenaline was pumping when I grabbed Vivi and lifted her into my SUV like she was a mission target I was shoving into my MH-60 Black Hawk helicopter to get to neutral ground and out of a war zone. Layers and layers of fabric like she's carrying the weight of every expectation that's ever been shoved onto her.

She stumbles a bit on the uneven path, and I steady her with one hand on her elbow.

"I've got it," she says, voice soft but obviously trying to maintain her independence.

"I know," I say. "Doesn't mean I'm not going to help."

I gather the train of her dress in both hands like it's a damn parachute and follow her up the walkway.

I notice the way her hair is up in curls, perfectly pinned in place, that I can only imagine would get her security checked through the airport at TSA.

We're halfway up the path when a voice calls out from the yard next door.

"Well, I'll be!" A familiar silver-haired woman in an aggressively floral rain jacket straightens up from her bare rose bush, pruning shears still in hand.

Vivi freezes, then offers a shaky smile. "Hi, Mrs. Fraiser."

Miriam Frasier. Miriam to me—but Mrs. Frasier to everyone else. I guess we made it to a first name basis at this point. "I didn't know you two kids were getting married. I thought you were marrying into that rich Seattle family. What were they called again? The Holidays?" The woman beams. "Well, good for you, sweetheart. Much better match, if you ask me. Did you know Trey came over and mowed my lawn most of last summer when Gerald was in the hospital for hip surgery?" she says.

Vivi glances over her shoulder at me, her eyes searching, "No, I didn't."

"Trey's a sweetheart," she winks. "And that little girl of his is the sweetest. Go Hawkeyes."

Vivi and I both repeat the sentiment in unison. "Go Hawkeyes."

"Always good to see you, Miriam," I say and then nod to Vivi to keep moving, my jaw tightening. The less we say, the better. "Your rose bushes are going to be the envy of the neighborhood this coming summer."

I hear Miriam give me an audible "aww, how sweet" and then stares down with pride at the bare sticks that will start sprouting leaves in a couple of months when spring hits. I keep walking with the time I just bought us.

Better match?

I shouldn't care, but something about that hits in a place I haven't let people reach in years.

When we're finally out of earshot, Vivi glances over her shoulder.

"Miriam? How did you manage to get on a first-name basis? I've known her for five years—ever since Isla moved in with Kaenan and Berkeley—and I'm still stuck at 'Mrs. Frasier.' Tell me your secret."

I shrug. "She says I remind her of her husband. He was a combat fighter pilot in the war."

"Really? Because I think it's more than that." Her brow arches. "I think she's got a crush. Do I need to warn her off now that she thinks we're married?"

I chuckle. "Why would you need to do that, Vivi? Afraid I'm going to run off with Isla's seventy-five-year-old neighbor?"

"Can you blame a girl?" She smirks. "We're practically newlyweds, and I already have to fight her off you. And no more cutting her lawn—it makes me insecure. Next thing I know, she'll have you in a speedo cleaning her pool this summer while she watches."

My eyes soften. She's teasing, but after the day we've had, I'll take it. "I don't think that'll be a problem. I only have eyes for you, darling." I gesture to the impossible yards of fabric she's wrangling. "Now, let's just worry about fitting this dress through Isla's front door."

She punches in the key code, but before the door can swing open, I lift a hand. "Hang on."

I slip inside first, scanning the entryway like muscle memory. I don't even know what I expect to find—Jameson lurking in the shadows? That mother-in-law Isla's been warning me about, ready to pounce?

Nothing. Just quiet.

I step back out and hold the door for her. "You'll be safe here,"

I tell her, voice sharp, controlled. The kind of tone I used overseas when I needed to keep a clean break.

Because if I let it soften—if I let her hear what I'm really feeling—I won't leave.

My fingers twitch with the urge to sweep the entire house before she goes inside. Top to bottom. Clear corners. Check locks. It's not rational. Not here in this neighborhood. I can at least say that no one was waiting in the front rooms or kitchen to ambush her.

Some things are hard to untrain. Years of military protocol is one of them.

"I don't know how to thank you," she says.

"You don't have to. Right time, right place, that's all."

I should go.

But I don't move.

Not until she walks into the house, her dress smashing in against the side of the doorway, but she fits. The last foot of her train passes through the threshold.

"Goodnight, Vivi."

"Goodnight, Trey."

Then I close the door behind her and hit the lock button on the keypad.

Only then do I force myself back down the steps, jaw clenched like it'll keep everything else from unraveling.

I don't even turn the engine on right away. Adeline is lost in a book she got from the library downtown, and I just sit there in the driver's seat, rain beginning to tap against the windshield again, wondering what the hell just happened.

And why the idea of leaving her there alone feels like I'm breaking a rule that's written into the marrow of my bones.

"Ready to go? I'm starving after ballet." Adeline says, shutting her book. "What's for dinner?"

"How about we order in tonight?" I ask because trying to pull something edible together for her tonight might be a challenge with my mind somewhere else.

"Oh, thank God," she says under her breath. I'm not exactly the best cook. "What can we order?"

"Whatever you want."

"Yes..." she says, throwing her hands into the air.

At least someone's content with how this night is going.

CHAPTER THREE

Vivi

I woke up the next morning to a memo email from the board with the subject line:

EMERGENCY MEETING at ten o'clock today

As if this weekend couldn't get worse, the board wants to meet about the runaway bride situation.

Although this is the last thing I want to do, it beats hanging out around Isla's while she continues to ask me questions that I don't know how to answer.

No clarity came to me after barely sleeping last night in her spare bedroom.

I head inside the office and slide my card into the door of the elevator to head up to the eleventh floor when I receive an indicator light I've never seen before.

I stare at the red light on the security panel, the same panel I've used every morning for the past eight years. The same company on the eleventh floor that I built from the ground up, turning a college nanny service into a multi-million dollar staffing empire.

"I'm sorry, Ms. Newport." Tyler, our head of security, a man I hired years ago, appears beside me. His usual warm smile is replaced with a forced one, professional and distant almost. "I'll need to escort you up."

"What do you mean 'escort me up'? Are we having technical issues with our card system today?" I ask.

Everything seemed to be working fine last week when I was here, but technical issues happen. It's part of working in a technological world, I suppose.

"It's just what I was told by Martin Howard. He should clear it all up in the board meeting."

"Martin Howard? You mean the interim CEO who's standing in for me while I take my—"

I was just about to say "honeymoon" when the realization hits me.

I'm not taking that honeymoon. I would have been there this morning. Waking up on the beaches of Greece with Jameson and the penthouse honeymoon suite that was booked for us by the Holiday's personal travel agent. But instead, I'm here on a drizzly Seattle Sunday for an emergency meeting with the board over me running away from my own wedding.

Fair enough. I'm sure they want to discuss how we will handle this in the press, and I have some ideas. First things first, we won't be needing Martin Howard in my CEO position.

"Right. He said that he will answer any questions you have. He just told me to meet you down here, Ms. Newport."

"You can call me Vivi," I remind him, for the hundredth time. over the course of his six years here as our head of security.

He just smiles back at me. He won't use my first name, but I'm just as stubborn and will keep trying.

We ride the elevator up to the eleventh floor, the light over the door illuminating quickly with each level we pass.

"I don't mean to speak out of turn, Ms. Newport, but if it's any consolation, I think what they are doing is wrong," he says.

My eyebrows furrow. What an odd thing to say.

The elevator dings, and the doors open just as he finishes. "What do you mean, you think what they are doing is wrong?" I ask as I step off the elevator and onto the eleventh floor. I look to my left where Tyler would be standing if he had gotten off the elevator with me, but he's not there. When I turn back, I see the doors closing again with Tyler inside. "Good luck," he says with a thumbs up.

Wait...what the hell did he mean by that?

I walk into the office and our front receptionist, Virginia, smiles at me, but it's not her usual smile. It's almost as if it's a consoling smile. Like I just buried a beloved family pet.

"Vivi, you're here. Thank God. I've been calling and texting you but your phone won't let me leave you a message. I tried your house phone, too, but I couldn't get through," she says, racing around the reception desk.

"My cell's been ... occupied." With hundreds of missed calls and texts from reporters, wedding guests, and most persistently, Genevieve Holiday. "And I spent the weekend at Isla's. Why, what's wrong?" I ask, not liking the deep frown across her face.

"They've been here since eight," Virginia says, falling into step beside me, voice low.

"Who? The board?" I ask, but I already know they are coming in.

"Yes, but also... Mrs. Holiday arrived with them."

"Of course she did," I say, because this day couldn't get worse. "No problem. Might as well get this over with."

"That's not all. The Holiday Industries board of directors are also here," I stop dead in my tracks, and she almost crashes into the back of me.

"All of them?" I ask.

She nods first, "Yes. All of them."

"Is Jameson here too?"

"No...haven't you heard?" she asks, her eyebrows scrunching together.

"Heard what?" I ask, unsure of where Jameson could be that it would be a shock I don't know.

"He's in Greece with..." She bites her lower lip as if she's scared I'm going to kill the messenger.

"With whom, Virginia?"

"With the wedding planner," she says in almost a whisper.

For a second, I swear I must have blacked out and heard her say "the wedding planner."

As in Natasha?

The same woman who can barely stand Jameson, who would physically cringe anytime he showed up for wedding planning. I'd spent months running interference for her—shielding her from the full force of Holiday family madness whenever I could—because I knew she had her own reasons for avoiding him. He'd been more than an ass, shooting down her questions about flowers or music with that dismissive, clipped tone of his.

So the idea that she would go anywhere with him—willingly—doesn't even compute.

"He left on our honeymoon with the wedding planner? You're sure?"

She nods vigorously. "I heard Genevieve practically yelling on her phone leaving what sounded like a less-than-happy voicemail for him, demanding that he return to the states and that if he attempts to use the paparazzi to get shots of him and the wedding planner canoodling on the beaches somewhere to ruin elopement wedding plans, she won't fight against the trust board to have him disinherited."

"Oh God..." I say, not meaning to say it out loud.

"Also, you should know that your key card didn't stop working—your office code has been changed," Virginia whispers. "I'm sorry, I couldn't—"

"It's fine." I cut her off, though nothing about this is fine. "I'll fix it all now that I'm back. Just...hold my calls while I figure this out."

I don't like how worried she looks. As if she knows more than she's letting on.

"The board is ready for you in conference room number three," she tells me.

I nod.

"I just wanted to thank you for everything you've done for me. You've been the best boss I've ever had, and I wanted to take a moment to say that," she says as she reaches around me and hugs me.

I'm taken off guard. Virginia has been with me for the last three years. I trained her having zero experience, and I was right to go with my instincts about her. She was worth the time spent training her. She's been a big asset to the team...but we've never hugged before.

This is new.

She finally releases me, and I smile at her. "Thank you for telling me. I do think we should discuss you moving into a bigger role in the future. I think you're ready for more responsibility. Let's discuss that next week, okay?"

She just stares back at me, tears beginning to well in her eyes as I start to walk down the hall toward conference room three. I'm absolutely confused by her reaction regarding her future promotion as I watch her over my shoulder.

What was that about?

I pause outside the conference room, squaring my shoulders, and take a breath through my nose and out through my mouth before turning the sleek back door handle. Through the glass walls, I can see them all—my board of directors mixed with Holiday Industries executives, and at the head of the table sits Genevieve Holiday herself, perfect in Chanel and pearls, not a hair out of place.

The room falls silent as I enter. Twelve pairs of eyes track my progress to the only empty chair—directly opposite Genevieve Holiday.

"Vivi." Richard Styles, head of my board, breaks the silence. "Thank you for joining us."

As if I had a choice.

"Given recent events," he continues, shuffling papers, and stands as if to address the entire room. He's tall and thin with jet black hair that's now starting to grey on the sides but he has a presence about him that demands a room take notice. "The board has made some temporary adjustments to company leadership."

"Temporary adjustments?" I repeat.

Martin Howard, the current interim CEO, jumps in. The polar opposite of Richard. Shorter, with more weight and dirty blonde hair where he isn't beginning to bald. "You were scheduled for a sixty-day absence during your honeymoon. The board feels it's best to maintain that timeline while we...resolve the current situation."

I never did like Martin, but he came with an impressive resume for the CFO position.

The current situation—that's what we're calling my runaway bride moment? "I'm still capable of running my company," I say, keeping my voice steady, on the verge of reminding Martin that we didn't make him take leave when his wife left him for his cousin last Christmas. "The IPO preparations are complete for going public, the Q3 projections—"

"Are excellent," Richard cuts in, his charming smile flashing as he attempts to squash the rising tension. "Which is precisely why we can't risk destabilizing investor confidence with leadership uncertainty."

"Leadership uncertainty?" Heat rises in my cheeks. "I built this company from nothing. I've never missed a target, never in all the years—"

"You missed your own wedding." The words crack like a whip across the table. Genevieve Holiday's perfectly painted lips curve into what might generously be called a smile. "Which, need I remind everyone, was a crucial component of the acquisition agreement when Holiday Industries bought the majority shares of Newport Staffing Solutions."

"An agreement I only accepted because—"

"Because you needed capital to go public," the head of Holiday Industries says. "Capital we provided in good faith, with certain expectations."

Like marrying Jameson. Like becoming the perfect Holiday wife to clean up his playboy reputation.

"The board has voted," Richard says, sliding a document across the table. "Effective immediately, you're placed on administrative leave for sixty days. Your accounts will be frozen until the situation resolves, and all Newport Staffing Solutions property must be returned, which includes your company Range Rover."

"Frozen? My car?" The word comes out strangled. "You can't—"

"We can and we have," Martin says, but won't meet my eyes. And now I know why I never had a good feeling about him. Something always rubbed me wrong.

"It's temporary, Vivi," Richard says, his voice calm. "Just until you and Jameson work things out."

Work things out. As if Jameson isn't currently in Greece with our wedding planner, ignoring calls from everyone, including his own mother.

"And if we don't?" I ask, though I already know the answer.

"Then the board will be forced to make permanent leadership changes, and Holiday Industries may take additional action as the largest stakeholders." Richard's tone turns a little more serious, but this is a serious threat he's suggesting. "You have sixty days, Vivi. Either you and Jameson marry, securing the merger and your position, or..."

"Or I lose everything." The words taste like ash.

"And Jameson will be disinherited from the family trust," Genevieve chirps in. "You both have a lot to lose."

"Your shares will remain yours," Richard offers, as if that's any consolation, considering I'd have a hard time selling those shares if Holiday Industries doesn't take it public. Not that I want to sell my shares—it just puts me in a tough position. "However," he continues, "operational control would transfer to the board's appointed CEO."

My hands clench under the table. Eight years of work. Eight years of solving not just childcare problems for parents needing help but now Fortune 500 companies that we staff and train employees for. Success after success, sacrifice after sacrifice, all built by my own hands.

Gone in two months if I don't marry a man who's using Natasha as a bargaining chip on a Mediterranean honeymoon.

"If there's nothing else?" I stand, gathering what's left of my dignity.

"Actually," Genevieve speaks up. "I'd like a word. Privately."

The parking garage is empty when we reach it, our heels clicking against concrete in perfect alternating rhythm. I head for my car, but Genevieve's voice stops me.

"You and I are going to have to work together, Vivi."

"And why do you believe that?"

"Because I have no idea what my son is planning, but this is a game of chess and he's using the press and Natasha as his checkmate. I think he might have offered her money just to stick it to both of us—you and me. He's trying to teach me a lesson at the very least, but in the end ..." She exhales, running a manicured hand over her face—the first genuine gesture I've seen from her. "He's made a mistake."

A mistake bad enough to make Genevieve Holiday nervous? That alone sends a chill down my spine. "What kind of mistake?"

"One that could cost him everything."

"The trust." Understanding dawns. "If he doesn't marry who you choose..."

"He loses everything. His inheritance, his position at Holiday Industries, his board seat." Her eyes lock onto mine. "The trust is very specific about arranged marriages. All Holiday children must marry their parents' chosen match or be cut off completely. It's how we've maintained our position for four generations. I've kept the board from finding out about Natasha. I hired a private eye to follow them around and make sure to pay off any paparazzi who get photos, but it will only keep us safe for so long."

"And if Jameson's caught with Natasha? What does that mean?"

"If the trust board determines that Jameson's actions in Greece show contempt against your betrothal, or that his misconduct damages the family name by gallivanting around with another woman, they won't hesitate to cut him out. They don't care if he's playing chicken, using Natasha to call my bluff," she says, raising an eyebrow. "What he fails to remember, is that I only have so much power over the trust."

"And if the trust pulls his inheritance?"

"Then his piece of the trust transfers equally to his siblings." Her voice hardens. "Which cannot happen. The board is already questioning my judgment. If I can't control my own son..."

She trails off, but I understand where she's going with this.

"If you can't control your son, they'll question your ability to arrange marriages for the other children," I finish. "And your position as matriarch."

"Precisely." She steps closer. "Which is why we need to fix this. Quickly, before anyone finds out."

Virginia knows but a quick text from me will keep her silent. She's loyal, and for now, she'll be my eyes and ears inside my own office that has turned against me.

"We?" I laugh without humor. "I'm not the one who took off to Greece with the wedding planner."

"No, you just left him at the altar in front of half of Seattle's elite." Her eyes narrow. "Which wouldn't have happened if you had just gone through with it and married my son like we planned."

Guilt twists in my stomach, but I push it down. "I left the ring."

"Yes, how thoughtful." She pulls out the ring from her bag. I stare at the massive diamond sparkling even in the dim lit parking garage. "I already cleared it with both boards. We are putting out a group statement that says that the merger and all of the wedding planning put you through too much stress and that you and Jameson have decided to elope in two months to the south of France, as was your dream to begin with."

She's pushing a narrative to feed the press. I never wanted to elope.

"Are you insane?"

"I don't know. Are you willing to lose everything?" She fires back and then hands me the ring. "You will wear this whenever you are in public so that everyone sees it and knows that the engagement is still on."

I let out a sigh. At this point, I have no choice. I take the ring from her...reluctantly.

"Have you heard from him?" I ask, hating the desperation in my voice. Not because I miss him—six months of engagement produced nothing more than a working relationship—but because my entire future hangs on his return.

"No." She puts her phone away. "But he'll come back. He has to. And when he does..."

"What? We just pretend none of this happened? That he didn't run off with our wedding planner while I ran out on our wedding?"

"That's exactly what we'll do." Her tone leaves no room for argument. "The press release is already written: 'Cold feet leads to intimate destination wedding.' We'll say you got overwhelmed by the publicity, that you and Jameson decided to elope quietly."

"And Natasha?"

"Will be generously compensated for her silence." Her smile turns sharp.

"Do you really think he'd take her out into public just to get the press talking?"

"I think my son is desperate enough to do something stupid." She straightens her jacket. "And I think you're smart enough to see your options clearly. Marry Jameson when he returns and produce a grandchild to carry on the Holiday name, or watch everything we've both built crumble."

She turns to leave, then pauses. "Oh, and Vivi? I suggest you find temporary employment. Two months is a long time to live on savings alone. Good thing you kept your townhouse because you'll be needing a place to stay. I'll have the moving company bring your boxes back to your place for now, but I wouldn't unpack too quickly."

Then I watch her head straight for her Town car with her driver stepping out to open her door.

I grab my phone out of my purse and dial Jameson's number, but it goes straight to voicemail. Then I send him a quick text:

I know you're probably mad at me, but call me when you can. We need to talk.

The Town car pulls out of the parking garage and back onto the busy streets of Seattle.

She's gone within minutes, and I stand there with a diamond ring in my hand that I can't seem to get rid of, an ex-fiancé who's not taking my calls, and a soon-to-be empty bank account that I'd better find a way to fill. And fast.

Perfect.

CHAPTER FOUR

Trey

The sharp crack of a hockey stick against ice echoes through the rink, and my body reacts before my mind can catch up. My muscles tense, ready to dive for cover. The metallic taste of adrenaline floods my mouth as my hand automatically reaches for a weapon that isn't there anymore.

But this isn't Kandahar. It's just Saturday morning youth team practice at the Hawkeyes' training facility. The only explosions here come from kids celebrating goals, and the only thing I need to protect them from is their own wobbly ankles.

I adjust my hearing aid, trying to filter out the sound of skates scraping ice, pucks hitting boards, and kids shouting. The device helps with the damage from the bomb that took half my hearing and my best friend, John Parker, but some sounds still slice through me like shrapnel.

"Uncle Trey! Watch this!" Adeline calls from center ice, her voice carrying over the chaos. She's working on her slapshot; the determination in her stance is just like my brother's.

I force my features into what I hope passes for an encouraging smile, though exhaustion pulls at every muscle. Three hours of sleep isn't enough to function, but nightmares don't care about coaching schedules or NHL playoff season.

"Looking good, kiddo!" I call back, noting her improved form. She's getting stronger, more confident. Tommy would be proud of her.

The thought of my younger brother sends a familiar ache through my chest. He should be here, teaching his daughter these things. Not me—the broken soldier who can barely remember to sign field trip permission slips and bake a store-bought lasagna without burning it in the oven.

With Adeline's nanny quitting on us two weeks ago to travel through Europe, it hasn't made anything easier. Luckily, between Isla and her mother-in-law, plus the two bye-weeks the NHL has, we've managed to get by for the last couple of weeks. But I'm going to need a nanny that I can trust with Adeline, and I need her soon.

"You look like shit," Kaenan Altman says, sliding up beside me with his clipboard. The sound of his skates cutting ice is crisp in my good ear. As head coach of the Hawkeyes sponsored youth league, the Little Hawks, he takes these Saturday morning practices as seriously as regular season games.

"Thanks." I adjust my hearing aid again, a nervous tick I can't shake. The background noise still overwhelms me some days, despite the VA's best efforts at adjustment. During Hawkeyes games, I usually just turn it off and rely on my other senses. I can feel a player skating up on my left flank better than I can hear him. Something you learn with fifteen years as special ops. You have to rely on more than sight and sound to get you through. "Rough night," I tell him.

He nods, understanding in his eyes. As a retired defenseman for the Hawkeyes and father of two, he gets that the transition from military life to civilian routines hasn't been smooth for me.

"Berkeley's looking stronger on her crossovers," I say, desperate to change the subject. His seven-year-old daughter glides past, dark curly hair bouncing under her helmet. She's the spitting image of him, same determined set to her jaw when she concentrates.

"Yeah, she—" His phone buzzes, and he checks it. "Isla's here. With Vivi."

My pulse quickens at her name. It's been a week since I dropped her at Isla's house, still wearing that wedding dress that made her look like something out of a Vogue front cover, even drenched head to toe from the rain. One week of wondering if I should have checked on her, gotten her number, done anything besides drive away like she wasn't my problem.

I guess technically, she isn't.

"How's she doing?" I ask, attempting for casual, but I'm sure I miss it by a damn mile.

"According to Isla, better than expected. The media's having a field day though. 'Newport Heiress Leaves Holiday Heir at Altar.' It's everywhere."

Of course it is. Because running from your wedding isn't dramatic enough without Seattle's gossip mill getting involved. I've seen the headlines myself, though I try to stay away from all media noise. Propaganda if you ask me. Especially when it comes to the military.

Not that I blame her. The look in her honey-colored eyes when she climbed into my SUV ... I've seen that kind of desperate escape before. In the mirror, every morning for months after the helicopter accident.

"Have you found a replacement for that nanny that dropped you on your ass two weeks ago?"

"Not yet. I made some calls, but so far no one's interested in keeping Adeline overnight when I'm out for away games."

"You should ask Vivi to hook you up with a nanny from her company."

The idea of asking Vivi for a favor right now when she just ran away from her wedding seems like shitty timing. I'd rather not.

"Uncle Trey," Adeline calls again. "Can you help me with my

slapshot?"

"On my way," I call back, grateful for the excuse to escape this conversation. The ice feels solid under my skates as I push off, the familiar sensation of ice cracking under me like it always has. Here, I know what I'm doing. Here, I'm not the broken soldier or the inadequate guardian. Just a coach teaching kids the game I love.

As I demonstrate proper form to Adeline, my mind keeps drifting to honey-colored eyes and a wedding dress in my back seat. To all the things I should have said, should have done.

Movement in the stands catches my eye, and there she is. Vivi. The sight of her hits me, knocking the air from my lungs. She's wearing jeans and an oversized Hawkeyes hoodie—probably Isla's—but she might as well still be in that wedding dress for how she makes my blood pressure skyrocket.

I scan her left hand automatically, searching for that massive diamond that was missing a week ago. She's too far away to be certain, but a ring that size would be visible from space. When she waves at Berkeley, I don't get the confirmation I'm looking for because she's wearing gloves. No way to tell if she's wearing Jameson's ring again.

The first time I saw her was at Oakley's, the night I signed with the Hawkeyes. She'd walked in with Isla, and I remember thinking she looked like she'd stepped out of a magazine—all long dark hair and curves that made my mouth go dry. A tiny thing with the biggest personality I'd ever seen. And I was hooked right then and there.

It wasn't just her looks that drew me in that night. It was the way she carried herself, confident but not arrogant. The way she'd make everyone within earshot laugh, her smile lighting up the whole damn bar. How she commanded attention without demanding it. Smart as hell too—I overheard her breaking down complex business strategies to some rookie who thought he could mansplain investments to her.

I considered making a move in those first few weeks after

meeting her. I was still new to town, new to the team, trying to get Adeline settled into our life on the opposite coast from everything she'd known in Florida. Then suddenly, Vivi was wearing Holiday's ring, and whatever opening I thought I had slammed shut.

Not that it would have mattered if she'd been single. Women like Vivi Newport don't end up with guys like me. Trust fund girls who summer in the Hamptons don't choose ex-soldiers who grew up dirt poor with nomad parents and barely finished high school before enlisting. Women who run multimillion-dollar companies don't want men who have to take sleeping pills to cut through the PTSD that keeps them up all night.

"Earth to Uncle Trey." Adeline waves her stick in front of my face. "You're supposed to be watching my form."

"Sorry, kiddo." I force my attention back to her stance, the other girls waiting for instruction. "Widen your grip a bit. Weight forward on your toes...yeah, just like that. Where's the net open?"

She glances up, analyzing. "Right corner—top shelf."

There's no goalie in the net right now, but I like where she's envisioning it. "Good eye. Now take the shot. Remember, your eyes guide your hands."

She fires off a shot that makes the net but misses her target... yet not by much. The other girls cheer anyway, the sound echoing off the rafters. My hearing aid whines at the sudden volume spike.

"Better?" she asks, skating back to me.

"Much better." I hold up my hand for a high-five then pat her helmet. "Just like your dad taught you."

Her smile dims slightly at the mention of Tommy. "I wish Mom and Dad were here."

The words punch through my chest. "Me too, kid." Every damn day. "But they're watching over us, so let's make them proud. Okay?"

She nods and skates back to join the team for a short scrimmage before we end practice. She's tough, like Tommy was. There's so much of him in her—the way she analyzes everything, how she notices details others miss. She's only nine, but sometimes she seems so much older. I worry about that, about how loss can age a kid before their time. God knows it aged Tommy and me, even though, as his older brother, I tried to shield him from as much of that as I could.

My eyes drift back to the stands. Vivi's leaning forward now, elbows on her knees, watching practice with genuine interest. She nods at something Isla says, and a strand of dark hair falls across her face. My fingers itch to brush it back, to touch her in any way that isn't shoving her into my SUV in her wedding dress. Unless she was wearing one to marry me...

"Fuck," I mutter, scrubbing a hand over my face.

Get it together, Hartley.

A laugh rings out from the stands—Vivi's laugh. The sound wraps around me like a vice grip. This attraction, this pull toward her ... it's dangerous. I'm barely holding it together between proving myself to the Hawkeyes, managing my injuries, and trying to raise a pre-teen who barely knew me when the courts handed her over. I spent most of her life deployed, and the rest living with the guilt that I left Tommy with our parents.

He was sixteen when I walked away, choosing the Army over staying to protect him. Despite that, he ended up becoming a NASA engineer. His wife was a labor and delivery nurse. They were giving Adeline everything I couldn't give Tommy—stability, safety, love—until a drunk driver ended both their lives in an instant. Adeline was with a sitter that night... Thank God for small mercies.

The last thing Vivi needs is a broken ex-soldier who has to watch YouTube videos to figure out how to do a French braid and who's already dreading the eventual period talk and tampon purchases. She deserves someone whole. Someone who can give her the life she was meant to have, not drag her down into my mess.

But when I look up again and catch her watching me, those dark eyes intense and curious, it takes everything I have to look away. The way she bites her lower lip, leaving a perfect indent in the glossy pink... Christ. I want to taste that lip, to feel it quiver with excitement against my tongue, feel her body melt into mine when I take her mouth.

"Hart!" Kaenan's sharp voice snaps me back. "You want to call that offside or what?"

Right. Coaching. Focus.

I blow my whistle and wave the kids back. "Reset at the blue line."

Adeline shoots me a look as she skates past. The same look Tommy used to give me when I was being an idiot. Which, these days, seems to be most of the time.

"You're distracted," she says during a water break, skating up to the boards where I'm standing. Her cheeks are flushed from exertion, hair escaping her low ponytail under her helmet.

"Am I that obvious?"

She grins, a smile that almost looks like Sarah's—her mother. "Only to everyone with eyes."

Sometimes I forget she's only nine. She's too perceptive for her own good.

"Watch your smart mouth," I say, but there's no heat in it. "How about you focus on your passing instead of my coaching?"

"How about you focus on coaching instead of staring at Vivi?"

Jesus. When did she get so bold? "That's enough out of you. Get back on the ice."

She shrugs, taking a long pull from her water bottle. "I still think I was right."

"Right about what?"

"What I told her in the car. After you picked me up from ballet." Her eyes sparkle with mischief. "About you two running away together."

A spark floods through my veins at the memory. Vivi in the back seat, that massive dress taking up half my SUV, looking at me like I was her salvation instead of just the sorry bastard who happened to be in the right place at the right time.

"You told her what?" My voice comes out rougher than

intended.

"That you two should get married instead. That she could live in our new house with the pool, and Berkeley and I could be cousins." She says it like it's the most logical thing in the world. "She's pretty. And she makes you smile. Like, really smile."

The observation knocks the wind out of me. Sometimes I forget how much she sees, how much she understands.

"It's complicated, kiddo."

"Adults always say that when they're scared."

I stop, staring down at this tiny piece of Tommy who somehow got his wisdom along with his eyes. "When did you get so smart?"

"I've always been smart. You're just slow." She grins up at me. "Like how you didn't notice Vivi couldn't stop watching you during practice."

My heart stutters. "She was watching the kids."

"Sure she was." She skates backward, a smirk that almost looks like mine across her lips. Great, now she's picking up my mannerisms. "Can we get pizza after?"

The subject change gives me whiplash. "Don't push your luck."

But as she rejoins the scrimmage, her words echo in my head. Vivi is watching me. The thought sends heat crawling up my neck.

"Ten minutes," Kaenan calls out. "Let's finish strong."

I focus on the kids, on correcting form and calling plays. Anything to keep my eyes from drifting back to the stands. But I feel her presence like a physical pull, drawing my attention no matter how hard I fight it.

When I finally give in and look up again, her seat is empty.

The sight shouldn't hit me as hard as it does. What was I expecting? That she'd wait around after practice? That she'd want to talk to the guy who couldn't even check on her after rescuing her from her own wedding?

"She had some kind of emergency," Kaenan says, reading my expression. "Apparently, running from your wedding creates some PR headaches."

Right. Because Vivi isn't just some woman who climbed into my car. She's Vivi Newport, CEO of Newport Staffing Solutions. The woman who turned a college nanny service into a multimillion-dollar empire. Who was about to merge with Holiday Industries before she left their golden boy at the altar.

"She doesn't need my complications," I mutter, more to myself than him.

"Maybe you should let her decide that." He pauses, studying me. "But it might be just as well."

I toss a stray puck into the bucket. "What do you mean?"

"I heard Genevieve Holiday hasn't stopped calling. Neither has the head of her board of directors. I'm not so sure that the whole thing is as wrapped up as it appears."

"You think she's going back to him?" The words taste bitter.

He shrugs. "I was at the wedding, standing with the groomsmen. When the planner raced up the aisle and told Mrs. Holiday that Vivi was gone. She looked more pissed than heartbroken when she found out. She told everyone it was postponed, not cancelled. I guess that's to be expected with your marriage being arranged."

Something cold settles in my gut. "What kind of arrangement are we talking about?"

"The kind where both parties have something to gain." He claps my shoulder. "Look, you're a good guy, Hart. A guy who gave up everything to serve his country. Who stepped up to raise his niece without hesitation. Who fought his way back onto the ice when everyone said he couldn't."

I look away, uncomfortable with the praise. "Anyone would have done that."

"But they didn't. You did." His voice softens. "Just something to think about."

Before I can respond, Adeline emerges from the locker room, her hockey bag dragging behind her. "Ready!"

The drive home is quiet, but my mind is racing. Vivi's empty seat haunts me, along with Kaenan's words about the Holidays.

The thought of her going back to that carefully arranged life, to that polished bastard who probably never had to fight for anything in his life...

"You should text her," Adeline says suddenly.

"What?"

"Vivi. You should text her."

I grip the steering wheel tighter. "I don't have her number."

"Isla does."

"Drop it, Adeline."

She's quiet for a moment, then adds, "Dad would want you to be happy."

That gets my attention. Tommy always did know how to get through my defenses, and apparently his daughter inherited that talent.

"I am happy," I lie.

"No, you're surviving." She kicks her feet against the dashboard. "There's a difference."

Christ. I can't believe this is what we're talking about on the drive back from practice.

"Since when do you know so much about happiness?"

She shrugs. "Since I saw how Mom and Dad were together. How Isla and Kaenan are. That's what I want for you."

My throat tightens. "It's not that simple."

"Only because you make it complicated." She pulls out her phone—when did she get so tech-savvy? "I can ask Berkeley to ask her mom for Vivi's number."

"Adeline." My warning tone has zero effect.

"Or we could go to Berkeley's birthday party next weekend. Vivi will be there."

I forgot about the party. Shit. I almost forgot...again.

"You're worse than your father, you know that?"

She grins. "Thanks."

We pull into our driveway, but I sit there for a moment, engine idling. The house looms before us---three bedrooms, two baths, and about a thousand reminders of how inadequate I am at this whole guardian thing. I bought it last month to honor my brother's wishes in his trust that Adeline grow up in a house and not a broken down bus on the edge of town like we did. And with it only being a few blocks from Kaenan's house, we've spent more and more time with them, giving Adeline some sense of family that I can't seem to give her myself.

But I didn't use any of the life insurance money that Tommy had in place to buy a house for her to live in. I bought the house with my own money and put every penny of the funds Tommy left for Adeline into a trust that she can access when she's thirty.

Providing for her isn't a hardship—it's a privilege. My brother and his wife picked me. There had to be a reason for that.

Besides, living in The Commons with all the other single players wasn't exactly the best place for her to grow up. Parties all hours of the night, women coming and going. She needs more of a "normal" life for a kid—aka, the gated suburbs that the Altman's call home and a lot of other retired Hawkeyes players that started families here.

"Uncle Trey?"

"Yeah?"

"Thanks for coaching my team."

A small smile stretches across my lips, and I nod.

"I'm glad we have something we can do together," I tell her. "Now get inside, squirt. Pizza, homework, shower, and then bed. We'll go get her a present after tomorrow's morning skate."

She grabs the pizza and races to the house to dodge the rain and then inputs the key code and walks inside.

I hope that Tommy and Sarah are watching like I told her they are...and that they don't regret leaving me with the very best thing either of them ever made.

CHAPTER FIVE

Vivi

Vanilla buttercream and chaos—that's what Berkeley's eighth birthday smells like. Through the sliding glass doors of Isla's kitchen, Seattle's signature February drizzle pitter-patters against it, but it doesn't stop the pack of kids racing through the backyard, their shrieks piercing the afternoon air. The bounce house is their haven from attempting to stay out of the rain...but it's a futile attempt. Yet none of them seems to care.

It's been a week since the board kicked me out of my CEO position, and the ticking time bomb of my upcoming elopement... to no one at this point, is now down to seven weeks away.

I still haven't heard a word from Jameson, and the few texts back and forth from Genevieve confirm that he's not talking to her either. His whereabouts are mostly being tracked by the private eye she hired to watch him.

The whole idea of hiring someone to spy on your son is a little cringy, or at the very least an invasion of privacy, but I get that his decisions don't just affect him, they affect his siblings as well. I just have to wonder if she has a private eye watching me too.

Good thing everything I've been doing is completely mundane and boring. I've never not had a job, and rearranging my furniture for the tenth time isn't cutting it. I need something to fill my time and pay at least my bare minimum expenses until the board comes to their senses and gives me back my position and my salary.

"Hold this." Isla shoves a frosting-filled piping bag into my hands while she adjusts the "Happy Eighth Birthday Berkeley" sign. The professional cake decorator nailed the hockey theme, complete with tiny fondant sticks and a Hawkeyes logo, but my sister can't help adding her personal touches. A condition caused by the fact that she's an athletic wear designer and perfection is her worst quality, though I can't blame her. It may not be genetic, but we both have it. "And while you're at it, spill. Have you gotten the board to change its mind?"

I pipe a small rosette onto the corner of the cake board, buying time. "I've been trying to get a call with Richard, but all he does is ask if I've talked to Jameson."

"Jesus." She steps back, examining the banner's tilt. "Well, keep my car as long as you need. You know that. I still can't believe they took your car. You still own a huge share of the company, and Jameson isn't returning your calls."

"They want it to hurt. Apparently, running out on your wedding creates some PR complications. Who knew?" I say, sarcastically, rolling my eyes.

"Speaking of running away before walking down the aisle, have you talked to Dad yet? He tells me that you're not returning his voicemails or texts. You should talk to him. Your board director respects Dad. Maybe he could have a word with Richard on your behalf."

"No way. I don't want Dad getting involved. Keeping him out of my business was the whole point of me marrying Jameson to begin with," I tell her and then glance around the room, realizing I haven't seen our father here yet. "By the way, where is Dad? He never misses the kids' birthday parties."

"He called and video chatted Berkeley this morning. His assistant personally flew down her gift this morning so he could watch her open it, but he was very vague about where he was. Said he'll be out of the country. I'm guessing that's code for getting married to a new wife somewhere because the US must cut you off at ten ex-wives, right?" Isla teases.

"It hasn't been that many," I say—though it's been at least six.

"So, if you're not going to use Dad's influence to get you out of this mess, what's your plan? Can't you just fire everyone on the board and be done with it?"

"That's the problem with creating a board of directors," I say. "The moment I did, I gave up total control. And now, with the Holiday merger, I don't hold the majority share anymore. It was part of the deal I made so they would take us public. The board can, and will, vote me out as CEO." The word tastes bitter. "So unless I can get Jameson to pick up the damn phone, I can kiss my corner office goodbye."

She adjusts the happy birthday for the hundredth time, tilting her head from right to left to decide if the placement is better. I swear it didn't move an inch. "Jameson still hasn't reached out to you though, right?"

"Nope." I pop the *p* with false cheerfulness. "He's too busy enjoying what should have been our honeymoon in Greece. With our wedding planner. Poor girl." I say under my breath. I owe her the biggest for all of this. I can't imagine what consequences of me walking out on my wedding cost her.

Her commission?

Her job?

Her freedom?

A burst of male laughter cuts through the kitchen chaos. Through the open concept layout, I catch sight of Trey in the living room, standing with Aleksi and Wolf. His dark blue Henley stretches across broad shoulders, and the sleeve tattoos I glimpsed at practice are on full display. Something warm coils in my stomach at the sight of him—all six-foot-five of raw power contained in faded jeans and careful control. He's gorgeous, but anyone with eyes can tell that. There's something else about him, though, that has always caught my attention.

Maybe the fact that he's a trained Special Forces Night Stalker bad ass who used to fly Black Hawk helicopters into combat war zones and who could probably kill a man forty different ways with his pinky alone. Yet the way he is with Adeline is so nurturing and sweet. Like a giant teddy bear.

And how—even though I've seen him punch a man straight off his skates with more force than anyone I've ever watched play—he's also the first guy on the ice to try talking down a fight. It's as if his fifteen years of military service came with a side of hostage negotiation training, because he's damn good at diffusing a situation before it blows.

He's a conundrum. A mystery.

And maybe I'm just curious enough to find out what makes him tick.

He's also the polar opposite of Jameson Holiday. Where Jameson is charming, charismatic, and professional, Trey seems authentic, centered, and mysterious.

"Earth to Vivi." Isla waves a hand in front of my face. "You were saying? About Jameson?"

I drag my attention back to her, though I swear I can feel Trey's presence like a physical pull. "Right. Well, apparently, we're planning to elope quietly in the South of France in seven weeks."

"Seven weeks?" She frowns. "That's specific."

"That's the ultimatum." The words come out sharper than intended. "Either Jameson and I marry by then, or the board votes me out and he loses his inheritance and his position as the head of Holiday Industries."

Before Isla can respond, Berkeley races through with a pack of sugar-high kids on her heels. "Mom! Can we have cake yet?"

"Soon, baby." Isla smooths her daughter's wild curls. "Go play with your friends."

I watch Berkeley dash off, her dark curls bouncing. She might not be Isla's by blood, but she's every bit her daughter. When Kaenan discovered his ex had kept their child secret until her death, he'd been devastated. Then fate—and my meddling—brought him Isla as Berkeley's nanny. Now they have this gorgeous home, Berkeley, and little Oliver. The kind of life I used to dream about before I traded romance for practical business arrangements.

Another burst of laughter draws my attention back to the living room. Trey's smiling at something Wolf Ziegler, the Hawkeyes' right defense, said, and the sight hits me like a sucker punch. He looks younger when he smiles, less guarded. More like someone I could ...

No. I can't go there.

"You know what the worst part is?" I lower my voice as another group of kids thunder past, looking to sugar up with Capri Suns. "I actually thought Jameson might call. Not because I deserve it for leaving him at the altar, but because we were partners in this. I screwed up leaving like I did, but now we both have something to lose. Why isn't he calling so we can make a game plan about how to move forward? I mean, for all I know, he's not going to come back, and we'll both lose everything. Maybe that's my punishment."

But would Jameson really do that? He's a fierce CEO. I've seen the way he handles a boardroom of investors with a calm yet charming demeanor. Never once have I seen or heard of him being vindictive, but I wouldn't blame him if he decided not to be with me. It's just that, to be fair, he loses more than I do in this.

Isla pulls me toward the pantry, away from little ears and prying eyes. "What exactly do you mean by 'something to lose'?"

I lean against a shelf of pasta, my eyes clamping down for a moment as I prepare to tell my sister about the complete shit show that my running away put into action. "The Holiday trust has strict rules about marriage. If Jameson doesn't marry who his parents choose, he loses everything—all the Holiday kids have to follow it. And it's not just his trust fund—his CEO position at Holiday Industries, his seat on the board, even his shares in the company."

"And your board?"

"They've wanted to go public for years. The deal with Holiday Industries would've given us the capital and connections to make it happen." I rake a hand through my hair. "Without it, there's no IPO. Which means I can kiss the stock options I was planning for my staff goodbye. Genevieve is already threatening to delay the IPO if I don't marry Jameson."

"They'll force you out," she finishes.

"Exactly. And the best part? While I'm stuck here dealing with their threats and the media circus, Jameson's living it up in Santorini."

"Lucky bastard," she mumbles. "Have you tried calling Natasha?"

"Her phone goes straight to voicemail." I pull out my phone, showing Isla the string of unanswered texts.

Movement catches my eye through the pantry's slatted door. Trey passes by, Adeline perched on his shoulders like she belongs there. His massive hands grip her legs securely, and despite his size, his touch looks impossibly gentle. The sight makes my chest ache, remembering how gentle yet strong they were when he helped me into the back of his SUV.

"Speaking of things you could be doing instead of wallowing..." Isla's tone turns sly. "Did you hear Trey's nanny quit?"

I keep my expression neutral, though my pulse jumps and my ears perk up. "Oh?"

"Mmhmm," she says, grabbing more decoration off a shelf and then pushes the pantry door open and heads back towards the kitchen island. I follow behind her. "Something about following her heart in a Sprinter van across the country." She begins to arrange the candles on the cake as if she isn't up to some meddling of her own. "You know, since you have nothing else to do for the next two months and you're destitute ..."

"Oh no... I know where you're going with this. Don't even think about it."

"What?" she says, shrugging her shoulders as if her suggestion is harmless. "You literally own a staffing agency for this sort of thing. Plus, you and Adeline already get along great at our movie nights, and you need funds." She glances toward the living room. "Besides, it might be good for you to focus on something else for a while."

Or someone else, as her tone implies.

"I can't." But even as I say it, I'm remembering how it felt in his SUV that day. Safe. Protected. Like for one moment, I could breathe.

"Why not?"

Because every time I look at him, I feel something I shouldn't. Because over the last week, since he was my getaway driver, I've thought more about those forest-green eyes and those hands gripping my hips than I did about Jameson in six months of engagement.

Because in less than two months, I have to marry someone else or lose everything I've built.

"It's just a bad idea. I haven't nannied for a family in almost a decade."

"Hold that thought," she says, staring at the cake. "It's missing something."

She heads back to the pantry, and then I catch Trey's eye again.

He makes his way over, and my heart rate kicks up. "Hey," he starts.

"Hi," I say back.

Really? A single syllable? That's all you're going to give him after he saved you from your wedding. I should be ashamed of myself.

He clears his throat. "How have you been?" he asks, his deep voice sending shivers down my spine.

"Fine, thanks." *Whoa, good job Vivi.* You can control a boardroom of ego maniacs, but you can't come up with more than two words to say to this man?

He nods in response and then glances down at his beer.

Say something you fool.

"I should thank you again for what you did for me—"

His eyes shoot back up to mine. "You don't have to thank me," he says. "I'm glad I was there to help."

"But I do need to thank you. I would have been stranded out there looking like a drowned rat if it weren't for those missing cufflinks." I try to lighten the moment. "Thank God for those ballet moms you were trying to avoid." I tease with a smirk.

His laugh is low, rich. "Trust me, you looked like anything other than a drowned rat. You looked beautiful." The words seem to surprise him as much as me, and I watch the muscle in his jaw tick as he realizes what he said.

"Thank you," I say quickly, trying to ease his discomfort. "So, Isla tells me you're down a nanny?"

"Yeah." He takes a long pull from his beer, and I find myself tracking the movement of his throat. "The nanny gave barely any notice. She fell in love or some shit with a guy online. She's off backpacking through Europe or something."

"It happens." I offer, though my own experiences with love have been less than stellar.

"Backpacking through Europe?" he asks.

"No," I laugh. "Falling in love."

He just shrugs as if he knows nothing about how falling in love just happens to someone.

"What? A tough ex-special forces guy like you doesn't believe in it?"

His dark green eyes lock onto mine, and the intensity has me wondering what it would be like to be pinned under him with his eyes only on me. God, it's been too long since I've gotten any. That has to be what this is about.

"Who said I don't believe in love?" His voice drops lower. "I believe in it...with the right person."

The way he says it, the way his gaze drops to my lips for just a heartbeat...heat floods my body. It has me wondering exactly what woman Trey would consider the "right person."

One thing I do know, this is dangerous territory. I'm not technically engaged anymore since he's not returning my texts or voicemails and is currently sharing a honeymoon suite with Natasha—or so I suspect—but as far as the Holiday family and my company are concerned, I have seven weeks to fix this mess and marry Jameson or lose everything.

I can't even think about what my life would look like if I fell in love with Trey Hartley. Not that he's offering it anyway.

Oh God, I'm spiraling.

"Just so you know, I set the record straight with Mrs. Fraiser. She does not believe that we're married," I tell him. "I told her the situation so you're in the clear."

She had looked very disappointed about us not being married, but said that she read the news about my situation and patted my hand, saying, "Maybe this was a gift to reconsider. And that maybe the universe was trying to tell me something."

Isla appears with a lighter for the birthday candles and a dozen hungry, sugar-deprived children on her heels.

"Time for cake!" she announces.

The spell breaks. Trey steps back into the crowd of other parents and Hawkeyes players, and I feel the loss like a physical thing.

Forty-nine days. That's all I have to either salvage my company or lose everything I've built.

Getting involved with Trey Hartley, in any capacity, would be like lighting a match in a room full of gasoline.

But as I watch him with Adeline, his arm slung over her shoulders, watching as Berkeley blows out her candles, I can't help thinking that maybe that's exactly what I need.

Something hot enough to burn...to remind myself that I'm alive.

CHAPTER SIX

Trey

The locker room chatters around me with the sound of players prepping to get back out on the ice after the second period. It's been a hard-fought game so far, but we're not even close to the end. I adjust my hearing aid, filtering through the erratic sounds of hockey game chaos: skates being sharpened, tape ripping, and the endless shit-talking that comes with playing any competitive group sport.

"Hart, how's the nanny search going?" Hunter asks, sitting on the bench to my right, strapping back on his shin guards. "It's got to be hard for her to lose Charlotte. It seemed like they were getting along."

What's hard is having another person leave Adeline's life so abruptly. I'm used to loss, but she shouldn't be. Not at her age.

"She's handling it," I say, unable to hide the frustration in my voice.

I hate how fast Adeline is having to grow up. I hate how many disappointments and losses she's been facing over the last year.

"She's a tough kid." Wolf chimes in from his stall. "She'll

bounce back through it."

I blow out a breath. "Yeah, but she's only nine. I don't like how mature she's being about it. I expected tears, or for her to throw something...but she didn't even give a bad attitude over it at all." It concerns me.

"Have you been looking around for a fill-in? Our next away game is coming up," JP Dumont asks.

"Yeah, I know. I have to figure out something fast. All the agencies I've called don't have anyone. No one wants to cover away games or evenings with the home games," I say. "Isla and her mother-in-law have been great this last week, filling in where they can, but I can't put that kind of pressure on them forever."

Even when Charlotte was Adeline's nanny, Isla and Kaenan's mom would jump in where they could if I needed a night covered for team events that Charlotte couldn't cover. Adeline jumps at any chance she can to spend more time with Berkeley.

"Speaking of help," Luca Popovich, our alternate right winger says, a shit-eating grin spreading across his face. "I heard at Berkeley's party last week that Newport Staffing is between CEOs right now. Maybe you could work something out with Vivi."

It's been a week since I saw Vivi at Berkeley's birthday party, two weeks since I dropped Vivi off at Isla's in a rain-logged wedding dress.

"Shut up, Popeye," I warn.

But apparently Wolf doesn't get the memo. "Come on, Hart. We all saw how you looked at her at Berkeley's party."

"I didn't look at her in any way."

"Bullshit." Hunter snorts. "You were watching her like a sniper on target."

They're not wrong. I'd tracked her movements all afternoon, cataloging every smile, every laugh. The way she'd helped Berkeley open presents, with Oliver perched in her lap, completely aware that every moment with her niece and nephew are precious. How she'd snuck extra cake to the kids when Isla wasn't looking.

"Besides," Hunter adds, "word is Holiday's living it up in

Greece with the wedding planner. Talk about Vivi dodging a bullet."

"How the hell do you know that?" I ask. I was at the same party and didn't hear anything about it.

JP chuckles as he walks by me, suited up and ready to go. "He overheard it from Peyton. The girls are just as bad as the Hawkeyes locker room. No one can keep a secret around here."

My jaw clenches. The image of Vivi in that wedding dress, rain-soaked and desperate, flashes through my mind. The way she'd trusted me without hesitation, climbing into my car like I was her salvation instead of the random asshole who just so happened to be there.

"Whatever's going on with Jameson, she's got enough on her plate, and she's overqualified for a nanny position. I wouldn't insult her by asking."

Coach Haynes saves me from further interrogation, striding in with his game face on. "All right, boys. Circle up."

We gather around, the familiar pre-game energy vibrating through the room. Coach's eyes scan each of us, landing on me last.

"Florida is playing physical tonight. They've got something to prove after we embarrassed them last year." He turns to me. "Hart, I want you on their top line. Shut down Erikson before he gets comfortable."

I nod. Erikson's their star forward, known for fancy stick work and a nasty right hook. Nothing I can't handle.

He discusses a few more changeups for some of the players, and then the room erupts in movement, players grabbing sticks and heading for the tunnel. I cut to the end of the line, adjusting my hearing aid one last time to lower the sound. The device helps with the damage from the Helicopter accident, but game nights are still a sensory nightmare.

The whistle blows, and everything else fades away. Time to remind anyone in the world who doubts me why Everett Kauffman signed me to the team as a walk-on with a lot to prove.

THE CROWD ROARS as we take the ice. The third period starts with Florida up by one. My legs burn from chasing Erikson around the ice, but I've kept him scoreless so far.

Erikson lines up for the face-off, smirking. "Getting slow, old man."

I ignore him, focusing on the ref's hand. The puck drops, and I win it clean, sending it back to Slade Matthews, our center and captain. We've played together long enough that he knows exactly where I'll be—cutting across center ice, drawing Erikson with me while Aleksi Mäkelin streaks up the boards.

The play develops exactly as planned until Florida's defenseman catches Aleksi with an elbow. The whistle blows, and suddenly I'm skating full force towards two hundred pounds of angry Floridian.

"That was clean." The defenseman shouts, shoving Hunter who's already in his face for hitting Aleksi.

Before I can intervene, gloves are dropping. I grab Hunter's jersey to pull him back while Wolf clocks another opposing player who's chirping in his ear. Last thing we need is our top defenders in the box.

"Save it for the scoreboard," I growl in Hunter's ear as Slade gets between Wolf and the other player.

The refs separate everyone. The player who hit Aleksi heads to the penalty box, and play resumes. But something's shifted. The hits get harder, the chirping nastier. With five minutes left, Erikson catches me with a late check that sends me into the boards. My bad shoulder screams in protest.

I push through it, like I always do. The pain's nothing compared to what I've survived. But when Erikson gets the puck in the neutral zone with thirty seconds left, my body betrays me. That split-second delay is all he needs.

The red light flashes. Florida's bench erupts. 4-2 with one

second left.

Game over.

The locker room is quiet afterward, everyone lost in their own thoughts. Coach Haynes' critique is brief but pointed.

"Hart." He catches me as I'm heading out. "Kendall's room. Get that shoulder looked at."

I want to argue, but the throbbing speaks for itself. Dr. Hensen wraps it, lectures me about playing through pain, then she clears me to leave. By then, most of the guys have already headed to Oakley's—our usual post-game spot whether we win or lose.

I text Adeline's temporary sitter—Isla's mother-in-law—to check in. Everything's fine. She's already asleep. I should go straight home, ice my shoulder, and try to figure out this nanny situation.

Instead, I find myself pulling into Oakley's parking lot. One drink won't hurt. And there aren't any nanny services I can call late at night. Though I've already tried most of the reputable ones.

I PUSH THROUGH the door at Oakley's. The place is packed with the usual post-game crowd—players, fans, and locals all mingling together, the bar music just loud enough to work as background noise without being overwhelming, the smell of beer and freshly showered hockey players mixed with long forgotten peanut shells fills the space. Wolf and Olsen are setting up at one of the pool tables, Hunter and JP are at the bar with their girlfriends, Cammy and Peyton, and the rest of the guys are scattered around. What I don't expect to see is Vivi Newport perched at a high-top table with Isla and Kaenan, laughing at something Aleksi just said.

My feet stop moving. She's wearing tight dark jeans that stretch across her perfect curves, and a puffy jacket with a fur-lined hood, her dark hair falling in waves down over her shoulder. The sight of her instantly soothes the ache in my body. How the hell does she do that?

She glances over her shoulder, and those honey-colored eyes lock onto mine. My pulse kicks up like I'm eighteen again, not a thirty-four-year-old ex-soldier with more baggage than the luggage terminal at LAX.

"Rough game?" she asks as I approach, concern flickering across her features.

"You were watching?" I ask.

She nods, and I swear her cheeks flush slightly. "Isla and I caught the third period after we got the kids settled at her mother-in-law's. That last hit looked nasty."

"I've had worse," I say, though my shoulder throbs in protest as I shrug off my jacket.

Her eyes track the movement, lingering on my arms where my T-shirt stretches across my biceps. When she bites her lower lip, heat floods my system and my cock twitches. Christ, this woman has an effect on me that no one has ever had before.

When Isla steals her attention away, I adjust myself under the table.

"At least let me buy you a drink," she offers. "To make up for that cheap shot Erikson took."

"I can't let you do that."

She arches an eyebrow. "Why not?"

Because every time you look at me like that, I forget all the reasons I should stay away from you. Because I have no idea if you still belong to someone else. Because I'm barely holding my life together as it is, with no extra room to take on something this complicated. Even if I wanted to, I can't give you the life you were raised with—a life you deserve.

"Because I drove you away from your own wedding. If anything, I owe you a drink." I try for lightness, but her expression shifts.

"Actually, I think you just made my point for me, getaway driver." She slides off her barstool with a teasing grin. "So what will it be? You'd better make it quick because otherwise, I'm going to pick for you, and I can guarantee that your beverage will be bright pink and come with a drink umbrella and a curly straw."

She's too fucking cute for her own good, and I know enough about her personality to be fully aware that she'll make good on her threat—that is, if Oakley even makes anything like that in his sports bar. If I don't want to lose complete respect from the guys and give them ammo to use against me tomorrow at practice, I'd better speak up with a drink I can chug in public...respectably.

"Beer's fine."

"Preference?" she asks with a lifted brow.

"Anything will do."

She heads to the bar, and I try not to watch the way she fills out those jeans in all the right places. The way those hips make my mouth water. What I wouldn't give to see my handprint painted red across her ass cheek.

One night with Vivi isn't the problem. It's the fact that one night won't be enough. And that's a cost she can't afford. She deserves someone whole—so does Adeline. They both deserve more than who I am.

"You're staring," Isla says, amusement dancing in her eyes.

I shift back quickly.

"No, I'm not."

I try not to make it obvious as I cut my sights over to the pool game where Wolf just kicked Olsen's ass and Luca is up next, but I know I was already caught red-handed.

"Yes, you are." Kaenan chimes in. "And she's my sister-in-law, so it's my duty to tell you to stay the fuck away from her."

Isla elbows him hard in the side with a death glare.

"What?" He whines and rubs his ribs though I'm sure she barely made a dent in the Hawkeyes' retired defender.

"Shut up. You don't speak for her," Isla mumbles, annoyed with her husband running interference.

I shoot him a warning look as if he'd better listen to his wife, but before I can respond, Wolf appears at my shoulder.

"Hart! Get over here. Popeye thinks he can beat me at pool. I need you to referee—pretty sure he's some kind of Russian mafia pool shark."

There's been plenty of rumors about Luca Popovich and his possible family ties to the Russian mob, but that's all it is. Rumors. Ones that Luca shrugs off with a laugh. All I know about Luca is that he's a two-time hockey Olympic medalist and moved to the US permanently when he was thirteen to train under one of the greatest hockey players to ever play the game.

"You just know you're about to lose," Luca calls from the pool table, already racking the balls. "Now let's get this ass-whooping over with. My beer's getting warm."

I glance at Vivi, still at the bar waiting for our drinks. "Give me a minute."

"Scared I'll win without witnesses?" Luca taunts.

"More like scared you'll cheat without them," Wolf shoots back.

Vivi returns with our drinks. A beer for me and what looks like a whisky sour for her, just as the first game starts. As she hands me the beer, our fingers brush. The contact sends an electric shock up my arm.

"Thanks." I take a careful sip, hyper-aware of her presence beside me.

"So," she settles onto a stool, "how's the nanny search going?"

Great. Even she knows about that disaster.

I blow out a breath.

"That good, huh?" she asks, reading my expression.

"My job isn't exactly normal. It requires overnight stays, weekends, and long hours. People have families too—I get it." I scrub a hand over my face. "But now I'm scrambling."

"What about nanny agencies? Have you called any of them?" she asks, watching Wolf line up his shot.

"I called a few, including Newport Staffing but no one had a nanny available for the schedule we need." I lean against the high-top, close enough to catch that fruity scent of her perfume. "Between away games and evening practices, it's been hard to find someone willing to work an odd schedule like that."

"Eight ball, corner pocket," Wolf calls out, then curses when he misses.

"Amateur," Luca taunts, circling the table casually as if he could do this in his sleep. He sinks three balls in quick succession while Wolf mutters a curse word under his breath.

Vivi stirs her whisky sour in her glass with a vacant look on her face.

"What?" I ask. She's thinking about something, I can feel it.

"Nothing." She takes a sip of the drink. "Just considering your situation. I understand why it's tough to find the right fit. If I had any control over my staff at the moment, I could help you, but as it is...I'm on vacation at the moment, or 'forced leave,' you take your pick."

That's when I notice it. The engagement ring for Jameson. It's back on her hand.

"Speaking of 'forced leave,'" Isla says, leaning into our conversation. "That means you have some availability for the next little while, right Vivi?"

Vivi moves quickly, and then Isla yelps and bends down like she's rubbing her shin. "What did I say wrong? I was just going to suggest that you could nanny for him," Isla mumbles angrily to Vivi.

"And you're so good about being subtle about it," Vivi says back and then turns to me. "Sorry about her. She thinks she's being helpful by sticking her nose in other people's business."

"It's not a big deal. Really. I would have never considered asking you. I'm sure you're busy. Vacation or not."

Vivi opens her mouth to say something in response when the waitress stops by and interrupts, breaking the moment, but it's fine. How much further could that have gone anyway?

Kaenan orders a round of wings for the table. I notice Vivi checking her phone, probably dealing with the media fallout from her almost-wedding. I've seen the tabloids about it. The urge to reach for her is almost overwhelming.

"You good?" I ask quietly.

She looks up, those eyes troubled. "Just more emails from the board. Nothing I can do about it tonight."

"Want to play the winner?" I nod toward the pool table, trying to distract her.

Her smile returns, though it doesn't quite reach her eyes. "Only if you're ready to lose."

"Big talk from someone who's never seen me play."

"Oh, I've watched you plenty." The words slip out before she can catch them, and her cheeks flush pink. "I mean, at games. Playing hockey."

The wings arrive, saving her from backtracking any further. Though I file away that admission for later. She's been watching me play pool when she comes to Oakley's? This isn't the first time I've seen Vivi here with Isla. Over the last eight months, she's come to plenty of home games, but I've kept my distance after she showed up with that same engagement ring on her finger.

An hour passes in a comfortable rhythm. Luca beats Wolf, then loses to Hunter. Vivi demolishes Hunter, proving she wasn't bluffing about her skills. I switch to water after my beer, conscious of driving later. When Vivi steps up to play me, the tension in the air shifts.

"Show me what you got, Newport," I challenge, racking the balls.

She takes her time choosing a cue, testing the weight. Her movements are deliberate, almost sensual. Or maybe that's just my imagination working overtime.

"Ladies first," I offer.

She smirks. "Such a gentleman."

She leans over the table to break, and my mouth goes dry. Those jeans should be illegal. The crack of balls splitting across felt echoes through the bar.

"Stripes," she calls, already moving for her next shot.

What follows is the sexiest game of pool I've ever played. Every time she bends over the table, my hands itch to grab her hips. When she brushes past me to line up a shot, the electricity between us is almost visible.

"You're up, soldier," she says after missing a tough bank shot.

I sink two before scratching. "Damn."

"Rusty?" She circles the table, studying angles. "Or distracted?"

Both. Definitely both.

The game stays close, but she beats me on a beautiful combo shot. Wolf whistles low.

"Damn, Newport. Where'd you learn to play like that?" he asks.

"College job. One of the first families I nannied for had a pool table and the dad was a world-renowned pool player. He taught me a few tricks so that, one day, I'd never lose to a bar full of hockey players," she teases, setting her cue in the rack.

"Holding out on us," I accuse, but I can't help grinning.

She shrugs, all false innocence. "A girl's got to have some secrets."

And she has no idea how bad I want to know every last one.

It's after ten when Kaenan starts gathering their things. "We should head out. Mom's got the kids so I get my wife to myself tonight."

Isla hugs Vivi. "Need a ride?"

Vivi instantly waves her off. "No way. I'm in the opposite direction from you guys. I'll just get a rideshare," she says, reaching for her phone.

"I can give Vivi a ride," I offer.

I'm technically going the opposite direction as I live only a few blocks from Kaenan and Isla, but it's late, and I'd rather know she got home safe than have her take a rideshare. I'm also not done with spending time with her, and I might be more than a little curious where she lives and if she's safe there.

Isla's eyes sparkle with something that looks suspiciously like triumph. "Perfect! Thanks, Hart."

As they leave, I catch Wolf and Luca exchanging looks as if I'm being obvious. I flip them off, which only makes them laugh harder.

"Ready?" I ask her.

She nods, and then I lay my hand against her lower back to lead her out of the crowded space, and it feels like I've done this with her a thousand times before.

The night air hits us as we exit, and she shivers slightly even with her large jacket on. Without hesitation, I shrug off my jacket and drape it over top of her. She looks up at me with surprise and something else flickering in her eyes.

"Thanks," she says softly.

I open the passenger door of my SUV, and the memory of her wedding dress taking up the whole backseat hits us both. A look of discomfort flashes over her expression as she climbs in and glances to the back seat as if she remembers the moment too. The smell of her perfume lingered in my car for at least a week, and every time I got in, I'd get an endorphin hit and then check my backseat as if she might still be there. Of course, she wasn't.

The drive starts quiet, but it's not uncomfortable. She gives me directions to her condo downtown, and I try not to focus on how close she is in the enclosed space. Or how my jacket looks wrapped around her shoulders. Or how easy it would be to reach over and drape my hand over her thigh.

"You're different from what most of your fans would expect," she says suddenly.

I glance at her. "That's because they don't know me."

"That's true, I guess." She turns slightly in her seat to face me. "They only see you on the ice. Everyone talks about your service in the military and how intense you are as a player. How focused you are all the time. And the tattoos..."

"What about the tattoos?" I ask.

"They just give you that hard edge," she quickly tries to cover it up as if she just insulted me, which she didn't. "I mean, they're sexy as hell but—"

"Sexy as hell?" I ask. Fuck yeah...now we're getting somewhere. "Do you find them sexy, Vivi Ann?"

"Hey...how do you know my full name? I only ever go by Vivi."

"It's in your CEO profile on Newport Staffing's website," I say, knowing I just gave myself away that I stalked her online. "I might have looked you up once." Or twice.

"Oh really?" A mischievous smile flashes across her face.

I just shrug. "Maybe. But let's get back to the part where you called me edgy, mean, and sexy."

She laughs. "You weren't going to let me sidestep that, were you?"

"Nope." I say simply.

"I was just saying that people think they know who you are when they watch you on the ice, but with Adeline ..." She trails off, studying my profile.

"But with Adeline...?" I prompt.

"You're gentle. Patient." Her voice softens. "It's a nice surprise."

The words hit something deep in my chest. "I'm trying. Most days I have no idea what the hell I'm doing."

"I think that's normal for any parent."

"I'm not her parent though." The admission is still painful to think about. Tommy and his wife should be responsible for how she is brought up...not me. With the years I had put into the service, I never had a serious girlfriend. Before Adeline came around, I thought that there was a good possibility that I would never have kids of my own. The fear of raising kids the way that my parents raised us...that was enough to make me believe that me not being a father was a good thing. But now that I have Adeline, I'm having a harder time understanding how my parents could have treated us the way that they did. "I'm just the uncle who got custody because there was no one else."

"You're more than that." Her hand touches my arm briefly, and warmth spreads from the point of contact. "I've seen you with her. You're exactly what she needs."

We pull up to her building, and I kill the engine. The silence stretches between us, charged with something that feels like it's been there since the first time we met—at least from my side of things.

"I'll walk you up," I say, already opening my door.

She doesn't argue, just leads the way to her front steps. The security light casts shadows across her face as she turns to face me. I don't like that she doesn't have a door man or a barbed wire fence with a moat filled with sharks with lasers on their heads, but those aren't the decisions I get to make. I'm not on her security team ... though I sure as shit should be.

"Thank you for the ride." She starts to shrug off my jacket.

"Keep it," I say, because the idea of her handing it back to me feels wrong. "It's cold."

She pulls it tighter around herself instead, and the sight of her wrapped in my clothes does something primal to my system. Like I'd give her everything I own in this world if she simply asked me for it.

"Trey..." she starts, then stops.

I step closer, unable to help myself. She tilts her face up to mine, and for one single moment, I let myself imagine closing that distance. Pulling her into me to taste those perfect lips that I've been craving for eight months. Pushing her up against her front door, wrapping her legs around my waist, and grinding into her to show her exactly what she does to me. How fucking bad I want her, in every way that I know will only leave her with regrets when one day she wakes up and realizes that she settled for me. That she could have had better. She could have had someone with a pedigree like Jameson Holiday.

She inputs the code on the side of the door, and as soon as the lock disengages, I lean forward and grip the door handle to open it for her. But then, without warning, Vivi's lips plaster against mine, her fingers sliding up to my hair and tangling in them. Pulling me closer to her. I go willingly like a sheep to slaughter. Letting her have whatever she wants of me.

Sweet, soft—she's every fucking thing I knew she would be.

Did she misread me reaching for the door? I don't give a shit right now because this woman just made my dreams come true.

I hook my free hand around her waist and pull her against me. A small moan passes through her lips, and then she releases my mouth and looks up at me with sex drunken eyes...up until she glances over and sees my hand on the doorknob.

"Oh no," she says instantly, covering her face, but I don't let go. I keep her pulled against my chest. "You were only opening the door. Oh my God, I read that wrong. I'm so embarrassed."

If I had known she would have thought I didn't want to kiss her, I would have let go of that damn doorknob. How does she not know that she just made my night with that kiss?

Scratch that, correction. She made my fucking life.

"Jesus, no... Vivi," I say, releasing the doorknob to pull her hand from her face. "I wasn't going to make an assumption that I could kiss you. But trust me, if I thought I had an opening tonight, fuck, Vivi... I'd..." I stop, I shouldn't go there, especially with the fucking engagement ring mocking me.

"You'd what?" she asks, her eyes pinging between mine, searching for something. "You'd do what, Trey?"

"We'd already be halfway to your bedroom, and you'd already be naked."

She takes in a sharp breath, her eyes dilating. *Yeah, baby, you like that, don't you?*

"What's stopping you?" she asks.

Besides the fact that you're not the kind of woman I can do a one-night stand with and the fact that I don't want to be the man you regret years down the line when you realize that a lifetime of childhood abandonment and trauma, mixed with fifteen years in the service seeing things that you can never imagine, means that I have a gaping hole missing from the man I should be. The fact that I'm not a whole person like Jameson Holiday. And if she has any shot left to salvage a relationship with the billionaire, I'll never live with myself if I stand between them.

"You're wearing his ring again," I say, straight to the point.

Reality crashes back in. I step back, releasing the rest of my grip around her, creating distance between us.

"This isn't what it looks like. Genevieve Holiday asked me to wear it out in public. There's so much you don't know."

"Even still. Sleeping with me would be a mistake. One that I won't let you make."

"You're not a mistake, Trey."

But I know better than she does. I would be, and that's not something I can live with. Not with her. "Goodnight, Vivi."

I turn to leave, already berating myself for letting this go too far. For wanting something I can't have.

"Wait!" she calls after me.

I pause at the bottom of her steps, not turning around. I can't look at her right now or I'll do something stupid like kiss her anyway. Like pick her up and find the nearest surface to show her how easily I could make her come for me.

"I could help," she says quickly. "With Adeline."

That makes me turn. "What?"

I mean, I'm technically between jobs right now. And Adeline already knows me ..." She's rambling slightly, which is oddly endearing. "I could fill in until you find someone permanent."

I stare at her, wrapped in my jacket, trying to process what she's offering. "You want to be Adeline's nanny?"

"Is that crazy?"

Yes. Absolutely insane. Having her around constantly, in my house, with Adeline ... it would be torture.

"You're overqualified," I say instead.

"Maybe." She takes a step toward me, stopping at the edge of her steps. "But I'm also available. And I care about Adeline, which I know is one of your biggest concerns. I can do overnights and long hours and away games. I can make sure she makes it to hockey practice and ballet class and piano lessons. And..." she hesitates. And then I realize that Vivi knows Adeline almost better than anyone I could hope to care for her. "Maybe we both need a distraction right now."

A distraction. Right. Because in less than two months, she has to make a decision that could cost her.

I should say no. I should walk away now before this gets complicated. Before I agree to something just to selfishly keep her close.

Instead, I hear myself say, "When can you start?"

Her smile is like sunshine breaking through clouds. "Tomorrow?"

I nod once, sharply. "I'll text you my address."

"You don't have my number."

"Right." I pull out my phone, trying to ignore how having Vivi's phone number gives me access to calling her, texting her. All things I should stay away from. From here on out, I need to keep it as professional as possible...for Adeline's sake—for Vivi's sake—and fuck, for my mental sanity too.

She puts her number in and hands it back. Our fingers brush slightly. Every touch with her makes me want more.

"Goodnight, Trey," she says softly.

I watch her disappear inside, still wearing my jacket. Then I lean against my SUV, letting out a long breath.

What the hell have I just agreed to?

CHAPTER SEVEN

Vivi

The board in my kitchen stares back at me as I take a step away from it, snapping the cap of my dry-erase marker back into place:

REASONS TO MARRY JAMESON

Written in big bold letters on the right side of the newly crisp white board that I just wiped clean of my wedding to-do list that I had crossed off before my wedding day, my to-do list seems so vastly different with one small decision:

~~Dress fitting on Tuesday~~
~~Confirm inbound flight with mom~~
~~Dress rehearsal Friday~~

And now the new list reads:

He's a great business partner
I gave him my word
I'll get to keep my CEO position

It's a start anyway. To remind myself every day why marrying Jameson is the right call. Thank God that I start for Trey today because I could really use the distraction.

I reach for my phone when a call comes through—Isla.

She must have seen the text I sent her this morning about agreeing to nanny for Trey last night.

"You did what?" Isla practically shrieks into the phone before I even have a chance to say hello.

I hold it away from my ear, wincing. "Good morning to you as well, my lovely sister. I may have offered to be Adeline's temporary nanny."

I also kissed a man who was doing me a favor and misread the moment, but there is no way I'm telling her that part. I'm still completely mortified.

"May have?"

"Okay, fine. I did." I say putting her on speaker as I set my phone on the counter to pull on my hoodie before heading off to Trey's this morning. Trey's jacket is still draped over my kitchen chair, and I'm trying very hard not to think about how it smells like him. "It made sense at the time."

"Well duh, I could have told you that last night before you kicked me in the shin. Thanks for that by the way—it's bruised."

"You'll live," I say, rolling my eyes at her exaggeration, though she can't see me. "And people think I'm the dramatic one," I say sarcastically.

"Okay, start from the beginning. When exactly did this happen?"

"Last night. After you left Oakley's with Kaenan, when Trey dropped me off at home."

My brain replays a birds-eye view of every moment with Trey, walking me up to my door, right up until the moment I told him I would be Adeline's nanny. The excitement I felt in my belly, something that's been missing with Jameson...or really, any of the last dead-end relationships I've had over the last decade. Not that Trey and I are in a relationship...obviously.

"And you're just telling me now?" The betrayal in her voice would be comical if I weren't already questioning my own sanity.

"At least I'm telling you. The attitude is unwelcome by the way. As it is, I've been trying to process it all myself." I walk over to my office off of the kitchen and grab my monthly planner so I can take notes today regarding Trey's hockey schedule and Adeline's extra-curricular activities. "God, what was I thinking?"

"I know what you were thinking. You were thinking about those rock-hard glutes and those massive, ink-covered arms," she says, and I can hear the smirk in her voice. "You don't have to tell me, Sis. It turns out you and I might have the same type."

"And what would that be?" I ask.

"Hot hockey players who know how to toss you around in bed and make you forget all about your cheating ex-fiancé."

That last part about the cheating fiancé was more specific to her experience than mine, but it doesn't stop the image of Trey on top of me in bed naked with hot, sweaty muscles and that smirk of his as he pants, thrusting into me. I feel a hot flush of desire pool low in my belly and goosebumps break out down my arms.

For the love of God, get a grip. He's just a man.

I shake my head, trying to dislodge the imagery.

"Not helping," I mutter, turning to head for the front door and then remembering I forgot Isla's car keys on the kitchen counter. I'm distracted. Something that rarely happens to me. I'm usually incredibly focused—every decision, every action created with precise intention. "Besides, I'm doing this for the money until the board reinstates me and because Trey and Adeline need help. No other reason."

God... I even think I moaned when I slid my fingers around the back of his neck and pulled him to me and felt his warm lips on mine.

I brace my fingers around my forehead and slam my eyes shut. I'm so embarrassed.

"So what are you going to do?"

I glance at my phone. No texts yet, though he has my number

now. The thought makes my stomach flutter like I'm sixteen again.

"I guess I'm going to be a nanny. It's been a while, but it's like riding a bike, and Adeline and I already know each other and get along really well. Not to mention that I built an entire company around connecting families with childcare. I should be able to handle one nine-year-old for six weeks."

"Uh-huh." Isla's tone drips skepticism. "And the fact that said nine-year-old's uncle is six-foot-five of pure muscle with a jawline that could cut glass has nothing to do with your decision?"

"He needs help," I say defensively. "And I need a distraction and something to keep my mortgage paid, at least for now."

"What's the distraction for? The fact that in six weeks you're supposed to marry Jameson Holiday? Or the fact that said fiancé is currently living it up in Greece with your wedding planner?"

"Both?" I groan, grabbing my purse and slinging the strap over my shoulder. Maybe I should be jealous that Jameson took Natasha on our honeymoon, but considering that he's using her as some kind of chess move to keep Genevieve from doing anything to force him home before the honeymoon is over, I'm more concerned that Natasha is in paradise with a man she despises. The whole thing seems off. But if Genevieve believes that Jameson paid her off to go with him, well, then it makes more sense. After the fact that I cost her a large commission and her job, I can't be all that shocked that she would have agreed to that.

And besides that point, I can't hide the fact that I don't have feelings for Jameson enough to be jealous...not like that anyway. Though this whole thing would probably be easier if I did. Still, I know that Jameson and I are a perfect match on paper.

In six weeks, if he ever returns, we'll marry and it will all make sense. "I don't know, Isla. Everything's such a mess right now. The board's breathing down my neck, the media won't leave me alone, and Mrs. Holiday keeps sending these texts about 'salvaging the situation.' At least this way I'll be too busy to obsess over it all."

"Too busy obsessing over Trey instead?"

Yep, I'm definitely not telling her about that kiss. She'll never let me live it down. My cheeks are already warming at the idea of seeing Trey again this morning after that happened. Will he let me pretend that it didn't happen? Or am I going to have to address the elephant in the room? I guess we'll see soon enough.

"I hate you."

"No, you don't." She pauses. "Just...be careful, okay? This could get complicated really fast."

"I know," I say as I head for the door, grabbing Trey's jacket off the chair as I head for my front door. I catch myself in the entry mirror. I look exactly how I feel—conflicted, confused, and completely out of my depth. "But maybe that's what I need right now. Something real. Something that matters."

"It worked for me," she singsongs. "I was so pissed at you for tricking me into nannying for Kaenan." She laughs. "But I guess I owe you one because it worked out better than I could have imagined. I can't even think of what my life would have been like if I had married dad's successor."

She's right. I do owe her one. Her words remind me that, even though this whole Holiday merger was my way of keeping Dad out of my business and stopping him from controlling me the way he tried to control Isla, I can't ignore how my wedding to Jameson mirrors Isla's engagement.

The only difference is that I picked Jameson. My dad didn't. I walked into an arranged marriage—but one I arranged for myself.

"Yeah, well, I doubt this will end with me married to Trey Hartley."

As soon as the words slip out, I freeze, and there's awkward static on the line.

"Vivi..."

"I didn't mean—" My phone buzzes with a text, cutting me off. "Hold on."

It's a text from Trey with his address.

My heart does a little flip that has nothing to do with the logistics of childcare.

"He just texted," I tell Isla. "Sending me his address."

"You're going over there today?"

"He needs a nanny now, and I have nothing to do until the board reinstates my position or Jameson comes home. Besides, I owe him."

"Right. Because you always offer to nanny for hot, single hockey players who rescue you from your own wedding."

"Exactly. Slap that on a bumper sticker. Goodbye, Isla."

Her laugh follows me as I hang up. I stare at Trey's text for a moment, then type out a response.

Great! See you soon.

Trey

Thanks again for doing this.

I hate how fast I grab at my phone the second I hear his response come through, and the dopey smile across my lips when I read his text.

Happy to help.

I set my phone down, then grab it again.

I'm bringing back your jacket.

Three dots appear, disappear, appear again. My heart pounds stupidly hard as I wait.

Trey

Keep it. Looks better on you anyway.

Oh.

I clutch my phone like a teenager who just got a text from her crush. This is bad. This is very, very bad.

And yet... I can't stop smiling.

SHOWING UP AT Trey Hartley's front door at seven forty-five a.m. wearing yoga pants isn't the most professional look for my first day as a nanny. But after tossing and turning all night, replaying that kiss and the heat in his eyes when he'd said, "We'd already be halfway to your bedroom," my usual polished CEO wardrobe felt wrong.

Besides, I'm not a CEO right now. Thanks to my board's "temporary reassignment," I'm just a woman trying to figure out how to nanny a nine-year-old while fighting an attraction to her uncle that could destroy Genevieve Holiday's plans.

I lift my hand to knock, but the door swings open first. Trey fills the frame—fresh from the shower, track pants hanging low on his hips, a Hawkeyes training shirt pulled tight across his chest. Ink teases up the strong column of his neck, just enough to make me wonder what's hidden beneath. His dark hair is damp, a few stray drops clinging to his temples, and he smells of clean soap and fresh coffee. The scent alone is enough to make my mouth water.

"You're early," he says, his morning voice rough.

"I'm always early. The habits of a CEO are hard to kill. I brought breakfast." I lift the bag of fresh bagel, egg, and ham sandwiches from Serendipity's like a peace offering, the coffee carrier balanced in my other hand. "Thought we could talk logistics before Adeline gets back from her sleepover."

"It smells good, thanks. I just got back from a run and a shower. I was going to make breakfast. You're just in time. Come in." He steps back, and I catch a glimpse of the tattoos wrapping his forearms when he reaches for the coffee carrier and bag of food to carry it for me.

I walk through, and Trey closes the door behind me. I wait

until he leads me down the hallway, and then I follow as he passes me.

This house isn't as big as the other players' in the neighborhood, but my townhouse could fit in it a few times over, but you get more for your money in the suburbs. Slade and Penelope live on the opposite corner of the neighborhood, Kaenan and Isla, only a couple of streets down, and Coach Haynes and his wife Juliet live in this neighborhood as well. It's a large gated community with gorgeous homes.

"So you run?" I ask.

"Everyday. Early morning. Four-thirty before morning skate."

"Like clockwork?" I ask.

"Routine is important while I'm still adjusting—"

He doesn't finish, as if he didn't mean to divulge that information.

What could he have meant? Adjusting as a father? As a professional player on an elite hockey team?

"Adjusting how?" I ask because I'm nosy...and because understanding his routines will better help me understand where I can help as a nanny.

Being a nanny isn't just an overpaid babysitter. Our job is to blend into the family as seamlessly as possible and to lighten the burden around the house wherever we can, especially when it comes to the kids.

"It's been taking some time to adjust to civilian life. I still feel like a fish out of water. A strict schedule and morning runs help keep me sane," he says. Then he shakes his head as if he couldn't have said that out loud. "Shit, I probably said too much. I don't talk about this a lot."

"No, I get it. And you didn't say too much. I can't relate to adjusting from military life to being an instant dad and professional hockey player, but I understand that early mornings and strict organized days keep me from spiraling out of control. Though my working conditions seem trivial compared to yours.

My office isn't a war zone."

He glances over his shoulder. "But isn't it?" he asks and then turns back as we walk through the living room and into the large kitchen.

I smile to myself. Sure, we both know his years in a special forces unit were far more dangerous than a heated conference room negotiation—although, in my world, things get ugly fast when the pastries run out and the coffee pot's empty. Still, I appreciate that he's not letting me downplay what I do.

Because my job *is* hard. The stress load is relentless, and when I'm not on my A-game, it's not just the company and shareholders who take the hit—it's the people who work for me. The staff who show up every day and make Newport Staffing Solutions the best staffing service of any of our competitors. I built this company from nothing, and those employees aren't just names on a payroll; they're the reason I fight as hard as I do. They've been here fighting with me. I know their families, their goals, and I care about their futures. If I lose control of the company, I lose the ability to protect them from the kind of careless decisions made by leaders who only see the bottom line. Like Martin Howard.

A company doesn't grow to where we are by winging it, and it certainly doesn't stay there without someone willing to go to war for it.

Meticulous plans and long hours are what got us here. And no matter what the board thinks, I'm still the right person for the CEO position because no one else loves this company as much as I do. It's my baby—starting it with my own sweat and tears to get it to this point.

I follow him through the house, trying not to stare at the way his track pants hang low on his hips. The layout is open concept, modern but warm. A few family photos line the hallway—mostly of Adeline with who I assume are her parents. There are only a couple of Trey, and I'm guessing his brother. One at his brother's wedding, another of Trey at the hospital holding a newborn Adeline while his brother beams beside him.

The last frame makes me stop. Trey's in full Night Stalker gear, standing in front of a Black Hawk helicopter with another man at his side, his arm draped over the guy's shoulder as they pose for the camera. The grin on his face is pure adrenaline, and something in my stomach flips. I've always told myself I didn't have a "type," but apparently I like a man in uniform. Because Trey? He looks just as devastatingly handsome in Army fatigues as he does in a hockey uniform.

Or maybe it's not the uniform at all. Maybe it's just him.

The pictures are hung with care, but they certainly lack a woman's touch.

"Your house is beautiful," I say, as he leads me to the kitchen island. "When did you move in?"

"Last month." He pulls out a bagel sandwich, sets it on a plate, and then hands it to me. "I wanted to get Adeline out of my apartment at The Commons before the end of the season. Give her some stability. It's what my brother would have wanted too."

The Commons is the luxury high-rise in downtown Seattle, only a couple of blocks from the Hawkeyes stadium, where most of the single Hawkeyes players live. Definitely not the best environment for a nine-year-old girl. Especially with the late-night shenanigans I can only imagine happening around there. The women sneaking out in the morning, still in their cocktail dresses or in a player's warm-up gear with heels in hand, isn't probably the best for Adeline to witness.

I can see why Trey wanted to get her out of there. I have even more respect for him than I did before I showed up this morning. Staying in The Commons would be easier for him with proximity to the stadium. Moving her here was clearly for Adeline's best interest. Not Trey's.

Right when I think I couldn't like him more, I learn something new about him and what he's willing to do for Adeline.

"Smart move." I help unpack breakfast, hyper-aware of his presence as he leans against the counter. "This neighborhood's great for kids. Close to her school and the ballet school down the road."

He nods. "And Berkeley's house. They've gotten close."

"They have." I smile, remembering how the girls have seemed almost inseparable since Adeline joined the Little Hawks when Trey got signed on with the team. "Isla says they do everything together."

"Yeah, about that..." He runs a hand through his hair. "Her recital's in a month. Charlotte was helping with costume fittings and hair and...well, all that stuff I know nothing about."

The admission carries an edge of frustration that makes my heart ache. Here's this fierce hockey player, this decorated soldier, brought low by the prospect of ballet buns and tutus.

"I can handle that," I assure him. "What else can I take off your plate?"

He pulls out his phone, showing me a carefully crafted schedule. "Morning practice at six means I leave by five-thirty. School starts at eight. Then there's after-school activities—hockey on Mondays and Wednesdays, ballet on Tuesdays and Thursdays. Piano on Friday afternoons."

I nod, mentally noting each commitment. "And game days?"

"Home games, I leave around four for pre-game. Away games..." He hesitates. "Those are tougher. Sometimes two or three nights away."

"I can do overnights," I say quickly. Maybe too quickly, but I don't want him to stress over any of this. I know what I agreed to. I remember Kaenan's schedule before he retired with Isla handling his days out of town with their kids. "I mean, I'm used to traveling for business trips, and I'm familiar with the Hawkeyes' away game scheduling. You don't have anything to worry about. I'm assuming it would be easier for Adeline's routine if I stayed here?"

"I think that would disrupt her life the least, if you're okay with it. You can have the bed in the master bedroom. I've never slept on it."

"You don't sleep in the bed? Even when you're home?" I ask, overstepping into nosy territory again.

He looks down at his coffee cup and then takes a sip. "No."

"Where do you sleep then?" I ask.

"In the living room—usually."

"Even when you host a lady friend?" I ask, the words slipping out before I can think better of them. "I mean—sorry—that's none of my—"

Trey cuts me off before I can finish my thought. "I don't bring women home. I keep Adeline's life free of any of that." His response is casual, as if answering the question doesn't bother him in the least.

"Never?" I ask, though I should just shut up. It's just hard to imagine, with all the women I've seen begging for his attention, that he doesn't bring any of them back to his place.

"Not in Seattle. The last thing I need is to unknowingly hook up with a teacher at her school or someone else she might interact with regularly."

"Or a ballet mom?" I tease, though now I'm far beyond overstepping because I'm on a fishing expedition to see if he hooks up with any of the moms throwing themselves at him.

"God help me..." he says, shaking his head. He knows I've seen his little fan club up close and personal. "That's exactly what I mean. It's safer to keep that part of my life on the other side of state lines."

"Meaning away games," I say, seeing where he's going with this.

Hooking up with puck bunnies during games out of state keeps Adeline's uncle's sex life from affecting her in any way.

I hate how the sound of him hooking up during away games makes my stomach sink. Nothing will ever happen between us because in six weeks' time, I'll be headed back down the aisle to Jameson unless somehow Jameson has a way out of this. Since he still hasn't returned my phone calls or his mother's, I'm guessing he hasn't.

"I'm sorry," I say, glancing down at my own coffee cup now. "I shouldn't have asked. It's none of my business. It just took me by surprise that you don't sleep in your bed. But I'm fine with sleeping on the couch too."

"I don't blush easily, Vivi. You can ask me anything you want. I'll answer truthfully. The only person I need you to keep that information confidential from is Adeline," he says. "I'll take the couch—you keep the bed. I'll be coming in late or early in the morning sometimes. It's better if you're upstairs so I don't wake you when I come in. Keep whatever you want in the walk-in closet. I don't have much in there anyway."

I just nod. The away game hookup admission is sticking with me—I wish it wouldn't.

"I should be fine with a duffel bag back and forth. Six weeks isn't that far away."

Trey's expression shifts. "About that. If you need to leave suddenly—if he calls before the time is up or you just can't do it anymore—I'd like to know as soon as possible so I can prepare her. Adeline's been through enough people leaving. I'd like to give her time to adjust."

The words hit like a punch to the gut. Of course that's his concern. After losing her parents, then Charlotte...I'm just another flight risk.

"I won't do that to her," I promise. "Whatever happens with Jameson, I'll give you the full agreed time."

He studies me for a long moment, then nods. "Okay. Let's talk about salary."

"Whatever you were paying Charlotte will be fine." The word comes out sharper than intended.

"Vivi, you're a CEO of a Fortune 500 company. I can't pay you a nanny rate. We'd both take offense."

"I still have some funds in savings. I just reinvested a lot back into the company, and I thought I would have the sale of my townhouse to pay back my savings, but I need to live there now. Whatever you were paying the last nanny will be enough for me to get by until—" I don't finish because the idea of what I might have to do to keep my company is still hard to swallow.

His lips twitch. He knows what I stopped myself from saying too. "I'll pay you what I think is closer to fair, considering your résumé."

I nod with a smile. "Deal."

He shifts against the corner, his hip resting against the countertop.

"About last night ..." he says, his eyes dipping to my lips, the tip of his tongue peeking out at the corner of his mouth to wet it. Then his eyes lock with mine again. "About that kiss."

"Yes?" I ask, feeling myself leaning into him.

"Adeline already has this fantasy about us." *She and I both,* I almost say out loud. "What I said to you last night, about fucking you...it was inappropriate considering your situation with Jameson. I don't want to confuse Adeline about what this isn't. She's already attached to you in so many ways—your connection to Berkeley and Isla—I don't want to see her disappointed when she realizes that you and I aren't going to end up together."

"Right... I get it."

"I realize that I don't think straight when I'm that close to you, and if Adeline ever witnessed another accidental kiss..."

"We'd get her hopes up...I understand," I nod. "No more kissing you on front stoops."

"Because next time, I won't be able to keep from doing what I promised I'd do to you."

My nipples harden under my hoodie, and heat pools low in my belly. "Trey..." I say, taking a step forward.

Then I hear the front door open, and he and I both freeze.

"Uncle Trey?" Adeline's voice sounds through the hallway, and then the sound of the front door closes behind her. "Why is Isla's car out front? I smell bagels."

"Isla's car? Where's yours?" he whispers quickly at me, eyebrows furrowed in confusion as Adeline's footsteps come down the hall toward the kitchen.

"I don't have one. It's company property."

"Those fuckers took it?" he asks, his eyebrows turning down

with anger.

I step back quickly, plastering on a smile as she appears in the doorway. Her dark blonde hair in a ponytail, her overnight backpack slung over one shoulder, and a smile stretching from ear to ear when her eyes land on me.

"Morning, squirt." Trey's voice carries a gentleness I'm learning to expect when he talks to her. "Look who's here."

"Vivi! I was hoping it was you!" she yells as she races across the living room into the kitchen, full speed for me, dropping her backpack on the floor with no regard for its contents, and then wraps her arms around my middle. She's tall for her age and with my five-foot-two in sneakers, her head practically comes up to my collarbone. "I knew you two were going to end up together. Are you moving in to live with us? Are you guys getting married? Can I be the flower girl?"

When I glance up at Trey for help, his eyes are locked on me, but he's covering up what I imagine is a smirk with his to-go coffee cup as he takes a sip. This is exactly what he's worried about, and I get it. He's right—no more late-night kisses, no getting too close and forgetting that all of this is temporary. If not for us, then at least for Adeline.

I wrap my arms around her back and quickly come up with a rebuttal since Trey has gone silent. Traitor.

"You would make for a perfect flower girl, but I have something even better than a wedding. How would you feel about me being your nanny for a little while?" I tell her, trying to redirect her as quickly as possible.

"You'd be my nanny?" she asks, confusion but maybe a little bit of hope in it.

"If that's okay with you," I say, suddenly nervous about her reaction.

That huge, beautiful grin that looks so much like Trey's flashes across her face again. "Yes! This is perfect. Now you can help me with my ballet bun because Uncle Trey is hopeless."

"Hey," he protests, halfheartedly.

"And can we make your special hot cocoa on the nights you watch me? Charlotte never could make it like you, and Uncle Trey could burn water." She begs. Trey opens his mouth to protest again, but then just shrugs.

"They don't teach Home Economics in boot camp?" I tease.

"Too busy dodging bed bugs and barfing up my own guts from running a marathon every day."

I smile over at him, and he smirks back.

"Wait!" Adeline says, pulling out of our hug, and then grips both of my hands in hers. "Does this mean we're going to have sleepovers too? Can we invite Isla and Berkeley some nights?"

I nod. "We'll ask, okay? That sounds fun."

"I know!" She climbs onto a stool, grabbing a bagel from Serendipity's bag, already spreading on cream cheese. "This is going to be the best having another girl in the house."

Trey checks his watch. "I've got practice. You two good here?" he asks.

The question is directed at both of us, but his eyes linger on mine. Checking one last time that I'm sure about this.

I am. Maybe for the wrong reasons, but I am.

"We'e good," I assure him. "Go be a hockey star."

He snorts, grabbing his keys. "Hardly. Adeline, behave for Vivi. And remember—"

"I know, I know." She rolls her eyes. "Brush my teeth, pack my homework, don't forget my ballet bag."

He drops a kiss on top of her head, then hesitates like he wants to say something else. Instead, he just nods and heads out.

The door closes behind him, and Adeline turns to me with a mischievous grin. "So...do you like my uncle?"

I choke on my coffee. "What?"

"Because he likes you. Like, like-likes you." She takes another huge bite of a bagel. "I can tell."

"Adeline..." I start, not sure how to handle this conversation.

"It's okay." She shrugs. "I won't tell him that you watch him when he's not looking."

Heat floods my cheeks as I glance down. Busted by a nine-year-old.

"Come on," I say, desperate to change the subject. "Let's get you ready for ballet. Show me this infamous ballet bun situation. We'll tackle it together."

She chatters the whole way upstairs about her upcoming recital, but my mind keeps drifting to Trey. To the conversation we had about how if we kiss again, he won't be able to hold back next time.

Six weeks. That's how long I have to be Adeline's nanny and help Trey find a replacement.

But as I help Adeline with her hair, taking in the lingering scent of Trey in every inch of this house and the sweetness of this little girl in my care, I'm starting to worry that walking away might not be as easy as I thought.

CHAPTER EIGHT

Trey

Four thirty a.m. and I'm already on edge.

My shoulder throbs from sleeping wrong on the floor again, but it's better than the couch where the nightmares come easier.

Something about the softness of the cushions makes me sleep harder, and then the memories flood back—carrying John's body from our Black Hawk that got shot down, watching him die in my arms as a rescue chopper came in, flying us over an endless sea to the nearest medic unit. I wake with night sweat in the middle of the night, remembering the explosion that took half my hearing, losing John on that mission. And then I lost Tommy within weeks. I'll never forget the look on my commander's face when he walked into my hospital room and told me what had happened to Tommy and Sarah.

I swore to him after John Parker died that I wasn't done. That I would do whatever surgery, whatever therapy I needed to do to get back out there.

The mission wasn't over, and John wasn't going to die without meaning—not on my watch. It was a long shot, the doctors told me—that I'd be able to walk, let alone regain most of my hearing back, but the odds have been against me since being born into the family that I was. I knew that I was made of something stronger than the X-rays or the CT scans or what doctors could prove on a clipboard.

But then my commander told me that he was issuing a medical discharge against my wishes, because my nine-year-old niece was now mine to care for. She was an orphan, and she would either go to me or to the state. My brother's will and trust denied our parents' ability to fight for custody. Luckily, they didn't know about the life insurance policy that my brother had for her. A life insurance policy that I put every penny back into a trust for her. They would have done anything they could to get their hands on that money

That's the moment it all sunk in. Everything I lost. It only took three weeks for a lifetime of hardening myself up to realize that you can never prepare for the worst three weeks of your life. John, then Tommy, and next...my military career. Adeline became my new mission—my new purpose.

My phone pings with a text.

Kaenan

I just picked it up. On my way to your place.

The sound of tires on wet pavement draws my attention. He can't be here yet.

Through the front window, I watch as Vivi pulls up in Isla's car. She steps out wearing black running tights and a fitted jacket, her dark hair pulled back in a high ponytail. The sight of her here, at my house, in casual clothes ... it does things to my control that I'm not proud of.

I open the door and step out into the cold February morning. "Good morning," I say.

She smiles as she walks up with two bags of groceries.

"Morning."

"Here, let me take those for you," I offer, reaching out to take the bags that she's clutching to keep anything from falling.

"Thank you. That would be great."

I take the bags, and her face shows instant relief. The bags are heavier than they look. "Damn, this bag is heavy. What the hell do you buy at the grocery store? Dumbbells?"

"Don't be dramatic," she says, then follows me in, closes the door behind us, kicks off her shoes, and hangs Isla's keys on the key ring by the door. The car she's been driving since the board took her company car.

In the kitchen, I set the grocery bags on the island, unsure of her plans with any of this.

"Let me know what you paid for it. I'll reimburse you for anything you spend."

"It was no trouble. Just some things for breakfast that I promised Adeline."

I turn back toward the grocery bag because all those curves of hers have me thinking about what I would like for breakfast... and the last thing either of us needs right now is for me to pull her up onto the island and show her what I'm capable of doing between her thighs.

I reach in and grab a bag of chocolate chips.

"What are these for?" I ask.

"I brought stuff for chocolate chip pancakes. But don't worry, I'm making her eggs and bacon too. I wouldn't sugar her up too much before school."

She thinks of everything. But that makes sense. This is what she used to do, and her company runs an entire fleet of nannies now.

"My breakfast skills are pretty much cereal or store-bought breakfast burritos from the freezer," I admit, following her into the kitchen. The way she moves through my space, like she belongs here... It's dangerous how right it feels.

She shoos me away from the bag with a playful smirk and

then starts to unload the rest of the contents. "Watch out Chef Boyardee, Trey Hartley's making a play for your job."

I try to keep my distance from her standing barefoot in my kitchen. Too close might kill me.

In less than two months, Vivi will marry Jameson Holiday and become the perfect corporate wife with charity brunches and country club tennis matches on her schedule just like she was born and bred for. And I'll go back to being what I am—a broken soldier trying his best to raise his brother's daughter.

"It could be worse. The pantry could be stocked with military-issued rations that taste like cardboard," I tell her, leaning against the granite countertop. "And trust me when I say, those are the good flavored ones that we'd all fight over."

"Stop, you're killing my fantasy of military life," she says, unpacking ingredients, her movements efficient and graceful. "The outfits, the food, the luxurious sleeping accommodations." She glances at me through her lashes. "I think I could pull off a tight military bun too. What do you think?"

The image of Vivi in fatigues, hair pulled back in a regulation bun, gives me a new set of fantasies about her. Not that I need anymore. She stars in all of them. My cock twitches, and I shift my stance behind the island.

"You'd make for the cutest damn soldier I've ever seen," I say. "You'd have a waitlist of men willing to watch your back. That I can guarantee."

And I'd have to fight every single one of them off. The thought shouldn't please me as much as it does.

She reaches for a mixing bowl in the top cabinet, stretching up on her toes. The movement pulls her jacket up, revealing a strip of tanned skin at her lower back. My hands itch to touch her there. Feel her soft skin against my fingertips.

"The cutest?" she asks, tossing me a look over her shoulder. "Did you ever date any women in the Army? I'm sure there had to be plenty of good-looking girls on base."

I move behind her before I can stop myself, reaching up

to grab the bowl she's struggling to reach. The heat of her body radiates through my thin T-shirt as I press against her back.

"Date? No." The words come out low, close to her ear. "I never dated any military personnel. The base is too damn small for that. That's how you end up with a broken nose, or worse."

She lowers back to flat feet, her ass sliding down my front in a way that tests every ounce of my control. I step back quickly, putting distance between us before I do something stupid like spin her around and make good on what I told her I would have done to her two nights ago.

She turns around to face me, the bowl now in her hands. "What about outside the military?" There's a slight flush coloring her cheeks where there wasn't before. "Any ex-girlfriends with a voodoo doll with your face glued to it and pins in your heart that I need to keep a lookout for cutting the brakes to your SUV?"

I laugh. "No, nothing like that." Though I'm sure there's enough people out there in the world that want me dead. Me and every member of my unit for the last fifteen years.

In fact, I wouldn't put it past my parents to have a voodoo doll of me. Ever since I gave up a probable first-round pick position in the NHL my senior year to enlist, they've made it clear I owe them for "wasting their investment." The letters and voicemails haven't stopped in fifteen years. They birthed me, they're broke, living in poverty, dad needs surgery—how could I be so cruel after they gave me and Tommy so much?

The state should have taken us away with how they would abandon us for weeks, sometimes months at a time, to panhandle or whatever scheme they had going on at the time in a different state. But I always made sure that no one ever found out. I made excuses to the ladies at the food banks where I'd ride my bike to get groceries for us. I'd lie to the schools when they asked to talk to a parent, or I'd use the money I'd make pulling weeds around town to get a bum to agree to take their call and pretend to be my dad for a six-pack of beer. I knew they would put us in a home—probably separate us because who wanted to take on two pre-teen boys?

But when they started seeing me win hockey championships with my high school team, and scouts started coming around, my parents set up a "home" for all of us. They pushed the happy family image, and my father loved flaunting me around town, telling everyone how much my contract amounts would be, getting our meals comped at restaurants, free shit for just showing up with me to places, and betting on my games.

So I did the one and only thing I could to hurt them. I took away their precious hockey star image, enlisted in the Army, and filed emancipation paperwork to make sure they were never tied to me ever again.

"Come on," she says, planting a hand on her hip. "You have to have some kind of juicy ex-girlfriend story to share so we're even."

"Even?"

She rolls her eyes at me like I'm being intentionally daft. "You're part of my runaway bride origin story, so it seems only fair that you share something equally embarrassing from your past." Her smile turns teasing. "Out with it. No one is lucky enough to have a drama-free life. Where are your closet skeletons, Trey Hartley?"

The playfulness drains from my body. My hands grip the counter until my knuckles turn white as memories flood back—not the ones she's asking for. Not the lives taken under my command. Not John bleeding out in my arms. Not the hospital bed where I learned Tommy and Sarah were gone while I was overseas with no way to have protected them.

"Trey?" Her voice softens, concern replacing the teasing. "Are you okay? Did I say something wrong?"

Am I okay?

Is something wrong?

How do I answer that? Where would I even begin?

And if by some miracle, I could somehow unload a lifetime of everything that's wrong with me, where would that leave us?

Would she pity me? Would she see the massive canyon

between our upbringings?

How I was raised with an outstretched hand for spare change my parents made us beg for as kids, while she grew up in a mansion with everything she could have wanted?

Will she see that I don't have the charisma and polish that Jameson has? Will she judge me for enlisting and leaving Tommy behind with my parents, forcing him to play hockey and live in the shadow I left? Will she think I'm broken—unfixable?

Am I broken and unfixable?

"Vivi... I—"

"Uncle Trey," Adeline's voice drifts down from upstairs, followed by the sound of small feet on stairs. "Is Vivi here?"

Vivi's eyes meet mine, understanding passing between us. Some stories aren't meant for nine-year-old ears. My stories aren't meant for anyone.

Yeah, I have skeletons. Skeletons that I'll never let anyone see.

"Yeah," I call out. "She's here."

Adeline appears in her penguin pajamas, rubbing sleep from her eyes. The sight of her like this, innocent and young. She looks so much like Tommy at this age that it almost hurts. His eyes would search mine, looking for me to fix everything. To tell him that we'd be okay until mom and dad showed back up. He believed me...every time. And then I left him.

I was supposed to protect him. To keep him safe. I failed him then, but I won't fail his daughter now.

"You're up early, squirt." I force lightness into my voice.

"I'm sorry, Adeline. Were we too loud?" Vivi moves to her side, gentle hands guiding her toward the kitchen.

"No, you didn't wake me. I was just so excited that you were going to be here this morning." Adeline's whole face lights up. "And you said if I got up early enough, we could make pancakes before school. I didn't want to miss it."

Vivi catches my eye, her smile soft. I can't help but notice how natural they look together.

"That's true, I did say that." She grabs a stool from under the island and Adeline follows her to the stove. "You're just in time because I was about to start them. Why don't you take a seat right here, and I'll let you add the chocolate chips? I'm almost done with the batter."

Adeline practically bounces onto the stool. "Yes, please!"

"I'd better go," I say to Adeline. "I'll see you later."

I head for the hallway but can't resist one last look at them—Vivi measuring ingredients while Adeline chatters about chocolate chip placement strategy. They look like they belong there, together, in my kitchen, in my life.

Then I hear a honk from outside. Shit... I almost forgot.

"What was that for?" Vivi asks.

I glance at her and then down to Adeline. "I forgot that Kaenan is coming by this morning to drop off something from his friend who owns a dealership downtown," I glance down at Adeline. "Should we go see what it is?"

Adeline's eyes light up, practically jumping off the stool and races past me towards the door.

"Come on," I wave at Vivi to join us.

"What dealership did Kaenan go to downtown?" she asks as we head down the hall. Adeline opens the front door and leaves it wide open, and I grab Isla's car keys that Vivi set on the key ring.

I watch the second that Kaenan pulls into the driveway, driving a brand-new Range Rover.

"Kaenan bought a new car for Isla? Because he's not the Range Rover type," Vivi says.

"Nope." Kaenan steps out of the front seat. He tosses me the keys, and then I toss him Isla's keys for him to drive back to his house.

"Morning Berkeley. Have a good day," he tells her and then heads for Isla's car and gets in, pulling out of the driveway and heading home.

"I'm so confused. What just happened?" Vivi asks.

I toss her the keys to the new Range Rover. She stares down at the key fob as if it's a foreign object that she doesn't know how it got there.

"The car is for you."

She whips her vision from me, back to the car. "For me? You borrowed a car for me to use while I nanny?"

"No, I didn't borrow it. I bought it for you. It's yours. Consider it a perk of the job, and I'll sleep better knowing that you have a reliable car of your own."

She stares back at me. "Wait...you're serious? You just went out and bought me a brand new Range Rover? The same make and model as the one I had before?"

"It's not a big deal."

"Not a big deal?" She gives a non-comical laugh as if that's the craziest thing she's ever heard. "You think a two-hundred-thousand-dollar car is not a big deal? I think you and I have different definitions of the meaning," she says, taking me off guard since, from what I know about her, she was spoiled with expensive cars, luxury clothes, and private schools most of her life as a Newport. Her reaction is surprising but also endearing. "This is a huge deal, and I can't let you give me a car."

"Too late. I put it in your name when I paid for it cash last night at the dealership. It's yours."

"It's so pretty!" Adeline's squeals, running for it. "I call front seat."

"I don't understand how this happened."

"Kaenan knows the Range Rover dealership owner. I asked if they had a brand-new white Range Rover on the lot. Like the one those assholes took. They did so I asked them to hold it for me. Kaenan drove down this morning and met him to get the car so I could be home when you got here."

"Oh my God... Trey. This is too much. Take it back. This is too much."

"Too late. It's already in your name. I signed the documents electronically last night. Consider it a bonus."

"I can't accept this."

"I'll feel better knowing that you have your own transportation and that you're safe."

I walk over to Adeline, who checks every pocket, every cup holder, oohing and awwing at everything.

"I have to go to practice. Love you. Be good." I say, bending into the passenger front side of the car and giving Adeline a kiss on the top of her head.

"We're not done with this conversation," Vivi says, walking up carefully towards the car as if it might bite her if she turns her back on it. "You can't just buy me a car with cash and act like it's nothing—no strings. What happens in two months when you get a new nanny and I go back to being the CEO of Newport Staffing?"

"Then I guess you'll have two cars, but at least one they can't ever take away from you again."

"Trey, this is too extravagant."

"I have more than enough money to buy you a car. I was paid well in the Army, and I made a lot when I was on active duty. I lived on base and didn't spend hardly anything. And now with my contract guarantee from the Hawkeyes...I'd need two lifetimes to spend all of it. I'm sure you're worth ten times my net worth, but I can assure you that I have more than enough to buy you a car."

She tilts her head at me as if this whole thing is ridiculous. "Trey—"

"Just consider it a signing bonus. You're grossly overqualified for the job anyway." I say, walking back to the house to grab my duffel bag that sits just inside. Vivi's on my tail the entire time, a little shadow I can't shake, and maybe I like giving her a reason to follow me around.

Maybe I need to piss her off with expensive grand gestures more often so she'll follow me around nagging at me. I'd take a lifetime of Vivi nagging...just tell me where to sign.

"Well, I don't know about ten times your wealth, but I can assure you that right now, that net worth isn't doing shit for me. In fact, it sort of has a noose around my neck."

I slide the duffel bag strap over my shoulder and then turn to face her, anger toward her board members bubbles up in my veins again like yesterday, when she said that her company took away her car. "If anyone is threatening you Vivi, or forcing you to do something you don't consent to, you'll tell me, right? I'll take care of it. You never have to know."

She looks up at me and blinks twice as if I just threatened to kill someone—which I sort of did. Sometimes I have to remember that when people see me, I can make them uneasy. My size, my tattoos, my military background. The last thing I want her to be is scared of me, but I do want her to know that I won't stand by if anyone ever tries to hurt her.

She sucks in her bottom lip, and then I see it—the kind of interest I see in some women when they know what I'm capable of. What I was trained for over the last fifteen years in the Army's special forces.

"This conversation still isn't over," Vivi threatens.

"Yes, it is because we've butchered the conversation at this point, but nothing will change the fact that the deal is already done and signed for. Now you two had better go in or the pancakes are going to get cold."

I force myself to leave before I can think too hard about how empty this house will feel when she's gone and how I need to fill it with someone else that Adeline likes to make the transition as easy as possible for her.

CHAPTER NINE

Vivi

I tap the marker against my chin, searching for something more personal to add to the dry-erase board in my kitchen. My "Reasons to Marry Jameson" list. Something that speaks to actual feelings rather than business strategy. The marker stays poised, but nothing comes.

My phone buzzes on the counter. A text from Genevieve Holiday.

Genevieve

He finally responded. Says he'll be back when the honeymoon is over, not a day before.

My stomach drops. I've been nannying Adeline for a week now, which puts me five weeks away from Jameson coming home. I was hoping that somehow he'd postpone—just a little longer.

Another text follows:

Genevieve

Fix this, Vivi. Or we both lose everything.

I set my phone face down, unable to look at it anymore. The marker squeaks against the board as I add one more item to the list:

He'll keep his inheritance

But for now, the word I'm keeping is to a little girl and her uncle, waiting for me to take her to ballet.

The ballet studio is already buzzing when Adeline and I arrive. Mothers in designer athleisure crowd the viewing area, their whispers following me as I help Adeline with her shoes.

"Isn't that the Newport heiress?" one stage-whispers. "The one who left Jameson Holiday at the altar?"

"Who leaves a man that gorgeous?" another asks.

"Maybe some secret lover? I heard that there was a getaway car waiting," another whispers.

I focus on Adeline's laces, pretending not to hear. But she notices.

"Don't listen to them," she says fiercely. "They're just jealous because you're prettier than they are and you're going to marry my uncle instead."

"Adeline..." I warn.

"Oh really? And why do you think that?" Isla asks.

"Because Uncle Trey bought Vivi a new car," then Adeline slaps her hand across her face. "Oh right, I wasn't supposed to say anything."

Isla's laugh carries across the studio. She's sitting in the bleachers. She and Berkeley got here before us and is clearly enjoying my predicament.

"Time for class!" I practically shove her toward the dance floor. "Go line up with Berkeley.

She skips off towards the other girls lining up along the balancing beam, leaving me to face the curious stares of Seattle's elite dance moms who overheard everything. I escape to Isla's side, pretending I don't see them watching me.

"Enjoying the show?" I mutter.

"Immensely." She hands me a coffee. "So...about this car situation."

"Don't start."

"A brand new Range Rover—same trim, color, and interior as the one that Richard took from you. That's quite a grand gesture."

"Hold on. How did you know that it's identical to my company car?" I ask, my eyebrows pointed as I side-eye her.

She just stares on at the girls across the room with a smirk. "Trey called Kaenan and asked."

I shake my head. The lengths he went to for me.

"But to be honest. I bet he would have gotten it right without Kaenan. Trey is incredibly observant, and when it comes to you, he doesn't miss a thing."

I shake off her words, though they land like she wanted them to.

"It's not that big of a deal. You're blowing it out of proportion," I say, taking Trey's stance when I tried to reason with him about buying me the car yesterday. "The car is just so I can drive Adeline around." But even I don't believe that excuse anymore.

"Right." She sips her coffee, watching the girls warm up.

"I do have to confess something, though," I tell her. It's been eating at me to have no one to talk to about this. I stare over at the other dance moms that seem to be chatting amongst themselves at this point and aren't close enough to be in earshot. "I sort of kissed Trey...on accident."

She nearly chokes and spins in the bleacher to stare straight at me. "You did what? When did this happen? How did he take it?"

"It was the night he took me home from Oakley's. He was reaching for the door, and I sort of ... thought he was leaning in to kiss me," I admit, both of my hands wrapping around the warm to-go paper coffee cup.

"And?"

"And nothing. We agreed that nothing more can happen because of Adeline," I say, and I wipe the light mauve lipstick stain from the opening of my coffee cup. "He's right. She's already too attached to the idea of us together."

"But you want it to happen again."

It's not a question. She knows me too well.

"It doesn't matter what I want. In five weeks, I have to marry Jameson or lose everything. To be fair, I don't even know Trey well enough to know if something between us would even happen if I was available to do anything about it," I show her Genevieve's text. "He's finally surfaced, by the way. Still in Greece with Natasha."

"Forget Jameson for right now." Isla's voice turns to reason. "Let's be honest for a second here. If you were available to date someone, do you really believe that you don't know if something would happen between you two?"

"I'm not sure if I would take the risk. I've had so many bad relationships. That was part of the appeal with Jameson."

"I know. You've had some real dud exes, and I get it." She nods. "But what do you really want?"

What do I want?

I want to keep my company and do what I promised my staff I would do. I want to prove I can succeed without my father's influence. I want to wake up excited about my life instead of dreading another day of corporate politics, power hungry board members, and a trust fund that will probably require any children that Jameson and I have to be forced into an arranged marriage just like he and his siblings.

I want Trey's hands on me again. His lips on mine. His voice in my ear telling me all the things he'd do to me if we didn't have to stop.

"What I want doesn't matter," I say finally. "Some of us can't afford to follow our hearts."

"That's dad talking." She squeezes my hand. "You're not that girl anymore, Vivi. You don't have to do what's expected."

But don't I? My entire identity is wrapped up in Newport Staffing. In proving I'm more than just a trust fund kid playing CEO. If I lose that, what do I have left? And how many people do I let down in the process?

"You should come out with all of us to the home game tomorrow night. I already told Trey I'd pick up Adeline so you might as well come out with us. Cammy got us Everett Kauffman's owner box."

"That sounds fun. I'll ask Trey tonight to make sure that's okay with him."

Then, in the corner of my eye, I see Adeline wave over at me.

"Watch this, Vivi!" Adeline calls from the barre. She executes a perfect pirouette, beaming with pride.

My heart squeezes, and I clap for her. Then I think about how it's not only Trey I can't have. In just over a month and a week from now, I'll have to leave her, too. Not in the physical sense. I'll still be around for girls' night at Isla's, birthday parties, and Little Hawks practices, but I won't be her nanny anymore. No more chocolate chip pancake mornings and a little girl taking up my entire passenger seat with all of her backpacks and after school gear. After what Trey said about people leaving her, the thought that I will be just another person to walk out of her life has heartburn rising in my throat.

The rest of class passes in a blur. Before I know it, Isla and I are standing from the hard bleachers, intentionally designed to hope that ballet parents won't stay, is my guess, and step down onto the wood flooring to wait for the girls as their instructor gives them all a hug, dismissing each one separately.

A woman steps up to us, giving Isla a tight smile, and then turns to me. I swear she looks familiar, but I can't place her. "Did I hear that you're Adeline's new nanny?"

"Yes, I am ... temporarily. I'm Vivi," I say.

"Theresa," she says, forcing a smile as if it's almost painful. Then I register her as one of the moms who practically chased Trey out to his car the day he saved me from my wedding, but I think I've seen her at Oakley's in her jersey before too? Now I see why Trey is concerned about accidentally sleeping with a dance mom or a teacher in this town. "Temporarily? I see," she says, a real smile coming to her cheeks now as if she's already glad to see me go. "It's too bad that Charlotte left Trey high and dry like she did. I offered to fill in whenever he might need me, but he never called."

"I can guess why," Isla mutters, under a fake cough.

"You okay there, Sis?" I say, slapping her back with a good amount of force a few times as if I'm helping dislodge a chicken bone from her lungs.

"Ouch!" she groans, stepping out of my reach. "You're hurting me."

"Anyway," I say, turning back to the ballet mom who offered to help with *whatever* he might need. I can read between the lines. "As you were saying?"

"I just didn't realize he found someone so quickly. How convenient."

I nod dramatically. "Almost like it was written in the stars—meant to be. The right place at the right time. That sort of thing."

Her smile fades quickly, and admittedly, I'm enjoying this too much. "Right..." she says, trying her best to keep her lips from pursing with annoyance that I'm clearly in the spot she was hoping to wiggle her push-up bra and fake Hermes handbag into. "Well, I'd love to get the girls together for a play date sometime. We are available most days and are happy to come to you to make it easy. I believe Trey just bought a house in the subdivision just down the road from us."

Oh, so now she's a stalker. This woman is a level of creepy and desperate that I can now see why Trey was happy to bring Kaenan his cufflinks and was more than happy to give away ballet duties to me.

"We could bring dinner to lighten your load. I have a foolproof casserole that I know Trey would love. He's off on Monday nights, right?"

"Oh God..." Isla mumbles under her breath.

Berkeley and Adeline run over to us after pulling over their jackets and track pants.

"You know what?" I say, helping Adeline put her backpack on her shoulders. "I'll get back to you, okay? Our schedule is a little crazy right now."

"Sure...right. Trey's heading towards the playoffs—very exciting," she beams. "Just let me know, we can be available anytime that works for Trey."

I look down at Adeline, whose eyes are wide as she subtly shakes her head "no" at my side.

"Of course. We'll see you around, Theresa."

The four of us turn and head for the exit.

"Please don't invite them over. Her daughter is rude, and she's terrible at ballet. Her mom pays double to keep her in this class."

"Why would she do that?" I ask as Isla and Berkeley hold the doors open.

Isla rolls her eyes. "You can't guess? Momma's trying to land an NHL player."

I shake my head and then hit the unlock on the car.

"See you girls tomorrow night at the game," Isla calls over.

I wave and climb in, Adeline already buckling her seatbelt.

"CAN WE MAKE pasta tonight for dinner?" Adeline asks, already heading to the pantry to grab the ingredients.

"Whatever you want, sweetie."

"And just so you know...Uncle Trey doesn't like casseroles," she says with a smirk.

I laugh. "Noted."

She chatters about her day while we cook, and I try not to think about how domestic this feels. How right. The front door opens just as we're setting the table.

"Something smells good," Trey calls out.

He appears in the doorway, fresh from the gym and a fitted T-shirt that does illegal things to his shoulders. His hair is pulled back in a backwards hat, the side of his hair still damp from his shower, and the sight of him like this—relaxed, at home—makes my heart stutter.

Why are backward hats so damn sexy?

It's the eighth wonder of the world.

"We made pasta!" Adeline runs to hug him.

"I can see that." His eyes meet mine over her head. "You didn't have to cook."

"Yes, we did. You're cooking was about to poison me," Adeline says, making a choking noise with her hands around her throat.

He chuckles. "Maybe we should drop you out of ballet and put you in drama school instead." He pats her head and then walks toward the fridge, pulls out a bottle of water, twists off the cap, and drinks half of it in one gulp.

"I second that decision," I tease.

"Oh yeah?" he asks. "Why is that?"

Trey plants a hand on the island and stares over at me as he downs the rest of his bottle of water.

"Vivi met Theresa today at ballet," Adeline says.

Trey takes a sharp gulp. "Oh..."

"Just a heads up. She knows where you live, and she really wants to feed you casserole." I tell him.

"You didn't invite her over, did you?" he asks with a look of concern on his face.

"God no. I'm not a masochist."

He relaxes. "Good. She's crazy, and I've been avoiding her since Adeline started ballet there."

I reach for the Parmesan cheese and begin to add a little more to the finished pasta.

Trey walks up behind me and reaches around me, plucking a hot penne noodle from the pot and plops it in his mouth. "Damn, that's good. I'm starving. But you didn't have to cook. I could have ordered in."

"We wanted to." I busy myself with the sauce to avoid staring at him. "How was the gym?"

He moves closer, reaching past me for plates, his hand gently sliding over my hip as if to keep me from stepping back into him. The heat of his touch sends electricity down my spine.

"Good. Coach Haynes thinks we're ready for tomorrow's game." His voice drops lower. "Isla's going to come get Adeline after school and bring her to the game tomorrow night. I already cleared it with her."

"Actually, about that." I start. "Isla invited me to tag along with everyone. I mean...if that's okay." I tuck a string of hair behind my ear. "You don't have to pay me or anything. I'd just be coming to watch the game for fun with the girls."

"Of course it's okay. You're always welcome at the games. Adeline has access to my season tickets anytime you two want to come without an invite from the wives."

Adeline walks over to take the plates from Trey to set the table, and he reaches over and ruffles her hair, making her giggle. "I always love having my loudest cheerleader in the stands."

"That's me!" Adeline beams.

"Biggest shit-talker out there too," he stage-whispers to me. "She's going to get me kicked out of a game one of these days."

"I learned it from you," Adeline shoots back.

"Is this ready for the table?" Trey asks, pointing to the bowl of pasta piled high.

"Yes, and the salad and green beans are ready too," I tell him.

He grabs as much as he can and heads for the kitchen table where Adeline is setting out napkins and silverware.

Then my phone buzzes as I remember the rolls in the pantry.

I stop and read the text.

Dad

You haven't returned my calls about the wedding. How are you holding up? What's going on with the board? I heard they kicked you out of the CEO position. Call me. Let me help.

But I still can't bring myself to take his call. To hear the disappointment in his voice. I remember how he treated Isla when she ran off from her cheating fiancé five years ago. They've patched up their relationship since, and he's trying with Berkeley and Oliver.

He set up a trust fund for both of them—no strings attached. Still, his expectations for his daughters are different from his expectations for his grandchildren. He was so happy that I was engaged to Jameson, and I'd be lying if I said the little girl in me wasn't happy to have his approval for once. The little girl who was abandoned by her biological father. Who grew up with a single mother who was barely making ends meet until she married Conrad Newport.

I leave my phone on the counter and head for the pantry, grabbing the rolls, and then head for the dinner table, where Trey and Adeline are dishing up. Adeline is already telling an animated story with her hands while Trey listens as if it's the most amusing story he's ever heard.

Right now, this is where I want to be—no distractions.

Because two months with them is all I get.

CHAPTER TEN

Vivi

The security guard checks our passes and waves us through to the executive level. Adeline practically bounces down the hallway ahead of us, her handmade HARTLEY jersey sparkling with the rhinestones she and Berkeley spent hours applying yesterday, while Berkeley decorated her custom ALTMAN jersey with her dad's retired number on the back that Isla designed.

"Wait up!" Berkeley calls, racing to catch up with Adeline. Oliver does his best to keep up. The girls' matching rhinestone Hawkeyes jerseys catch the overhead lights, throwing tiny rainbow prisms across the walls.

"Girls, no running!" Isla calls after them. "And watch out for your brother. He's following you," she warns, but they're already around the corner, all three of their giggles echoing off the walls.

I adjust my own jersey—also bedazzled, though I tried to protest. Not because I don't love all of their hard work—and what girl doesn't love a little sparkle—but because wearing Trey's name on my back and his number feels oddly personal. Maybe because I'm not just a fan, I'm his nanny, and to pretend there isn't sexual tension between us would be silly and potentially dangerous to our working situation if one of us gives into it. We're too old for games anyway, and Trey's concern that anything happening between us could hurt Adeline is a valid reason not to let anything go beyond a working relationship. "They'll get lost," I say, moving faster to follow.

"Berkeley knows where they're going." Isla loops her arm through mine. "She's been coming here since she was two. Besides, Cammy's already up there waiting for them with goodie bags. Hawkeyes stickers, hats, foam fingers, and coloring books."

The engagement ring on my left hand catches the light, and I resist the urge to take it off. Genevieve's texts were clear—wear it in public or risk everything falling apart faster. Somehow, it feels heavier tonight, more constricting than it did for the six months Jameson and I were engaged. Now it feels especially out of place with HARTLEY stretched across my shoulders.

We reach the owner's box, and I take it all in. I've been to games before, dozens in the Hawkeyes stadium, sitting in Kaenan's season ticket seats with Isla, but I've never been up here. The space is massive, easily able to hold a hundred people, though tonight it's just the usual crew, some of the legal team and corporate employees, players' wives, girlfriends, and families.

Floor-to-ceiling windows stretch across the entire front wall, offering a perfect view of the ice below. The walls are decorated in team colors—turquoise and black—with jerseys from every player mounted in between. A massive mahogany bar with an illuminated blue top that looks like ice dominates one wall, while a buffet that could feed half the stadium lines another.

"Vivi! Over here!" Cammy, Brynn, and Penelope wave from one of the high-top tables along the windows. It's only half the crew, but some of the wives, like Coach Haynes' wife, Juliet, sit in her husband's seats with her brother, opting to be closer to the ice.

Adeline, Berkeley, and Oliver are already loading plates with everything from sushi rolls to barbecue ribs and everything in between.

"This is..." I trail off, taking it all in as I follow Cammy and Isla to the buffet table.

"Different from the regular seats?" Isla finishes.

I nod. I've watched dozens of games from the family section, but this feels more intimate somehow. Like I'm crossing over into a territory only meant for someone who's close to the team...or in my case, close to a player.

"Come on." Isla tugs me toward the buffet. "Let's get food before face-off."

As we load our plates, I catch snippets of conversation around us.

"Did you see what that reporter wrote about Trey's stats?"

"The playoffs are going to be intense this year."

"I can't believe Everett Kauffman hasn't been here much. Where is he?"

That last one has me curious too. Everett Kauffman, the new Hawkeyes owner, has been as elusive as Jameson with his lack of correspondence back to me. I know how these circles work in the Hawkeyes world—how fast gossip travels, how quickly assumptions become truth. Sure enough, when I turn around, several WAGs are watching me with poorly concealed interest. I've known these women for too long for them to hide anything from me, and if they've been talking to Isla...they're all sitting there wondering if I'll be the next one to join the WAGs roster.

Everyone here's heard about my runaway wedding, but I'm hoping the conversation doesn't come up, because the truth is, I have no idea what to say at this point.

"Vivi!" Peyton, Hunter Reed's girlfriend and the host of the sports podcast *Bleacher Report,* waves us over. "Come sit with us. The girls said you're helping out Trey? Thank God, poor Adeline. Having Charlotte drop them like that...it really sucked."

"It's just temporary. Until he can find a replacement," I say, forking a spiral noodle from the pasta salad and taking a bite.

"How is it going with Adeline? She's really the sweetest. I hate how much she's gone through," Cammy says, her voice low, checking to make sure Adeline isn't close enough to hear us, and then chomps down on a carrot dipped in garlic hummus.

"We're still getting our schedule down, but so far we haven't hit any issues."

Isla snickers. "You mean besides the ballet mom trying to use her kid to get her claws into Trey? Or how about the fact that Trey bought you a brand new Range Rover and you won't admit that things are heating up between you two," Isla offers up, while she takes a sip of the lavender blood-orange kombucha that the wet bar has on tap up here.

What is this place? Seriously? I'm half expecting them to roll out an entire pig roasted on a spit at this point.

"Thanks for the subtlety, Sis..." I say with a scowl. I love these girls, I do, but their men are the biggest gossips in the locker room, and if even one of them says anything about Trey and me to a Hawkeyes player, there is no stopping the rumor mill. It's worse than the sorority I went to in college. Even those girls can keep a better secret than this group can. I just hope the tabloids don't get their hands on any of the gossip circulating in the Hawkeyes stadium.

"Just paying it forward," she grins, reminding me that I sort of did something like this to her when I was trying to get her to see that Kaenan was the guy she was meant to be with when she first started nannying for him.

"What?" Peyton perks up, her jaw dropping. "I'm not even sure which one to start with. Crazy dance mom or grand gesture purchases."

"So, what's going on with you two?" Penelope Matthews—team GM and wife to the Hawkeyes' forward, Slade Matthews—asks as she returns from the buffet, clearly having kept one ear on our conversation the entire time.

"Nothing. I just have some time off from work for the next little while and he needs someone to help with Adeline until he finds someone else. That's it."

"Well, that jersey looks good on you," Cammy says with a

knowing smirk.

Before I can respond, the lights dim and the crowd below roars. The team skates out for warm-ups.

"Uncle Trey!" Adeline presses against the glass. "He's on the ice."

I glance down as the announcer calls each of their names. Then I see him. Trey Hartley, number fourteen. The same number I've watched score countless goals, throw bone-crushing checks, and carry my niece around on his shoulders at team barbecues.

"Earth to Vivi." Isla nudges me. "You're staring."

I tear my gaze away, but not before I catch Trey looking up at the owner's box. Even from this distance, the heat in his eyes makes my skin tingle.

God help me. This is going to be a long night.

I watch him as he moves with lethal grace. Power and control wrapped in tattoos and layers of protective hockey gear.

"Admit it. You're glad you're here and not in Santorini with Jameson," Isla says, standing next to me with Berkeley, Adeline, and Oliver on the other side of me, elbow deep in blue cotton candy and a mountain of nachos and cheese, not paying attention to us as their eyes are glued to the ice and the players.

"You know I can't say that. I might lose my CEO position, and even worse, I might have cost Jameson his entire inheritance and family standing."

"Then look at that ring on your finger," Isla says gently. "And then look at that jersey on your back. Which one feels more like you?"

Before I can answer, Adeline jumps with excitement.

"Uncle Trey scored in warm-ups," Adeline announces, blue cotton candy already staining her lips and fingers. "Did you see that?"

"I saw," I say, helping her settle her snacks on the high-top tables near them. "Are you going to share any of that?"

She tears off a piece of cotton candy and holds it out. "Only because you're wearing his jersey."

I accept the sugar with a laugh, trying to ignore the fact that I miss this—miss being a nanny—being part of a family. Every minute with Adeline feels like I'd never get sick of this ... being with her.

The lights dim again, and the team circles up for final instructions. Trey glances up one more time, and this time I'm sure he sees me. His eyes lock onto mine for just a moment, but it's enough to send heat flooding through my body.

I catch Isla watching me with knowing eyes.

"What?" I whisper.

"You know," Isla says as we wait, "some things are worth more than corner offices and merger deals."

I touch the ring on my finger. "Some things aren't our choice to make."

"Everything's a choice, Vivi." She squeezes my hand. "You taught me that, remember?"

But as the puck drops and Trey takes his first shift, I can't help wondering what this life would look like. Hockey season, owner's boxes, jersey and cotton candy with Adeline, little league, ballet and drama school. Being a part of this tight-knit group of WAGs that Isla has been a part of for so long. Having Trey and Adeline to come home to every night after a long day.

Something exactly like the man who just laid out an opposing player to protect his teammate, then glanced up at the owner's box like he was checking to make sure I was watching.

The game moves fast, a blur of bodies and flashing skates. But I can't take my eyes off number fourteen. Every time Trey hits the ice, the energy in the owner's box shifts. These people have watched him play dozens of times, but there's something different about him tonight.

"He's showing off," Cammy whispers, nudging me with her elbow.

"What? No, he's not."

But even as I say it, Trey dekes past two defenders like they're standing still, his movements fluid and controlled. The crowd rises to their feet as he breaks away, nothing between him and the goal but sixty feet of ice and a goalie who suddenly looks very nervous.

"Go Uncle Trey!" Adeline screams, pressed against the glass. Blue cotton candy stains mark her fingers where they leave prints on the window.

The shot comes fast—top shelf—and the announcer's voice cracks with excitement. "Hartley with the bottle rocket!"

The crowd roars as the goalie's water bottle flips off the top of the net and skitters across the ice.

I've heard the term enough times to know what it means, but this is the first time I've actually seen it happen in a game.

A bottle rocket isn't just a goal—it's hockey slang for the kind that hits so clean, so hard, and so perfectly placed that it sends the goalie's water bottle flying off the net. It's skill, speed, and just enough flair to make everyone's jaw drop.

Trey raises his stick, gliding past our glass. His eyes find mine, and for a moment, everything else disappears—the roar of the crowd, the flashing lights, even Adeline jumping up and down beside me. All I can feel is the heat in that look.

"Did you see that?" Adeline tugs on my jersey. "Did you see what he did?"

"I saw." My voice comes out breathier than intended.

The final horn sounds.

Hawkeyes win 4-1.

"Can we wait for him?" Adeline asks as the crowd starts to clear out.

"Of course." I help her gather her things, wondering if I'll ever be back here again, but that seems unlikely. "He said to wait until after media."

We head down and wait, watching as the players all file in nicely fitted suits, all of them waving to their families as they walk past. The moment Trey walks by us, his eyes sparkle when he sees Adeline waving with her entire body. And then he looks up at me, the same heat from the owner's box floods my system, and then he's gone again. Headed in for interviews that I'm sure he hates, but he has a lot to celebrate tonight. He had a great game.

Finally, as player after player returns out of media and leaves with their family, Trey is the next to emerge.

"Uncle Trey." Adeline launches herself at him. "You were amazing. Did you see me watching? Did you see your jersey? We made them ourselves!"

He catches her easily, swinging her up onto his hip like she weighs nothing. "I saw." His gaze drifts to my matching jersey. I turn around so that he can see Adeline's rhinestone work on mine too. His eyes linger on his name stretched across my back. "You both look great."

I swear I don't blush, but the look in his eyes says he sees the way those words affect me.

"Ready to go home, squirt?" Trey asks, setting Adeline down.

"We can drop you off if you want to head to Oakley's to celebrate with the team," I say.

"Or you could come home with us and we could have movie night," Adeline says.

"Movie night? This late?" I say back.

He looks at her and then at me. "Actually, a movie night sounds good. How about we stop for ice cream first?"

I don't bother to tell him all the junk food she already ate today and how I'm worried she is going to be sick tonight, because these two are in their own world, and the bonding between them is more important than anything else.

"Yes!" Adeline squeals.

We follow him through the player's exit, but the moment we step outside, camera flashes explode around us.

"Ms. Newport!"

"Over here!"

"Where's Jameson?"

"Are you and Hartley—"

Trey's arm comes around me, pulling me against his side, and he yanks Adeline back onto his hip as he guides us through the crowd quickly. The solid wall of his body shields me from the worst of it, but I catch snippets of questions:

"Is this why you left Jameson?"

"What does the Holiday family think?"

"How long have you two been together?"

Adeline's arms tighten around Trey's neck, and I wrap my hand around her leg in front of Trey to try to comfort her in any way that I can. I have no idea how she's going to react to all of this. The paparazzi can come for me all they want, but they'd better stay away from her.

"Why are they yelling at you?" she asks, voice trembling.

"Because they don't know how to mind their own business," Trey growls, the sound vibrating through his chest where I'm pressed against him.

Hawkeyes' security steps in quickly, forcing the reporters back. But their cameras keep clicking, capturing every moment—Trey's protective stance, Adeline clutching my hand, the way we move as a unit through the chaos.

"Almost there," Trey murmurs, his breath warm against my ear.

We reach his SUV, and he helps Adeline into the back seat before opening my door. The reporters are too far away at this point to get any good photos, but it doesn't change the fact that they were there, taking photos of us.

I close my door, and Trey walks to his side, getting in next.

"Maybe I should just take her home and you can—"

Trey cuts me off. "No, they're not ruining our plans—right, squirt?" he asks Adeline though I can tell he's trying to gauge how affected she is after that. I doubt something like that's ever happened to her before. "And I'm right where I want to be." His voice drops lower, meant just for me.

I look over my shoulder from the front seat as Trey watches her from the review mirror.

She nods. "That was crazy. I've never seen them go nuts like that," she says.

Frankly, neither have I. I've never had the press after me,

except for the night after Jameson and I got engaged. They all wanted to get a photo of the ring after Jameson and I stepped out of a high-end restaurant.

Optics, as Genevieve would tell me after. No doubt she planted the paparazzi.

"But are you okay?" I ask Adeline once we're moving.

She nods, though her usual bounce is subdued. "I didn't like how they yelled at you."

"Sometimes people forget their manners when they're trying to get a story," I explain, reaching back to squeeze her knee. "But we don't let them stop us from having fun, right?"

"Right." A small smile returns. "Ice cream helps too."

Trey's laugh fills the car. "That's my girl. Always thinking with her stomach."

The convenience store's fluorescent lights buzz overhead as we crowd around the ice cream freezer, debating flavors like it's a matter of national security. None of us is in agreement.

"Look," Trey says, pointing at the rows of pints, "they even have cookie dough in the front. Clearly the superior choice."

"Only because basic people keep buying it," I tease, reaching past him for Rocky Road. The smell of his deodorant and something uniquely him fills my nostrils, and I take in a deeper inhale. "You probably order vanilla lattes too."

He gasps in mock offense. "I'll have you know I take my coffee black. Like my soul."

"Your soul isn't black," Adeline pipes up from where she's pressed against the glass, breath fogging up the door and then she draws a heart shape into it. "It's probably mint chocolate chip colored."

"Betrayed by my own niece," he says, reaching in for a pint of cookie dough.

"Face it, Hartley. You've easily picked the most boring flavor."

"Yeah, well, at least I don't put rocks in my ice cream."

"They're not rocks," I protest. "They're almonds. And marshmallows. And chocolate chunks."

"Sounds like trail mix had an identity crisis."

"Says the man who thinks elevating a boring flavor like vanilla is by adding chunks of tasteless raw cookie dough."

Adeline grabs mint chocolate chip and then heads to the register. Trey pays for it all, and then we're back on the road, heading home.

Adeline talks movie options the entire way to their house.

The minute we step through the door, Trey tells Adeline to change into pajamas first and shower off quickly. She groans but does as she's told while Trey heads for the kitchen, grabbing spoons. I head for the couch to get the Disney movie we all agreed to in the car queued up, and then I walk to the downstairs bathroom to grab a hairbrush and a hair tie.

As I walk out, I still hear Trey rifling through the kitchen as if he doesn't know where the utensils are.

"Need help in there?" I call out.

"I think I can handle spoons," he replies, and I can hear the smile in his voice. "Though according to Adeline, I can't be trusted with anything more complicated than cereal."

"She's teasing you. For a guy who's known for shit talking on the ice, you sure take a nine-year-old's chirping pretty hard."

Before he can respond, Adeline bounds down the stairs in penguin pajamas that I recognize from my first day here and wet hair from the shower. Has it really only been three weeks? It feels like I've been a part of this family forever.

"Ready!"

"Here. Let's braid your hair so it doesn't get tangled tonight," I call her over and point to the floor in front of me.

She skips over and plops down, grabbing her ice cream and squeezes her shoulders between my thighs as I brush out her hair and give it a quick French braid.

Trey comes in, handing out spoons to all of us.

"Done," I say as I add the hair tie to the end of her braid.

She feels it and turns around, her eyes wide. "It feels so cool. No one's ever French braided my hair since mom."

I instantly worry she's going to burst into tears, but she doesn't. It almost seems like nostalgia, and the memory of her mom is more calming than anything.

She wedges herself between Trey and me on the couch as I start the movie.

Ten minutes in, Adeline's head starts to droop.

Twenty minutes in, she's completely out, mint chocolate chip melting in its container.

"I should probably get her to bed," Trey whispers.

I nod, gathering the half-eaten pints while he scoops her up. She doesn't even stir, just burrows into his chest like she belongs there. The sight makes my throat tight.

In the kitchen, I hear his footsteps on the stairs, then the soft click of her door. Every sound is familiar now. I know which step creaks, which cabinet hinges need WD-40, how the dishwasher makes that weird clicking noise when it's almost done.

I'm putting the ice cream away when he returns, filling the kitchen doorway with his presence.

"It's getting late. You can stay here tonight if you want. You can have the bed upstairs," he offers.

Though the offer is tempting, I don't have anything to wear in the morning, and staying here with him under the same roof feels like a bad idea if we're trying not to complicate things more than we already have.

"I should head home. Check on my plants," I say, though we both know that's not the reason. Besides...I don't have any plants, and if I did, with my work schedule, they'd be dead already.

"Right," he says, understanding in his eyes. "I'll walk you out."

I grab my purse and slip on my shoes before we walk to my car in silence.

He opens my door, and I step around him. "Thank you."

"About tonight...those photographers..." he starts before I slide into the car he bought me. "Is that going to cause problems for you? What they assumed about us? The photos?"

"I don't think so." I fidget with my key fob. To be honest, I'm not sure. The media has been trying to get information on Jameson's whereabouts and our wedding plans since I ran away. I just didn't think that the finance world and the sports world would have overlapping media coverage, but I should have considered it. The Hawkeyes are on the main stage, and so is the Holiday/Newport wedding. "At least I was wearing his ring like Genevieve wanted. A bare finger would have caused more problems."

His eyes drop to my left hand, and something dark passes across his features. "Right. The ring."

"Though I was wearing the wrong last name on my back, so we'll have to wait and see what the press decides to do with that."

"I don't think that's true," he says.

"What's not true?"

"That you were wearing the wrong last name." His voice drops lower as he steps closer. "Hartley looks damn good on you. And unlike Holiday... My last name comes with a jersey, season tickets, and free cotton candy."

I smile, my heart thumps against my chest. He's close enough now that I can see the flecks of gold in his green eyes.

"How could a girl pass up an offer like free cotton candy?" I tease.

He steps closer again, his finger brushing a strand behind my ear. His thumb brushes over my jaw line, feather soft. I take a deep swallow, knowing this is the moment Trey kisses me again.

Instead, his touch lingers just long enough to make me ache.

"Careful, Vivi," he murmurs, a slow, knowing smile tugging at his mouth. "I get my hopes up easily. Don't tempt me to make that jersey permanent." He lets the words hang there, then adds, low and rough, "But if that ever interests you...you know where to find me."

Then his gaze drops to the ring again, and he steps back.

My stomach drops, disappointment instant.

He stares into my eyes, but we both know I have no control over this any more than I can control when Jameson is coming back or how the board decides to handle the CEO position.

I suck in my lower lip and glance away for a moment, not wanting to show the hurt in my eyes, because it's not fair to him.

"Goodnight, Trey," I say.

"Goodnight, Vivi. Drive safe."

Then he closes my door, and I watch in my rearview mirror as he stands in the driveway, his hands buried in his front pockets, his eyes watching me go until my taillights disappear around the corner.

CHAPTER ELEVEN

Vivi

After dropping off Adeline at school this morning, grocery shopping, and dropping off every legal document I have in my possession about my position as CEO, my rights as a stockholder, and the marriage agreement documents that I signed with Genevieve and Jameson, I'm exhausted.

Yvanne said that she's going to pore over everything and see if there are any loopholes or rights that I'm not aware of. Anything to stop them from being able to terminate my CEO position if I don't marry Jameson.

I slide into my car, glancing at the time. After all of that, I need to get back on the road, get to Adeline's school for pick up, and take her to ballet on time.

Thankfully, I packed her backpack with her tutu this morning so that she can change at school.

Just as I take a deep breath, my phone rings.

"Good morning, Mrs. Holiday—" I say, seeing Genevieve's number highlighted on my phone.

"Is it a good morning? Did you enjoy yourself last night? The press certainly did."

I quickly rack my brain about what she could be referring to. "I'm not sure I understand—"

"The Hawkeyes game. That Hartley player certainly seemed comfortable wrapping his arms around you to shield you from the press. What is going on, Vivi?"

Oh shit. The memory of Trey's protective stance, his massive frame blocking photographers as we left the arena, his jersey hanging loosely on my frame...it probably didn't look great.

"It's nothing. He's a family friend whose nanny dropped out on him last minute, and since I don't currently have a position at the moment, I've been helping him out with his niece."

"You do have a position, Vivi. Getting my son to come back before your futures are both ruined. Not gallivanting around with some war-hero heartthrob hockey player and his niece, getting photographed in his jersey with my son's ring still on your finger. This isn't good news. What if my son had seen these photos?"

"War-hero heartthrob...?" I ask.

How much does she know about Trey?

"It was the headline they were going to publish this morning until I stopped them. Can you even begin to understand what an uphill battle that would have been to fight against publicly? He would have gotten the sympathy, and everyone would have wanted him to win you over. Instead of the billionaire playboy image my son needs to shake. Not to mention Jameson's disappearance from all social circles. It's not a good look, Vivi."

She's right. I have no idea how this would look to Jameson, though he's also in Greece spending our honeymoon with another woman...or at least I assume they're still together at this point. I haven't heard anything from either of them.

"I know, I'm sorry. I didn't realize the press would recognize me and put two and two together."

"It's literally what the press gets paid to do. Make connections, whether they're true or not. And a scandal like this? Big money."

"You're right. I should have been more careful."

"Lucky for you, my private eye caught the photographers and paid them for the images last night before they could go public and ruin everything I'm trying to do. My son didn't see these, but I'm warning you Vivi, the press is out for anything they can get about you and my son. A scandal with a Hawkeyes player or Jameson taking the wedding planner on your honeymoon would sell for far more money than the story that you two are quietly marrying in the South of France when he returns. You both need to take this more seriously."

Her examples have me wondering if the private eye she has watching Jameson in Greece has paid off photographers as well.

"Have you gotten confirmation that Jameson and Natasha are still together?" I ask, still worried about Natasha and how I must have cost her everything. She has to hate me at this point.

"I'll just put it this way. You both are costing the Holiday trust fund more money in photography payoffs than has ever happened in the history of this family, and I expect you both to do better in the future. Do I make myself understood?"

So he and Natasha are getting photographed together. I want to ask follow-up questions, but I suspect they won't be met with warmth and openness at this point. I just want to know that Natasha is doing fine and doesn't blame me for ruining her commission that would have paid for everything she needed.

"Yes, Mrs. Holiday. I understand."

"Good." The line goes dead.

I stare at my phone for a long moment, guilt and frustration warring in my chest. The rain patters against my windshield as I sit in Seattle traffic, already running late to pick up Adeline from school before ballet. The weather called for a thunderstorm, and based on the dark clouds looming over the city, I think that's likely.

That's when I feel it—the telltale thump followed by the rhythmic flapping of rubber against asphalt. The steering wheel vibrates under my hands as I ease onto the shoulder of I-5, hazard lights casting an orange glow through the sheets of rain.

"No, no, no..."

Seattle's signature March drizzle has evolved into a proper downpour, drumming against the roof like artillery fire. Through the windshield, brake lights blur into red streaks as traffic rushes past, throwing up walls of spray. Each passing semi rocks my car, reminding me how exposed I am out here.

I climb out, immediately regretting my choice of a silk blouse as the rain soaks through to my skin. The rear left tire isn't just flat—it's shredded. Fantastic.

Back in the relative safety of the driver's seat, I dial my company's emergency assistance line that we offer to all of our clients, just another perk, water dripping from my hair onto the leather. The dispatcher's voice carries that forced cheerfulness I used to insist on during training.

"Newport Staffing Solutions, Roadside Assistance, how may I direct your call?"

"Hi, this is Vivi Newport."

A pause. "Oh. Ms. Newport..." Her voice drops to barely above a whisper. "I'm so sorry, but Mr. Howard sent a company memo that you're currently cut off from all company services. Including roadside assistance."

The bastard. Of course he did. "You're kidding? Is there any way you can connect me to Richard's line?"

He's the only one who can overturn Martin's decision.

"Unfortunately, he's out on vacation this week." Another pause. "I'm really sorry, Ms. Newport. This isn't right."

Marcus from security, Virginia, my receptionist, and now our dispatcher in Roadside Assistance all see how this company policy about me is wrong. How does the board not see this? They're undermining me at a company I built.

I hang up before my frustration shows. Two hours minimum for a tow truck, they tell me when I call. Perfect. Apparently, I'm not the only person in the Seattle area with a shitty day piling up and in need of roadside assistance.

Next, I text Isla.

Flat tire on I-5. Any chance you can grab Adeline with Berkeley?

Isla

Of course. Where are you? Do you need me to come get you?

No, I'm fine. Just stuck in this mess. Tow truck's coming... eventually.

Isla

You sure? Kaenan can come.

Really, I'm good. Just keep Adeline distracted. I'll meet you at ballet if I make it.

Isla

If you're sure...but text me updates or I'm sending search and rescue.

Finally, I call Trey. It goes straight to voicemail—he's at practice and I know they can't have their phones on them, but I still feel like I need to let him know what's going on and that I have Adeline's pickup and ballet handled.

"Hey, it's me." I try to keep my voice steady despite the chill setting in. "Just letting you know I got a flat tire, but Isla's getting Adeline. The tow truck's coming since my asshole Interim CEO suspended my access to our maintenance department as well," I blow out a breath, realizing that I'm rambling. "Sorry, you don't need to know any of that. I just wanted to keep you in the loop."

It's less than a few minutes before he calls back.

"Where exactly are you?" His voice carries that command tone that makes my spine straighten automatically.

"I'm fine, really. Two exits down from the stadium. The tow truck will be here in a couple of hours."

"Vivi." The way he says my name—soft but firm—makes my pulse jump. "Which side of the highway?"

"Northbound. But you don't need to come."

"Send me your location and don't move."

The intensity in his voice sends a shiver down my spine that has nothing to do with my wet clothes. "Trey, you're at practice. You can't just leave in the middle to help your nanny with a flat tire."

"Watch me."

I hear the sound of his SUV roar to life. "I'm not leaving you on I-5 for hours. Traffic moves too fast—it's dangerous. A semi could swerve into the shoulder and rear-end you. I'm already pulling out of the Hawkeyes parking lot."

I pin my location and send the link. "Got it. Stay there. Don't get out of the car for anything, do you understand?"

"Yes," I tell him, my chest flooding with relief, not realizing how bad I needed someone to show up for me right now. Of course, it would be him. Running out on practice even though it could cost him time on the ice for the next game.

He hangs up without another word. Ten minutes later, his black SUV pulls up behind me, hazards flashing.

I start to open my door, but his voice carries through the rain. "Stay in the car! Don't come out here."

He's already moving to my trunk, lifting the gate, and pulling out the spare tire into the compartment. "If someone hits us, you're safer in the car. Don't get out. Not for any reason." His eyes are on me through my rearview mirror. He waits for me to nod, and then he gets back to work. I watch him work efficiently despite the downpour. He squats down by my rear left tire, his T-shirt clings to his broad shoulders, rain dripping from his hair as he works with the car jack and starts pulling off the lug nuts quickly.

"You shouldn't have come," I call out my window. "The tow truck is coming, and Isla has Adeline covered."

"You're a sitting duck on I-5 in this weather." He doesn't even look up as he pulls off the old tire and then replaces it with my spare. "Now stay inside where it's dry. I'll have this done soon. I'll pick you up a new tire tonight. I don't want you driving more than you have to on this spare."

Something about watching him work—those capable hands, the focused set of his jaw—does things to my insides. He moves with military precision, each action deliberate and controlled. Within minutes, he's lowering the car back down and putting everything back in the truck, closing the back gate of my car for me.

When he appears at my window, rain dripping from his nose, I can't help myself. I've never been more turned on in my life.

"What's the name of that interim CEO?" He asks, his voice rough.

"Why?"

"Because I'd like to have a word with him about leaving you stranded on the highway."

The protective growl in his voice sends heat straight to my core. "As much as I'd love to see that, he's not worth your time."

"You're worth every second," he says, voice low and lethal, like the ex-soldier that he is. "You might not be mine, but that doesn't change a damn thing. As long as you're in my care, you're under my protection—fully. That means your safety is on me."

He steps closer, gaze sharp. "And I don't hesitate. I don't blink. If anyone so much as thinks about hurting you..." A muscle ticks in his jaw. "I'll handle it. No limits. No mercy."

"Don't hurt him," I say, almost afraid for what Martin just unknowingly stepped into. The idiot is lucky that Adeline wasn't with me. I can't imagine how Trey would have reacted if this is how he is when I blow a tire with just myself in the car.

"He's fucking lucky you're okay."

The words land low, more lethal than the thunderstorm raging around us—rough enough to steal the air from my lungs. He's dripping rain, chest heaving like he's holding back something bigger than the weather, and the way his eyes lock on mine makes it impossible to think of anything but him.

Lightning flashes and I catch the hard lines of him—soaked T-shirt plastered to muscle, jaw clenched, every inch of him coiled and dangerous. The storm might be raging outside, but the one in me is worse.

I should tell him to finish the tire. I should thank him and shut the door. But my pulse is in my throat, pounding like it's daring me to do the reckless thing.

And then I do. The dam inside me bursts, spilling out in one reckless move. My fingers curl into his soaked shirt, fisting the wet cotton as I yank him down until his mouth crashes against mine. He tastes like rain and raw need, lips cold but burning fast, and when he groans into the kiss, the sensation shoots down my body, heat pooling low in my belly—reminding me exactly where I need him. Denying this was never an option. He's everything I keep trying to convince myself I can't want.

"Careful," he murmurs against my mouth. "My hands are covered in grease."

"I don't care." I tangle my fingers in his wet hair, drawing him closer. The rain soaks through my blouse, but I barely notice. "You came for me. No one's ever done that."

His greasy hands find my hips, leaving black smudges on my jeans as he deepens the kiss. He slides them down to my ass, gripping hard enough to make me gasp, pulling me against the door panel. A passing truck honks, the blast of air rocking my car.

"You're lucky we're in public," he growls against my lips. "Or this wouldn't stop here."

"I'm not so sure I would count that as luck," I say, pulling back to search his eyes.

We stay frozen like that for a moment, his hands possessive on my body, my fingers tangled in his wet hair. The air between us is buzzing with electricity that has nothing to do with the lightning.

He lets out a guttural groan that makes my thighs clench. "I'm leaving before we end up in the back seat of this Range Rover." He pulls back slightly, though his hands don't leave my body. "Don't pull out until I do. Traffic's moving fast—at least I'll take the hit if someone comes up on us too fast and rear-ends me."

"Trey—"

"Not until I move into the lane first, Vivi," he demands, no argument.

I nod, watching as he picks up the ruined tire. "Send me your office address and the asshole's name."

"You won't be able to get up to the eleventh floor anyway."

"Failure's not an option," he says, spinning back around to head for his SUV, clearly on a mission.

"Please don't waste your time," I call after him, my head out the window, watching him get further and further away from me.

"Send it, Vivi Ann." The command in his voice is thick, like he's used to barking orders and having people follow them without question.

So I do as he asks, watching in my rearview mirror as he tosses the tire in his backseat. Within minutes, he finds an opening and pulls out onto I-5. I follow his lead, accelerating quickly. Then I see him take the exit to my office, and my stomach flutters with equal parts anticipation and concern.

I have no idea what he's going to say to Martin, but something tells me this isn't going to be a polite conversation.

CHAPTER TWELVE

Trey

The damaged tire rolls around in the back of my SUV as I navigate through downtown Seattle's afternoon traffic. The fancy high-rise that houses Newport Staffing Solutions looms ahead—all glass and steel and corporate success. The kind of place that probably has a doorman who'll take one look at my tattoos and assume I'm lost.

But I'm not lost. I know exactly where I'm going and what I'm doing. That flat tire could have been dangerous at highway speeds. The fact that some corporate asshole denied her access to her own company's emergency services because she didn't go through with an arranged marriage... It makes my blood boil.

I park in the visitor lot, ignoring the valet's offer to take my keys. The tire is heavy as I haul it out, but I've carried worse through worse conditions. Besides, I want this Martin guy to see exactly what kind of damage he risked by leaving Vivi stranded.

I see a card reader for the elevator, but then a florist with reception flowers hops on an elevator, and I jump in behind her like I'm meant to be there. She smiles, not realizing that I didn't scan in.

Her eyes quickly scan me and my wet clothes. "It's wet out there, huh?" She says, making small talk.

"If it wasn't, it wouldn't be Seattle," I say. She chuckles and then steps off on the third floor. I take the elevator up to the eleventh, per Vivi's text.

The lobby of Newport Staffing Solutions looks like the kind of office Vivi would have designed. This is the kind of place she belongs. All marble and modern art. Not making pasta, barefoot in my kitchen. This is exactly what you'd expect from a multimillion-dollar staffing empire. There are touches of Vivi everywhere. The warm colors. The comfortable seating areas. The wall of "Employee of the Month" photos mixed with candid shots of company events.

She built this. All of it.

Pride mixes with something darker in my chest. This is her world—corporate luxury and business success. So different from my life of military service and hockey violence. What can I possibly offer her compared to this? I knew this was what I was up against, but to see it is a reminder that I might have her right now, but I can't keep her. It wouldn't be right.

But then I remember her face just now, watching me change that tire in the rain. How she pulled me in for that kiss, not caring about grease or dirt or what anyone might think. For that moment, she'd wanted me—just me, exactly as I am.

Newport Staffing's logo spans the reception area in elegant script. A perfectly polished receptionist looks up from her computer.

"Can I help you?" Her eyes widened at my appearance, her eyes scanning over my full sleeve tattoos up my arms, visible from my T-shirt that's soaked from the rain and stained with grease spots. It's easy to guess I'm not their usual clientele.

"Martin Howard's office."

"I'm sorry, the CEO doesn't take walk-ins." She pastes a professional smile. "You'll need to make an appointment."

I give her my best media-trained smile. The one that doesn't reach my eyes. "Don't worry. This won't take long."

Before she can stop me, I'm past her desk and through the glass doors marked "Executive Offices." Her heels click frantically behind me, but I've outmaneuvered better opponents than a receptionist in stilettos.

"Sir! You can't—"

I find Howard's office easily—the biggest one with the best view. The nameplate on his door might as well read "Stolen from Vivi Newport."

The door opens before I can kick it in. Martin rises from behind Vivi's desk—because it is her desk, no matter whose nameplate is on the door. His eyes bulge at the sight of me: six-foot-five tattooed hockey player holding a damaged tire and fifteen years of special forces training in my stance.

"Who the hell—"

I slam the tire onto the desk, sending papers flying. "This could have killed her."

He backs up a step. Good. He should be afraid.

"I don't know what you're talking about." But his voice wavers slightly.

"Vivi Newport. Ring a bell? You cut off her access to Roadside Assistance." I lean forward, bracing my hands on the desk, leaning into his space, my eyes locked on his. "Her own company's services. The company she started from scratch. The one that pays for your fancy ties." I glance down at the ugly swirl print he's wearing. "Though I strongly suggest you rethink your pattern choices in the future."

He clears the fear out of his throat. "Ms. Newport is on administrative leave." He tries for authority but can't quite manage it. "Company policy clearly states—"

"Company policy?" I laugh, but there's no humor in it. "You mean the policy you created after she left Holiday at the altar? The one designed to push her out? Nice little takeover you maneuvered there, but I can't wait until she's back in her rightful spot and she fires your ass for insubordination."

His face reddens. "Now see here—"

"No, you see here." I lower my voice to the tone that made insurgents talk in dark rooms. "I've seen men killed for less than what you did yesterday. Letting her sit exposed on that highway, vulnerable to any drunk driver or road rage incident..."

"Are you threatening me?"

"Threatening you?" I smirk. "No. I'm promising you that if anything ever happens to Vivi Newport because you deny her access to these services, what happens to you won't be a threat. It'll be a guarantee. And trust me, I'm the last asshole that you want to underestimate. I know how to make a body disappear without a trace."

He swallows hard. "I'll call security."

"Go ahead." I straighten back up, sliding my hands off of Vivi's desk that he stole from right underneath her. "But first, you're going to reinstate her access to all company services. And you're going to do it now."

"You can't—"

"I can." I tap the tire. "And I will. Because next time, it might not be just a flat tire. And I promise you, if anything happens to her while you play power games with her safety, what I do to you will make Special Forces interrogation look like a kindergarten timeout."

The door bursts open as security finally arrives—two rent-a-cops who look like they've never faced anything more dangerous than a drunk executive.

"Everything okay here, Mr. Howard?"

Martin's eyes dart between me and the security guards who I can tell with the way their sizing me up, don't want anything to do with me. I guess they aren't that stupid after all.

Martin weighs his options—piss me off more and see what consequences come out of it for him or tell his guys to stand down and not make a scene.

"Fine. I'll put out the company memo to reinstate her benefits," he says, slumping back into his chair and then looks to the security guards. "It was just a...discussion about company policy. You can go."

I smile again. "Glad we understand each other."

The security guards trail me to the elevator, but their stance screams amateur. I make a mental note to call some ex-military contacts about upgrading this place's security. Vivi needs better protection, whether she ends up marrying Holiday or not, and I'll make sure she gets it.

Back in my SUV, I pull out my phone.

All taken care of. You're approved to use the services now.

Her response comes quickly.

Vivi
Oh God, what did you do?

Don't worry about it. He saw my side of things. P.S. We're getting you better security here.

Vivi
We?

See you at home.

I hit send before I can overthink that last word.

Home.

Not my house or Adeline's house, but home. Like Vivi belongs there with us.

The realization of how hard and fast I'm falling for her is terrifying, but then again, I knew this would happen if I ever got involved with her. I knew it from the first time I met her.

I want it to be her home. I want her there every morning,

making pancakes with Adeline. Every night, curled up on the couch watching Disney movies with her God-awful taste in ice cream. Her in the stands wearing my jersey at every home game, and every moment in between.

But this isn't about what I want. It's about what's best for her. And maybe what's best isn't a broken down ex-soldier who sleeps on the floor because beds are too soft after fifteen years of war. Whose left hearing is all but nonexistent, and the scars on my body from combat show the hard life I've lived.

Nothing like how she grew up. Nothing like country clubs, trust funds, and summer homes in the Hamptons.

The kind of life Jameson Holiday can give her.

Technically, with all of the money I saved in the military and my hockey contract, I could afford that lifestyle if she really wanted it, but it's not who I am, it's not who Adeline is. We don't fit in that world, and I can't force it.

My phone buzzes again.

Vivi

Thank you for today. For everything.

Three dots appear, disappear, then appear again.

Vivi

And yes, I'll see you at home.

The words make my chest tight. Because in five weeks it will mean something different. She'll be living in Holiday's mansion, wearing his ring, building the perfect life everyone expects of her.

And I'll be here, sleeping on my floor, raising my brother's daughter, trying to forget how right it felt to have Vivi in our lives—for just a minute.

I drive past the exit that would take me to practice, heading instead to a security firm run by my old squad mate, who turned from special forces to hired mercenary, to private security company, and now even owns a helicopter charter business. Because even if I can't keep her, I can make damn sure she's protected.

The thought feels like shrapnel in my chest, but I push it down. I've survived worse. I'll survive this too.

But as I park outside Lawson Security Solutions, I can't help wondering if survival is enough anymore.

CHAPTER THIRTEEN

Trey

My duffel bag sits by the front door next to Vivi's overnight bag. Mine packed for three days on the road, hers for three nights here with Adeline.

I never like the idea of leaving Adeline, and ever since the tire situation that happened on I-5 last week with Vivi, I dislike it more. With Martin reinstating Vivi's use of the benefits, after I strongly encouraged him, I feel better at least, and Kaenan is only a couple of blocks away if they need help with anything else.

It's crazy how fast time is flying by. With only four weeks left until Jameson is supposed to return, it feels like time is on team Jameson.

"And then we need to return these books to the library," Adeline says, pulling out a stack from her backpack to show Vivi. "It's my favorite place in the whole world. Mom used to take me every week in Florida."

The mention of Sarah catches me off guard. Adeline doesn't talk about her parents often. I know it's painful for her to discuss, but I think she worries about me too. Sarah loved reading, and she passed that onto Adeline. The library was something they did together since she was little. I've tried to make sure that she has access to the library whenever she wants to go.

"Then we definitely need to go," Vivi says, her voice gentle. "Maybe we can find some new ones too?"

Adeline's whole face lights up. "Really? Can we get ice cream after? Like Mom and I used to do?"

"Of course," Vivi says with a smile, setting a plate of eggs, bacon, and sliced strawberries. "Maybe we can add it to our weekly schedule if you want."

"Are you sure you're good with everything?" I ask, though I know she is. She's handled everything we've thrown at her like the professional she is.

"We're fine," she assures me. "We're watching the San Diego game at Penelope's with all the girls on Thursday night. Apparently, she's ordered enough food to feed half of Seattle."

"That sounds about right." I smile, remembering how Penelope always goes overboard for away game viewing parties. And with us playing our biggest rivals, the San Diego Blue Devils, I have no doubt Penelope is going all out. "Just...call if you need anything."

"We've got it handled, I promise. Now go. You'll miss wheels up."

I bend down to kiss the top of Adeline's head. "Be good for Vivi."

"I'm always good," she protests.

"Uh-huh." I ruffle her hair, earning a squawk. "Love you, squirt."

"Love you too." She hugs me tight. "Score a goal for me?"

"I'll do my best."

At the door, I pause. Vivi stands in my kitchen, Adeline beside her talking about what they are going to make for dinner. They look like they belong there. Like this is how every morning should be.

"Trey?" Vivi's voice pulls me back. "You're going to be late."

"Right." I grab my bag. "See you in three days."

The drive to the private airport passes in a blur of Seattle rain.

"There he is!" Aleksi calls as I walk across the tarmac to catch up with them, my shoes splashing in the shallow puddles. He and Scottie are already heading for the plane, bags over their shoulders.

"Hey man," Scottie calls over his shoulder.

"Thought you were going to miss the flight," Aleksi teases.

And then I see Aleksi's face, shiny yellow masks under his eyes.

"What's that shit on your face?" I ask.

Scottie rolls his eyes. "Don't ask," he mutters under his breath.

Hunter runs across the tarmac to catch up. I guess I wasn't the last one to show up.

"They're under-eye masks. My mom sent them from Finland. They're twenty-four karat gold. A foolproof skincare regimen is important." Aleksi pats his bag defensively. "Don't worry, I brought enough for all of you."

"All a man needs is his Dramamine and an ocean waves soundtrack," Scottie counters, already wearing his noise-canceling headphones around his neck. "I'll be sleeping like a baby before wheels up. Wake me up when we land."

Hunter pats Aleksi's arm. "I'll try them. Peyton has some like these. We wear them on our weekly movie nights."

Aleksi beams back, happy to have an ally. "Hold on, I'll get a set for you now." He rifles through his bag as we all keep walking and pulls out a small package for Hunter. "Here you go."

Hunter takes no time pulling the sticky golden eye masks off their sheets and places them under his eyes like he's done it a hundred times before. Then Hunter turns to me with a wide grin.

"How do I look?"

"The gold really brings out the color in your man bun," I tell him.

Aleksi pats Hunter's shoulder. "Let Hart have his laughs...and his crow's feet."

Scottie chuckles and then pulls his noise-canceling earphones over his ears as he goes first, taking the steps up the jet. Hunter goes next but turns back to Aleksi behind him before taking his first step. "Give me a pair of those for when Scottie falls asleep. Let's see how well his Dramamine works," Hunter whispers, already planning his next prank—Scottie his next victim.

I follow them up the stairs, finding my usual seat across from Slade Matthews. Our captain looks up from his tablet as I settle in.

"How's Adeline doing with Vivi?" he asks.

"Good." I stow my bag. "They're getting along great," I say, and then flop into the aisle chair.

"Yeah? Heard about the press ambush after our last home game." He sets his tablet aside. "And about you being her getaway driver from that wedding."

I freeze. "How did you—"

"No secrets in the Hawkeyes family." He shrugs. "But that shouldn't be a shock to you by now."

To be honest, people knowing about me being the getaway driver doesn't affect me at all...but for Vivi, it might be a different story if it makes it outside of the team.

"I was in the right place at the right time," I say, because it's the truth.

"That might be true, but you don't have a poker face at all when it comes to her. You've got it bad. I should know what it looks like." His voice drops lower as other players file past. "Just don't forget that she's still wearing Holiday's ring."

The reminder feels like a blade between my ribs.

"Four weeks," I say quietly. "Then she marries him."

Slade studies me for a long moment. "You're going to let her walk away like that?"

"What choice do I have? The situation's...complicated."

"I had a complicated situation with a coach's daughter who thought I blackballed her from her Olympic dreams. You don't have to tell me about something complicated. Still, life's too short to have big regrets like letting the right person go."

The captain cuts us off, announcing our departure. Right now, the only thing I should be thinking about is beating Boston tomorrow and then San Diego in three days. Everything else will have to wait.

CHAPTER FOURTEEN

Vivi

"The contract is iron-clad, Vivi." Yvanne spreads the papers across her mahogany desk in her downtown office. Her notes and highlighted areas cover the entire thing. "I've had three other firms look at it. They all say the same thing."

I lean forward in the leather chair, studying the document that's effectively holding my future hostage. My signature looks foreign to me now—the careful loops and swirls of a woman who thought she was making a smart business decision by signing a contract that the trust required before Jameson and I got married. Additional documents I signed regarding my honeymoon time off and my agreement to the interim CEO. The board and its responsibilities, originally designed so that no one person could take over the company. And here I am, the one who's being kept out.

The irony.

"There has to be something." I run a hand through my hair, a habit I picked up from Trey. "Some loophole or clause we can use."

"The merger agreement is tied directly to the marriage

contract. If you don't marry Jameson within the specified time frame, Holiday Industries can exercise their option to take controlling interest." She taps a particularly dense paragraph of legal jargon. "And the board has the right to remove you as CEO. You'll still retain your ownership of your shares, but there's nothing else we can do. The board has to agree to this and right now, they're playing nice with Holiday Industries."

"But it's my company. I built it from nothing."

"And you made a decision to get Holiday Industries involved in order to push Newport Staffing public—you created a board and signed this agreement." Her voice softens. "I tried, Vivi. My partner, both of our paralegals...we've all been over every word for weeks. But whoever drafted this knew exactly what they were doing."

My phone buzzes—another missed call from my father. His voicemail notification pops up immediately:

Vivi, I heard you're still planning to go through with the wedding. Call me. I want to support you however I can.

Support me? I have no doubt that Genevieve is in my father's ear too. A family connection to the Holidays only furthers the Newport reach, and vice versa. In all other ways, this union between Jameson and I would make both of our families stronger. That's what my father had expected for Isla and me as we grew up. That's why I wanted to do this all on my own, and in the end, I landed right where he always wanted me.

What was even the point of working sixty-hour weeks for the last decade to prove I was more than just a Newport name when I just paid into the exact future he wanted for me?

Before I can delete the message, a text comes through.

Genevieve

We need to start planning the wedding in France. I've found several venues that would photograph beautifully. My PR team is drafting the narrative now. Call me.

Then a barrage of photos and links to venues start to blow up my phone. Some with rolling hills, some with vineyards, a gorgeous fifteenth-century castle, and a venue three stories tall made of glass. More keep popping through but I ignore them, setting my phone face-down on the desk, unable to look at it anymore.

"What happens if Jameson doesn't come back?" I ask. "He hasn't answered anyone's calls in weeks."

"The contract doesn't specify which party has to initiate the wedding. Just that it has to happen within the timeline." Yvanne makes another note. "Though I suppose if he stays in Greece indefinitely..."

"Then I lose everything anyway." I slump back in the chair. "I have no control over this situation. Perfect."

"There might be one other option." She hesitates. "But you won't like it."

"At this point, I'll take anything."

"Your father—"

"No." I stand up, pacing the length of her office. "Absolutely not."

"He has the resources to buy out Holiday Industries' stake. And let's be honest...he's the best negotiator we know. It's possible they would consider selling to him. From what I know, he helped them close a huge deal years ago that saved the family's trust because he knew the right people. It would void the merger agreement and the marriage contract if he can convince Genevieve to pick a new bride."

"The problem is the Holiday trust has its own board, and they are making Jameson pay for this. They're making an example for the other kids in the Holiday family. And my father bailing me out would put me right back under his control which was the entire point of making the deal with the Holidays." I shake my head. "I'd rather marry Jameson."

She doesn't argue. We've been friends since freshman year, when we both pledged to the same sorority and became roommates. She knows that everything that comes from my father comes with strings. "Then I suggest you start looking at venues in France and try to convince Jameson to come back."

My phone buzzes again.

Adeline

Can we go to the library after school? Please? 🥺

The request comes when I need it the most. I can't control whether Jameson comes back or not. The best thing to do right now is pick up Adeline from school and have a girls' day, just the two of us. Get lost in the library and pick up some greasy food on the way home before Trey's game in Boston tonight which we'll stream just the two of us when they take to the ice later this evening.

"I have to go." I check my watch. "School pickup."

Yvanne's eyes soften. "How's that going? The nanny thing?"

"It's..." I trail off, unable to find words for what it is. Wonderful. Terrifying. Everything I never knew I wanted. "Complicated."

"Because of Trey?"

Heat floods my cheeks. "I've never been with anyone like him."

"You've taken on so much, and then he steps in and takes care of you," she says as if she can read my thoughts.

"Exactly. But it doesn't matter." I gather my things. "I have to marry Jameson."

"Unless he doesn't come back."

Wouldn't that be a fantasy come true? That somehow it works out and we don't have to marry. But he still hasn't returned a single text or voicemail I've sent.

"He'll come back." I head for the door. "He has as much to lose as I do."

But as I drive to Adeline's school, I can't help wondering what would happen if he didn't. If he chose to lose it all instead of marry me. If he decided some things were worth more than family expectations and trust fund requirements.

Adeline's waiting at pickup, bouncing on her toes when she sees me. "Can we go? Please?"

"Of course." I help her into the car, grateful for the distraction from my own problems. "What section do you want to look at first?"

"Fantasy." She buckles herself in. "Mom used to take me every week when I was little. We'd spend hours in the kids' section."

My heart squeezes. "That sounds nice."

"It was." She's quiet for a moment. "The smell of old books reminds me of her. Is that weird?"

"Not at all." I adjust the rearview mirror to see her better. "Smells are powerful memory triggers. Like how fresh-cut grass always reminds me of summer vacation."

She nods, considering this. "Uncle Trey says the smell of jet fuel reminds him of deployment. But he doesn't like to talk about it much."

The casual mention of Trey's service catches me off guard. He rarely mentions it, and I've learned not to ask.

The library parking lot is nearly empty when we arrive. Inside, the familiar smell of books and quiet conversation wrap around us like a warm blanket. Adeline leads the way to the children's section, navigating the shelves like she's done it a thousand times.

"Mom always let me check out five books," she says, running her fingers along the spines. "One for each weekday."

"That's a good system."

She pulls out a worn copy of *The Lion, the Witch, and the Wardrobe*. "This was her favorite. She used to do all the voices."

I settle into one of the small chairs, watching as she carefully turns the pages. "Want to tell me about her? Your mom?"

She's quiet for so long I think she won't answer. Then, "She was funny. Like, really funny. She could make anyone laugh, even Uncle Trey when he was being grumpy. And she always smelled like cupcakes because she baked all the time."

"She sounds wonderful."

"She was." Adeline hugs the book to her chest. "I'm glad you came with me today. Sometimes it's hard to come here because it makes me miss her. But it's easier with you."

The simple honesty in her voice makes my throat tight. "Thank you for sharing this with me."

She sets the book aside and starts browsing again. "Uncle Trey tries, but he doesn't really get the library thing. He says books are too quiet—he likes noise better."

"The silence probably reminds him of things he'd rather forget," I say softly, more to myself than her.

She nods. "That's what Mom used to say too. That's why she always brought him cookies when he came home on leave. Said sweet things chase away bad memories."

My phone buzzes again—another text from Genevieve about venue options. I ignore it, focusing instead on Adeline as she builds a stack of books.

I pull a few of *The Lion, the Witch, and the Wardrobe* books to my corner. Maybe reading it at night together would be comforting for her. My mother used to read it to me too. Maybe we both could use a dose of nostalgia right now.

We spend the next hour picking books, Adeline telling me stories about her mom—how she'd do silly voices during bedtime stories, how she'd leave notes in Adeline's lunch box, how she'd dance in the kitchen while baking.

By the time we check out, my phone has three more missed calls from my father and two texts from Genevieve. Still nothing from Jameson, and that has me both worried and relieved. Watching Adeline clutch her books to her chest as we walk to the car, eyes bright with memories and possibilities, I can't bring myself to care about any of it.

"Pizza?" I suggest as we head for the car. "I think we've earned it. The Hawkeyes take to the ice in thirty minutes to play Boston, so we have to hurry home."

"Yes! That sounds good," she beams, running the rest of the way to the car. "Can we call him after the game to say goodnight? I miss him."

"I know he would love that."

My phone buzzes again—Genevieve, asking about flower arrangements for the wedding.

I leave it unanswered, focusing instead on Adeline's chatter about which pizza toppings. Right now, this is what matters. Everything else can wait.

CHAPTER FIFTEEN

Vivi

It's been a couple of nights since the Hawkeyes beat Boston in a close game, and now they play San Diego tonight before heading home.

Driving up to Penelope's house, a line of luxury vehicles already fills the circular driveway—other wives and girlfriends arriving for game night. The three-story mansion that Slade bought her after they got married to start their family looms ahead, warm lights glowing from every window.

"There's Isla's car. Berkeley's already here." Adeline squeals.

She's already unbuckling, practically vibrating with excitement.

We use the side entrance that leads straight into Penelope's massive chef's kitchen—a space bigger than Trey's entire first floor. That might be an exaggeration, but it's big. The smell of various cuisines hits us immediately: garlic and ginger, melted cheese, grilled meat, and something sweet I can't quite place.

"You ladies outdid yourself. Good God," I stop short, taking in the spread. The marble island disappears under stacks of dishes that all the girls made or brought. A buffet of delicious snacks. A chocolate fountain burbles in the corner, surrounded by strawberries, marshmallows, and pretzel rods.

I've never been to a WAGs party without tons of really good food. It's something this group prides themselves on. I set down the cupcake platter next to the desserts that Isla asked me to pick up from the bakery before we came over.

"I might have gone a little overboard with the food," Penelope appears from the butler's pantry carrying serving spoons. Her long blonde hair is piled in a messy bun atop her head, and she's wearing Slade's hockey jersey. "The playoffs are coming up, and I cope with food."

"You didn't," I lie. We'd need to invite the entire neighborhood over to make a dent. "It's perfect, and you always do a great job.

"Well, here, help yourself, girls, and then find a spot out in the living room. The game starts in twenty minutes."

The great room beyond the kitchen is already full of wives, girlfriends, and kids. Multiple flat screens are mounted on the walls, each showing pre-game coverage for the San Diego game the boys play tonight. The largest screen dominates the main wall above a stone fireplace.

"Vivi! Over here!" Cammy waves from the massive sectional. She's already settled in with Peyton and Isla, an array of snacks spread across the coffee table.

Berkeley appears as if summoned, grabbing Adeline's hand. "Come on! We're building a fort behind the couch!"

I help Adeline fill a plate before letting her run off with her friend. The sound of children laughing mixes with pre-game commentary and adult conversation—a familiar sound of game night.

"Perfect timing," Peyton says as I sink into the cushions. "We're planning Kendall's birthday surprise. She gets back with the guys tomorrow, and we want to do a girls' night."

"Ooh, where are we thinking?" I'm grateful for the distraction from my own problems, and a girls' night sounds fun. I'll just have to check with Trey before I can agree to anything to make sure he doesn't need me for that night.

"I was thinking Ground Zero." Cammy's eyes sparkle with mischief. "I already called. They have one of the roped-off VIP sections still available to book for next Friday night."

"And the guys?" I ask.

"No boys allowed." Peyton grins. "It's about time we had a proper girls' night. No hockey talk allowed."

"I'll talk to Kendall when they land," Cammy offers. "Get her on board."

"Speaking of plans..." Isla touches my arm. "Can we talk for a minute?"

I follow her into Penelope's formal dining room, away from the pre-game excitement. A massive crystal chandelier hangs above the middle of the mahogany table. Family photos line the walls—Slade with the Stanley Cup, their wedding day, vacation shots of them.

"How did it go with Yvanne?" she asks softly once we're alone.

I sink into one of the high-backed chairs. "Not great. The contracts are iron-clad. My only option is ..." I trail off, unable to say it.

"Dad?"

I nod. "Yvanne thinks he could buy out Holiday Industries' stake. Since they owe him from years ago when he called in a favor with the mayor of Seattle to help them out of a real estate venture that went bad. But you know what that would mean."

"You'd be back under his control." She squeezes my hand. "But is that worse than marrying someone you don't love?"

"At least with Jameson, I'd still have some independence. Dad would..." I shake my head. "You remember what it was like. The constant oversight, the 'suggestions' about how to run things that turn into decisions made the next morning you walk in, the threats to pull funding if we don't do exactly what he wants with the company."

"I remember." She studies me. "But what about what you

want?"

What I want.

The answer comes instantly: Freedom to marry who I want, the white picket fence family in a subdivision like this. Having some level of family/work balance.

But I can't have it all. I have to make sacrifices for the company I'm building or sacrifice the company I'm building for the family I want. I can't have both. At least with Jameson, there is an expected family he and I will have together. It's better than nothing.

"Game's starting!" Penelope calls from the other room.

We return just as the puck drops. The first period is brutal—hard hits, missed opportunities, growing frustration on both benches. I watch Trey closely, seeing the tension in his shoulders even through his pads.

"Come on, Uncle Trey!" Adeline cheers as he takes another shift.

But nothing seems to click. By the third period, they're down by two, and the mood in Penelope's living room has shifted from excited to tense. When the final horn sounds, the loss feels personal. The camera pans to Trey as he skates off, and the disappointment on his face makes my chest ache.

"Time to head home?" I ask Adeline, who nods sleepily.

I say goodnight to all the girls and promise to let Peyton know if I can make the party at Ground Zero as soon as I talk to Trey.

The drive home is quiet, both of us lost in our own thoughts. At home, we change into pajamas and settle onto her bed with one of our new library books.

"Can we ask if Uncle Trey is going to be home tonight?" she asks as I open to the first page.

"I don't think they are coming home until tomorrow morning, but let's text him and see. He might still be trying to finish post-game stuff."

Someone wants to know when you're going to make it home.

His response comes quickly.

Trey

We're trying to leave tonight, but the weathers bad. Stuck on tarmac. Won't make it home before she's asleep. Tell her I love her, and I'll see her in the morning.

"He's delayed," I tell her gently. "But he says he loves you and he'll see you in the morning."

She nods, though disappointment clouds her features. "Will you do the voices like Mom used to?"

My heart squeezes. "I'll try my best."

We make it through three chapters before she drifts off, curled against my side. I ease away carefully, tucking the blanket around her. My phone buzzes as I close her door.

Isla

Maybe it's time to consider Dad's help. Is spite worth marrying someone you don't love?

I put my phone on vibrate and toss it onto the couch without responding. The answer isn't what I want to face right now.

The kitchen is dark and quiet as I open the freezer, seeking comfort. Three pints of ice cream stare back at me—my rocky road, Adeline's mint chocolate chip, and Trey's cookie dough. I stare at his cookie dough.

I probably shouldn't eat it. Not just out of principle for it not being my ice cream, but also because of the fact that I called his taste in ice cream "boring." I also still have half a pint of rocky road available to eat.

The trouble is, rocky road won't hit the craving I need to satisfy. If he isn't set to be home until early in the morning, I probably have enough time to purchase a new pint of ice cream tomorrow before he knows that I ate his boring ice cream. Otherwise, I'll have to eat my own words too, and if I know Trey... he'll gloat so hard it will be hard to show my face here ever again.

I grab his, making a promise to myself to replace it first thing before he finds out. I don't bother to examine the possibility that the act of eating this ice cream is because I've missed him for the last three days. No, absolutely not. Because if that were true, what the hell am I going to do when he's out of my life for good and I have a new last name that's not Hartley?

Curled up on the couch with my guilty pleasure ice cream and equally guilty pleasure reality TV, I don't hear it at first—the faint sound of four digits getting typed into the outside keypad.

My body freezes—heart hammering against my chest.

I glance toward the door, but there's no movement. Just silence.

I hear the keypad chime a successful input and then the handle jiggles.

I suck in a deep breath. God, I wish Trey were home.

I bolt upright, standing up on the couch for better leverage up higher than my protective attacker. I could grab my phone, but the cops won't be here in time so I grab the spoon like a weapon, ridiculous as it is. I'll protect Adeline and this house to the death. Trey would be proud of me.

I hear the sound of the door swing open. "Shit," I whisper, and then there's a thud as something drops on the floor just inside.

A duffel bag...a Hawkeyes duffel bag.

Then Trey appears, looking rumpled and travel-worn, his bag in one hand and confusion on his face. Even exhaustion, but goddamn it, he's the best thing I've seen all day.

"Vivi?" he asks, eyes narrowing at the way I'm gripping my spoon like a dagger high above my head to rain it down on some intruder.

I exhale hard, my shoulders easing, lowering my spoon weapon and clutching at my heart. "Jesus. You scared the hell out of me."

His brow furrows. "I texted you when we landed. Said I was heading straight home. We got stuck on the tarmac at the airport so I couldn't tell you that we were going to make it home tonight."

I grab my phone, flipping it over. Sure enough, the missed message is there.

"I turned it to vibrate. I didn't see it," I say, and then notice something unusual on his face. "Are those...gold eye masks?"

He looks down quickly, hiding his face from me as he yanks them off quickly. "Shit. Forgot to take them off after the flight. But they work—don't tell Aleksi I said that."

His eyes land on the pint in my hands. "Is that my ice cream?"

I clutch it closer. "Maybe."

"You hate cookie dough."

"It grew on me." I take another bite, taunting him, watching his eyes narrow. Why the hell am I egging on a trained ex-special forces operative? I have no idea. "I was going to replace it before you got home," I explain.

"Hand it over, Newport."

"Make me, Hartley."

His grin turns predatory as he stalks toward me, unzipping his Hawkeyes jacket and tossing it to the side of the living room and squares up to me. All muscle and power. "Last chance."

I leap off the couch, heart hammering, legs already thrumming with anticipation. The thrill hits fast and sharp—he's going to chase me, and I want him to. I clutch the ice cream like a shield and flash him a daring smile over my shoulder.

"You'll have to catch me first."

"That can be arranged." He launches over the couch with military precision, and I shriek—half startled, half giddy—as I take off toward the kitchen, laughter bubbling in my throat.

He chases me down the hallway, and I duck into the dining

room, sliding behind the table.

"You forget I did recon in worse terrain than this," he calls, flanking the other side. "You're not going to win this."

"I've got home-field advantage," I quip, darting into the front hallway and doubling back toward the living room.

He nearly catches me at the stairs, but I fake left, then veer right, laughing as he curses under his breath.

"You're fast," he calls, amused. "It must be because you're so much lower to the ground."

"Are you calling me short?" I gasp, feigning insult through breathless laughter.

"Not short—just pocket-sized. And don't get it twisted." He smirks. "It's one of my favorite features of yours."

"Flattery won't get you this ice cream."

"Then I guess I'll have to take it from you."

He closes the distance, grabbing me by the waist as I attempt to cut through the kitchen again. I scream-laugh as he hauls my back against his chest, lifting me effortlessly.

"Caught you," he says, breathless but triumphant.

"You cheated."

His mouth finds my ear, and he whispers, "Not cheating if I win fair and square, Vivi Ann."

If I had been standing, my knees would have given out with how sultry he said those words to me. The heat of his mouth against my neck, the thumping of his heart through his chest against my back.

He tosses me back onto the couch, following me down until I'm pinned beneath him.

"Give me a bite," he demands, bracing his arms on either side of my head, his breath warm against my cheek.

"You want a bite?" I scoop up some ice cream with my spoon.

"You know what I want."

I shove the spoon in his mouth, both of us chuckling. But as he swallows, something shifts. The playfulness evaporates, replaced by the same tension that's been growing between us.

"Was that good?" I ask.

He nods, "It tastes even better when you're under me."

His eyes search mine. No words, but we don't need any. I know what he's asking.

His eyes drop to my lips. "The ring ..."

I pull my left hand between us—it's bare. "You'll never see it on my finger again unless I have to for public appearances. There's nothing between us tonight."

I need to at least know what it would be like to be with him, even if tonight is all we have, and I have to walk down the aisle to someone else in four weeks. I can't live with regrets that I didn't at least give us one night.

His eyes flash—surprised, maybe hopeful—and then his lips crash into mine.

Desperate. Hungry. I know the feeling. His mouth moves with urgency, tongue sweeping into mine, tasting of cookie dough and weeks of pent-up desire. I want so badly to have a chance with him, but how can I have it all?

I part my legs on instinct, and he takes my cue, sliding his hips between my thighs, grinding against me. His hands tug my legs higher around his waist, locking us in.

His hand slips under my shirt, fingers pausing at the hem of my bra like he's waiting for permission.

I nod against his mouth.

That's all it takes. He palms my breast with one hand, rough and warm and possessive, while bracing his weight with the other. I feel every inch of him pressed against me through the thin barrier of our clothes.

I grab the hem of his T-shirt, and he yanks it over his head in one swift motion. A set of dog tags hangs from his chest, and his body—scarred, solid, and beautiful—knocks the breath from my lungs.

He's a survivor. A fighter. If not for the hearing aid, you'd never know how much he's been through. But I see it all, every story etched into his skin.

"Your turn," he says.

In seconds, I'm topless. Shirt and bra gone. He drags my leggings down and off, and when his sweats hit the floor, we're down to a thong and boxers.

He groans at the sight of me, then dips his head to my nipple and sucks, slow and purposeful. I arch into him with a soft whimper.

His hand skims down my stomach and slides beneath my thong. My knees open wider for him as his finger slides through my wet folds. He groans and sucks on me harder as his fingers explore my center.

"You have no idea how many times I've imagined you like this." My breath hitches at his admission. "You, naked beneath me. So fucking beautiful. Letting me have what I want from you."

"What do you want from me?"

"I want everything."

He sits back on his heels and hooks his thumbs into the waistband of my thong, dragging it down my legs and tossing it aside. "This is mine tonight," he mutters, echoing his words from weeks ago.

Then he stands, pushing down his boxers, and my breath catches at the sight of him—tall, broad, thick, and already hard for me. My mouth goes dry, wondering how good he'd taste in my mouth.

I sit up and reach for him, but he stops me, gripping the base of his cock as he leans in to whisper, "Not tonight. Tonight, I'm the one doing the work."

He reaches for his wallet in his sweats discarded on the living room floor and pulls out a condom.

"You came prepared," I tease, heart thudding.

He gives me a look that's all hunger. "I've been prepared since the first morning you showed up in those tight ass leggings on your first day."

He tears the foil and rolls it on with practiced ease, then lowers himself back between my legs, kissing me like he's starving.

I feel the blunt tip of him press against my entrance, and my body arches instinctively, wanting more.

He eases in slowly, giving me time to stretch around him. Inch by inch, he sinks into me, and I'm already moaning, the pressure delicious, the stretch exactly the way I knew he'd be.

"You're so tight," he grits. "Fucking hell, I knew you'd feel like this. Knew I'd lose my mind."

He bottoms out, holding still, his arms holding strong around me, his teeth grinding as he adjusts trying to hold it together. His forehead rests on mine.

He groans, pulling out just enough to slam back in, hard and deep.

My gasp turns into a moan, and then I'm lost—rocking beneath him, clinging to his shoulders, drowning in the feel of him.

He fucks me like he's claiming me. Like he doesn't know if this is the only time we'll get, so he's going to make it count.

His hand slides to grip my ass, lifting me into his thrusts. "You'll tell me if I'm hurting you? I'll stop."

"If you stop," I pant, "I will kill you."

That earns me a grin, and then he thrusts harder, deeper. "That's my girl."

The pleasure builds slowly, climbing in waves. His hand snakes between us, thumb circling my clit. I cry out, clenching around him.

"Not yet," he growls, slowing his thrusts. "Hold it. I want you to come apart with me."

"I—I don't know if I can."

"Yes, you can." He kisses me, tongue sweeping in to swallow my moans. "I'm right here. I've got you. Just hold on a little longer."

He thrusts harder, hitting that perfect spot again, and I feel it—right there, on the edge. His dog tags swing between us, clinking softly. His breath is hot against my cheek.

"Are you going to come on my cock?" he pants. "Going to let me feel you squeeze me while I fill this condom so hard I forget my name?"

I shudder, legs wrapping tighter around him. "Yes. Trey, please—"

"Then take it," he growls. "Come for me, Vivi."

It crashes through me like wildfire. My body arches, and I cry out his name as I clench hard around him, my orgasm tearing through every nerve ending.

"Fuck," he grits. "Vivi—shit—I'm—"

He slams into me once more and then his thrust holds a rhythm, coming hard with a deep, guttural groan against my shoulder that vibrates through his chest. His arms lock around me, holding me tight as his tip pulses inside the condom, hips twitching with every aftershock.

We stay like that, tangled and breathless, until the world slowly rights itself.

He kisses my cheek, my jaw, my collarbone. His movements slow as worship and praise.

"Jesus," he murmurs. "I've never come that hard ..."

I brush his hair back from his face. "Yeah. Me either."

He finally pulls out and disappears down the hallway. I hear the bathroom faucet run. He returns with a warm towel and wipes between my legs gently, then discards the condom before grabbing a throw blanket off the armchair and pulling me into his lap on the couch.

We sit in silence, his fingers tracing lazy circles on my bare back.

"I missed you," he says finally.

I blink. "After only three days?" But the truth is, I missed him too, which is why I stole his ice cream.

He presses a kiss to my shoulder. "Still missed you."

I nestle closer, tucking my head under his chin. "You said you were prepared since I started ... You must have thought this would happen?"

"I know what I wanted to happen, but things with us aren't exactly straightforward, and the conversation we had about

Adeline on your first day," he says, tucking his free hand behind his head. "I knew this would complicate things. I certainly didn't come home tonight thinking this would happen."

I bite down on my lips, nervous now, my fingers finding a tattoo on his pec to swirl around to keep my attention off his eyes before I ask, "Do you regret it?"

"No, of course not. Why would I regret having the best sex of my life with you?"

"I don't know. Because you just said that sex makes everything between us more complicated."

I can feel his eyes on me. I glance up to find concern in his eyes. "Do you mean because what I said about Adeline and how I don't want her to see us together and get attached?"

"Oh my God, Adeline," I say, pulling the blanket up higher as I attempt to peek over the couch down the hall.

He laughs, kissing my temple. "Relax. She has a fan on all night and sleeps harder than the undead. She didn't hear anything. I wake before the sun which will give us more than enough time to sneak you upstairs before she's up."

"I don't want to traumatize your niece. Maybe I should just go home to be safe."

"She won't ever know this happened, and I don't want you to go home. I want to wake up and make breakfast with you. Please don't leave. I'm not ready to let you go yet."

I smile at the words, heart aching in the best way. "I'm not ready to go either."

I feel his hand stroke up my spine as my eyes start to drift shut.

"And just so we're clear, there is nothing about these moments with you that I'll ever regret," he says and then kisses my forehead. "Now get some sleep," he says quietly. "I've got you."

And for the first time in a long time, I believe him.

CHAPTER SIXTEEN

Trey

The first light of morning breaks through the living room windows, and for the first time in fifteen years, I slept through the night on the couch.

Vivi is still asleep, her head resting on me like an angel. We put our clothes back on after our second round because once wasn't going to be enough for either of us.

I stare down at her, not knowing what any of this means for her but knowing that I'm still not a whole man who can offer her what she deserves. I'm still broken and bruised, but I'm also selfish, and being with her for as long as she'll let me is something I can't walk away from if she offers it. Even if it's only the next four weeks.

Vivi's eyes begin to flutter open, and then those golden amber eyes are back on mine. "Good morning," she says.

"Yes, it is."

"You're still here on the couch. I figured you would have taken off for your run by now."

"Yeah, me too. I've never slept in this late in... I can't even remember how long.

She smiles up at me, and we both know what kept me on this couch all night—her.

"What do you have going on today?" she asks.

"Breakfast with my girls and then the gym with the guys," I tell her.

"Sounds good." She smiles, wiggling back into the side of my arm.

And I love that she's not pulling away.

I bend down and kiss her. Her hand reaches for my cheek and then curls around the back of my neck, pulling me tighter against her.

"Uncle Trey?" Adeline's voice carries down the stairs.

We spring apart like teenagers caught by parents. Vivi nearly falls off the couch, with a thud and then an "ouch" trying to yank the blanket we're both stuck in off of her.

"Here. I'm down here," I call back, jumping off the couch and trying to straighten up the cushions, but Adeline is quicker than I thought, and she's already heading down the hallway.

Thank God we dressed last night.

"Oh, you're both down here already," Adeline says, wiping the sleep from her eyes.

Vivi snorts. "Good morning, Adeline," she says, then disappears down the hall, grabbing her overnight bag and hightailing it upstairs. I hear the moment she closes my bedroom door behind her.

She looks around suspiciously. "Is that Vivi's phone?"

Shit. "She must have left it last night after putting you to bed."

"Uh-huh." She crosses her arms, looking so much like Sarah it hurts. "And is that her sweater on the floor too?"

Double shit.

"Go brush your teeth, squirt. I'll start breakfast."

She rolls her eyes but heads back upstairs. "Whatever you say, Uncle Trey."

I hear the shower upstairs. Vivi is washing away the evidence of our night together. Like it never happened. Like in a month, she won't be walking down the aisle toward someone else.

My phone buzzes—a text from Slade.

Slade

Still on for the gym this morning?

Reality crashes back in. I have the guys to meet up with. Games. Playoffs are coming up. A nine-year-old to raise. I can't afford distractions, no matter how beautiful they are or how right they feel in my arms.

But as I hear Vivi humming in the shower, I know that no matter how much I convince myself I'm capable of staying away from her, especially now that I know what she tastes like, the more I know...I'm a damn liar.

Vivi

THE HOT WATER cascades over my shoulders, but I can still feel Trey's hands there. His mouth. His everything. My body aches in the best way—tender nipples from his talented tongue, the sensuality between my thighs where he took me.

I trace the light bruise on my hip where he gripped me, pulling me harder against him as he thrust up into me. The memory alone makes the heat pool low in my belly all over again.

God, I'm in trouble.

Because it wasn't just sex. It was the way he held me after. How safe I felt falling asleep in his arms.

"Get it together," I mutter, reaching for my shampoo.

But I can't. Because now I know what it's like to have him. To be his. To feel him come apart inside me while whispering my name like a prayer.

A knock at the bathroom door makes me jump.

"Vivi?" Adeline calls. "Can you help me with my hair before school? Uncle Trey's terrible at braids."

"Sure, honey. Give me five minutes."

I rinse quickly, trying to look like I didn't just have mind-blowing sex with her uncle on the living room couch. When I emerge in my robe, she's waiting with her brush and hair ties.

"So..." she starts as I begin sectioning her hair. "Did you and Uncle Trey kiss or something last night?"

I nearly drop the brush. "What?"

She catches my eye in the mirror. "Uncle Trey's smiling. He never smiles this early."

"I...um..." How do you explain this to a nine-year-old?

"I told you that you two are perfect together." She shrugs. "I think you two should just get married already, and then you could live here with us all the time. Plus, I think he sleeps better when you're here."

My hands freeze mid-braid. "What do you mean?"

"He doesn't like me to know, but I've caught him sleeping on the floor in the living room before when I had a nightmare and came down to find him. He doesn't sleep in his bed or on the couch. He goes for a run and a shower before I even get up usually, but this morning he was still lying on the couch with you." She picks at a loose thread on her sleeve. "Dad used to say he has trouble sleeping because of the war stuff."

My heart squeezes. Not only because she wants the best for her uncle, but because of the fact that he sleeps on the floor and he spent the entire night asleep with me on the couch. I shouldn't read into it even though it's hard not to. What does it change though?

And of course, she notices these things. She's more perceptive than any of us gives her credit for. Was this what Trey was worried would happen if he and I got too close in the house where Adeline might see it?

"Your uncle is tough, and the sleep thing is probably just his usual routine. I wouldn't worry about it, okay? I know he wouldn't want you to."

She nods.

"There," I say, as I finish her braid. "All set."

"Thanks." She hugs me quickly. "Don't forget we have ballet today."

Right. Ballet. Normal life. Not whatever fantasy world that Trey and I had last night. I need to shake it off and get back to work.

Upstairs, I find clothes I'd packed for today and get dressed quickly. My phone has three missed calls from Virginia and a text from Isla about meeting the girls at Serendipity's later.

I call Virginia on her private cell.

"Oh thank God you answered," she says after one ring, in a hushed tone.

"Why, what's going on? And where are you?"

"I'm in the ladies' room," she says, her whisper echoing. "It's the only place Martin can't follow me."

"Martin? Follow you? What the hell is going on over there?" I ask, concerned for Virginia having to hide in the bathroom to talk to me.

"Nothing like that, only, I think he knows that half the staff doesn't like him, and the other half is just better at lying. The thing is, I just can't stand by anymore and watch him ruin everything. He changed the water dispenser order from spring water to distilled, the coffee maker is gone because he said the afternoon crash is killing productivity, and he dismantled the party planning committee because he said we spend too much money. I think he's just jealous because we won't let him in on it."

I head down the stairs, and I hear Trey and Adeline chatting in the kitchen.

Trey's making breakfast—shirtless, because apparently the universe hates me. The muscles in his back flex as he flips pancakes, and all I can think about is how those muscles felt under my hands last night. Then I remember that I'm on the phone with Virginia.

"Right, okay. It sounds like he's trying to penny-pinch a little bit. It's not what you're all used to, but it's temporary," I tell her, hoping to make her feel better.

Trey turns when he hears my voice, and then he sees that I'm on the phone. "Coffee's ready," he says gently to not interrupt.

I nod and smile.

I pour a cup, trying not to stare at the tattoos etched up both arms, across his shoulders that I've seen peeking above his T-shirts. I had never considered tattoos particularly sexy before, but with Trey, I want to personally take my time to lick each one. "Thanks," I say back.

I hear Virginia blow out a breath. "I know, but it's just that. That's why I'm calling. It's gotten worse—way worse."

"How much worse could it get?" I ask.

"Mrs. Vanderbeaker called for a fill-in additional nanny for her annual Fourth of July party. She wanted an extra for the entire three days of the party plus an extra pastry chef and head chef for the entire weekend."

Mrs. Vanderbeaker is one of those pain in the ass clients that asks for the extra mile, which is never convenient, but she has four separate homes around the country, and we fully staff each one with butlers, housekeeping, a nanny, and two chefs for whenever she wants to travel back and forth. Not to mention the three assistants we staff her with who travel with her wherever she goes.

She pays us a lot, and I try to always accommodate her. Plus, she treats my staff well and tips them well. They are always happy to get more hours with her when they can.

"This is typical for one of our premier clients. Mrs. Vanderbeaker asks for this every year for the Fourth of July, Thanksgiving, and Christmas. I'm not sure what the issue could be," I say.

"He told her no," she says flatly.

And that's when I just about lose my mind. I knew that putting the CFO in my shoes was the wrong idea. He cares more about the bottom line than understanding the actual nuts and bolts of how we've become the leading staff agency for our niche in the state.

"What do you mean he told her no? Mrs. Vanderbeaker is responsible for at least ten percent of our premier clients. We've always made her happy because she brings us a lot of revenue."

"I know...which is precisely what I told him when she called me after their phone call and asked me if there was some kind of mistake. I went to him immediately and explained that you have always honored her special occasion requests because she is an elite member."

"And what did he say?" I ask, assuming he must have realized his mistake.

"He told me that it's time this company trains its clients a little better and that Newport Staff is starting with her."

My soul just about leaves my body the moment she says it. "Train our clients? Is he insane? Mrs. Vanderbeaker has the kind of weight to push around. If she leaves, all of her minions who make up a massive portion of our portfolio will leave and sign with our competitor."

"Thus, the reason for this call. What should I do?" she asks.

I think for a second. This is my company, and I am still the CEO, no matter what the hell Richard or Martin thinks. I'm the one who built it and landed big fish clients like Mrs. Vanderbeaker and her friends by offering them a service they couldn't resist and customer service that's above what anyone else in our field is willing to offer.

I won't let it go down like this. Not if I can do something about it.

"What did you tell Mrs. Vanderbeaker when she called?"

"I told her that you were on leave looking at venues in France for your elopement with Jameson and that's why Martin took the call, but that she is your most important client and I would personally have you call her back while you're tromping through gorgeous vineyards."

"You're brilliant. Thank you for thinking so quickly on this. You might have just saved our client from leaving and taking her followers with her. I'll call Richard and make sure he understands to slap some sense into Martin since Martin isn't taking my calls right now. I owe you big."

"Just get back here, and soon. I can't take much more of this.

I'm a little worried he's going to fire me if he finds out that I told you, and I'm not the only one who's worried he's going to fire us for our loyalty to you."

When I look up for a moment, I see Trey is watching me. Listening in with curiosity.

"You're not getting fired, Virginia. I may not be the current CEO, but I won't let that happen. Tell anyone you talk to who seems worried that I won't let him get away with firing any of my staff as retaliation."

"There's a rumor going around that he's planning on cutting your Christmas bonuses because they are too costly. A lot of people are really worried about that since they depend on those extra funds to help get them through a very expensive time of the year."

I can't even believe I am hearing this. These Christmas bonuses mean so much to our staff, and it's one of the things I've always done to show our appreciation and make their loads a little lighter around the holidays to make it a more enjoyable and stress-free time for them.

This is exactly why I knew our CFO couldn't handle the CEO position. Sometimes money is spent on employees as an investment into your future working relationship.

"Squash that rumor whenever you hear it. Reassure them that I will be back in the CEO position way before Christmas, and bonuses will definitely be happening. Just stay strong and keep the front office as united as you can until I can get back to work."

Now the fantasy I had of telling the board and the Holidays to kiss my ass and run away with Trey is out of the question, even if it was only that...a fantasy.

Walking away from the CEO position at Newport Staffing means letting down a lot of staff members who have been with me since the beginning and have never let me down. I have to show up for them.

"Thank you, Vivi. Just come back soon, okay? We all miss you."

We hang up, and I shake my head at how quickly everything

is falling apart without me.

"You're good at this whole CEO thing, aren't you?" Trey asks.

"If almost losing one of the biggest clients we have is what you consider good, and my employees think that we're going back on our promises...then we should work on your standards."

He chuckles. "I mean, you have a team that's so loyal she hid out in a bathroom to call you. And she has enough faith in you that she believes you're the only one who can save the company."

"Maybe it means something."

"It means you're a good leader. You understand that the client is more important than the bottom line and that the people who work under you feel you will have their back when they tell a client you're going to fix something, because Virginia believes that you will. You told her that you're coming back, and she believes you. I knew you were good at your job, I just didn't realize how good," he says, his eyes on mine. "Now I've seen it. You need to save your company—whatever it takes."

I want to ask him what that means for us, but with Adeline sitting at the island, I can't. For now, it means I have to set my sights on marrying Jameson, unless some Hail Mary comes out of nowhere and saves us both from a loveless marriage.

"Thank you for seeing all of that in a four-minute phone conversation."

"I saw it before that... This just confirms it." And then he turns back to the stove, working a frying pan.

Something in him, believing that I'm good at what I do, has my chest swelling with pride. It's all I've ever wanted. For people to see me as Vivi Newport, CEO, not as one of the Newport sisters who must have gotten where she is with her daddy's money.

Trey seeing that means more to me than he'll ever know. But holding onto it means I have to let him go when Jameson gets back.

No more ice cream chasing around the kitchen. No more impromptu sex on the couch when he catches me. No more grease stains on my ass where his hands have been.

"Something smells good. I thought you didn't cook?"

"Uncle Trey stole your recipe for the pancake batter," Adeline announces, sliding onto a stool. "Let's see if he can pull this off and impress you."

He turns towards us and sets a plate in front of her. Now I'm gifted with the front view of Trey, the tattoos over his pecs and the dog tags that I didn't get to read last night. "Keep that up and you can make your own breakfast, squirt."

The domesticity of it all makes my chest ache. This is what I want—morning teasing and shared coffee and family breakfast. Not some arranged marriage in France with a man who's currently ghosting everyone from Greece.

"I should get going," Trey says, checking his phone. "I'm meeting some of the guys at the gym."

"Right." I busy myself with my coffee. "I'll drop Adeline off at school, and then I've got ballet covered later."

He nods, heading upstairs to change. When he returns, he drops a kiss on Adeline's head.

"Be good for Vivi."

"I'm always good."

He snorts, then hesitates by my chair. For a moment, I think he might kiss me too. Instead, he hesitates, his eyes shift to Adeline who's watching us with a coy smile, and then he squeezes my shoulder gently instead.

"See you tonight?"

I nod, not trusting my voice.

After dropping Adeline at school and sending off an SOS text to Richard that we have to talk, I head to Serendipity's. The coffee shop is already full of WAGs when I arrive.

"There she is." Cammy waves me over. "We were just talking about girls' night."

"At Ground Zero," Peyton adds. "This Saturday for Kendall's birthday—no boys allowed. You in?"

I slide into a chair. "I'll have to check if Trey has plans or if I can take the night off."

Peyton nods. "Perfect, just let me know. I'm going to book us a VIP lounge so we don't get hassled like last time."

"I'll know tonight," I tell her.

"Speaking of Trey," Cammy says, a glint in her eye.

I nearly choke on my latte, panicking that somehow I have "Trey and I had sex last night" stamped on my forehead. "What about Trey?"

"Oh, please." Isla rolls her eyes. "We all saw how he looked at you during the home game last week. And now you're wearing his shirt."

I glance down, realizing I grabbed one of his Hawkeyes training shirts by mistake this morning instead of the new work out gear that Isla sent me from her new line. Heat floods my cheeks.

"It's not... We're not..."

"Honey." Cammy leans forward. "We've all been there. The 'it's complicated' phase. Trust me... that phase fades fast, and then before you know it, you're living with the man and planning a future. Right, Peyton?"

Peyton chuckles. "Don't trust a Hawkeyes boy. They're like quicksand. They suck you in faster the more you struggle."

"I'm not struggling, and he's not sucking me in." Unless you count what he did to my nipples, I think to myself. "In four weeks—"

"In four weeks, you have a choice to make," Isla says softly. "The question is, what do you really want?"

My phone buzzes—another text from Genevieve about wedding venues. This time, flower arrangements. I ignore it.

"I don't even know what I want right now. Except that I know that my company is in trouble, and the only way to fix it and to save Jameson's situation is to get married."

"Just think about it." Isla squeezes my hand. "Sometimes the right choice isn't the easy one."

Right now, I don't even know if there is a Trey and me. He knows I'm leaving in four weeks, and it's not like he's asked me to give it all up for him. Even if he did, I'd have to think about my employees and clients who are counting on me.

For today, I just need to focus on getting Richard to fix the mess that Martin is making, and then maybe I'll have time to figure out the rest.

Chapter Seventeen

Trey

It's been a week since I had Vivi beneath me on that couch, and I'm losing my goddamn mind.

Every morning, she makes coffee in my kitchen, barefoot, knowing where everything is better than I do. Like she is meant to be here. Every evening when I don't have a home game, I watch her and Adeline run through bedtime routines like they've been doing it for years, chattering and laughing the entire time. And every night, I walk her to her car and then sleep alone on the floor, replaying the way she felt wrapped around me, the sounds she made when I was buried deep inside her.

But it was more than that—more than the sex. It was the way she looked at me, the trust she gave me, every touch of hers on my skin that felt like tattooing her fingerprints on every part of me that she owns now.

I'm standing in my living room doorway, watching Adeline and Vivi work through a dry run on her ballet recital hair and a costume fitting on the new tutus that they picked up today after class to make sure no alterations need to be made before the big day.

"Hold still," Vivi says, bobby pin between her teeth as she works on Adeline's bun. "Almost got it."

Adeline stands perfectly still in her pale blue tutu, the layers of tulle making her look like a tiny ballerina doll. Blue tights, satin slippers, even a little tiara that catches the light when she moves. But it's not my niece that has my attention completely captured.

It's Vivi, kneeling behind her, tongue poking out slightly in concentration as she secures each pin. She's changed into comfortable clothes after picking Adeline up from school—yoga pants that hug her curves and another one of my Hawkeyes shirts that she's stolen from my closet. Her dark hair falls in waves down her back, and I want to run my fingers through it like I did the other night.

"There." She sits back on her heels, admiring her work. "What do you think?"

Adeline looks from side to side, admiring herself in the mirror. "I look like a real ballerina!"

"You are a real ballerina," Vivi corrects gently. "The costume is just for fun. The work you put in during class is what makes you a ballerina."

This is what Adeline needs. Someone who sees her, who makes her feel special. Someone who doesn't just go through the motions but actually cares.

Someone like Vivi, who won't be here much longer.

My phone buzzes, breaking me out of my thoughts.

I answer the call, putting it on speaker. It's probably something to do with the Little Hawks anyway. "Hey. What's up?"

"Quick question for you," Kaenan says. "Mom wants to take Berkeley to Disneyland for spring break. Two nights, fly down Friday morning, back Sunday afternoon. But Berkeley's driving her crazy, begging to bring a friend."

I can already guess where this is going.

"Specifically, she wants to bring Adeline. Mom's fine with it. Apparently, one nine-year-old is the same amount of chaos as two, and Oliver just chases the two girls around. She says it's no trouble. What do you think?"

I look over at Adeline, whose smile is so bright and wild, and I already know that I can't say no.

"Can I go?" Adeline's voice rises an octave as she processes what she's hearing. "Can I go? Please, Uncle Trey."

She starts bouncing, making Vivi laugh as she tries to keep the carefully constructed bun from falling apart.

"Adeline, careful," Vivi says, chasing her with more bobby pins. "Your hair!"

I pull the phone back up closer to my mouth. "Yeah, that's fine with me. But she better be on her best behavior and not cause any trouble for your mom."

I say it to Kaenan, but my threat is focused on the little ballerina twirling around my living room with excitement.

"She was born to be a grandmother. She's happy to do it."

Adeline lets out a shriek of excitement that probably rattled windows three houses down.

"I take it she's happy?" Kaenan's laugh carries through the phone.

"That's an understatement. Text me the details, and I'll make sure she's packed and ready."

"Will do."

I hang up to find Adeline practically vibrating with excitement while Vivi starts taking out Adeline's hair since there's no use at this point, and it was only a trial run to make sure they were ready for her recital in two weeks.

"Disneyland!" Adeline bounces again. "I get to go to Disneyland with Berkeley!"

"If you keep moving like that, you're going to go to Disneyland bald," Vivi threatens, but she's smiling.

"This calls for celebration hot cocoa," Vivi announces once she finishes taking out the hair pins. "And a movie. What do you think?"

"Yes!" Adeline squeals. "Can I pick it out?"

"Yes, but after you get dressed in pajamas and hang up the tutu in your closet so it doesn't wrinkle," Vivi tells her.

Adeline disappears upstairs to change out of her recital costume while Vivi starts the hot cocoa.

"You spoil her," I tease as she walks by me.

"Oh and you don't? I'm not the one sending her to Disneyland for spring break."

She turns back, a slight smile over her shoulder as she heads for the pantry to get everything started. I follow her in, but then make a beeline for the refrigerator, already remembering that she'll need milk for her recipe.

We meet by the stove, her arms full of sugar and bittersweet cocoa powder. I set the milk down next to her and then reach for the nutmeg and cinnamon from the spice cabinet above her head.

"You've been watching," she says, setting a large sauce pot on the stove.

"I notice a lot of things when it comes to you. Like how you haven't worn his ring since what we did on the couch."

Her breath hitches, and before I've thought better of it, I close the space between us—hands braced on either side of the counter, boxing her in.

Her back presses lightly against the edge. "Are you scared of me, Vivi?"

Her gaze lifts, steady but warm. "No. I'm just scared of you stepping away for good."

Something primal coils in my chest, but then the pounding of small feet on the stairs breaks the moment like a gunshot.

Adeline bounds down the stairs finally, and we spring apart like we're on fire. Vivi busies herself with the hot cocoa while I put distance between us, adjusting myself before my niece appears.

"Perfect timing," I manage, completely oblivious to the tension between Vivi and me. "Ready for the best movie night ever?"

"Ready," Vivi says, her cheeks flushed but her voice steady.

We settle onto the couch—Adeline between us like a tiny chaperone, hot cocoa in hand filled to the brim with mini marshmallows. I'm hyperaware of every movement Vivi makes, of every time her eyes linger on me, of every smile or laugh she and Adeline share.

Twenty minutes into the movie, Adeline's head starts to droop. Thirty minutes in, she's completely out, curled against my side with her empty mug still clutched in her hands.

"She's beat," Vivi whispers.

"Ballet prep is exhausting work." I ease the mug from Adeline's grip. "Let me get her to bed."

I carry her upstairs, going through our usual bedtime routine even though she's unconscious—tucking her in, checking that her nightlight is on, cracking her door just how she likes it. When I come back downstairs, Vivi's cleaning up the kitchen.

"You don't have to do that," I say.

"I don't mind." She rinses the mugs in the sink. "Besides, I should probably head home soon anyway."

The thought of her leaving makes panic rise in my throat. "Stay."

She turns to face me, and I can see the conflict in her eyes. "Trey, we could have easily gotten caught last time. And you're right, she's already so attached. We both are. I can't stand to hurt her any more than I'm already going to."

"Just stay. We don't have to do anything. I'll keep my hands to myself, I swear. " I run a hand through my hair. "Just stay."

She's quiet for a long moment and then nods. "Okay, I'll stay upstairs."

"Good."

"I've been meaning to ask about next Friday night. The girls want me to come out for girls' night—Kendall's birthday at Ground Zero. It's the same weekend that Adeline is going to Disneyland. I'm guessing you won't need me?"

Something cold settles in my stomach. Ground Zero is the kind of club where assholes go and hit on any woman in sight. The thought of Vivi there doesn't sit well with me, but it doesn't matter what I want.

This is her life. Her friends. I have no right to be jealous or possessive. Soon enough, she'll be someone else's, making hot cocoa in a different kitchen, with kids of her own that don't look like me.

"You should go," I say, and I mean it. "Have fun with the girls."

"Yeah?" she asks, a sparkle in her eyes. "I mean, I figure you won't need me with Adeline gone."

Won't need you? Nothing could be further from the truth, but saying it out loud won't help anything. Guys like me don't get to keep girls like her. Not with backgrounds so vastly different.

"You deserve a night out with the girls. It sounds fun."

She smiles at that. "Kendall's been so busy with the team and extra sports medicine conferences. She deserves this," she says, then adds, "I should head to bed. I have a lot to do this week. And you have early practice in the morning."

I nod. "Goodnight, Vivi."

"Goodnight," she says and heads for the staircase. I listen for the sound of her heading up to my bedroom, and for once, I don't have to watch her taillights drive away with my hands glued inside my pockets to keep me from chasing after her, begging her to stay.

At least tonight I can sleep easy knowing that she is safely asleep upstairs where I can protect her. Even if the person I have to protect her from the most...is me.

CHAPTER EIGHTEEN

Trey

The fights are halfway over when Aleksi walks through Kaenan's front door, freezing at the sight of Kendall's G-class Mercedes in the driveway.

Most of us have been here since the start, but Aleksi got tied up at a charity event earlier today—signing sticks and hats for underprivileged kids in the area. Good cause. The kind a lot of us players get behind.

He points toward the window like the car just cut him off in traffic. "Why is Kendall's ride out front?"

Kaenan doesn't look up from the screen, settling deeper into his recliner. "Relax. She's not here."

Aleksi's brows lift. "Then where—"

"Dropped her, Isla, and the rest of the girls at Ground Zero an hour ago. Kendall's birthday." Kaenan takes a slow pull off his beer.

Aleksi rocks back on his heels, grinning like he's already plotting something. "So what you're telling me is...we're sitting around here when we could be there?

"Girls' night," Kaenan says flatly. "The hell we should. Girls only. Isla was adamant. So park your ass and watch the fight," he says, pointing to an open chair for Aleksi to take.

Aleski motions to the TV, "The fights are practically over."

Scottie walks back to the couch with his second plate full of pizza and two beers, plopping down next to JP, who's already on his third beer and a full plate of BBQ wings. "We're looking out for you, bud. Kendall will kill you if you show up. You'll scare off any guy that looks in her direction."

Aleksi shrugs, trying for casual but his jaw's already tight. "It's her birthday. I don't care who she dances with."

Wolf nearly chokes on his beer. "You have it so bad you can't even see straight. You'd get us kicked out for sure."

"Bullshit."

"Oh really?" Hunter leans forward, that shit-eating grin. He loves giving Aleksi shit for his crush on the team doctor whenever he can. "So you'd be totally fine watching some drunk asshole grind up against her in whatever barely-there mini skirt she's probably wearing?"

Aleksi's hands curl into fists. The muscle in his jaw ticks like a time bomb.

"Knowing Kendall," Luca adds helpfully, "she's probably wearing that black number that barely covers her ass. The one from Penelope's New Year's party."

"Fuck," Aleksi mutters, rubbing his forehead, like he's trying not to think about what Kendall looks like tonight in a club full of guys all checking her out.

Kaenan's phone pings. "It's your lucky day. Isla said that the bar is getting crowded. They're going to finish their drinks and a few more songs, then they'll be ready to go."

Aleksi instantly grabs his keys from his pocket. "Perfect, tell them I'm already on my way."

Hunter gets up from the couch and reaches for his jacket. "We'd better all go to keep his stupid ass from fucking up the girls' night."

"No one's buying your shit, Reedman," Aleksi calls over his shoulder to Hunter. "You just want to go dance with your girl."

Hunter grins. "So sue me. Peyton's a great dancer."

I fall in line behind them, trying to convince myself this has nothing to do with making sure no drunk college kid is putting his hands on Vivi. The guys already suspect I've got it bad for her. The last thing I need is to confirm it.

But the thought of some asshole pressing up against her, breathing in her ear, touching what I already know feels like fucking heaven...

She's not mine, I remind myself as I follow behind Kaenan who's not happy about this.

Unfortunately, the fact that she's not mine won't stop me from wanting to break the hands of anyone who tries to touch her.

"You coming, Hart?" Wolf calls from the driveway.

"Yeah." I grab my keys. "Someone's got to keep you idiots out of trouble."

Kaenan and I take our SUVs since we're the designated drivers tonight anyway. Plus, we'll need seats to bring the girls back home with us.

If I'm relieved to get to make sure no one's dancing too close to Vivi, I sure as hell won't be telling any of these assholes.

GROUND ZERO IS exactly what you'd expect from Seattle's hottest dance club—music blaring, lights flashing, packed wall-to-wall with bodies moving to bass that vibrates through your chest. The kind of place that exists for dancing, drinking, and hooking up.

I have no fucking idea why the girls love this place.

We find a booth near the VIP section, trying to look casual. But Penelope spots us immediately, shaking her head as she marches over past the velvet rope of their VIP section where most of the wives are sitting and chatting. She's all curls and killer heels and the kind of look that could stop traffic. She intercepts Slade halfway across the floor. Her finger jabs into his chest, her mouth moving in a tight, silent tirade that I can barely hear over the bass: *You promised no boys allowed.*

Slade tries to charm his way out of it, but Penelope's not buying it. She glances toward the booth, catches the rest of us loitering like idiots in enemy territory, and shakes her head so hard her earrings flash in the strobe lights.

Hunter grins from beside me. "She's gonna make him sweat for this one."

"Good," Kaenan mutters, sliding into the booth like a man settling in for the long haul. "We're here to keep Aleksi from doing something dumb. We sit, we drink soda, we watch the fight on my phone, we go home. No bothering the girls."

I nod like I agree. I don't.

Because the second my eyes find Vivi across the floor, every plan I had to keep my head down goes straight to hell.

She's in black. Not the kind of black that blends in. The kind that makes you look twice, then again, then forget your own damn name. The dress is short, the sleeves barely there, the neckline just enough to make me think of how she'd look out of it, sprawled naked on my bed. Her hair's loose, catching the light when she throws her head back laughing at something Kendall says as they all sway together in a protective circle as if not to let any male intruders into their group.

And she's moving, nothing wild, just this easy, natural sway like she doesn't even realize half the men in the room have clocked her.

My jaw tightens.

She's not mine. I've been telling myself that for weeks. She's got an expiration date stamped on her time in my life. But none of that stops my chest from tightening at the thought of some drunk asshole pressing up against her.

I take a long sip of my club soda, trying to focus on anything else.

Hunter elbows me. "You've been staring at her for three minutes straight."

"I'm making sure she's safe," I lie.

"Right. And I'm only here for the good music and heavily poured drinks."

I ignore him, but I can't ignore the way my pulse kicks when a guy in a button-down starts moving toward Vivi and Kendall. He's tall, broad, and clearly thinks he's the answer to their good time. I'm halfway out of the booth before I realize Kendall's already waved him off without missing a beat.

Still, my hands curl into fists.

Kaenan gives me a look. "Sit your ass down."

I do...for about thirty seconds.

Because now Kendall and Cammy head for the VIP section to get a drink to cool down and Peyton's dragging Vivi toward the center of the floor as the DJ drops something with a bass line so deep it rattles my teeth. She's laughing, moving in time with Peyton, her hips swaying, eyes half-lidded with the rhythm.

I'm done pretending.

"Are you ready to get in there?" Hunter asks.

"Let's go," I say.

By the time I reach her, she's just turned, hair sweeping over one shoulder. Her eyes widen slightly when she sees me, then narrow in mock disapproval.

Hunter slides in between us and Peyton, and Peyton looks more than happy to have a new dance partner.

"Thought this was girls' night," she says over the music.

"Then you shouldn't be here," I counter.

Her mouth curves. "Pretty sure that's not how it works."

I step in closer, one hand finding the curve of her hip, testing. She doesn't move away. If anything, she leans back into me, her body fitting against mine like it's been waiting for this.

"Tell me to go," I say, against her ear.

She doesn't. Instead she turns around, giving me her back. She just starts moving again, and I move with her, my hands braced low on her waist, feeling the heat of her through that thin strip of fabric. The crowd disappears—it's just the two of us, locked in the same slow, steady rhythm.

Her perfume's driving me insane. So is the way her ass brushes against me with every shift of her hips.

"You're playing with fire," I tell her.

"Maybe I like the heat." Her voice is low, meant for me alone.

The song changes, slower, heavier, and she doesn't step away. My hands slide a little lower, thumbs stroking the bare skin at the small of her back.

"Is this a warning or an invitation?" I ask.

"Depends. Are you going to behave?"

"No."

She huffs out a laugh, but her body presses into mine, hips rolling against me in time with the beat.

"Dangerous game, Hartley."

"Baby, you have no idea," I say pulling her tighter against me.

"Are you always this cocky on the dance floor?" she asks.

"Only when I'm dancing with you."

The crowd seems to shift around us but nothing matters. Neither of us seem to notice anything but each other.

"You've been watching me since you walked in," she says.

"Been watching you longer than that. Weeks. Every damn day in my kitchen. Every night you leave before I'm ready to let you go."

She breathes out at that, which steals a little of her balance. "You make it sound like you're the one suffering."

"Sweetheart, I'm barely holding it together."

Then she leans back, her head against my shoulder, her mouth brushing my jaw. "My townhouse is only ten minutes away."

My hands tighten on her hips. "You sure you want to say that to me right now? Because what I want to do to you tonight isn't acceptable for public consumption."

She smiles up at me. "I wouldn't have if I didn't mean it."

"Say it again, Vivi. Tell me how close your house is."

I already know where it is. I've dropped her off before, but this isn't about the logistics. Her house could be ten hours away and it still wouldn't stop me from driving us straight there, right now.

Her lips curve, wicked and soft. "Ten minutes, Trey."

That's all it takes. I entwine my fingers through hers and start cutting us through the crowd. She muffles back a giggle like she thinks it's funny how easy it is to break me like that. And I don't mind. Maybe she should know that when it comes to her, my self-control is hanging by a thin thread, ready to snap at the smallest touch from her.

And not just because I want her body. Fuck... I want so much more than that.

I spot Kendall at the edge of the crowd, and she's not alone. Aleksi's got one hand braced at her hip, his mouth close enough to say something that makes her laugh hard enough to throw her head back. He's grinning like a man who just won the lottery.

It's not likely that she's going to let him get any closer than that tonight, we've all heard she has a no-dating-players rule, but Aleski is a good guy and I hope someday, she gives him a shot. Though I doubt that night is tonight.

Good, I don't want Vivi hating me for taking her away and ruining Kendall's birthday. Besides, it's the end of the night. The club will be winding down in an hour, and the look of discarded drinks at their VIP tables means they must have had a good time before we all showed up.

We pass the booth where Kaenan's camped out, nursing what's left of a beer and keeping an eye on the room. I lean in. "Can you get everyone home without my car?"

He glances at our joined hands, then smirks. "Yeah. Don't worry about it. Just go."

I don't even bother with a thank you. I'm already pulling Vivi toward the doors, the cold air outside hitting my skin like a slap.

She laughs softly, breath fogging in the night. "Are you always this impatient?"

"With you? Definitely."

I don't let go of her hand until we're in my SUV. And even then, when I open her door, my fingers brush her thigh before I step back. She slides in, eyes glittering in the dim light, and I swear I can still feel the heat of her on my palms.

The engine rumbles to life, headlights sweeping the emptying lot. Ten minutes feels like forever. But I'll make it.

CHAPTER NINETEEN

Vivi

The drive takes exactly nine minutes, but it feels like hours with Trey's hand draped over my thigh the whole way, his thumb brushing the bare skin where my dress has ridden up. He doesn't say much, and neither do I, but the air in the SUV is thick with all the things we're going to do once we're inside.

We hit my street and my pulse spikes. The moment the garage door closes behind us, we're out of the car—his door slams, then mine, then he's there, taking my keys from my hand like I can't be trusted to manage a lock right now.

I barely get the door shut before he's on me.

Lips, teeth, hands—everywhere at once. My back hits the wall, my purse slides to the floor, and his mouth crashes into mine like we've been holding this in for years instead of weeks.

"You're sure," he rasps against my lips, already dragging the hem of my dress higher.

"If you stop now, I might actually die, and then you'll have that on your conscience forever."

That earns me a low chuckle, and then I'm being walked

backward through my own place, bumping into furniture as we kiss like we're trying to ruin each other.

We lose the rest of our clothes in a blur. My bra clasp snapping under his fingers until I'm only in my thong. He shoves his jeans down and kicks them across the room, giving my hands access to him. He's thick and hard, and when I wrap my hand around him, his head drops to my forehead with a curse. "Wait until I get you to the bed. You touching me like that could end this all too quick," he warns.

"We wouldn't want that to happen," I say. He shakes his head. "Shower first? I'm still sweaty from dancing all night."

"Oh yeah...we can make that work."

He grins and then lifts me up, carrying me upstairs to my bedroom, just like he told me he would the night we first kissed. My arms wrap around his neck, my lips not leaving his for a single second. I feel weightless in his arms, completely protected, like there is nothing in this world that would make him drop me.

By the time he walks up through my bedroom and into my bathroom, he's stripped out of his boxers, and I've lost my ability to form coherent thoughts at the sight of him. It's not the first time I've seen him completely naked, every inch of bare skin covered in muscle, tattoos scrolled all over him, a set of dog tags dangling around his neck.

He reaches past me and turns on the water and lets it run while he takes a knee and painfully slowly hooks his fingers into my thong and pulls it down my thighs to my feet. I step out, and then his mouth is on me again.

Steam begins to billow from the shower, the water warm enough now.

He lifts me back up before stepping into the shower, pinning my back to the tile.

The first kiss in the water is deeper, wetter, hungrier, and when his hands slide down to cup my ass, lifting me, I hook my legs around his waist without thinking.

His mouth leaves mine to trail down my neck, teeth scraping

lightly before his tongue soothes over the spot. "Been thinking about this all night," he says against my skin. "The way you moved against me out there..."

"Trey..." My head falls back when his hand slides between us, fingers finding me already wet.

"Fuck, you're ready." He kisses me again, slow and deep, while his thumb circles my clit. His other hand braces me against the tile, holding me exactly where he wants me as his fingers work me with steady, deliberate pressure.

I gasp into his mouth as the rhythm builds, my hips rolling helplessly. The heat from the water and the heat from him blend until I can't tell which is making me dizzy.

Every stroke of his fingers feels more deliberate now, his thumb circling with just enough pressure to have my thighs clamping tighter around his waist. The slick slide of his skin against mine under the spray is maddening. All muscle and heat and control.

He drags his mouth from mine, kissing along my jaw and down the column of my throat, letting the water pour over both of us. His teeth scrape lightly at the hollow of my neck, and I swear my knees would buckle if he weren't holding me up against the wall.

"You feel that?" he murmurs, curling his fingers inside me until he finds the exact spot that makes my breath hitch. "Right there?"

I nod frantically, nails biting into his shoulders as another wave of heat coils low in my belly. My head tips back against the tile when he does it again, this time with his thumb keeping perfect rhythm against my clit.

The steam makes my skin hypersensitive. Every droplet that trails down my body feels like it's pulling me closer to the edge. His chest is pressed so tight to mine, I can feel the steady thud of his heart, matching my own erratic pulse.

His lips find my ear, breath hot despite the mist between us. "You're close. I can feel you shaking."

I am. Everywhere. My legs, my stomach, my voice when I try to speak and only a broken whimper comes out.

He grins against my skin, slow and wicked. "Let go for me," he says, voice low and rough.

The command breaks me. My back arches off the wall as I come, hard and fast, clutching at his shoulders like he's the only thing keeping me upright. My thighs tremble around his hips, water streaming over us as every nerve ending sparks.

He keeps his fingers moving, coaxing me through it until the sharp edge fades to a slow, delicious throb. Then he eases his hand away, holding me close while I bury my face in his neck, breathing him in under the steam.

He kisses my temple. "The shower worked, didn't it? Do you feel cleaner now?" he teases.

"There was nothing clean about what you just did to my body. That was dirty through and through, and you know it," I say.

There's a glint in his eyes and a smile across his lips that tells me he enjoyed every moment of it...and so did I.

"Fair enough. Then I guess I get to wash you up."

He reaches past me for a loofa and my dragon fruit body wash.

"I'll do you—you do me," I tell him, grabbing my second loofa.

"That is the idea," he smirks.

After we finish washing up, Trey steps out and grabs big fluffy towels for both of us from the bathroom cabinet. He slides one around his waist and has one open and ready for me to step out of the shower and into.

He wraps me up as soon as I step out.

His hard cock tents his towel, and I know he must need a release just as bad.

"Maybe we should take care of that," I say, gesturing to the towel.

"I've never agreed more with anything in my life."

I barely have time to towel off my hair before he takes my cue, catching me around the waist and guiding me backward toward the bed. The room smells faintly of my shampoo and the steam we carried with us from the shower. The low light catches on the drops still clinging to his shoulders, running down over muscle and ink.

His smirk fades when I sink to my knees between his legs, pulling his towel down until it crumples around his feet.

"Vivi..." There's a warning and plea in his voice.

His cock twitches at the anticipation, and he jerks gently when I take him into my hand.

Then I guide him to my lips and open wide for him, taking him fully into my mouth without breaking eye contact. The taste is familiar and new all at once—my dragon fruit soap from the shower still lingers on his skin, but underneath is salt, heat, and the faintest trace of him that makes my pulse jump. I sink lower, my lips stretching around him, and he tips his head back with a low groan.

My hand works in tandem with my mouth, stroking slowly, even passes as I suck him down like a straw. His fingers slide into my hair, not forcing, just holding, guiding, like he can't help but need that connection.

My mouth waters at the feel of him filling me, the steady weight and heat pressing against my tongue. I'm already wet again, my body primed and eager just from the way he reacts.

"God, that's good," he rasps, the roughness in his voice scraping deliciously along my nerves. "So good."

I love the way he enjoys my mouth. Watching a man like Trey—all controlled force and unshakable presence—melt under my touch is intoxicating. Seeing him like this, his breath hitching, his grip tightening...it gives me a rush I didn't know I craved. It's not just turning him on—it's undoing him. And it makes me greedy for more.

When I swirl my tongue over the head, his fingers tighten in my hair. "Stop."

I pull back, lips tingling, a little taken aback. "You didn't like—" I've always been confident about this part of me, about knowing what I'm doing.

"I liked it too much." His voice is gravel and heat as he reaches for his jeans, tearing into a foil packet with his teeth. "I'm not coming until I'm inside you, and the way you took me down your throat...I wasn't going to last much longer. You're very talented with that tongue."

I wipe the saliva from my mouth, pulse still racing, content to bask in the rough edge of his praise.

His praise still hums through me when he rips open the condom with his teeth, the sharp sound loud in the quiet room. My pulse stutters. There's nothing casual about the way he rolls it on, no teasing, no delay, just a man with intent.

"Up here," he says, his hands firm on my waist as he guides me onto the bed.

The sheets are still warm from the shower steam clinging to our skin. I lean back against the pillows, watching him come over me like a shadow, all broad shoulders and heat. He settles between my thighs, his hand sliding up the inside of my knee until my legs open without thought.

His hand slides between my thighs, and I jolt when his fingers find me, already slick. He strokes lazily, circling my clit just enough to make my hips lift, but never quite giving me what I want.

"You're wet for me already," he says, like it's the best thing he's learned all night. His eyes are locked on mine, his touch maddeningly slow. "Is this how turned on you get from my cock?"

I bite down on my lip, almost worried he'll think I'm too easy, but the wicked grin that spreads across his face tells me getting that wet from giving him oral is a turn on for him too.

"And here I thought I'd have to work for it."

"You do," I manage, even though my voice shakes.

That earns me another grin. Dangerous. Knowing. His fingertips trail lower, dipping into me for just a second before sliding back up. My thighs twitch at the teasing glide.

"Trey ..."

"Hmm?" His tone is all innocence, but his thumb presses just enough to make my breath stutter.

"Stop teasing."

"I like teasing," he says, leaning down until his lips hover over mine. "I like watching you squirm for it."

Another slow slide of his fingers has me gripping his shoulders, arching against his hand. "Please," I whisper.

"Please what?"

My patience snaps. "Please fuck me."

The groan that rumbles out of him feels like a reward. He positions himself between my thighs, his tip pressing at my entrance. The first push makes my breath catch, my body stretching to take him.

"Good girl," he says, keeping his gaze on me like he doesn't want to miss a single reaction. "I'll never get tired of hearing you say that to me."

He thrusts into me further, pulling a moan from my lips. His teeth grind at the feeling of being inside of me.

"Christ, you're tight," he mutters, like he's talking to himself, his gaze fixed on where we're joined. He holds there, buried halfway, like he's savoring the moment—or giving me a chance to adjust.

The weight of him inside me is almost unbearable in the best way, and my thighs tremble against his hips. He's already pulled one orgasm from me and left my body sensitive and ready for another release after having him in my mouth.

"Move," I whisper.

The corner of his mouth lifts. "You sure?"

"Yes," I breathe.

Impatient. Needy.

He sinks the rest of the way in, slow enough to make my toes curl, deep enough to knock the air out of my lungs. A low sound slips out of me—part moan, part gasp—and his own breath hitches in response.

For a beat, neither of us moves. His hand braces beside my head, the other hooked under my thigh to keep me open for him. Then he starts, deliberate and controlled, each thrust measured like he's mapping every inch of me.

Every time he pulls out, the drag makes me shiver. Every time he pushes back in, it's deeper, thicker, more consuming. My hands roam over the solid planes of his back, nails catching lightly when he hits just right.

The air between us is heavy. I catch his gaze, locked on me like he's memorizing every inch of me. My pulse kicks harder, because I want to remember every moment of feeling like this with him.

"So this is what it feels like," he says, his voice panting through every thrust.

"Like what feels like?" My voice is barely a whisper.

"When you fit someone like they were made for you."

My throat tightens so fast it's hard to breathe, the words hitting somewhere deep. How am I supposed to leave him now? How can I go through with a wedding to a man I don't love when I feel this pull to Trey?

Before I can recover, he thrusts again—deep, slow, deliberate—and my body just breaks for him. The coil inside me snaps, heat flooding every nerve until I'm arching into him, clinging to him, my core squeezing him so tight it's almost unbearable.

He's right there with me, holding out until my release drags him under. His hips jerk, a guttural groan tearing from him as he spills into me, both of us trembling through it until all that's left is the sound of our ragged breaths filling the room.

He kisses me tenderly. "Are you okay?"

I nod, but the truth is, I'm not sure if I'm okay. The sex was incredible, better than I've ever had with anyone else, but it's not just sex with us. There's more to this, and we both know it. Whether Trey wants to realize what he just said in the heat of the moment, it still feels true. We do fit together like we were made for each other.

He slides over to the side and I see the dog tags around his neck. I gently pick them up in my hand to look at them.

"John Parker?" I say, reading the name, confused as to why it doesn't say Trey Hartley.

His eyes drift over to the dog tags. "My best friend. He died in the explosion that took out my hearing."

"Trey..." I say, knowing that there is no way for me to understand the loss and pain he must have gone through that day. I stare back down at them. "Are these the same ones you wear every day?"

"Yeah," he says softly, as if the memory is taking it back somewhere, "I don't have mine anymore."

My eyebrows stitch together. "You don't have them anymore? Did you lose them in the explosion?"

He shakes his head. "I buried John with mine. I kept his. He saved my life that day. I wouldn't be here without him."

I'm just about to ask him to elaborate when he sits up gently. I let go of the dog tags with so many more questions unanswered.

"I should get rid of this condom, and we should both wash up," he says. "How about a snack before round three?"

I get the hint.

Story time is over.

Whatever I want to know about Trey is his story to tell, and I have to live with the fact that he may never want to share that day overseas when he lost his best friend. I just wish he knew that I'm here for him, whether or not he ever feels ready to tell me.

The truth is, in a couple more weeks, I'll be married to someone else. That is ... if I can go through with it after knowing what it feels like to "fit someone like they were made for you."

He slides to the end of the bed and then he walks over and gives me his hand to help me off the bed. We both enter the bathroom—Trey discarding the used condom into the trash and both of us wiping up quickly.

He comes up behind me and wraps an arm around my middle, lowering his mouth to the side of my neck and kisses me in front of the mirror.

I was afraid that asking about the dog tags would put a damper on the rest of the night, but Trey is back and flirty as ever.

I grab my robe, and he wraps a towel around his middle before we head downstairs.

"WHAT SOUNDS good?" I ask as I open the fridge.

"Anything that's easy. I only get another day and a half with you before Adeline gets back so whatever gets us back upstairs is fine with me," he says, poking around to look through the dining room, office, and living room that are on the lower level.

There are still boxes from when the movers brought back everything I packed and moved to Jameson's before the wedding.

I like that he's curious about my place. Jameson has only been here once in the six months we were engaged and never looked around. Maybe because he figured I was going to put the townhouse on the market since I was going to move in with him.

"You have a lot of unpacked boxes," he says.

"Yeah, well..." I say as I open the freezer and pull out a pint of cookie dough ice cream. Okay, I've lost it, I know. "I'm not sure that I should unpack them at this point."

It's not lost on me that I never put the townhouse on the market. Even after Genevieve gifted us one of the mansions in the Holiday Trust as our wedding present. Maybe I knew something then and I wasn't willing to face it?

Trey heads back towards me, as casual as ever, but I can see that my answer to not unpacking the boxes is the reality that neither of us want to discuss right now.

Instead, he glances at the pint of ice cream, and I see the smirk start to form. Cue Trey's gloating.

"Cookie dough ice cream..." he says, walking up and taking one of the two spoons I laid out. He pops off the top and takes a big spoonful. "You know, someone once told me that this is the most boring flavor of ice cream on the face of the planet."

I grab the pint from him, taking my own spoon and scooping a bite. "Yeah, well now it tastes like you."

His smirk deepens. "So, basically, you're saying I've converted you. My influence is powerful."

"You wish," I say, but the grin tugging at my lips gives me away.

He leans a hip against the counter, eyes narrowing playfully. "You didn't even *like* cookie dough before me. Now you've got a pint in your freezer. What's next? Wearing my jersey to bed? Trading your wine nights for hockey game replays with me on the couch?"

I roll my eyes. "Don't push it."

"Too late." He digs for another bite, but instead of going back to the counter, he wanders toward the fridge like he's just casually taking in the space. My stomach does a little flip when I realize where he's heading.

And sure enough, he stops dead in front of the dry erase board propped above the nook where I usually drop my purse and hang my keys. Sticky notes littering a small corkboard that hangs on the wall. And next to it? The dry erase board where I have my list for going through with the wedding.

But he's already reading it out loud, slow and deliberate, like he's savoring each word. "*Reasons to marry Jameson...*" He turns, one brow arched, spoon still in his hand. "This should be good."

He starts to read the list out loud.

"He's a great business partner."

Trey tips his head, eyes glinting. "Mm, bet I could be better."

He reads the next one. "I gave him my word."

He makes a low sound in his throat. "You've given me a lot more than that in just one night." He looks over his shoulder and winks.

"Oh my God, Trey..." A nervous chuckle bubbles out. I'm not sure if I like him reading this list now.

He takes another bite of ice cream and then continues.

"I'll get to keep my CEO position." One corner of his mouth lifts. "You'd keep it with me too. Just give me five minutes in a locked conference room with your board of directors—hell, I'd have them promoting you."

"CEO is the top position, and you're not allowed to go anywhere near the board after the way you handled Martin Howard."

"I got him to change his mind, didn't I?" he asks, a twinkle in his eye. So sure of himself. I hate how attracted I am considering the Martin situation could have made things worse. Still, I've never had anyone stand up for me like that.

"He's well connected." His brow arches. "So am I. Different kind of connections, but they'd definitely keep life interesting. And if you ever needed to get broken out of a Colombian prison... they'd be the people you'd call."

"Lovely..." I mock.

He just smirks and takes another bite before passing me the pint of ice cream to share. I take it and scoop another bite for myself. The intimacy of sharing one ice cream might be silly but it makes the post-sex snack break that much better.

"My father approves." Trey snorts, taking another spoonful of ice cream. "Not sure that's the flex you think it is, baby."

He's right. My father's approval shouldn't matter to me, and yet... I can't shake it. We're not even blood related, and still I feel like it's programmed in me as a daughter to seek his good opinion with everything I do.

Is it so wrong that I want to imagine that his chest swelled with pride when he told his buddies on the golf course that his daughter Vivi's company made it on the Forbes list? Is it so bad that I want him to brag about me at the country clubs he frequents, that his daughter built an empire all on her own without Newport money?

Is there something wrong with me that I just want my father to be so proud that he truly believes that I'm worthy of the Newport name for everything I did without his influence and money? That not marrying Jameson Holiday wouldn't be so bad. That maybe a life like Isla's is something I deserve too.

The one thing I am sure of...Conrad Newport loves me. And if I ever have questions about it, I can look back at the divorce papers he signed with my mother where he negotiated more money to her than he would have had to, in order to ensure that I got to keep his last name.

He's just a creature with old habits he can't kill. He needs control, and the older I get, the more I realize that I'm more like him than I want to admit. Isla has tried to get me to see this for years.

I wish I could stop secretly looking over my shoulder to make sure he's watching my every accomplishment. I wish that the moment Genevieve suggested an arranged marriage between her son and me, I hadn't immediately thought about how pleased my father would be for a Newport/Holiday union.

The more I think about it, the more I wonder what I've been truly doing for me, and what I've actually been doing to try and make him proud—show that I belong in this family. That I'm a Newport through and through.

I'm so lost in my own head that I don't notice Trey studying me until he taps the spoon against the pint.

"You're overthinking again," he says, voice low but sure, like he's already decided that whatever I'm chewing on can wait.

"I'm not overthinking, I'm just—"

"You are," he cuts in, stepping closer until his hips press into the counter beside me. "Eyes got all far away, shoulders went tight. I've seen it enough to know when I'm losing you to whatever war zone's in your head."

"It's not that ..."

"Vivi," he says, soft but firm, tilting my chin up with the back of his fingers. "We're not doing that tonight. Not when I've got ten more things I want to do to you before sunrise."

Heat rushes up my neck. "Ten more things?"

"Okay, I lied. Eleven more." His smirk curves slow. "And I

know you're going to enjoy every single one." He dips down just enough for his lips to brush my ear. "In fact...I bet no one's done a couple of them to you, and a few are illegal in three countries."

I try to scoff, but it comes out shaky. "What about the ice cream?"

"You're right. We should make sure it goes back in the freezer. We'll need more sustenance for round four. We don't want this melting." He takes the pint from my hands, presses the lid back on, and drops it in the pull-out freezer. Then he hooks his arm around the backs of my thighs in one quick, fluid motion. The world tilts as I'm thrown over his shoulder, robe falling against the backs of my legs.

"Trey!" I laugh, pounding lightly at his back.

He heads for the stairs like a man on a mission. "Cookie dough just made me hungry for dessert." His hand slides over the curve of my ass. "And by dessert, I mean your pussy. I haven't eaten you yet, and I'm starving."

My laugh turns into a breathless sound I can't name, my fingers curling into the back of his shirt as he takes the steps two at a time.

The next morning, I wake alone—but there's a note on the bedside table.

Went for a run. Be back soon.

Padding downstairs, I stop cold at the sight of the dry-erase board.

Next to *REASONS TO MARRY JAMESON* is a fresh heading in Trey's blocky handwriting.

REASONS TO STAY WITH TREY:

Best sex of your life

Lifetime supply of cookie dough ice cream

Adorable niece to spoil

Season tickets to the Hawkeyes

The front door opens.

Trey steps in, all tattoos, sweat, and muscle, pulling out his earbuds. His chest rises and falls from his run, and he grins the second his eyes hit mine.

"I see the new list," I say.

"Figured, considering everything, I deserved representation."

"Best sex of my life?" I scoff, purely to tease—though nothing could be truer. I've never had it this good. Not in chemistry. Not in connection.

"Well," he says, voice dropping as he stalks closer, "if you're not convinced after last night and my couch, I'll just have to prove it again."

Before I can react, he's tossed me over his shoulder *again*, my squeal echoing off the walls.

"Where are you taking me?" I demand, laughing as he starts up the stairs.

"To the shower. Where else?"

CHAPTER TWENTY

Trey

My truck still smells like Vivi's perfume as I head to practice, the memory of this morning's shower fresh in my mind. The way she looked with water cascading down her body, steam rising around us as I pinned her against the tile. How she gasped my name when I lifted her, her legs wrapping around my waist ...

Focus, Hartley. You've got practice in twenty minutes.

I hit the hands-free button on my steering wheel, calling Kaenan's mom's cell. It rings twice before I hear the chaos in the background.

"Hello?" Mrs. Altman's voice carries over squealing and what sounds like the Indiana Jones ride sound effects.

"Hey, it's Trey. Just checking in on Adeline."

"Oh, hi Trey. Hold on, she's right here. Girls, come say hi to Uncle Trey!"

There's a shuffle, then Adeline's breathless voice: "Uncle Trey. We went on Space Mountain three times. And Berkeley screamed so loud that people three rows back laughed."

"Did not," Berkeley protests in the background.

"Did too."

I can't help smiling at their excitement. "Sounds like you're having fun, squirt."

"So much fun. We met Belle and Ariel and Snow White, and we're going to see the fireworks tonight, and tomorrow we're going to California Adventure, and—"

"Breathe, kiddo."

She giggles. "I miss you though."

"Miss you too. But I'm glad you're having fun."

"Vivi would love it here," she says. "Maybe we can all come together next year."

My chest tightens. There won't be a next year. Not with Vivi. In less than four weeks she'll be Mrs. Jameson Holiday, living in their mansion, attending charity galas instead of Disney trips. Board room meetings instead of ballet recitals.

"Maybe," I say, because I can't bear to crush her hopes. "Be good for Mrs. Altman, okay?"

"I will. Love you!"

"Love you too, squirt."

The call ends and reality crashes back in. Four more weeks. That's all we get before this ends. And though I wrote all of those things on the dry erase board, I know I'm not in the running. I can't be, even though I want to be.

I'm not even sure what I can offer her. I made the list up against Jameson but it was all for fun. To make her laugh, and yeah...maybe to make her remember that I'm still here, but I'm not a contender against Jameson, and we both know that.

Even if I were, I can't let her give up her company for me. Maybe she won't resent me today for it, but she'd resent me eventually. When she realizes that with the accident with John Parker, losing my hearing in my left ear, losing the military, and losing my best friend...and then my brother and his wife...a part of me is missing. She deserves all of someone.

I couldn't even bring myself to tell her about John and what happened that night though she wanted to ask. Because I know that telling her means showing her the holes in me that can't be put back.

No...I have to give her back to the world I took her from that night that I drove her away from her wedding. I got to keep her for a little bit, but she was only ever on loan, and my terms are up. Only, I have a few more weeks with her and tonight, I'm going to ask for it all...even if it means it ends after that.

I need to know I had her...once.

The locker room is already full when I arrive, guys suiting up for practice. Wolf spots me first, a wide grin spreading across his face.

"Well, well, look who finally showed up."

"Shut up," I mutter, heading for my stall.

"Good night?" Hunter asks innocently.

"None of your business."

"Aw, come on." Luca throws a roll of tape at my head. "Share with the class. Did our boy finally seal the deal with the runaway bride?"

I catch the tape without looking. "You want to keep your teeth? Be a little more respectful. She's more than a runaway bride."

"Touchy." Wolf whistles low. "Must have been good."

"Leave him alone," Aleksi calls from his stall. "Some of us like privacy."

"Oh, like you and Kendall last night?" Hunter shoots back. "Real private. You were on her like a fly on shit. She couldn't shake you."

Aleksi flips him off, but there's no heat in it. We all saw how happy Kendall was to see him. Whether it was the booze or just loosening her resistance to him, I can't be sure.

"Maybe our boy has a shot in hell after all," JP says.

The locker room busts out in laughter.

A text comes in from my friend at Lawson Security Solutions.

Callum Lawson

All set with the security team. Did a full assessment of the current security system and you're right. It's shit. My guys tested it twice this week with easy accessibility to disarming and break through without detection. I'll have a full scope of suggested measures we can implement as soon as you're ready.

Thanks man. I appreciate it.

Now I just have to convince Vivi to hire Lawson's team. Once I show her all the security breaches that Cullum and his team found, she'll understand why she needs to make the move.

Callum Lawson

I also have everything ready for tonight. I'll send you the details for when you arrive.

I owe you big for this.

Nerves spike up at the thought of tonight. Of sharing something with Vivi that I haven't shared with anyone outside of my unit, but if I want to ask her to share more of her time with me before this is over, I need to share something of mine.

Callum Lawson

Count us even for saving my life ten years ago over there. Looking forward to meeting your Adeline ... and your girl.

She's not my girl.

And she'll never be.

Callum Lawson

Yet, you mean. If any woman has a shot with Trey Hartley and doesn't take it, something is wrong with her.

Thanks again.

Callum Lawson

You got it, brother.

I grab my phone for one last text as the team starts to file out.

Are you available to do something with me tonight?

Vivi

Vivi: Yes. I'd love to. What do you have in mind?

Are you afraid of heights?

Vivi

Isn't everyone? But I can manage depending on what it is.

> **Dress warm. Meet me at my place at eight. You'll be safe, I promise.**

I stare at the last sentence, then lock the screen. There are promises you shouldn't make. That's one of them. I make it anyway because I will do anything in my power to protect her... even if it kills me.

ꙮ

I FOLD TWO wool blankets with the same precision I once used to fold maps—corners lined up, edges sharp. There's comfort in that.

The picnic basket Isla lent me gets stocked like a mission kit: charcuterie, grapes, chocolate truffles I'll pretend I didn't buy just because she told me Vivi likes them, and a thermos of hot cocoa made exactly the way I watched her make it in my kitchen—because where we're headed is windy and can get nasty, especially at night.

I check the flashlight. Then the backup flashlight. The med kit. The flight bag.

And I run the fuel numbers again, because there are two things I never screw up: checklists and the people I take into the air.

The driveway sensor pings, and my pulse does something stupid. Her white Range Rover turns in, headlights sliding across the front of the house. When she kills the engine and steps out, it hits me in a way that's almost physical. The jacket she's wearing is mine. Hawkeyes black, my number on the sleeve. She doesn't even notice she's put it on like a claim.

"Oh good," she says, rounding the Rover and beelining for me. "You're feeding me. Thank God, I'm starving," she says, letting out an exasperated breath as if she hasn't eaten all day, and it's cute as hell.

I don't wait for permission. My arm is around her waist, her smile widening a split second before I kiss her. Her lips are still warm from the heater in the car that she, no doubt, had cranked up, and they taste like watermelon ChapStick making my mouth water for so many reasons. Her fingers find my hair and tug, and the back of my neck lights up like it remembers every place she's ever touched.

When I break for air, her eyes are shining. "Well, hello to you too."

"Hi." My voice comes out rougher. "I only have one complaint."

"Already?" She bites back a grin. "Do tell."

"You can't wear that jacket and expect me not to forget the plan and carry you upstairs." My thumb slides against her lower lip. "You're not playing fair."

"I wouldn't protest to the new plan," she says softly.

I breathe once. The smart thing would be to lose the night in sheets. But the sky is clear. I did not get a helicopter and clear a private landing just to be undone by denim and a smirk on my doorstep. "I've got something to show you." I drop a quick kiss at her temple. "We'll do both."

"Both?"

"Trust me."

"I do," she says, and that does more damage than the jacket ever could.

I load the basket and blankets into the back. She slides into the passenger seat like she's always belonged there, tucking her feet under her, palms open on her thighs like she's done it a thousand times in my car before. As if she's just along for the ride. As if she'd go anywhere I decide to take her with complete trust.

On the console between us, her hand inches toward my forearm until her hand lies on top. I take her cue. If she wants to touch me, then I get to touch her too.

I reach across the console and hook my hand around her inner thigh, so damn close that if I stretched out my pinky, I could run a finger down her jean-clad pussy. But I won't take it there, because if I do, we'll never make it to my surprise.

She glances down at where my hand grips around her, my thumb making soothing strokes and then she turns in closer and smiles up at me, her hand still resting on my forearm. And that's how we stay for the entire drive to Lawson's—anchored to one another, neither letting go.

"So where are we going?" she asks, already smiling because she thinks she's clever enough to guess.

"Somewhere with a view."

"That's vague."

"It's on purpose."

She watches my profile like she's trying to decode a classified brief. "Waterfront? A rooftop? Oh! The space needle?"

"If I told you, then it would ruin the surprise."

"Mean," she says but grips my arm tighter as if she doesn't want me to pull my hand off her thigh. Doesn't she know that it would take a goddamn army to pry me away from her? "How high are we talking?" she asks, glancing out her passenger side window as if she'll find the answer out there.

"High enough. I want you warm." I cut her a look. "Too cold?"

She sinks deeper into my jacket like an answer and drags the collar to her nose. "Smells like you."

I swallow. "Good."

City lights stack themselves into glass and steel. We turn into the Lawson building's underground and come up through a lobby that looks like brushed chrome and money. Security nods us through, and I flash a pass that isn't about money at all.

The moment the elevator doors part, I can feel the shift in Vivi. She clocks the LSS signage, the discreet cameras, the hush that comes with competence. "Is this—"

"Lawson Security." I press my palm to the reader at the next door. "My friend owns the place."

"Friend?"

A voice carries from the end of the corridor. "Hartley!"

Callum Lawson is exactly as I left him: too sharp around

the edges, eyes that were older at twenty-five than most men get at fifty. He and I collide with a hug that's a *check* more than a greeting. He claps my back once, like a heartbeat.

"You must be Vivi," he says, turning a smile on her that lands just this side of charm. He always did well with the ladies off base back in the day. It feels like a different lifetime now—a different world. Ten years flies by when so much has happened in between. "I've heard good things."

She puts out her hand. "I'd say the same about you, but he doesn't talk." Vivi gives me a look that is equal parts accusation and affection.

Callum chuckles with a nod. "Vocational hazard. We're not supposed to talk about a lot. It's a hard rule to shake once you're on the other side."

"Yeah," I mutter, more to him than to her. He understands better than most. As an ex-special forces and then a hired mercenary for a number of years, there's a lot he can't talk about.

He tried to convince me to leave the Army and come work for him, but I couldn't leave my unit. My loyalty was stronger than the dollars in my bank account. Besides, I have more than most. The kind of money I could have retired on and lived a more than comfortable life with Adeline, but I'm like a workhorse...I need something to do or I'll go crazy locked up in a stable all day. I need a job that pushes me physically and mentally, and that's where hockey came in.

I didn't just walk on to the rink for tryouts with physical ability that I had stored for the last fifteen years, just waiting to use it. I stepped onto the ice with the same determination that I did on every mission. With failure not being an option and out-skating, out-working every other player who had more natural talent than me who were also vying for the same spot.

In the Army, as a Night Stalker, failure means everyone you are responsible for dies. I stepped out on the ice with the same mindset that I did every time I clicked into that five point harness of my Black Hawk. With failure as no option.

We pass through one last door and the air changes. It's cooler, the wind is howling up this high, but there's excitement thrumming between both of us. The rooftop is a clean rectangle of tarmac with a circle of paint where the city meets the sky. The helicopter sits like a legal weapon of power and strength, charcoal with the Lawson insignia small on the tail.

Vivi stops dead. "We're going on that helicopter?"

"Yep," I say.

"You paid Cullum to take us on a ride for our date?"

"No, baby. I'm flying. No one takes you for a ride but me," I say, not caring how possessive I sound.

I glance over, and she's grinning. She grips my free hand with a squeal she tries to muffle back with her excitement.

"I can't believe you did this for me. No one's ever done anything like this. You're certainly full of surprises, Trey Hartley."

"You haven't seen anything yet," I tell her, squeezing your hand. My other hand carries the picnic basket and my flight bag. "I want to share something with you that's important to me. Something that I've never shared with anyone else besides John. Is that okay with you?"

She glances at my chest as if knowing right where John's dog tags rest. "More than okay."

The last thing I want to do is open up more about John—about losing my brother and Sarah, about my injuries, surgeries, losing most of my hearing in my left ear. But if I want more of Vivi, I have to offer her more of me first. She needs to understand why I am who I am.

Callum runs Vivi through the quick brief like he's got good news he's not allowed to give. I help her into the five-point harness up front. She's in the co-pilot seat, headset cupped over hair I want to fist, chin tilted at the horizon like she was born to look at it.

When I step into the left seat, my body exhales. There are places your muscles remember better than your mind. My left ear is a dead zone, so I adjust the radio in compensation. Hands move without thinking: battery, fuel, lights, aux. The engine spools. The blades grab air and turn it into sound. Not a roar—*a thrum.* A pulse that matches mine.

I glance over, and Vivi's watching my hands. "You look different," she says into the mic, her voice intimate in my headset.

"How?"

"Like you just...slid into yourself." She laughs softly. "That makes no sense."

"It makes all the sense. This is where I feel the most like myself. Where I don't have to pretend to be someone else." She nods in understanding, and then I ease us light on the skids, lift, and the rooftop falls away so smoothly her breath catches but doesn't turn to fear. I level and bring us forward. The city opens like a map and now I'm back to a world I understand better than ballet buns, school PTA meetings, playoff wins, and small talk. I know this world in the air better than I know myself. As if part of me is missing when my feet hit flat ground.

"You hear that?" I ask.

She tips her head, listening as her eyes stare out into the dark night above us and the gleaming Seattle lights below us.

"It's quiet," I say. "Lots of sound. No noise."

She turns back to me, her eyes on mine. "I think I finally get it." Her hand finds my forearm where my sleeve pushes back from the watch. "This is your happy place."

"Yeah." It's not a sentiment I use or know well but she's right—it's my happy place. It sits easy in my mouth up here.

We bank toward the Sound. The water is ink with a scatter of city reflection, the boats like little moving galaxies. We skim the Space Needle, the stadiums, the shipyards, the bright grid of downtown lights and cars moving. She says *wow* a dozen different ways, and each one hits me like fuel.

"What's the mission tonight?" she asks.

"Give you something you'll never forget."

Silence hums across the channel. "I won't forget you," she says finally, voice smaller. "That's already done."

I could crash us with less impact than that line has on my

chest. I want to reach for her hand, but there are rules up here. I follow them. I point out landmarks like I'm not memorizing the look on her face more carefully than anything on the ground.

Being in the sky is what I love, but being with her? There's no sentiment, no feeling big enough to describe it.

I bring us down on a private pad owned by one of Callum's wealthy clients. Someone who owes him a favor I'm better off not asking about. It juts out over a peninsula of rock and low shrubs, with a view that goes wide open. The city sprawls to the south, mountains rise to the east, and water stretches in every other direction. It's quiet here, except for the wind and the soft tick of the engine cooling. I cut the power and wait for the blades to stop before I let myself really look at her.

She pulls off the headset. "That was insane. I've only ever seen the city at night like that when I'm flying back home from a business conference. But that? That was a totally different experience."

"Yeah," I say, feeling stupid for not being able to build a better word.

We leave the helmets in the cockpit. I haul the basket, the blankets.

We walk a short rise to a flat spot where the rock gives way to flattened grass, and I lay the first blanket, then the second. The wind blows at the corners but the wool blankets I chose are heavy and stay down...mostly.

I open the basket of food, and she laughs when she starts going through it all, seeing what I packed for us. It's a random list but far more food than we'll ever eat. I didn't leave a single thing off the list that Isla suggested.

She grabs the thermos that she's seen from home out and looks at me to answer for the contents of it.

"Your hot cocoa recipe."

"You made cocoa?" she asks, delighted.

"Don't act surprised," I say, pouring into tin mugs. "I pay attention."

"I know you do. You don't miss a thing," she says, and it's not teasing—it's a truth she lays between us like another blanket.

I pour us each a cup of it and hand one to her.

We both stare back at each other as we angle the paper cups to our lips, waiting for the other to try it.

"Moment of truth," I say.

"We'll try it at the same time," she instructs, and I nod. "One...two...three."

We both take a sip and neither of us make a spit take.

"Mmm," she says, and it's not lost on me that she's shocked it's palatable.

I finish my sip, and I'm surprised too, even though I'm the one who made it. "It's not as good as yours, but it's not burnt."

She nods. "Well would you look at that? Turns out your cooking skills aren't a lost cause after all. He can be taught, ladies and gentlemen."

"You think Adeline will believe us?"

"Nope," she says.

We both chuckle for a second, and then we start on the food.

We eat, trading bites. She bumps my knee with hers; I lean into it like gravity. When the truffles come out, she picks one up and holds it to my mouth. Chocolate melts against my tongue while I look at her looking at me, and I have to breathe through it because now I'm thinking about the way she tastes with sugar on her lips and nothing else in the world to interrupt.

"How long have you been flying?" she asks when the silence gets too loud.

"Long enough," I say simply, but I know that the curious look in her eyes means that being vague won't fly with her anymore. I remind myself that there are reasons why I brought her out here other than just a helicopter ride. I take a deep breath. Here goes nothing.

"Right, well, after my first deployment. My commanding officer noticed that I had a head for instruments, hands that didn't shake, and a lack of fear that's probably more reckless than brave,"

I say. "I don't know. Maybe it's the way I was raised that almost felt like I was on borrowed time anyway. My commander suggested I apply for the SOAR Night Stalker program. 'They could use a kid with a death wish' were his exact words to me. So I did. And then I passed."

She touches my left ear, gentle. "And your hearing?"

I could lie. I could redirect. But I make myself do neither. "Left ear went sideways after a blast. The right ear compensates. In the air, it's all headsets and habit."

"I think it's more than that. It's instinct, it's second nature. You don't look like you have to think about any of it. It's so natural that it almost seems like there's no end or beginning between you and that helicopter. Like you're one unit."

I didn't have to explain it. She just sees everything that I feel but can't verbalize.

And that's when I know it. That's the moment when I realize that Vivi's the one...the only one, and I'll have to give her up, but I won't until the minute I have to. Not a second sooner.

"You said John is the only one who understood?"

I nod once, stare out over the water instead of at her. "We were flying low over Kandahar—night op, low visibility. I had John in the back—my crew chief, my brother in every way but blood. We'd done this run a hundred times. It was an extraction mission. Pick up our unit and get the hell out of there. Just as John and I landed, the blast hit."

The sound and concussion of the hit is still in my bones, even years later. "We hit hard but it would have been worse if we hadn't touched down. I woke up upside down, completely disoriented. I didn't know what was up or down at first. Alarms screaming in my headset, fuel in the air so thick it burned my lungs. My shoulder was half torn out of its socket, my ear ringing so bad I couldn't hear anything else. For a second I thought we were both dead, and I woke up in hell."

Her fingers are still around her mug.

"Then I heard him first, yelling at me to get the fuck out.

He called my name two or three more times, waiting for me to respond. By the time I got my bearings and got out of my seat, trying to see him through the smoke and fire, he was there—slumped forward, helmet cracked, blood down the side of his face. He must have passed out from smoke inhalation after he called out my name. He wasn't dead. Not yet. He was unconscious but breathing. And that was it. My mission changed to saving him. I cut him free the best I could with my arm still dislocated, got him over my shoulder, and ran." I remember it all so vividly that I almost want to stop telling her because it feels like I'm taking her there with me, and I don't want her anywhere near it.

"I can't even imagine what that must have been like," she says, urging me on.

I don't want to continue but I need her to understand why I am the way I am. I have to keep going.

"I could hear on the radio attached to John. The unit saw the explosion and called in a new extraction team. The explosion started a fire around us, and they couldn't find a way in. I ran in the direction they were giving coordinates for, though I had no way of knowing for sure if I was going in the right direction. I was still suffering from vertigo, smoke inhalation, and bleeding internally. If it hadn't been for thinking I could save John, I don't think I'd have made it twenty feet with my own injuries. But I knew he needed me, and that was enough to keep moving."

"Adrenaline," she whispers.

I nod.

"They say mothers have lifted cars off their children when adrenaline hits like that."

"It's the only way I would have made it out. Without that desperation to get John to safety, I wouldn't have made it. The unit was too far away at that point. The new rescue team wouldn't have made it to us before the inhalation or fire would have killed us."

She blows out a heavy breath, and I feel that same weight in my chest.

"We made it to the extraction point. Got on the medevac. I

thought we'd pulled it off. Thought we'd get to the medical base, and I'd sit by his bed and watch him wake up. But halfway there... he stopped breathing. I was holding him when it happened."

Vivi's eyes are glossy now, fixed on mine like she's afraid to blink.

"Without John, I wouldn't be here. He's the reason I made it out. The reason I keep going. Because I know that if John were still here, he would kick my ass if I ever gave up. So I wear his dog tags so that I never forget. And I buried him with mine." I tap my chest where they hang. "Every time I think I've got nothing left in me, I feel the weight of those tags, and I remember that I have more in me than I think I do."

For a second, she just looks at me. No blinking. No nervous shifting. No pretending like she knows what to say. Just that steady, unflinching gaze that makes me feel like she sees every piece of me, even the parts I keep under lock.

"After all of that, how do you get back in a helicopter like today?"

"Because I don't associate the helicopter with John's death. That Black Hawk saved more lives than it ever lost," I tell her. "John and I were one of the most successful extraction teams out there. The hundreds of wins outweigh the bad. Completing a successful mission becomes an addiction. You always want just one more, no matter how many you've had. It's the losses that keep you up at night. But we knew the risks. We knew one day it might be us."

"What made you do it for fifteen years like that?"

"Knowing that there are still men out there, special forces teams that need you to show up and get them out of hostile situations. Without you, they die. That's what makes you get up every day and climb into a Black Hawk, not knowing if you're ever coming back."

"That's why you're so protective. It's deeply ingrained, isn't it? Me, Adeline, the guys on the Hawkeyes. You show up when someone needs you. For a flat tire, for a late hit to your goalie, to a little girl who isn't yours, but you love her as if she is."

"I can't turn it off."

"That's because it's not taught...it's who you are, Trey. And it's beautiful."

"I would have stayed in if Tommy hadn't died. I'm not the one who made the call, he did. Losing John and Tommy all in a month was more than he thought I could recover from."

"You retired for her?"

"I wish I could say I made the decision for her, but it was made for me. I was lying in a hospital bed—multiple surgeries on my shoulder, knee, ear...after the explosion. I had been there for a month in the VA hospital overseas in Japan, trying to come to terms with losing John, when my commander came in and told me that he had just gotten a call. My brother Tommy and his wife died in a car accident the night before from a drunk driver. I was now her guardian, and my commander issued a medical discharge."

Her lips part slightly, but she doesn't interrupt.

"I don't tell a lot of people about my time in the Army," I admit, my voice low and even. "I don't let them see any part of it, especially not Adeline. But whatever the hell this is between us makes me not want to keep anything from you. I want to tell you everything, even if it means you see the worst part of me."

Something flickers in her eyes—relief, maybe, or recognition—and then she moves. Sets her mug aside and climbs into my lap like she belongs there, knees bracketing my hips, hands cupping my face.

"I don't know what this is either," she says, her voice steady but thick. "But I know I feel safe with you. I want to know everything you'll tell me. I want to take care of you like you take care of me."

My hands come up to her waist, anchoring her to me. "Then give me two weeks. Every minute we can get before the world catches up. No holding back. No pretending."

Her mouth curves, not quite a smile but close. "Two weeks," she repeats. "All in."

"All in," I echo, and then I'm kissing her like the deal's sealed in blood and heat. That neither of us can go back on our word. A vow. As good of a vow as I'll ever get from her, until she vows her life to Jameson.

Her hands are in my hair, her knees bracketing my hips, the weight of her pressing me into the blanket. She shifts just enough to drag across me, and my body answers in a way that has nothing to do with patience. Her jacket slips to the ground, my palms sliding under her shirt, fingers splaying over the heat of her back.

She rolls her hips once, slow and deliberate, and my breath punches out. I grip her ass, guiding the next movement, and she follows, riding me through layers of denim until I can't remember why we're still wearing anything.

When I break from her mouth, she's flushed, lips parted, eyes bright with want. "Hold on," I tell her, and she barely has time to draw a breath before I've got my hands under her thighs, lifting her. She laughs—breathless, startled—arms looping around my neck as I carry her the few steps to the helicopter.

The jump seat creaks under us when I set her down, pulling her forward until she's straddling me again, knees braced on either side. The close quarters press us together from shoulder to knee, the faint tick of cooling metal surrounding us. Her fingers hook in my shirt, yanking it over my head, and then her mouth is on my neck, teeth scraping lightly.

I get her jeans open, shoving them down just enough, my hands greedy on bare skin. She tugs at my zipper, freeing me, and then she's sinking onto me, slow enough that my head falls back against the seat.

"There's no condom between us, Vivi," I warn, though I wish I could keep my damn mouth shut because, fuck me, she feels good bare around my cock.

She stops and stares back at me. "I'm on birth control." Her words are cautious as if her answer might not be an acceptable one.

Instead, I respond by pulling her mouth back down to mine.

The first roll of her hips is almost gentle, testing, and then she finds her rhythm, grinding into a deep press, the angle perfect in this tight space. My hands find her waist, then her hips, guiding her even though she's already moving exactly how I need her to.

The sounds in here are different—soft creak of the seat, the breathy hitch in her throat, the faint jostle of metal when her hips rock harder. Every shift drags heat through me, winding tighter. I slide one hand up under her shirt, cupping her breast, thumb brushing over a peaked nipple until she gasps.

Her forehead drops to mine, breath mingling, our bodies locked together in a rhythm that feels less like fucking and more like we're claiming each other. Relentless until the air is thick with the smell of sex, and I could live in it. Live in this moment with her.

When she starts to tremble, I hold her there, rolling up into her until she comes with a soft cry that shudders through both of us. I follow, burying myself deep, holding her in place as the release rips through me. Filling her body with hot white heat. Filling her with me. No protection between us. No barrier to keep me from her.

She stays draped over me, breathing hard, her hair falling around us like a curtain.

After a moment, she tilts her head, her mouth curving. "Tell me...is this the first time you've fucked in a helicopter?"

I huff out a laugh, still catching my breath. "Yeah. First time." I brush my lips over hers, lingering. "But everything feels like the first time with you."

Her grin widens. "Good answer."

I kiss her again, slower this time, and when I pull back, I keep my forehead against hers. "This," I say, "is by far my favorite memory in a helicopter."

Her smile softens, and for a second, I let myself believe we'll get a hell of a lot more firsts before the clock runs out. Two more weeks left.

Chapter Twenty-One

Vivi

I can't remember the last time I slept this little and felt this happy.

Maybe never.

The light in Trey's bedroom is soft, angled across his sheets, and I'm sprawled right in the middle of them with the faintest soreness humming through every muscle. My body feels wrung out in the best possible way. We didn't so much sleep as drift between touches and quiet words, half-dreams that dissolved into more kisses, more heat, more of him between my thighs and no condom.

I love the feeling of him bare. No barrier. Just him, me, and the friction.

My phone buzzes on the nightstand. I reach for it lazily, expecting a work email or a text from Isla.

Dad

I know you're still ignoring me, but we need to speak before Jameson's back. I'm in New York. I'll be back in a few days. It's important.

I stare at it for a beat, my stomach tightening, before locking the screen and sliding it face down. Not today. I'll deal with him later. Today is mine. Ours. I still have two weeks with Trey, and I'm not letting my dad take up any mental space of how the Holiday marriage merger is the best business decision I will ever make.

The smell of coffee wafts into the bedroom from somewhere down the hall. I roll out of bed, tugging on one of Trey's shirts and a pair of leggings, and follow it to the kitchen. He's already there—barefoot, hair still a little damp from his shower after his early morning run. How he had the energy to pound six miles of pavement after he pounded my pussy for most of last night, I have no idea. The man isn't human.

I just stare back at him, appreciating the way his T-shirt stretched over his shoulders makes me want to crawl back into bed immediately and take him with me.

"Morning," he says, sliding a mug toward me.

"Barely." I sip and sigh. "This might be the only thing keeping me upright right now."

His mouth tilts in that way that makes me want to kiss him before I've even had breakfast. "You seemed pretty upright last night."

I give him a slanted glance. "You're impossible."

A text pings on my phone, and I glance over.

Isla

Dinner tonight with us, Penelope, and Slade? You two available?

I grin to myself at the thought of Trey and me getting invited on a 'couple dates' as if we're already considered one unit.

"And yet, here you are. All mine for two weeks." He smirks and takes a sip of his own coffee.

I try to scowl at him and fail. "Two weeks," I echo, like saying it out loud makes it more real.

He nods. "For the next two weeks, you're my girlfriend."

My stomach does a dramatic swirl that almost gives me vertigo, but in the best way.

"I'm sorry, did you just say girlfriend?"

"I've never had one before, but I think that's how this works," he says. "We're more than just fucking...aren't we?"

I hide my stupid giddy grin behind my coffee mug, pretending to take a sip. "Yeah, I guess so, but if you're my boyfriend for the next two weeks, what exactly are we going to do about Adeline?"

He thinks for a second, his eyes scanning the ceiling for an answer.

"I don't want to keep things from her. I'm just not sure how you explain to a nine-year-old that we're only together for two weeks?"

"I'm not sure either, but we have tonight to try and think of something."

"Or," he says, "we could spend tonight making sure you can't walk straight tomorrow and let the talking happen later."

The sip I'm taking nearly goes down the wrong pipe. "Later, meaning when she walks into your bedroom in the morning and sees me sleeping in it with you? That's not a strategy."

"There's only one strategy I'm interested in tonight." His gaze drags over me, lingering on the hem of his shirt stretched over my thighs. "Two weeks, Viv. My strategy is to milk every last damn hour out of that body."

He watches me over his mug, eyes hooded, like he's already mapping out the next twenty-four hours. Which is unfair because I'm instantly imagining it too. And that is how I end up texting Isla "yes" to dinner and then needing to go home to shower, do a face mask, and pretend I got more than forty-two minutes of sleep.

Besides, he has game tapes to review and hit the gym before dinner.

By late afternoon I've picked a dress that reads "respectable dinner" from the front and "he's going to have his hands all over me later tonight" from the low plunge in the back. Hair up, gloss on, and tiny gold hoops. I leave the love bites he left all over my body mostly covered because I'm not a masochist, and I'm already anticipating Isla pouncing on me the second I step into the house, but every brush of fabric is a memory and I'm smiling like an idiot when Trey pulls up. I don't think I've ever been this excited for a date before. Even if it is just dinner at my sister's with two other couples.

"I could have just met you at your house. You drove all the way into town just for me to end up at your house tonight anyway."

"Yeah, but I like picking you up. It feels more like a date. And this way I get to keep you until I take you home tomorrow morning. I like that you can't leave."

"Oh, so this is a kidnapping?" I tease.

"Absolutely." He says it so straightforward without the faintest amusement that I laugh.

Then his eyes do that slow sweep that melts my knees. One hand on the wheel, the other sliding to my thigh like muscle memory. There's a heat in his touch and a calm in it, too, the kind of steady that says *I've got you*. He doesn't say a word about the dress. He just drags his thumb once, skimming high enough to brush over my panties under my dress, making me a promise for later.

"You're going to make it impossible to focus on dinner," I tell him, my hips trying to follow his thumb.

"My needy girl can't wait a few hours for me to fuck her again, can she?"

I shake my head, my tongue wetting my lips at the way he called me his girl.

"Then let me give you a preview of what's waiting for you tonight."

Trey slides my panties to the side, the warm rasp of his fingertips against my skin sending a ripple of anticipation through me. His hand is steady, confident, like he knows my body better than I do, and when he slips one finger into my slick heat, my knees go weak and hot heat pulls in my belly.

The hum of the tires on asphalt blends with the low rumble

of his voice. "Relax for me."

I melt back into the seat, the cool leather a sharp contrast to the heat pooling between my thighs. He adds a second finger and then curves them just right, finding that spot that makes my breath catch, then adds a third, stretching me until my thighs tense and I whimper at the fullness. Not as much as his cock stretches me, but it's still so good that I know I won't last much longer.

"That's it," he murmurs, dragging his thumb over my clit in slow, deliberate circles that make my hips lift for more. "You get wet so fast for me, Vivi Ann. You have no idea how hard I am right now. I barely touch you, and you're dripping at the thought of me fucking you."

A car passes in the opposite lane, headlights flashing through the cab, and it hits me—we're out here, in the open, and no one has a clue what's happening. The thought sends a fresh wave of arousal through me.

He works me with a rhythm that's unhurried but devastating, alternating between deep, curling thrusts and light, teasing strokes. My hand fists in his T-shirt, pulling at the fabric like it'll anchor me.

"Trey—" My voice is barely a whisper.

"I've got you, baby. Let it happen."

And I do. It starts low and tight, spreading until it crashes over me, my back arching as his fingers keep me there, milking every last shudder. The world blurs. The road, the headlights, the city beyond—all gone until I'm nothing but sensation.

I'm still trembling when he pulls his hand away, sliding my panties back into place with a slow, possessive touch. I catch his smirk like he's proud of how quickly he turned me into pudding, and then get up out of my seat and lean over him. Wanting him to feel as taken and owned as much as he just made me.

"Your turn."

His jaw flexes. "Vivi, I didn't expect you to return the favor. You don't have to."

I want to mark him with my mouth, make him melt under

my control. Two can play this game—and I bet I can make him come faster than he just made me.

"Eyes on the road, soldier. Let me take care of you."

I make quick work of his fly, the heat from his body hitting me as I free him. He's thick, hard, already flushed at the tip, and the taste of him, slightly salty, makes my mouth water. I take him in slow at first, letting my lips seal around him before sliding deeper.

He exhales hard, one hand gripping the wheel, the other reaching over and grabbing my ass that's up in the air as I kneel on the passenger seat. The engine hums under us, the SUV thick with the sound of my mouth working him and his groans egging me on.

"Jesus...you're gonna kill me," he grits out.

Every few strokes, I glance up at him, catching the way his eyes narrow, his knuckles tightening on the wheel like he's barely holding it together. His hips start to lift in small, controlled thrusts, pushing him deeper, and I suck down harder, giving him every inch of my mouth I can.

"Fuck, Vivi...don't stop," he grits out, voice rough.

I hum against him, and that's it. His fingers tighten in my hair, his breath stutters, his hips jerking as he spills into my mouth with a low, wrecked groan that makes my core clench all over again. I swallow every drop, licking him clean before tucking him back into his jeans.

By the time we pull into Isla's driveway, my lipstick's gone, my cheeks are flushed, and Trey looks like he'd skip dinner entirely if I let him. He kills the engine, leans in close, and sticks his tongue in my mouth. Mashing our mouths together, both of us desperate for one more taste.

"You just wrecked any possibility of me thinking about anything but what you just did for the rest of this dinner. And if I fake a flu bug to get you out of the house and back to my bed...just go with it, okay?"

"Got it. I'll take your lead, commander," I say, smoothing my dress like I didn't just come apart in his passenger seat and make him lose it behind the wheel.

He looks down between his thighs and pulls something out from between them. "Here, you forgot something."

He hands me my earring, the one I didn't even notice had fallen out while I was sucking him dry.

I take the earring and then glance at Isla's front door.

"Oh God...I don't stand a chance in there. These girls are a pack of wolves that will smell out my bullshit when they ask if we've been sleeping together."

Trey opens his door as I try to quickly finish and then comes around to open mine.

"I'll be outside with the fire and sharp objects," he reminds me. "You'll be safe," he says and then reaches out for my hand to help me out.

I roll my eyes. "That's not what safe means."

He looks at me, mouth curving. "It does when I say it."

Isla's front door barely clicks shut behind us before she's grinning like she already knows something.

And okay, fine...she probably does.

Penelope's there too, leaning in the doorway to the kitchen in a fitted sweater and that smirk she's famous for. I swear she could make someone confess to a murder with just one look.

"Hi ladies," Trey says to Penelope and Isla. Then he bends down and whispers to me, "I'll be out with the guys. Code word is 'cookie dough' if you need to be rescued. Godspeed."

And then he's gone, walking past all three of us until he gets to the large glass doors leading to the outside patio where Kaenan and Slade are already grilling.

"You look...refreshed," Isla says, dragging me in for a hug that lingers just long enough for her to assess exactly how "refreshed" I am.

Penelope's gaze sweeps from my hair to my outfit. And then she raises an eyebrow as if my outfit just gave away what Trey and I did on the way over.

"What?" I say, doing a quick sweep of my dress for myself, but nothing's a miss, as far as I can see.

"Come on already. Get in here," Penelope says, turning to head back for the kitchen, Isla on her tail.

The second we get into the kitchen, Isla begins to pour generously. "We're doing red. You'll need it for what's coming."

I lift a brow as I take my glass. "Should I be scared?"

"Only if you've got something to hide," Penelope says, grabbing her wine glass that looks like she already drank half of it, and then perches on a stool. "Which...judging by the fact that you're glowing like you just got back from a spa weekend..." she says, tilting her head. "Or a marathon session between the sheets... yeah, you've got something."

I take a sip big enough to qualify as a gulp. "You can't tell that from just looking at me."

"You basically just admitted it so fess up," Isla says, topping off her own glass. "Speaking of confession. We want to know how last night went."

I try to keep my voice casual. "It was nice."

Penelope snorts. "*Nice* is what you call a rental car. Not a date. Not sex."

I shrug, trying to focus on my wine, but my gaze flickers to the glass sliding door. Outside, under the patio cover, Trey's standing at the grill with Kaenan and Slade, beer in one hand, tongs in the other. He laughs at something Slade says, his head tipping back, and even from here I feel that stupid low swoop in my stomach.

Like clockwork, his eyes cut to me.

Like he felt me looking.

And just like that, I'm back in his passenger seat, the sound of his voice in my ear, his talented fingers...

"Hello?" Isla waves her fingers in front of my face. "We want details about your date last night with Trey."

I grab a cube of cheese from the charcuterie board just to have something to do with my mouth besides smile like an idiot.

"He took me out on a helicopter and showed me Seattle at

night, and then we had a picnic on a mountain top. Not a big deal." I grin.

Both of their eyes go wide.

"He flew you in a helicopter for your date?" Penelope says. "And you're trying to convince us that you didn't screw his brains out after? How new do you think we are?"

"And I already know he packed your favorite things for your picnic basket because he borrowed it from me. The little stinker wouldn't tell me what he was planning. I've been dying over here."

"Okay, maybe more happened in the helicopter, but a lady never kisses and tells." I take a sip of my wine, and damn her, it's good.

They both squeal with excitement and do some kind of victory dance that looks like this must be the second bottle of wine for the night.

"Please for the love of God, tell me that you two are dating now," Penelope pleads. "Because I have been dying to make you WAGs official since Isla got inducted into the group."

Even though technically we're "dating," I can't be that honest with them because, to be fair, Adeline's not the only one who might get hurt when Trey and I end this in two weeks. These WAGs girls all get really attached to each other and to give them false hope that Trey and I are a real item would be cruel.

"It's just casual. I still have to marry Jameson in two weeks or he and I lose everything. Nothing can happen between us, and it wouldn't be fair to Adeline."

Penelope juts out her lower lip like she's disappointed but understands, while Isla looks almost mad at me.

"Vivi, you're going to throw everything away to marry Jameson. He won't make you happy. Can you truly agree to this for the rest of your life?"

"Neither of us know if I won't be happy with him. I might," I say, trying to sound hopeful.

Sometimes I wish she could just face the truth like I have and grin and bear it, even if she's not happy about it.

I know she gave up her company to be with Kaenan and then she started the sportswear company, bouncing back into a new brand that she loves, but it still was a sacrifice. What she forgets is that Jameson loses everything too. And not just a company. He loses his family and five generations of his wealth that should be passed down to him.

None of this should be taken lightly, though I know she's just worried that I'm going to end up miserable in the long run. Maybe I will, but no one is guaranteed anything, and I have to make the best decision I can.

Trey and I have only agreed to two weeks as it is. It's not as if Trey is down on one knee asking me to choose him. I'm not even sure if he would if I weren't in this situation. There are too many questions that I can't ask because that reality isn't a possibility anyway. Not unless Jameson doesn't show up in two weeks and leaves me to clean up the mess, while his family trust disinherits him.

"Let's just have a nice dinner and talk about something else," Penelope says, trying to cut the tension, but neither Isla nor I have broken our stares on each other. That's when the guys walk in, Kaenan with a platter of grilled food that smells amazing.

The three men head for the kitchen, all smiles, but I see the moment their eyes dart around the room sensing that they just walked into something.

"Everything okay in here?" Slade asks.

"I'm sorry that I said anything. I don't want to mess up tonight," Isla says.

Trey walks over close to me. "Cookie dough?" he whispers.

I shake my head. "We're fine...really."

I don't want this to ruin our night either. I love my sister, and she loves me. She's worried, and I get it. I felt the same when she thought she had to go back to Colorado and marry her cheating fiancé. I know exactly how scared she is for me, because I was in her shoes five years ago.

I just wish she could see that I don't have an out. Not one

that doesn't cost Jameson and I both something substantial. This decision doesn't just affect me and Jameson. It affects Genevieve, Jameson's siblings next in line, the trust, both boards, and lastly, my staff and clients who need me back.

Trey and Adeline did fine before I came around, and they will do fine when I'm gone, even if it kills me to think of the lucky woman who gets to step into my place. Who gets to sleep next to Trey for the rest of her life and take Adeline to the library.

"Okay, well the food's hot so let's eat. Dive in everyone," Kaenan instructs. "There are chicken and veggie kabobs, coconut shrimp, and grilled pineapple. Help yourselves."

"Good. I'm glad that's all cleared up because can we *please* talk about what the heck is going on with Aleksi and Kendall for a second?" Penelope says, grabbing a plate to dish up.

We all start loading our plates as everyone takes a shot at their predictions for Aleksi and Kendall. We sit around the dining room table, and the night turns into one of the best. The guys share funny locker room stories and everyone is laughing. Trey grips my thigh under the table every once in a while to check in, and I love that he wants to touch me constantly, keeping us connected.

Finally, the night winds down, and I give both of the girls a huge goodnight hug promising to get together at Serendipity's this week. Trey tells Kaenan that he'll be back tomorrow to pick up Adeline when his mother brings the girls back tomorrow, and then we're out the door.

"You okay? It looked pretty tense when we walked into the kitchen earlier," Trey asks as he walks me to the passenger side of his SUV.

I can't tell him that Isla's mad that I'm choosing Jameson over him since Trey has never even offered more than the next two weeks. I can't afford to start that thought process or the conversation around it with Trey.

"It's fine. Just normal sister stuff. She and I are fine...I promise."

He opens my door for me and I slip in, but he keeps his eyes on me as he shuts the door. He doesn't look like he completely believes me, but what choice does he have?

He walks around the front of the car and slides in. "Well then, are you ready to go home and finish where we left off?" he asks, with heat in his eyes.

"Yes," I say dramatically. "Take me home."

He smiles and then pulls out of their long driveway.

Just as he heads down the street, I hear my news notification ping on my phone. An urgent update.

I glance down—just a preview of a headline:

JAMESON HOLIDAY'S JET SPOTTED RETURNING TO THE U.S.

The bubble around me wavers for a second.

And with a short delay, so does Trey's phone. He comes to a stop sign and glances down quickly, and then his eyes are on me.

Neither of us says a word. We just stare at each other for a moment.

Not tonight. Not here. I still have two weeks, and I'm not letting Jameson take one second of it from me.

CHAPTER TWENTY-TWO

Vivi

The first thing I notice when I wake is how quiet the house sounds without skates clacking around the mudroom and a grumpy nine-year-old humming Disney songs while she hunts for her other sneaker. Trey left at dawn for morning skate, a kiss pressed to my temple and a murmured, "Eat real food today." Adeline's due home this afternoon.

I was going to use the quiet to do normal things to prepare for Adeline coming home and a fun full week of activities for us for do. I still need to take care of the laundry, a grocery run—maybe stock up on those cinnamon granola bars she demolishes in two days.

I'm mid-pour on my coffee when my phone buzzes across the counter.

Richard Sterling

Emergency board meeting. 11 a.m.

I stare at the text, the words "emergency" and "board meeting" feel ice cold. It doesn't take a genius to guess why. The push alert from last night is still echoing in my head.

Jameson Holiday's jet spotted landing in the U.S. Is the prodigal son finally returning?

Of course he's "returning." Of course there's an emergency. And of course I have to be the one to stand in front of a table of people who think my personal life is a business lever you can yank like a slot machine.

I drain my coffee, tug my hair into a low knot, and swap Trey's T-shirt for a black sheath, blazer, and flats I can actually move in. If I'm going back into my building on a Monday morning, I'm going in armored.

ꕥ

THE ELEVATOR DOORS on the parking level slide open just as a town car nose inches past the concrete pillar and glides to a stop. The rear door opens. Chanel jacket. Pearls. Immaculate blowout not even Seattle's March "wetness" can touch.

"Mrs. Holiday," I say.

"Vivi," she returns. The driver falls in two steps behind her like a shadow. "Shall we?"

We cross the marble lobby together, two women who currently dislike each other for very different reasons, and I brace for the humiliation of my key card throwing a red denial light again.

It doesn't.

The panel clicks green, and the elevator opens.

I blink. Try it again just to be sure. It turns green, again.

It shouldn't make my eyes sting, but it does. Not because the board suddenly gave me back the keys to my own kingdom—because obviously someone did. The who is a coin toss between the man who left before dawn with a kiss, and that "friend" of his who owns a private security company and treats rules like suggestions.

Martin Howard wouldn't have done this for me. But he might have done it if Trey asked/forced. Or if Callum Lawson felt like flexing from his couch for sport and is pulling in another favor for Trey.

I file it away. Not the place. Not the time. But I pocket relief to use on Trey later as a thank you.

Genevieve and her driver file into the elevator with me. "I'm guessing you know what this briefing is about?" I ask as the doors close, and I push the eleventh floor.

"Of course. I'm the one who called it," she says, exuding the confidence of a woman in her position with that much power. "Jameson is back in the States." She lifts her phone, the screen flashing an itinerary. "He touched down in New York and is claiming he's closing the deal he started in Greece before he returns to Seattle."

"Claims," I echo.

She ignores my question. "We need to prepare for his arrival."

"But he's not in Seattle yet?" I ask to clarify.

"Not yet. But I expect him in before the next two weeks are up as per the trust and the board's instructions. Though the board wants this deal to go through and may be willing to give him more time to close. That's something I will be asking today."

I knew this deal was important to the Holiday board of directors, but I didn't realize that it's this big of a deal that they would potentially be willing to push back our set date for the business deal on a chain of hotels.

"I knew that's why Jameson pushed for our honeymoon to be in Greece—so he could work on getting the owners to sell to him. But I thought it was a lucrative passion project, not some massive venture."

"It's the kind of venture that would dramatically move the profitability of Holiday Enterprises and it opens other doors. It's a big deal."

"So we're still pretending that everything is on track for us to elope in two weeks?" I ask, trying not to sound as annoyed as I already am about having to lie just to save a job for a company that I started.

In the elevator, our reflections are pinned side by side in polished chrome, our differences on display. Her pearls glowing, my irritation simmering. She taps a manicured finger against her bag. "Pretending is our only option until my son remembers who he works for."

"His mother?"

"The trust," she says without apology. "Try to keep up."

The doors slide open on eleven, and the temperature in my body drops five degrees. Virginia looks up from reception, eyes wide, relief skating across her face.

"You're in," she whispers when I pass. "I don't know how—"

"I do," I whisper back, and then I'm moving because conference room three is already full.

Holiday Industries has colonized the left side of the table with navy suits and watch faces you can see from the next building. My board sits on the right, looking like they got invited to a party and realized too late it's a funeral. Martin Howard is at the far end, neat as a paperclip but he does shudder a little when he sees me—the product of a visit from my boyfriend, no doubt. Richard stands when I enter, a politician's smile already in place.

To be fair. I don't even blame Richard. He's doing exactly what he believes is in the best interest of the company, and that's precisely what he was hired to do. Only giving Martin Howard my position was a terrible decision.

"Vivi." He gestures to the empty seat opposite Genevieve, because of course. "Thank you for coming in on short notice."

"As if I had a choice," I murmur too low for him to hear me, but I don't follow his suggested seating arrangement. I walk over to where Genevieve's driver just pulled out her seat, and I sit next to her.

She and I don't see eye to eye about plenty of things, but in this moment, she's the closest thing I have to an ally in this room, so I'll be sitting next to her.

She glances over at me as her driver helps push in her chair. There's almost a softening in her facial expression, and it's the first time that I realize we're both the only two here who have no one on our side.

My company doesn't have my back, and she doesn't have the backing of Holiday Industries or her family trust on her side.

And though she's trying to force me to marry a man I don't love, once upon a time, I gave her my word, and if we play our cards right, in a couple of weeks I'll be her daughter-in-law and banding together could make us unstoppable.

We need each other and, in this moment, I realize that she and I aren't really all that different. She's fighting for her family... for her son. And I'm fighting for my company...my own baby in a way.

Twelve faces swing in unison toward Genevieve and me sitting there together, our spines board straight as if we're here to play ball. I lace my fingers on the table and keep my shoulders back.

Richard steeples his hands. "As you've likely seen, there's been new...movement. Jameson Holiday has returned to the U.S."

"Landed in New York," pipes in a Holiday director I don't recognize. He's the kind of man who treats his voice like a gavel. "He's at The Whitmore. We have him on a schedule to meet with legal and finalize the Greek acquisition. Then we intend to fly him west as soon as this evening."

"Intend," Genevieve says. "So he still isn't answering your calls either."

I hold back my desire to high-five her for that bitch slap of a response.

The man blinks, unused to being interrupted. Genevieve's mouth twitches. "Regardless," she says, "this is our window. We are moving forward with a controlled re-entry into public view. Tonight, if we can manage it."

"Tonight," I repeat.

Richard slides a folder toward me. "Our communications team has drafted a few hints to drop into the gossip columns to go out. 'Insider close to Jameson said that he's on his way back to his blushing bride after working on a new venture. Someone close to the family says that Vivi has her final dress fitting this week and she can't wait for their nuptials that are all set to take place in France next month.'"

I press my tongue against my cheek, knowing I should bite my tongue instead of speaking, but I can't. "So the plan is to feed the beast."

Richard leans in, softly. "Optics, Vivi. We all know this isn't ideal. We just need to get through the week."

I think of Trey this morning, before light even touched out on the pavement, tugging on a hoodie, kissing my forehead like I'm the thing he doesn't want to leave. Of Adeline's pink backpack waiting by the door because she asked me to "pretty please check if my homework folder is still there." Of the way my access panel just flashed green after weeks of red.

"Walk me through this," I say, because I want them on record. "Jameson lands here—when?"

"We're not sure," the Holiday director admits. "But the trust is not currently willing to push the timeline back."

Genevieve's diamond-clad wrist rests lightly on the table. "Which means," she says smoothly, "we have less than two weeks to convince the public that my son and Ms. Newport are happily engaged and on schedule for their elopement."

Richard nods. "We have talking points prepared for both of you, Vivi. Outfits, appearances, even which events you'll be 'seen' together."

I glance down at the folder in front of me. *Blushing bride. Final dress fitting. Can't wait to marry the love of her life in France next month.* My stomach turns.

"And if Jameson doesn't make it back in time?" I ask, looking straight at Richard.

"Then we have a problem," he says without missing a beat. "One the trust is unlikely to forgive."

Which is code for: *You lose your company, and he loses his inheritance.*

"Optics, Vivi," Richard adds, like he's offering reassurance. "We all just need to stay on script."

I keep my expression polite, but my nails press into the folder. Isla's words come back to me: "Is this worth it?" *On script* means I smile while Jameson gallivants around the world with our wedding planner, then play bride-to-be when he strolls back into town.

Though I am the one who left him at the altar. I have no leg to stand on here.

Genevieve leans forward. "This only works if you sell it. No cracks in the foundation and no hesitation. You'll wear the ring in public, attend all scheduled appearances, and, when the time comes, stand beside him like nothing ever happened."

My gaze flicks to her, and I catch something almost like a warning in her eyes. She's not giving me a choice—she's reminding me there isn't one.

I swallow my pride and nod once. "Fine. Just tell me when and where."

It's the only concession I can make without giving them the satisfaction of seeing me fold.

"Good," Richard says, like I've just agreed to a spa package instead of a hostage negotiation. "We'll have a detailed itinerary by this afternoon. Until then, I suggest you rest up. It's going to be a busy two weeks."

The meeting moves on to legal language and brand protection strategy. It's another half hour of executives discussing my life like it's a marketing campaign. The France wedding bringing in other opportunity for cross promotion of Holiday Industries, sponsorships coming in for brand deals, news outlets begging to be invited to cover the elopement. I sit through it all, spine straight, hands folded, letting them think they've got me right where they want me.

Because they do.

For now.

When we're finally dismissed, I gather my folder and push

back from the table. Genevieve stands when I do, falling into step beside me as we leave the conference room. It's not camaraderie anymore, just choreography.

In the hallway, she murmurs just loud enough for me to hear, "Two weeks, Ms. Newport. Don't waste them. Then the work really begins. If you do everything I tell you, you and Jameson will have a happy and fulfilling life together."

"Forced to marry?"

"I too was arranged with Jameson's father. It wasn't easy at first, but we did come to love each other in our own way. I found myself in my children and being the matriarch of this family. And someday, that responsibility will rest on your shoulders as the first Holiday wife. It's a lot of responsibility, but I trust that you, of all people, can do it."

I don't say anything else. And then the Holiday director calls Genevieve back for a private conversation.

I keep my chin high as I head for the elevator, but my pulse pounds in my ears. Two weeks to sell a lie. Two weeks to keep my company. Two weeks before this whole thing either explodes...or swallows me whole.

CHAPTER TWENTY-THREE

Trey

Adeline hits the front door like she's been shot out of a cannon, sneakers squeaking across the mudroom tile.

"Vivi!" she shouts, ditching her backpack and making a beeline for the kitchen.

I'm a few steps behind her, taking my time. The first thing I see when I hit the doorway is Vivi leaning down, arms open wide, smile bright enough to light the whole damn room.

"You're home. Finally, I missed you." There's a sound of relief in Vivi's voice.

Adeline launches herself in, and Vivi catches her like she weighs nothing, hugging her so tight I almost hear the air leave her lungs. It's not just the normal missed-you hug, either. There's a way Vivi's holding her, chin tucked into Adeline's hair, eyes closed for a beat too long, that has something in my chest pulling tight.

"How was Disneyland? Tell me all about it. I want to hear everything. Here, let's make you a snack. Are you hungry?"

"Starving," Adeline says, because she's a growing nine-year-old who's always starving.

Vivi reaches for Adeline's hand and pulls her to the kitchen.

"Can we have a movie night tonight and cuddle on the couch? All of us?" Adeline asks.

"You just got home, and I know Vivi has a busy week—"

But before I can say anymore, Vivi looks me square in the eye and shakes me off. I figured with everything she had to get done today before Adeline got home that she would be exhausted. Especially since I haven't let her get much sleep over the last few nights.

"That sounds like a great idea. I don't know about you, but I could really use a cuddle and a movie night with all of us on the couch." There's so much sincerity in her eyes, and almost...a sadness in them too, as if she's already missing nights like this with us even though we still have two weeks. "Should we send Uncle Trey out for pizza and ice cream for us?" she asks, and then her eyes are on me.

I get the hint. She wants time with Adeline, and something about it has me concerned. What happened today? I'm sure she missed Adeline, but something in the way she's watching Adeline, hanging on every word as she slices up apples and scoops a dollop of hazelnut spread on a plate for them to share, it has the look of someone who's trying to memorize every moment, every word, as if she won't have many more.

"Will you Uncle Trey? You've already heard everything in the car. You won't miss any of my stories."

Vivi looks up at me, too, and I nod. She needs this time with her, and I know that Adeline needs it too. After all, two weeks isn't going to be nearly long enough. Not unless somehow... Jameson doesn't return home and we get to keep her.

But with that push notification we both saw last night—that I guess we're not going to acknowledge exists—Jameson is already on his way home.

I head for the front door, keys in hand, armed with my wallet and demands for pizza and ice cream.

BY THE TIME I make it back, the scent of pizza and cold air clings to me, my fingers numb from carrying too many grocery bags on the same hand.

The living room light is dimmed, the flicker of the TV casting shadows across the walls.

They're already curled up together on the couch, sharing a blanket like they've been doing it for years. Adeline's head rests on Vivi's chest, her knees tucked up, the half-empty snack plate balanced on the coffee table. Vivi's fingers are moving lazily through Adeline's hair—long, slow strokes that make my niece melt against her like a cat soaking up the last bit of sun.

I stop in the doorway and just...stay there.

Not moving. Not breathing too hard. Just watching.

The sound from the TV is low, the steady rhythm of the rain against the windows even lower, and the only thing I can really focus on is how *right* they look together. Vivi's body curves around Adeline like she was made to be there, like her only job in the world is to keep her safe.

Adeline mumbles something, too quiet for me to hear, and Vivi's lips curve in a smile so tender I feel it in my chest. Her hand doesn't stop combing through Adeline's hair, slow and steady, like she's memorizing the feel of every strand.

Something in my chest twists, hard.

I've seen Vivi handle crises on the phone, reporters, and PR dumpster fires like she was born to win them, but this—this is the most natural I've ever seen her. Like she belongs here. Like she belongs with us.

And the worst part is the small voice in the back of my head whispering that she's holding on because she knows she won't get to do this much longer.

Her gaze drifts up and catches mine. She doesn't move, doesn't speak, but something in her eyes asks me not to ruin it.

Not to pull Adeline out of her arms or break the moment.

I nod once, slow, and finally step forward. The floor creaks under my weight, and only then do I clear my throat, holding the pizza box like it's the only excuse I've got for interrupting.

"Dinner's here," I say, and my voice comes out rougher than I mean it to.

Adeline perks up just enough to grab a slice before curling right back into Vivi's side, pulling the blanket up to her chin.

I sink into the armchair, the smell of melted cheese and the sight of them together wrapping around me like a vise. Two weeks. That's all I've got. And if Jameson Holiday walks through the door, I lose this. I lose her.

And I don't know if I can let that happen.

It's selfish, I know, but I'll never know unless I ask. I'll let us have the next two weeks together, letting her see what I can give her though I know what she'd have to give up to be with us isn't a small thing.

What Slade said on the jet comes back to my mind.

"Life's too short to have big regrets like letting the right person go."

CHAPTER TWENTY-FOUR

Trey

"My hair hurts," Adeline stops in her tracks as the three of us walk through the middle school auditorium that the ballet school rented for the night for the recital.

Vivi turns back to see Adeline putting her hand on the top of her head.

She takes the few steps back toward Adeline and crouches in front of her near a row of perfectly lined folding chairs, chairs that I already anticipate will kill my back tonight.

Vivi's fingers move sure and gentle while girls in tulle and glitter shuffle by like nervous swans.

"Too tight?" Vivi asks.

"A little," Adeline admits, breathless, eyes bright with the kind of nerves that are half terror, half rocket fuel.

"Okay, ballerina. Hold still." Vivi eases a pin, smooths the hair that's already perfect, and somehow makes it more perfect. "How's that?"

Adeline blinks, tests a head tilt. "Better."

I'm useless with bobby pins. I carry the garment bag, the

emergency snack pouch, and the water, and I try not to breathe too loud because every breath feels like it might knock the whole night off course. I've been to every practice, every dress rehearsal. I've tied shoes and fluffed skirts and pretended to understand what a tendu is. But this—the small, quiet know-how of fixing a too-tight bun without making her feel wrong—is the kind of magic I don't have. Vivi has it. She just...has it.

"Hey," Vivi says, tapping the tip of Adeline's nose. "Look at me."

Adeline does. Vivi lowers her voice like she's sharing a classified brief. "You go out there and you have fun. If you forget a step, smile. If you trip, smile bigger. If you feel scared, look for us... we'll be right there." She tips her head toward me, and the way she says "us" lands so deep in my chest I can physically feel her words. "You've already nailed it."

Adeline nods like she's swallowing hard. "Okay." She points a serious finger at me. "No yelling. You promised."

"I don't yell," I say, even though apparently my supportive clapping counts as "too loud."

Vivi stands, brushes glitter off her emerald dress that's pooled all around her. Tight fitting to show off her killer curves, but not too tight that it's too revealing for a little girl's recital, then reaches for my hand without looking, like it's obvious and natural and not the kind of touch that makes the whole hallway sharpen into focus. I curl my fingers around hers and feel something settle that's been rattling in me for years.

This last week has been...I don't have the word for it. It wasn't perfect, because life isn't. But it was the closest I've been to feeling like I'm exactly where I'm supposed to be. Morning coffee and her bare feet. Practice and texts that make me want to skate faster. Adeline's laugh in the truck, Vivi's head on my shoulder at midnight. The helicopter. The rooftop. Her saying I need you into my mouth like a vow.

I've already decided that I'm going to ask her to stay, and tonight, after the recital, I'm going to ask her to pick me. It's selfish.

I know it is. But I keep seeing the future, and it looks like this: Vivi leaning over to fix Adeline's bun, a hand finding mine in a crowd, the three of us eating pizza too late on a school night because we forgot how to be strict. If she wants this too, I can't let her go without asking. I'll live with the regret forever if I don't.

"We need to find our seats," Vivi says. "Five minutes to curtain."

Adeline does one last skirt sweep, then she's off with her class, a flutter of tulle swallowed by the stage manager and a mother with a headset who looks like she's about to launch a space shuttle.

We find our seats. Middle row, aisle, the good ones you get when you're the person who refreshes the ticket page at exactly a minute after twelve a.m. on a weeknight, on the on-sale date, and is willing to fight a lawyer from Bellevue for the seats. The auditorium smells like dust and hairspray. The air hums with "shh" and the thump of tiny feet backstage.

Vivi's hand finds mine again the second the lights dim. It stays there. Her thumb strokes once against my knuckle when the curtain rises.

There she is. My kid, center left, eyes scanning the dark like she's looking for a lighthouse. I lift our joined hands slightly. Vivi wiggles her fingers. Adeline spots us, beams, and I feel my throat get tight. She turns back to the audience, chin up. The music swells. They begin.

She's not perfect. Her fourth position is a little too third, and in the second phrase, she loses the count for a breath and then finds it again. But she is fearless. Grace and guts all mixed together—a mixture of Tommy and Sarah...and maybe now, a little of me. At the end of the choreography, she nails the turn she has been practicing in the kitchen for two months, lands it clean, and the little grin she tries to hide is a dead shot to my heart.

Vivi is all in beside me—applauding quietly, whispering "you've got this" to a child who can't hear her and somehow will anyway. She leans forward when Adeline crosses the front of the stage, the kind of lean you only give when a piece of you is up there. Our shoulders touch. And right then I know—if I let her walk out, I'll never forgive myself. I have to ask her to stay.

The last pose hits, music fades, applause starts. I'm careful. I clap the way she taught me. Enthusiastic but not *Trey at a playoff game*. Vivi laughs under her breath, squeezes my hand. "Proud of you," she teases.

"Of who?" I ask, but my eyes are on Adeline, who's soaking in the noise like sunlight. She was born for an audience, and I know she'll thrive in this world.

The curtain drops. The house lights bump up. Parents surge for the aisle in a way I have no interest in getting involved with. We hang back, let the rush flow. I turn to Vivi, and she's already looking at me. Whatever's been weighing on her since yesterday... It's softer now. Softer, not gone. I almost say it. I almost say, "Come home for good. Pick us."

Then the doors at the back creak open. I shouldn't be able to notice such a small change in the room considering the two hundred people moving around the auditorium and the chatter happening all around us, but I do. I was trained to notice suddenly, and the way the air shifts when danger is nearby pricks my senses. I can feel in my bones when a bad hit is coming, but my eyes find the motion immediately. A man steps inside, pausing in the shadow of the doorway like he's late and trying not to draw attention.

Jameson Holiday.

He's not in a tux. This isn't a gala entrance. He's in navy slacks and a white button-down shirt with the sleeves rolled up, and every woman who passes by him stares a little longer than they should, especially with their husbands at their side, but I know there's no threat for them. Because Jameson Holiday is only after one woman in this room ...

Mine.

He doesn't look rested. Not the kind of rested you'd assume two months in an oceanside honeymoon suite in Santorini would make you feel.

He scans the room once, taking his time, and when he sees

us, sees her, he lifts his chin a notch like a man walking into a negotiation he expects to win eventually.

The decision I made—to ask her to pick me—slides out from under my feet like bad ice.

He's here.

And everything I think I can give her, and everything I want to give her, comes with a cost she'll have to pay every day for the rest of our lives together. It's not just her company. It's a family trust, a board, siblings. Generations. Adeline can't be the reason she loses all of it. I can't be the reason she loses all of it. I can't live with her regretting me, the decision she made to give it up to live a simpler life than what she was born for, just like I can't hold Adeline back from the star she's destined to be—and I won't.

If Adeline were ever in Vivi's shoes, and she asked for my advice, I'd never let her pick the man in my shoes. The war vet who lost part of his soul the day everyone he loved died. The man who's struggling to keep it all together. A man with no family ties besides Adeline.

I'd tell her to pick the man in Jameson's shoes. The man who can give her everything she deserves. A family of means and influence, but at the very least...for good or bad, an archaic trust fund trying to marry off its generations to further gain...but still a family.

A family that understands how Vivi grew up. What she needs. What she deserves. And will take her and her business further than I ever can.

I'd tell Adeline to pick him. Because I love her...and I love Vivi.

Bitterness scrapes up, ugly and hot. I shove it down so hard my chest hurts.

"Vivi," I say discreetly.

She follows my gaze. Color drains from her face and then returns in a controlled flush like she put it there on purpose. Her hand tightens in mine. That one squeeze tells me everything—she doesn't want to go. She wants to stay. God help me, I want to let her.

"Go talk to him," I hear myself say.

Forcing the words out of my mouth no matter how bitter they taste.

Her eyes snap to me. "Trey—"

"It's okay." It isn't. "He came a long way. You should hear what he has to say. We knew this was coming."

She shakes her head, tiny, the kind that means "please don't make me." People are watching. Dance moms with big hair and bigger opinions have started clocking the joined hands, the domestic lean, the way we walked into this gymnasium earlier tonight as a family of three and will leave, broken. They see a story they want to tell later in the parking lot.

"It's too early. He wasn't supposed to come back yet," she pleads.

I do the one thing guaranteed to get her to protect herself. I make myself the wall she has to push through.

"We had a good time, didn't we?" The words taste like metal. "We're cutting it a little short, but we both got something out of this. And now he's back, and it's not like you can let Martin keep running your company. There's a lot at stake, and Jameson is finally back to help you fix everything. This is how it's meant to happen."

She goes very still. "You don't mean that."

"I do." I make my face into the one I wore in briefings when a soldier wanted a different answer than the one that would keep him alive. "This was fun. We needed it. But it doesn't change reality. We both have jobs to do, and we need to get back to those lives."

She flinches away from me as if I raised a hand at her. It cuts me deep. Right through the ribs.

My free hand balls into a tight fist, doing everything I can not to take every word back and wrap her in my arms, and tell her that I love her. To tell her the truth about what I really want—"choose me, and I will do anything to make sure you never regret it." But she will regret it. Maybe not this year, or the next, or five years down the road, but someday, the novelty of being with me will wear off. She'll resent me and the life we have, and then someday, she'll leave. It might as well be today before I've given her everything I have left.

The man in the doorway is a trust with her name on one check and her father's on another and a board waiting to eat my girl for breakfast if she hesitates.

This is protection. This is love, even if it all feels like I'm going against my own DNA. Against every cell in my body.

"Go," I say again, softer, trying to make it hurt less...and failing.

"But Adeline, and the Hawkeyes season. You don't have a fill-in nanny." She's desperate to come up with an excuse to stay, and it's breaking me not to let her find us a way out of this.

I had stopped looking for a nanny. Stupidly, I gave up on the search to find anyone better than Vivi. Maybe it's because I didn't want to find anyone to replace her. Maybe I didn't want to come to the realization that Jameson would come back. I don't know.

I come up with a lie quickly. Something I know that will push her to the edge.

"That ballet mom with the casseroles said she can help with Adeline until the Hawkeyes finish the season. Which is convenient since I guess she already knows where I live."

I force out a light-hearted snicker as if the convenience is comical, or that nothing about replacing her as a nanny is bothering me in the least, but nothing could be further from the truth. And the look in Vivi's eye says she doesn't find any of this funny.

She lets our hands fall, breaking apart. For a second, she doesn't move. Her eyes redden, but no tears fall. She won't let herself cry, not now, though I can see in her eyes that I broke something in her.

Something that's breaking in me, too.

Maybe it was hope?

Or maybe it was something even deeper than that.

"You're right," she finally says, defiance in her eyes. She lifts her chin, and I try not to draw attention to the fact that I see it wobble with emotion just a little before she reels it back in. She won't let me see how much I just hurt her... but I already know what I've done. "We both got what we wanted. It's time to face the facts of what we are and what we obviously never were. This was never supposed to last. We only agreed to the nanny position until Jameson returns, and you only offered me your bed for two weeks, and now that time is up."

The way she says it, as if all I wanted from her was sex, has me biting the inside of my cheek to stay quiet. If I tell her that I fell in love with her before I ever laid a finger on her, it will only make this harder than it has to be. I have to let her down to make sure she walks away.

When I don't challenge her assumptions, she pulls her shoulders back and turns away from me, heading up the aisle toward him like a woman heading into weather she can't outflank but will face without running.

She's stronger than me.

I sit down because my brain doesn't trust me not to run full speed towards her and yank her off her feet, tossing her over my shoulder, hauling her out of this auditorium until we reach my car. Driving her and Adeline out of this place, looking for higher ground, somewhere I can better defend from to keep her with us.

The chatter in the auditorium swells and blurs, but the blood in my ears swishes louder, the sound of my heart beating against my chest drowns out the noise. I can't watch her leave anymore. My vision switches to him. His eyes aren't on her either. They're on me.

We stand like that for what feels like eternity. No words, but we don't need any. She belongs to both of us, and neither of us at the same time, and we both know it.

Then we both cut our attention to her as she finally makes it up to him. The EXIT sign, looming over their heads, illuminating the fact that this is where Vivi exits my life.

I can't hear the words. I don't need to. I know the shape of that conversation. I know how compromise sounds when a man like him is holding the ledger.

"Uncle Trey!"

I turn. Adeline barrels out from backstage in her cover-up, cheeks pink, eyes still glittering with the high of stage lights and crowd applause. She launches into me before I can stand, all elbows and joy. I catch her and the joy cracks me right down the sternum.

"You were amazing," I say, and it's a relief to tell one true thing out loud. "The turn? You nailed it."

"I know," she says, pleased, then wiggles away enough to peer around me. "Where's Vivi?"

I look past her. Vivi's still with Jameson. He has a hand half-lifted like he's about to touch her arm and then thinks better of it. Good.

"She's...talking to someone."

Adeline follows my line of sight. Her face changes. Not confusion. Not yet. Something colder. She swings back to me so fast I almost miss the first hot tear in her eyes.

"Don't let her go," she says, fierce and small. "You have to fight for her."

The auditorium tilts. I lower to one knee so we're face-to-face. "Hey. We don't talk about fighting at a recital. Coach's rules."

She doesn't smile. Her hands fist in my jacket like I'm the one trying to leave. "She loves us."

"I know," I say. But hearing Adeline say it only makes it feel more hopeless. "And we love her."

"Then why are you letting her walk away?" Her voice cracks on "away," and it takes everything in me not to pick her up and walk straight through the wall to stop what's happening at that EXIT sign.

I can't say any of that to a nine-year-old who has so much to learn and has already lost too much. She doesn't need to think of the fact that a life with us might not fulfill Vivi. And the truth is a life with me might not fulfill Adeline either, but right now, she and I are all we have.

So I do the thing a coward does and call it protection.

"Because sometimes loving someone means making sure they don't lose themselves," I say. "Even if it hurts."

"That's dumb," she says, furious. "You're dumb. It's all your fault she's leaving us. You could have stopped her, and you didn't."

I can see that her raised voice is starting to gain attention.

Even Vivi turns to look in our direction. Though I don't think she can make out the words, the tone in Adeline's voice is coming through clear. She's mad at me.

"I can't just stop her from living her life and going back home."

"We are her home, and you messed it all up."

And then she spins around and runs for the side exit. I grab our things sitting on the chair and chase after her. I glance over quickly, seeing Vivi notice it. I see the moment she's about to chase after me and Adeline, but I hold up a hand to tell her to stop.

Not because I don't want her help, but because this is more about Adeline and me than it is about Vivi. We have to learn to rely on each other—no one else.

As I chase after Adeline in the dark and the rain, her bun starts to fall out. Symbolizing everything that's happening tonight, giving me flashbacks of seeing Vivi in my review mirror in her wedding dress, running in the rain toward my SUV.

I was going to ask Vivi to pick me tonight.

Instead, I told her to go.

Maybe at the end of the day, what I really couldn't handle was the idea that Vivi would pick me and that I would let her down. I wouldn't be enough for her with all my missing pieces, and I'd have to live with failing...again.

Like I failed John that night. Like I failed Tommy when I left him to join the Army.

Maybe the person who can't live with my own regrets and resentment...is me.

CHAPTER TWENTY-FIVE

Vivi

Every step toward Jameson feels like walking on hot coals.

Not because of him. Because of what I'm walking away from.

Trey's words are still in my head, sharp and deliberate. *This was fun. We needed it. But it doesn't change reality.*

As if that's all it was—fun. As if the last month of movie nights, the sleepovers, the secret grins, watching each other in every room where we'd pull apart didn't mean anything.

Jameson stands in the doorway. Exuding confidence from every pore in his body, no other reason than just because that's the man he is. Every woman in this auditorium is always well aware of his presence.

He's calculated but in a sophisticated and intelligent way. He didn't even step into the auditorium, as if he knew that he didn't technically belong, but his presence alone would be enough to bring me to him.

Navy slacks, a white shirt with the sleeves rolled, and hair just this side of perfectly styled—like he's run his hands through it more than a few times today. It makes him look less like the immaculate man from our engagement photos, who's been featured on Forbes magazine and is the face of the Holiday brand.

Instead, he looks more like someone who's been...moving. Busy. Distracted.

Like something has been weighing on his mind lately. And I suppose losing your trust fund, family, and status could do that to a person.

When I stop in front of him, his gaze sweeps over me. Not in the lingering, hungry way Trey does, but like he's taking inventory. Cataloging who I am in this more casual yet form-fitting maxi dress. A dress I knew Trey wouldn't be able to keep his hands off of. Not my suits. Not my gowns. Not the carefully constructed public image that certainly made Genevieve more interested in me as a match for her son. Instead, I'm dressed for a softer world. Trey's world.

One I wasn't ready to leave.

"Jameson...you're back."

"I couldn't let you have all the fun, now could I?" His tone carries a faint amusement, but his eyes are assessing.

"I'll admit, it's been a walk in the park since you left for Greece," I say, playing along. "But I suppose I can share. I'm a team player, after all."

A woman passes a little too close, her eyes darting to him. He doesn't look at her. We wait until she's gone before resuming.

"I'm surprised to see you here. I didn't think ballet recitals were your style."

He grins with a light chuckle. "No, they aren't. I just needed to see you two together," he says, and it smacks me in the gut. His tone is calm but clipped. "You and Trey. For myself."

There's a flicker of something in his eyes I can't name before he continues.

I'm about to word vomit an apology for running out on the wedding, about everything that's happened so far, though he did take our wedding planner on our honeymoon for two months. And maybe if Geneveve had let me see Jameson before our nuptials, maybe I wouldn't have ran. Maybe he could have reasoned with me like he always does, and I would have remembered all the reasons we agreed to marry. Then none of this would have happened.

But then Adeline and Trey wouldn't have happened. And as much as I'm hurting right now with how Trey dismissed our time together so quickly as a fling, I don't regret anything with him. Not a single moment, not a single touch.

But before I can utter a single word, he speaks up, taking my opening.

"I've already arranged for your reinstatement as CEO—immediately. They never should've had the power to remove you in the first place. Virginia briefed me in full. Martin Howard is gone. I personally made sure of it."

It takes me a second to absorb the speed of it. No negotiation. No request for my side. Just done.

"Gone—" I start, then stop. "You've already fired him?"

"Yes. Effective this morning. You can start back tomorrow."

It's all efficiency. No wasted words. Typical Jameson.

I glance over my shoulder at the sound of what I think is Adeline's voice coated in distress. She's standing in front of Trey, her hands in fists at her sides. I can't hear her words, but I feel them. Trey is bent to one knee, talking low, his mouth set in the grim line I've seen in post-game losses and bad news calls.

It's enough to make me turn and run to them. To soothe whatever issue she's facing and help to squash it quickly, assuring her it will all be alright and hold her in a tight hug.

I want to choose them.

But Trey's voice in my head says "Go."

And he didn't just mean to Jameson.

I glance toward Trey again, just in time to see Adeline tear toward the exit. Trey grabs their things in a panic and chases after her, his long strides eating the distance. My muscles tense to follow, but Trey catches my eye mid-chase and lifts a hand. A silent "Don't."

It's enough to root me in place.

I turn back to Jameson. My voice is steadier than I feel. "I need a ride home."

He doesn't comment. Just nods once and steps aside so I can pass.

THE RIDE IS quiet, the kind of quiet that fills with all the things you should say to the man you left at the altar and with whom you're about to make wedding plans.

Finally, I break the silence.

"I should apologize," I say softly. "For leaving. For... everything. I know I set all of this in motion."

His jaw works once before he answers. "Before Natasha came to my mother and whispered that the bridal room was empty, I had never considered having a choice."

That pulls my eyes to him. "A choice?"

"I was groomed from birth to know my mother would pick my wife. That's why I've never had a serious relationship, and I was labeled a playboy billionaire...which, fairly, I earned. But why bother with dating anyone seriously when I knew how it would end?" He exhales through his nose, steady but not entirely at ease. "I didn't pick you myself, Vivi, but my mother did a good job. I know you'll make a good wife, and I'll be a good husband to you. More than that," he continues, "I'll be a good partner. Now that I'm back, I'll make everything right."

I look at him, searching for... something. Warmth and certainty. But there's a thread of distraction there, like part of him is somewhere else entirely. However, I do believe that he means what he says. I've never heard or seen him ever go back on his word. Not on a business deal or otherwise, and we both have to face it...this is a business deal.

We pull up to my townhouse. I reach for the door handle but pause. "Is Natasha okay?"

He doesn't answer right away. "I don't know. She left Greece before I did. Didn't say where she was going. Didn't say anything at all."

The way his jaw tightens tells me it bothers him more than he wants to admit.

Before I can push further, he shifts gears entirely. Back to business as usual. Another product of the way he was raised...I assume.

"I'm going to set a meeting. You, me, and my mother. Just us. Our marriage is a private matter, no matter what the board and the trust think. We'll discuss everything that needs to be handled, though as I understand it, the wedding has now turned into a bigger circus than before."

"It's for the optics," I tell him, using his mother's tone.

He gives a humorless chuckle. He's probably as sick of hearing the word "optics" as I am.

"I'll be in touch soon."

And then he's gone, leaving me standing on my front steps, wondering if I just got my life back...

Or if I'm about to get back the life I don't want.

CHAPTER TWENTY-SIX

Trey

The worst part about leaving for an away game isn't the travel, the crappy hotel beds, or the schedule that chews you up and spits you out.

It's the silence.

Adeline didn't say a single word to me before I left this morning. She didn't even look at me when I told her goodbye. Vivi wasn't there—hadn't been since the recital—and I'm the one who made sure of that.

I told her I'd take the dance mom up on her offer to help with Adeline until the season's over. I didn't. Hell, I never even called the woman. I'd rather set the house on fire than put her in charge of Adeline. Instead, Isla and Kaenan's mom said they'd help me limp through the last couple of months of the hockey season until I can find a proper replacement over the summer break.

But none of that changes the fact that I lied to Vivi. Or that I've got a nine-year-old giving me the kind of cold shoulder you only get from someone you love.

The guys are already on the plane when I climb aboard.

Slade's across the aisle, scrolling on his phone. Scottie and Olsen got a deck of cards out. Hunters already passed out from the Dramamine with a face covered in gold eye masks. Wolf and JP are zoned out with their headphones on, and Aleksi and Luca are in a heated discussion over which restaurant in Chicago has the best pizza. I drop into my seat, nod, and put my earbuds in before anyone can try small talk.

I'm not in the mood to fake normal.

BY THE TIME we hit the locker room pre-game, I've gone through my warm-up routine twice and still feel like my body's lagging behind my head. Usually, I'm dialed in by now. Tonight? I'm skating in mental mud.

"Jesus, Hart, you look like you're heading to a funeral," Aleksi mutters, taping his stick. "Vivi got your balls in a vice these days or what?"

I glare, but it's half-hearted. "Shut up and play your game, Mäk."

He smirks like he hit a nerve. Maybe he did.

The coaches give us the usual rundown, keys to the game, reminders about matchups. I nod along, but my brain is replaying the recital. Vivi in that dress. Adeline grinning between us like she already knew we were a family. And then me, the idiot who pushed Vivi into the arms of someone else.

The thought of her in his Bellevue mansion, strutting around barefoot in his kitchen, making him hot cocoa, her things hanging in his closet, her Range Rover in his driveway, her sleeping in his bed—the thought of it all drives me fucking insane, and there's nothing I can do about it.

The puck drops, and my legs don't listen. I'm a half-second late on every read. The opposing winger blows past me like I'm a rookie—which I am, but I've never showed it like I am tonight.

By the second period, it's not just me noticing.

"Wake the hell up, Hartley!" Coach Haynes barks as I get back to the bench after a sloppy shift.

I don't even have an excuse. I just drink water and keep my eyes on the ice.

Next shift, I try to overcorrect. Throw my weight into a hit I should've just angled. The ref's arm goes up instantly. Two minutes for interference.

Fuck.

My head's not here, and I know it. It's on Adeline's silent treatment and the idea that someone other than me has his hands on Vivi.

Sitting in the penalty box, I grip my stick so tight the wood might splinter. In my head, Adeline's voice is screaming at me. *Fight for her, Uncle Trey.*

And all I can do is stare at the ice, powerless to do anything about it.

We lose 5-2.

And none of those two points had anything to do with me.

The handshake line is quick. Post-game medias worse. I give them all the standard answers. *We've got to clean up the mistakes. Back to basics. Focus on the next game.* Every sentence feels like sandpaper in my mouth.

I barely uttered a word during dinner with the team and even less by the time I get to my hotel room. I sit on the edge of the bed, Hunter, my roommate, still out with the guys, and finally pull out my phone.

No messages from Vivi.

I have no idea why I thought there might be. I don't deserve anything from her, but I was hopeful.

Two from Isla. Pictures of Adeline at their kitchen counter, covered in flour, grinning with Kaenan's mom over a plate of cookies.

I stare at the photos for too long. Relief that she's smiling, in a place with people she feels safe with and have her best interest at heart.

I toss the phone on the nightstand and lie back, staring at the ceiling. I've taken harder hits than tonight's loss, but none that left me feeling this hollow.

I pick my phone back up and scroll, mostly out of habit. That's when the headline hits me.

NEWPORT STAFFING MOGUL SPOTTED BACK IN WEDDING WORLD — VIVI ANN NEWPORT SEEN AT BRIDAL BOUTIQUE WITH FRIEND

The photo is clear enough to stab me right through the chest. Vivi, walking into a high-end bridal shop, hair loose over her shoulders, sunglasses pushed up like she's trying not to be recognized. Beside her, Yvanne is mid-laugh, holding the glass door open.

But it's the glint of Jameson's ring on her finger that sears into my brain.

She's wedding dress shopping. And my stomach wrenches at the thought of her trying on a gown for a wedding meant for anyone but me.

I zoom in. Her mouth is curved into an almost smile, but her shoulders are tense. I know that posture. It's the same one she had at the recital before she walked toward Jameson.

The article underneath speculates whether Jameson's return means the wedding is back on track, how this could "reunite two of Seattle's most powerful families." There's even a throwaway line about "no sign of Hawkeyes winger Trey Hartley, though sources say the pair had been spending significant time together during Jameson's absence."

I shut the screen off. Toss the phone on the bed hard enough that it bounces twice.

It shouldn't matter. She's not mine. She was never mine.

Later, I scroll to Isla's number and hit call. She answers on the second ring, the sound of pots clanging in the background.

"Hey, Trey," Isla says warmly.

I have no idea how much Vivi told Isla what I said to her or how we ended things, but she's not giving me any indication. She's staying neutral and I know if not for any other reason, it's for Adeline.

I appreciate her for that.

"Is Adeline around?" I ask.

"She's here. Hold on." I hear her voice lift, calling across the room, "Adeline, Uncle Trey's on the phone."

There's a pause, then faint but clear, "I can't come to the phone right now."

Never in all the away games I've played has Adeline ever missed my calls. I know this isn't because she's busy. She doesn't want to talk to me.

Isla comes back on the line, a smile in her voice. "Sorry, the girls are fingers-deep in homemade slime and glitter. Can I have her call you back before bedtime?"

"Sure." But we both know she won't.

Still, I'm relieved. She's not barricading herself in her room, refusing to talk. At Isla's, she's not the kid who just lost another adult in her life. She's just... a kid.

I cling to that, even if it doesn't make the photo of Vivi going into that bridal shop hurt any less.

"Hey, tough game tonight. Are you alright?" she asks.

"Yeah, just a bad night. I'll do better tomorrow."

We say quick final goodnights, and then we both end the call.

At least Adeline knows I called. I won't let her pull away from me too far, but I also know that she needs some space to vent, and I'm happy that she has a safe place like the Altman's to do it in.

We'll get back to normal—eventually.

We need each other. More now than ever.

Chapter Twenty-seven

Vivi

The game was brutal. I didn't mean to watch, but there I was, curled on the couch with my laptop open, pretending to work while secretly streaming the Hawkeyes feed. The announcers didn't hold back:

What the hell is going on with Hartley tonight? Worst game of his season. Coach Haynes can't be happy about this.

My stomach sank with every missed pass and heavy hit he didn't return. Whatever he was feeling out there, I could feel it here.

I push away from the counter, coffee in hand, intending to disappear into my office for the rest of the day when my eyes snag on the dry-erase board by the kitchen door.

The columns are still there.

REASONS TO MARRY JAMESON

REASONS TO STAY WITH TREY

I stare at Trey's messy handwriting under his side of the list—little things he'd added, teasing, knowing it made me smile. I pick up the marker without thinking. My chest aches, but my hand moves anyway, writing the only thing that matters. I write it in big, bold letters:

I LOVE HIM

The words blur for a second before I know I just need to get out of the house and head into my office. The one that Jameson got back for me five days ago. Everything put back in its rightful place.

I walked into the office with Virginia practically burning Martin's nameplate he covered over mine. She had my office looking exactly as I had left it by the time I walked in that morning.

Of course, I marched her down to HR that very minute and did what I should have done before I got kicked out of my CEO position. I told them to give her a raise and that she is the new client concierge. Her job is to make sure that account managers are doing their best for our clients, and if they have any requests for other services or anything we can do to make their lives easier, she's there to make sure it happens.

But she's still at the reception desk when I walk in this morning, training her replacement.

"Good morning, ladies," I say as I walk by Virginia and the new hire, about whom I have a really good feeling.

"It is a good morning isn't it?" Virginia says back as I walk down the hallway to my office, taking a deep, happy breath.

Home at last.

But it doesn't feel quite the same as it did before. And not because Martin tainted it.

In my office, I sink into my chair, fingers tapping absently on the desk, when my phone buzzes.

Yvanne

Thanks again for coming to the bridal shop with me two days ago. Was it weird? With everything on pause until you hear from Jameson?

No. I'm over the moon for you. That dress is going to be gorgeous for your wedding next year.

There's a pause, then...

Yvanne

Have you heard from him yet?

Jameson? No... but I've been so busy getting my office back on track, I haven't noticed.

It's a lie. I've been holding my breath every time a text notification comes through.

A knock at my door pulls me out of my thoughts. Virginia pokes her head in, practically glowing. She's been on cloud nine since I walked back into the office five days ago, after Jameson fired Martin.

"Cullum Lawson is here to see you," she says, bright and chipper.

"Great. Send him in."

I stand, smoothing my skirt, and come around my desk to shake his hand.

"Thanks for coming on such short notice."

"Anything for Hartley," he says easily, then glances down.

"Finally, he put a ring on your finger. Guess Hartley's not as stupid as he looks."

I blink. "I'm sorry...what?"

"He proposed, right? Between you and me, I thought he was going to propose that night on the helicopter the way he talked about you."

"Engaged...to Trey?"

"Aren't you?" He tilts his head, like he's genuinely confused. "The man's in love with you. Pretty much told me you were the one without actually saying it. He said you were out of his league. But you know Hartley...he's not great with words."

"Right..." My voice comes out slow, dumbfounded.

Callum smiles like he hasn't just detonated my afternoon. "Well, how about a walking tour? I can show you the plans for your new security systems."

"Callum...my security clearance last week..." I start, giving him a chance to say it without me accusing.

He grins. "Trey told me to keep an eye on you no matter what happens to him. *Matter of national security*, he said. When your brother pulls in a favor like that, you don't ask questions. He and John extracted me and my unit out of one of the deadliest nights I've ever seen. They were told to turn around, and they disobeyed orders to get us out. I owe him my life and the lives of five other men. There's no favor he can't ask."

He leans. "Might have hacked into your systems last week... maybe." He winks.

"Cullum, last thing. My current security team. They've been loyal to me..."

"No problem. With a little training we'll have them up to par. No one gets let go—I understand."

Callum leaves me with a thick folder of blueprints, a list of installation dates, and a head still buzzing. I walk him out, exchange polite goodbyes, and then shut my office door behind me.

The room feels too quiet.

I sit back at my desk, but the spreadsheet open on my monitor blurs. My brain keeps looping over his voice.

The man's in love with you.

Told me you were the one.

Trey, who hasn't called. Trey, who pushed me toward Jameson with a cool, steady voice, as if we'd been nothing but a passing fling. Trey, who, apparently, went out of his way to make sure someone he trusted had eyes on me no matter what happened.

I press my fingers to my temples, trying to make sense of it. He didn't tell Callum he loved me. Of course he didn't. But Callum's the kind of man who reads between the lines for a living.

The clock on my desk ticks louder than I remember it ever doing before. I force myself to answer three emails, skim through a vendor proposal, and sign off on payroll. It's busy work—just enough to keep me from spiraling out of control, but it doesn't work for long.

By the time I shut down my computer, the sky outside my office windows is streaked with pink and gold. The building is quiet on the eleventh floor. Virginia slipped out an hour ago, humming under her breath about date night.

I grab my bag and pause at the doorway. Scanning the hallway of empty offices and an empty front reception. My life is back in place, but the feeling of loneliness settles over me during after-hours.

It should feel like enough.

Instead, all I can think about is a man who isn't here, the little girl I should be going home to make spaghetti with and braid hair before bed for, and the three little words I scrawled on a dry-erase board this morning like a confession I'll never be brave enough to say out loud.

CHAPTER TWENTY-EIGHT

Trey

Adeline hasn't looked me in the eye since I got home yesterday from out of town.

Not at breakfast, not in the car, not when I asked about ballet practice. Just one-word answers here and there and the sound of her bedroom door kicking closed behind her. At least she's not slamming them anymore.

I told myself to give her space. She's a kid, not a soldier in my unit. She doesn't need me pushing her to talk before she's ready.

But the truth? I hate it.

Hate the silent treatment from her more than any injury I've ever played through.

I'm mid-set at the gym, the clang of weights from the other guys in here with me and the smell of sweat sharp in the air, when my phone buzzes with Isla's name. I don't think, just answer.

"Hey, what's up?"

"Trey..." her voice is tight, almost shaky. "It's not me. It's Kaenan's mom. She went to pick up Adeline from school..."

Something cold threads through my veins. "What about her?"

"She... she's not there."

The dumbbell in my hand drops to the mat with a dull thud. "What do you mean she's not there?"

"They called her out for early dismissal, but she never came out. The principal, Berkeley, and Kaenan's mom have been looking for her for twenty minutes. She's not on the grounds."

My vision narrows. My heart's in my throat.

"What do you mean she's not there?"

"Her teacher said she was in class the entire day. She left with all the other students out to the sidewalk for pick-up, but no one else has seen her."

"Fuck," I curse.

"I'm on my way to the ballet studio to see if she went there. Kaenan is headed to your house to see if she got a ride home." I can hear Isla's voice getting shaky. "Can you check the stadium? Maybe she went there?"

"Jesus..." I say, a fear I've never known radiates through me. "Yeah, I'm here, I'll check and then I'll meet you wherever you are. Just keep me in the loop, okay? We're going to find her, Isla."

I tell her to keep my cool, but I have no idea if we will.

"What's going on?" Slade asks, the rest of the guys starting to circle.

"Kaenan's mom went to pick up Adeline. She wasn't at school. No one has seen her since class was dismissed."

"We'll help. Where do you want us to check?"

Everyone runs for their keys and duffel bags. A group of my Hawkeyes family ready to disperse at the drop of a hat.

"I don't know. I'm going to check the rink and see if she came here."

Slade starts to bark out locations to each of the guys.

"I'm starting a text chain. Give your location and a confirmation if you find her," he tells them.

In minutes, we're all running out of the gym. I see Penelope and Cammy racing out of the elevator too. They must be on the text thread.

"I called security to tell us if Adeline shows up here," Cammy yells to me, and then she and Penelope are out the glass doors.

But there's only one person I want to call right now.

I scroll through my contacts as I race to the rink, though it's too far from the school unless she took a taxi. Still, I have to mark it off the list. I have to know she's not here.

I hit dial on Vivi's name, and it only rings once before she picks up.

"Trey...you called. I've been wanting to—"

"Vivi, I'm sorry. I know we have a lot to talk about, but I need your help right now."

"Of course, what is it?"

"Adeline's missing. Kaenan's mom went to pick her up. She left the school or was taken from the school. No one's sure."

"Oh my God, Trey." The panic in her voice evident.

I take a deep breath and admit what I should have at that recital. "I need you, Vivi. I need you to help me find her."

"Of course. I'm in my car right now. I'm turning around." I hear the squeal of her tires. I don't know if she just flipped an illegal U-turn in the middle of the road, but whatever she did, she wasn't waiting.

"She's been so mad at me for letting you go. She wanted me to tell you not to leave with Jameson. It's been a week of silent treatment...and then this. I just don't know where she would run off to."

There's a gasp on the other line. "I know where she is."

"Where?"

"Meet me at the library. I'm only three minutes away."

I drop my duffel bag and run full steam until I'm in my SUV, cranking the engine and peeling out of the parking lot.

I find a spot on the curb, making it to the library in record time. And that's when I see her—Vivi.

Racing down the street from wherever she found a parking spot too. She doesn't see me yet, but somehow, seeing her, I know we're going to find her. She'll never give up until we do.

I jump out of my SUV and run towards the front door of the library. Vivi barely beats me there. She yanks open the door, and I grip it to keep it open until I can come through.

"The kids' section. Where her mom always used to take her. She said it's the safest place she feels."

We don't even say "Hi" or "Hello" or "How are you doing?"

We both have one goal and one goal only.

To find our girl.

Vivi

WE CLATTER DOWN the library's front stairs, Trey's heavy footsteps beside me, both of us getting shushed by the librarian. Neither of us slows down.

Halfway to the children's section, I spot her—dirty blonde hair peeking out between two low shelves. I throw an arm out across Trey's chest.

He halts, frowning. "What? Why are you stopping me?"

"She's right there," I whisper, pointing.

I glance up at him, and the relief that flashes across his face nearly undoes me. My throat feels tight.

God, I want to kiss him. After everything—after thinking, even for a moment, that we might have lost Adeline—the adrenaline is one thing, but it's more than that. It's clarity. The most important thing in the world to me is right here. Him and her.

Hearing Callum say Trey was in love with me...that he thought Trey might propose... It has me seeing him and a future with him differently. But the reality is still messy. I still have my company to fight for. My life's still riddled with complications.

Right now, there's only one priority. Adeline.

"Give me a minute with her, okay?" I whisper.

He nods, but tension rides his shoulders. Every part of him is itching to scoop her into his arms. I know because I feel the same way, but if she were running from him and came here, seeing him won't have the reaction he wants.

He exhales. "I'll text everyone and tell them we found her."

I nod and step toward her aisle, careful not to rush.

At the end of the shelf, I pause. "Hi there."

She jumps, eyes wide, until she recognizes me.

"Vivi."

"Fancy seeing you here." I keep my tone light, my voice just above a whisper. "Looks like it's my lucky day. Mind if I come sit with you for a second?"

Her face lights up. Until she glances past me and spots Trey through the opening in the bookshelves. He has his head down, thumb moving over his phone.

"Oh. You brought him?"

I ease down onto the carpet across from her, the colorful spines of picture books lining the shelves between us. She's curled up in a beanbag, knees tucked, a book open in her lap but clearly unread.

"You had everyone worried sick, you know," I say gently.

Her cheeks turn pink. "I didn't mean to."

"I know." I rest my elbows on my knees, leaning in a little. "There are a lot of people who care about you, and everyone just wants you home safe."

Her eyes flick toward Trey's shadow at the end of the aisle. "I ran away because he wouldn't listen to me. You two were happy," she blurts. "You were holding hands, and cuddling, and flirting with each other..."

I bite back a sigh, my heart tugging. "I know. And I'm sorry if we confused you. Sometimes adult stuff is...hard. It doesn't always go the way you think it will."

She frowns—trying to understand but not liking the answer.

"We didn't want to hurt you," I continue softly. "I'm sorry if we did. But Trey isn't responsible for me going back to work. And..." I hesitate, then decide gentle honesty is better than letting her guess. Besides, she knows about the wedding I ran from. After all, she aided and abetted, although technically I didn't commit a crime. "I made a promise to Jameson. One I need to talk to him about. That doesn't mean you and I can't still hang out."

Her head lifts a little. "You mean we could still have movie nights? And come to the library together sometimes?"

"I think maybe you, me, and Uncle Trey could sit down next week and make a plan that works for everyone, so that you and I could still spend time together. What do you think?"

"That could be good." She pauses. "Do you think Jameson will let you come over, though, if he knows that you and Uncle Trey are in love?"

The air between the shelves stills.

My eyes lift—almost against my will—and there's Trey. Already watching me. His phone hangs forgotten in his hand.

He heard her. Of course he did. And he's not looking away. His gaze is steady, searching...like he's waiting for my answer. Or bracing for it.

My pulse thuds in my ears. For a beat, I forget we're in a library. Forget we're in the middle of a missing-child search.

I turn back to her, my voice quieter than before. "I guess I'll have to talk to Jameson about that. But for now...how about we focus on dinner, bath time, and homework before bed?"

"Okay," she says, a little disappointed but knowing that's the best she'll get after running away.

I glance back at Trey. That's his cue.

He steps closer, crouching down at the end of the aisle. "Hey, squirt. Can I have a hug?"

Adeline gets up, crossing the space between them. Her arms wrap tight around his neck. "I'm sorry I ran away."

"And I'm sorry this has been hard on you," he mumbles against her temple as he squeezes her tighter. "Just talk to me next time, okay? We only have each other. We have to work things out, even when we're mad."

I hate the way he says only *each other*—because I want so badly to be part of that we.

"How about pizza at Isla's?" Trey offers. "She texted me. Wants to give you a big hug. She's just happy you're okay. They're ordering for the search party."

"Can Vivi come?" Adeline asks.

Trey glances at me, his expression unreadable. "She's welcome if she doesn't have other plans."

"I would love—" I start, but my phone pings. I glance at the screen in case it's someone from the search.

Genevieve

I will be hosting a brunch tomorrow at my house to discuss wedding plans with you and Jameson. See you then.

"I would love to..." I start again, softer. "But I have a long day tomorrow and need to get a few things done. Rain check?"

Adeline's disappointment is obvious, and I see it in Trey's eyes as well, until he hides it from me. Burying like the true soldier he is.

"Okay. Rain check," she says, then turns toward the door.

Trey moves to follow her, but stops, waiting for me to catch up.

"Thank you for today," he says quietly. "I wouldn't have thought to look here. You know her better than anyone. I owe you."

"You would have, Trey. Give yourself more credit. She's loved without conditions or expectations...that means more to a little girl than you realize."

"That sounds like experience."

I nod. "Everything my father ever gave me or Isla came with strings."

"But you grew up with money and opportunities. We grew up differently."

"Maybe," I say. "But I stopped taking my father's help when I was in high school. That's why I took Genevieve's deal to marry

Jameson. So that I wouldn't have to ask my father for the money. My father's goal is to control everyone within his wingspan...and it's a long wingspan. Both Isla and my mother moved on without us once they found other men to take care of them. You might have grown up with less money, but no one has a perfect childhood. And mine wasn't charmed either."

"I didn't know any of that."

I shrug. "Adeline hasn't had it easy with her parents' passing, but at least she's loved freely by you for just existing—without parameters."

We walk out together, all three of us, before splitting at the curb—me in one direction, them in the other. A perfect metaphor for the life I'm living. And I'm tired of it.

And then I remember something. "Trey...the Range Rover," I say, of the car he bought for me when I didn't have one.

"Keep it," he says, turning back to look at me. "I'll sleep better at night knowing that there's one thing of yours they don't own."

I know he didn't mean for that to hit straight to the heart. But it does.

He's the only man in my life who has given me something with no strings. No ulterior motive. He gains nothing except for peace of mind that I'm taken care of in some way.

And he's right. They own too much of me.

But I guess he does now too. He owns a part of me that I can never offer Jameson.

CHAPTER TWENTY-NINE

Vivi

Genevieve's text had been short, sweet, and laced with the kind of power-play punctuation only she could manage.

"I will be hosting a brunch tomorrow at my house to discuss wedding plans with you and Jameson. See you then."

Wedding plans.

As if the last month hadn't been a dumpster fire I was still trying to stomp out in heels.

By the time I make it through the gates and up the sweeping driveway, I've told myself three times that this is just business. My life has been one long series of brunches with people who smile while sharpening the knife under the table anyway. I should be used to this by now.

The house smells like furniture polish and some flowers that she probably has flown in on a weekly basis for her floral arrangements. Money well spent, I'm sure all her garden club friends would say.

Sunlight pours in through the floor-to-ceiling windows, catching on every gilded frame and piece of crystal. My heels are barely off the marble foyer when I hear laughter coming from the sitting room.

I follow it, bracing for Jameson's smooth politician's smile and Genevieve's measuring eyes.

But when I round the corner...

My feet stop.

So does my breath.

Jameson is on the white settee, elbows on his knees with a smirk, my father in an armchair with a satisfied smile as if his negotiation tactics worked again. Both of them staring back at Genevieve as she pours herself a cup of tea.

"Well, this was all a surprise but you're right, the board will agree. It's all worked out and we should celebrate," she says. "Jameson, I still expect an elopement in the South of France. Everything's already set and promises have been made to sponsors and the press. And you will play your part as the groom perfectly."

"Of course. There's just the matter of the bride," he says. "She hasn't agreed."

"She will. Let me know if I can help in any way," my father says.

The sight of my father is an unwelcome addition to an already miserable venture.

I clear my throat, and then all eyes are on me.

The world tilts in the space of a heartbeat.

Genevieve is positively glowing, all but clapping her hands as if the universe just handed her the most perfect brunch centerpiece. "Darling, come in. We have news."

"Vivi," Jameson says, setting down his cup of tea and rising.

"I see the planning is underway without me. Already with the celebration. I should have guessed. Between the three of you, I suppose I was unneeded anyway. You can go ahead and send me the flight details for France. No point in my staying any longer as I see I must have stepped in on your celebration."

I turn as if ready to stomp off.

"Vivi, wait," Jameson says, heading towards me. "I need to

talk to you privately."

I debate heading for the exit, anger bubbling at the thought that my father got his way in the end. Controlling everything he touches. I stand there instead because I still control myself, and I won't allow my emotions to get the best of me.

Jameson walks up to me. He looks tired almost, but unlike when I saw him at the ballet recital, there's a softness to his eyes this time. Almost as if relieved.

He walks to me and gently puts his hand on my arm. "Can we talk for a second?"

I nod and follow him as he leads me down the hall of his mother's opulent home.

The moment he stops and turns around to face me, I stop too, crossing my arms over my chest protectively.

He takes a deep breath. "There's a lot to tell you, and also so much I can't say yet."

"How about you start with our wedding plans. That's all I really need to know. I won't run away this time," I tell him.

He gives a soft smile. "I believe you, but I'm not sorry that you did in the first place."

My eyebrows stitch together. This is not what I thought was about to happen. "I don't understand."

"You're in love with Trey Hartley, aren't you?"

"How do you know that?"

"I saw the way he looked at you when I showed up at the ballet recital. And I saw the way you looked at him."

"Jameson...it doesn't matter how I feel about Trey. I'm here now. I'm ready to get married and do what we agreed to."

"There won't be a wedding, Vivi. At least...not between us."

I stare back into his eyes. Searching for what he means.

"But I just heard that Genevieve still expects the wedding in France? The press? The sponsors? I heard her say, 'This calls for a celebration.'"

"There will be a wedding. Or at least I hope there will be. But first, I have to find Natasha and propose. If she'll still have me."

"I'm so confused. You showed up six days ago at my ballet recital to tell me that we were getting married. When did this happen? How did this happen? I..."

I'm in such shock that I let him lead me out of the room.

"I can't exactly tell you everything. Not until I talk to Natasha first."

"I don't get it. What happened in Greece? I thought she hated your guts."

He laughs. "She did at first. It's a long story. I offered her the money she lost on the commission to come with me. She didn't want to come at first, but she needed the money."

My stomach sinks at the idea that I'm the cause of Natasha having to agree. "I cost her that commission she needed for medical bills. She must hate me," I say.

"She doesn't hate you. But she agreed to come with me, and I used her as a threat to my mother. That if she tried to drag me back to the US before the honeymoon, I would flaunt Natasha in front of every paparazzi I could. I thought that if I had enough time to get the deal in Greece done before I had to come back, I could use it to buy the trust and the board out of requiring us to marry."

I nod. At least that part makes sense, and I place my hand on my forehead, hating how I cost her that commission. "I got her fired, didn't I? And she really needed that money."

He pulls my hand from my forehead. "It's fine. You don't have to worry about her. I've got her taken care of," he grins. "Despite my being an ass to her by taking out my frustrations about the wedding on her trying to plan it, I fell in love with her in Greece, and I need to find her and tell her."

"You could have mentioned these plans to me so I could have...I don't know, been at least supportive. I was here getting berated by two sets of board directors and your mother."

"Well, I had to stand up in front of four hundred people while my bride ran off with the left winger for the Hawkeyes."

I suck in my lower lip. "Okay...we're even."

He chuckles, and then I smile. A little weight lifting off both of our shoulders.

"My plan was to convince the hotel chain to sell to me, and I was going to use the deal to leverage the board to let us both out of the marriage. Even your father showed up and helped me close the deal."

"My father came to Greece to help you?"

"He sensed why you were marrying me. I guess your mom and Isla both gave him hell at the wedding that you, entering into an arranged marriage, was his fault. When you wouldn't return his phone calls, he flew out to find me to convince me to call off the engagement. He didn't know how deep you and I both were into it."

"So that's why he was overseas and not at Berkeley's birthday party. He was with you in Greece."

"I'm guessing so. He did a deal years ago with the CFO, and he's the one who got us a meeting with the owner."

"And Natasha?"

"I convinced her to fall in love with me. It took a while," he grins. "The board will see it my way soon enough. You're off the hook."

"So that's it then. You and I are free?" I ask, a smile wanting to break across my lips, but I'm too scared to believe this is all true. That I'm free to be with Trey and Adeline.

He nods. "But you and I are still business partners, so we'll be seeing each other around."

I leaped forward and hugged him. Something he and I have never done before unprovoked by a press camera.

"Thank you. I can't even tell you how relieved I am," I tell him, fighting back tears.

"We're better business partners."

I nod. "You'll make some lucky girl an amazing husband."

"I just hope Natasha thinks that, too."

"She will," I nod. He gives a warm smile, and I realize just now...I think Jameson and I might have just become friends.

Which should work to my advantage when I need help getting

Richard to reinstate me. If Holiday Industries puts him back in his position, he'll have the power to put pressure on Newport's board of directors.

"Your father is the one who made this happen. Without him, I wouldn't have closed that deal. He's also the one who made me realize that I needed to fight for Natasha no matter what it cost."

"He did?"

"Maybe talk to him? I don't know what you two went through, but he didn't have to show up in Greece. He loves you, Vivi."

"Here," I say, pulling off his ring and handing it back to him. "This is hers now."

"Thanks. I already bought her a ring I chose myself. If she agrees to marry me, we're going to start new traditions."

I smile. "I like the sound of that."

I hear footsteps behind me, and I turn to see who it is.

It's my father.

"Hi," he says.

"Hi," I say back.

"You haven't returned my calls."

"I thought you were going to berate me for running out on my wedding."

"I just wanted to help."

"You went to Greece to help Jameson close that deal so I wouldn't have to marry him. I thought you wanted the Newport/Holiday family merger. I don't understand why you would have helped Jameson get out of it."

His expression softens. "Because I love you. The moment you ran out of that wedding, I knew something was wrong. And your sister and mother laid into me at the wedding, saying it was all my fault. That I put too much pressure on you. That you were marrying Jameson Holiday to make me happy."

"But you were happy. You sent me seven dozen roses to my townhouse when you heard about the engagement."

"Those roses I sent were an attempt to be supportive. I wanted you to know that I will always support your choices. I didn't do that for Isla, and I regret that still to this day."

My throat tightens. "This merger is your dream, though."

"I'm tired of being on the outside of your life, Vivi. Looking in, but never getting the relationship with you that I want because of the mistakes I made with you...and with Isla. I'm not that man anymore, but you won't let me prove it to you, and I don't blame you. That's why I tried to stay away. I thought maybe someday, you'd come to me when you were ready. When you got engaged, I thought if I supported you instead of telling you I was worried you were making the wrong choice—like Isla almost made because of me—you'd let me close again."

I swallow. "So you went to Greece to help Jameson?"

"Yes. I thought if I could help him get the deal done, you'd be off the hook. You weren't taking my calls, but Jameson was more than happy to let me in."

There's a pause, and then he says quietly, "I know about Trey. Isla told me and asked me not to screw this up for you."

I laugh. "She is very protective."

"And I know why you two have had to be for each other. You know that I grew up poor. I built everything on my own, and the best gift I thought I was giving you girls was to make sure that you made the best business decisions you could make. I thought I knew what was best to protect you, and I've been wrong so many times."

"I know you love me. I just want a father, not a business partner."

He nods. "Can we start fresh?"

I nod and step forward, wrapping my arms around his neck.

"I am proud of you, Vivi Ann," he says, and then I think of Trey. The nickname he always uses.

Genevieve finally peeks in her head. "Everyone okay here?"

We let go at the same time, but the healing has already started. We both nod at her.

"Well, I still have brunch available if anyone is interested. We may not be family now, but I have a sense that this will be a long and successful friendship between our two families.

My dad nods, but I pipe up. "Actually, I have someone I need to go see."

Jameson leaves to grab a jet to go find Natasha, and my father follows Genevieve back into the living room. They're already discussing a new venture together, but I have somewhere else to be too.

Now I just have to see if the man I love and the little girl who has my heart still have room for one more.

CHAPTER THIRTY

Trey

Adeline's been quieter than usual all evening.

Not the cold, locked-behind-a-door quiet she had last week. This is softer—like her mood's gone gray around the edges and she doesn't know how to pull herself back into color.

I lean against the doorway of the living room, watching her curled into the corner of the couch, knees tucked under her chin. She's flipping channels without actually watching anything.

I clear my throat. "What do you think about hot cocoa night? Extra whipped cream. Marshmallows the size of baseballs. And maybe a Disney movie with a talking animal sidekick."

Her mouth twitches at the corner. "Only if I get to pick the movie."

"Done."

That earns me the smallest of smiles. Good. I'll take it.

In the kitchen, I pull out the cocoa ingredients that I've tried to memorize. Milk, cocoa powder, nutmeg, cinnamon, sugar, and...I try to remember the last one by memory, but it doesn't come to me. My hand hovers over the cabinet where I shoved a folded scrap of paper weeks ago. Vivi's hot cocoa recipe. She'd rattled it off like it was nothing—like it was just sugar and cream and cinnamon. But I know better.

I take a look at the list. Oh right...vanilla.

There's magic in the way Vivi does everything. It's in the way she stirs without looking, the way she hums when she "eyeballs" the measurements, the way she always hands you the first mug like she's been waiting all day to see your reaction. You can't write that kind of magic down.

Still, I pull out the pot and set it on the stove. I head to the fridge and grab the whipped cream and then the marshmallows out of the pantry. Even the peppermint sticks Adeline loves. I line them all up on the counter. Maybe some part of me is hoping—hell, *needing*—to be ready if Vivi ever walks back through that door.

I'm measuring out the cocoa when there's a knock at the door.

It's too early for the Chinese we ordered in, and I'm not expecting anyone. My stomach does something strange—tight and light at the same time.

I try not to get my hopes up. For all I know, it's just a neighbor asking to borrow a cup of sugar.

When I open the door, my world tilts.

Vivi's there.

Her hair is in a ponytail, catching the light from the porch, eyes bright but steady. She's not dressed for a meeting or an event—just jeans...and my jacket.

She doesn't ease into it. Doesn't give me a chance to breathe before she speaks.

"I hope I'm not interrupting anything," she says, nibbling down on her lower lip as if there is anything in this world she could interrupt.

"You're not. Adeline and I were just about to start a movie, and we ordered food."

"The engagement's over," she blurts out. "Jameson is proposing to Natasha...or is going to try to? Or..." She shakes her head as if she's getting off course. It's cute when she's flustered. "I'm not actually sure what's going on, but I don't care. Either way, what it means is that the wedding is off. And I love you. I want to be here. With you. With Adeline. No deals. No deadlines. Just... us, if you still want me."

For a second, I just...stand there. The world's narrowed to her voice and the cold air at my back.

She stands there, breathing like she ran a marathon searching my face. "Did I miss my chance?"

Finally, I step forward, my hand braced on the doorframe. "Vivi, do you have any idea how long I've wanted you? Since the first day my eyes locked on yours the night I met you at Oakley's. Hell, since the second you climbed into my SUV without knowing it was me, I've been in love with you, even if I didn't fully understand that yet. You've been it for me. But I thought you deserved better."

"Better than you? What in this world is better than you?" she asks, her eyebrow stitching together as if there is no reasonable answer.

"I've been holding back because I didn't think I was whole enough to give you what you deserve. I've been broken for a long time. My childhood, growing up alone, losing John, abandoning Tommy...life has a way of carving pieces out of you and not giving them back. I thought the best thing I could do for you was keep my distance. Let Jameson give you the life you were raised for. A life you deserve."

I step closer, close enough that I can smell the faint hint of her perfume. A smell I've become completely addicted to.

"But I was wrong. I realize now I'm whole with you. You carry the part of my soul I thought I'd lost for good. You're what makes this house a home. You're the missing piece of our family. Without you, it's just me and Adeline surviving. With you, we're living. You complete us, Vivi. You're my heart."

Her eyes are shining now, tears balanced but not falling. "Trey..."

I cup her face, my thumbs brushing her cheeks. "I love you.

I'm not letting you go again. If you'll have me, I'll spend every day making sure you never have to wonder where you belong."

She smiles through the tears. "I already know that I belong with you."

So I kiss her. Soft, at first—just the barest press of lips.

A test. A promise.

And when she melts into me, my hands slide to her back, and I pull her closer, deepening it until there's nothing between us but the thud of my heart and the warmth of her mouth.

When I pull away, my forehead rests against hers. "You're home now. That's all that matters."

A small voice cuts in. "Told you that you two were in love."

We break apart to find Adeline leaning against the hallway wall, a smug grin on her face.

Vivi laughs, a wet little sound that makes my chest ache. "Hi, sweet girl."

Adeline bounces on her toes. "Are you staying?"

Vivi glances at me, and I nod. "Yeah. She's staying. This is her home now."

I motion toward the kitchen. "I was about to make hot cocoa, but I realized even if I had your recipe written down perfectly, it wouldn't taste the same without you. So how about the three of us make it together?"

Adeline lights up like it's Christmas morning. "Yes."

Vivi's smile wobbles. "I'd like that."

We spend the next half hour in the kitchen, shoulder to shoulder, the scent of cocoa and cinnamon wrapping around us. The empty Chinese food takeout containers we share together litter the island as a reminder that this house is lived in with a family that loves each other.

Adeline is in charge of marshmallows—three for her mug, two for mine, and three plus an extra one for Vivi's. Vivi stirs while I warm the milk, her hip brushing mine every so often like she's reminding me she's really here.

When the mugs are ready, we pile onto the couch, Adeline

tucked between us under a blanket. She picks the movie. Something animated and loud, but I barely register it. I'm too busy memorizing the feel of Vivi's knee against mine, the way her fingers curl around her mug, the sound of Adeline's quiet giggle when Vivi adds more marshmallows to Adeline's mug when they think I'm not watching.

Halfway through, Adeline leans into Vivi's side, eyelids drooping. Vivi looks down at her, brushing hair off her face with the gentlest touch. My throat tightens because I know, without a doubt, this is what I want every night for the rest of my life to look like.

When the credits roll, I carry Adeline to bed. She mumbles something about extra marshmallows in the morning and is out before I can answer.

Back in the living room, Vivi's still curled under the blanket, her mug empty, eyes on me.

"I meant what I said," she whispers. "I love you. And I'm not going anywhere."

I drop to one knee—not for a proposal, not yet—but because I need to be level with her. My hands wrap around hers, thumbs stroking the backs.

"I've been through battles, injuries, and the kind of loneliness that makes you think you'll never feel whole again. But tonight, with you and Adeline in this house...I've never been more certain. You're it for me, Vivi. The life I want, the family I need, the home I never thought I'd have. You're all of that."

Her eyes brim again, and this time the tears fall.

I kiss her hands, one by one. "Stay. Build this with me. I don't care about the rest of it. The company, the past, the mess we started in. We'll figure it all out. Just...stay."

She nods, laughing softly through her tears. "I was hoping you'd say that."

And when I pull her into my arms again, the world finally feels right.

CHAPTER THIRTY-ONE

Trey

Six Months Later

The day after Vivi walked back into my life, with Jameson's engagement ring nowhere in sight and her first words to me being *I love you*, she moved into my house like she'd always belonged here.

I know because I physically drove her back to her townhouse the next morning and packed every suitcase I could find in her house full of her things and hauled it all back to my walk-in closet that is now ours.

We didn't make the move one hundred percent official. Her townhouse was still her house, technically. She kept some clothes there, used it as a workspace when she needed to focus without me or Adeline interrupting her, and...yeah, we definitely christened every surface in that place over the past six months. The townhouse became our unofficial love shack and her occasional home office.

Over the last six months, she hired a new CFO whose priority is employees first, clients second, this time. She and Jameson successfully restructured the board of directors' power, knocking them down a notch and requiring at least higher vote percentages from the stockholders before making the kind of decisions they did with Vivi's CEO position and Jameson's position as the head of Holiday Industries.

Jameson and Natasha used the already perfectly planned elopement in the South of France. The press had a field day, eating up the Cinderella type story that, of course, Genevieve and her PR team spun. Genevieve got the optics she wanted, and the billionaire playboy narrative was officially dead.

Though as hard as Jameson and Genevieve have tried, they still haven't been able to get the trust fund lawyers to agree to abolish the arranged marriage stipulation for Jameson's siblings.

Two months ago, Vivi called the realtor. Last week, she signed the papers. And tomorrow, the new owners take possession of her townhouse.

Today is the final moving day.

The driveway is packed—my SUV, Vivi's Land Rover, Slade's truck, and the moving van our friends rented for the day. The Hawkeyes turned up in full force, boxing, hauling, and cracking jokes. Vivi bribed them with pizza, beer, and her triple-fudge brownies, which probably explains the speed of the loading process.

By early afternoon, the van is full, half the stuff already headed to a storage unit, the rest bound for our house. When the last load gets driven off, the place feels hollow. The walls echo.

Our friends say their goodbyes in the driveway, loud and full of plans for dinner later this week. Adeline hugs everyone twice. Then the last truck pulls away, and it's just me, Vivi, and the townhouse she's about to hand over for good.

I should've proposed earlier, maybe back when she told me she loved me in my doorway. But I held back. Partly because I didn't want her to feel like she was trading one engagement for another. Partly because I wanted to make sure that when I did it, I did it right. Because Vivi deserves my best effort.

But the longer she goes without my ring on her finger, the

more I can't figure out why I haven't just done it already. Frankly, if I could go back in time, and I know what I know now, I would have proposed to her the night we met in Oakley's...before Genevieve arranged everything with Jameson. But maybe we both needed to go through that to know that this is right between us.

Maybe it all happens for a reason.

And I'm not letting any other asshole have the chance to put a ring on her finger.

"Adeline's over at Isla's for the next few hours," I tell her casually as she drops the last box onto the kitchen counter. "She wanted to give us time to...I don't know... 'say goodbye to the old place,' as she put it."

Vivi grins, pushing a strand of hair behind her ear. "Sounds like your niece has been talking to my sister."

"Maybe." I lean against the counter. "Or maybe she just knows her uncle has a plan."

Her eyes narrow as if she knows I'm up to something. "A plan?"

Instead of answering, I walk to the far side of the kitchen, where the old dry-erase board leans against the wall.

She notices immediately. "Trey... you didn't."

Oh, I did.

On the left side I erased her list the same week we decided to be together, but I kept mine up there to remind her of all the reasons I'm the right one. And every once in a while, I add something to it, which always makes her laugh.

The list keeps on growing with more items.

Adeline needs you

We like your cooking

I can't imagine the house without you

But there's a new one at the bottom, in red marker:

Because I want you to be my wife

Her lips part, breath catching. "Trey..."

I take a step closer. Then another.

"I've been holding this in since the day I met you," I say, my voice low but steady. "I wanted you before I knew your last name. I wanted you before I knew how much you'd change my life."

I stop right in front of her, my hand lifting to tuck that same strand of hair back again.

"I'm whole because of you, and now I need to be able to look up in those season ticket seats and know that the last name you wear on your bedazzled jersey is yours too."

Her eyes shine, and I know I've hit the truth dead-on.

I pull the ring from my pocket. Not one that screams "society engagement," but the one I spent two weeks designing with a jeweler downtown. Simple, timeless, still WAGs size approved, and hers.

"Vivi Ann Newport, will you stay with us forever?"

She laughs through a sob. "God, yes."

I slide the ring onto her finger. It fits like it was always meant to be there.

She's in my arms a heartbeat later, kissing me like she's trying to make up for all the time we wasted not saying what we really felt.

When we finally break apart, I mutter against her hair, "You know, I was going to bribe you into staying a little longer."

Her lips brush my jaw. "Oh really? With what?"

I grin. "One last hurrah upstairs before we lock up."

Her answering smile is pure mischief. "Lead the way, Hartley."

I don't lead. I scoop her up, her laugh ringing through the empty townhouse as I carry her up the stairs two at a time.

The bedroom door swings shut behind us, and the rest of the world disappears.

EPILOGUE

Vivi

Five minutes until I marry the man I love.

The bridal suite is bathed in gold from the afternoon sun streaming through wide-open French doors. A breeze carries the scent of peonies, garden roses, and lilac—the bouquet I chose, in my colors, with my florist. Outside, laughter drifts in from the lawn where guests sip champagne under white parasols.

This isn't Genevieve Holiday's ballroom in February. It's a sunlit villa in July. My day. My way.

The mirror reflects a woman in a sleek, form-fitting gown with a low back and a sweep of silk that hugs every curve. The kind of dress I always pictured, without layers of tulle to hide behind. My hair is loose, the way Trey likes it, and my veil is delicate lace that catches the light.

When I lift my hand, the diamond on my finger glitters, sending a shiver up my spine. Not a "disco ball of bad decisions." This ring makes me feel alive every time I see it. Chosen by him. Worn for him.

"Much better," my mom says from the doorway, her dark eyes

warm as they roam over me. "You look like you." Then, with a teasing smile, "I know I said there's always a wedding number two, but I didn't think you'd take me up on it so soon."

I laugh, my chest light. "Well, you were right. Again."

Behind her, Isla and Yvanne bustle in, both in soft champagne-colored dresses. Isla's cheeks are flushed from herding people, and Yvanne's hair is pinned in a sleek twist that screams competence even at a wedding. Adeline trails behind them in a dress that matches theirs, her bouquet of baby's breath clutched in both hands. She beams at me like she's keeping the world's best secret.

When they leave to join the procession, I turn to my mom. "I want to see Trey."

Her brow lifts. "You know it's bad luck."

"I think we've had enough bad luck to last a lifetime."

She chuckles and disappears, returning moments later with him—though his palms are slapped dramatically over his eyes. "I can't look. I've got a superstition to uphold."

My heart hammers. "Trey Hartley, get over here."

He takes two steps, still covering his face. "You're not getting cold feet, are you? Because if you are, just tell me. I'll be the guy in the running SUV waiting in the parking lot. Your getaway driver for life."

I cross the room, hook my fingers around his wrists, and tug his hands down.

His jaw goes slack. His throat works around a swallow like he's forcing back tears. "Vivi... you look..." The words fail him.

"I just wanted to see you before we say I do."

"I'm glad you did." He steps closer, voice low. "Anything you want today, it's yours."

I take a breath. "Can I have John's tags? I'd like to honor him today. After all, he's the reason you're here with me."

He nods, pulls the chain from beneath his tux, and hands it to me. I wrap it carefully around the silk-bound stems of my bouquet, just like I told my florist I would. I planned it all along, but I wanted to ask him in this moment.

"There," I say, looking up at him. "Now we're ready to get married."

"I love you, Vivi Ann Newport."

"I love you too."

THE MUSIC SWELLS outside, the signal it's time. My father's arm is warm and steady as I loop mine through his. He grins down at me, pride radiating from every line on his face.

As we step onto the sunlit aisle, the world narrows to one man waiting at the end. Trey's broad shoulders square when he sees me, but it's his eyes—shining with unshed tears—that hit me like the first time I realized I loved him.

Every step forward feels like a piece of the past falling away. No running. No doubts. Just the sun on my skin, the bouquet in my hand, and the man who makes our house a home waiting for me.

This is the healing all of us needed.

And this time, I'm walking straight into forever.

BONUS SCENE

Vivi

Nine Years Later

Our house is louder than ever—though at the moment, it's not from the two toddlers running around. They're finally asleep upstairs. No, the noise right now is from the cluster of people crammed into our living room, all here for the same reason: to celebrate Adeline's high school graduation.

She's standing in the middle of it all, grinning in her cap and gown, her long dirty-blonde hair twisted up in a bun that looks suspiciously regulation-friendly. I know because she's been practicing it for months.

She's going into the Army. My first baby—the one who made me a mom before I even knew I was one—is following in her uncle's footsteps to become a helicopter pilot.

When she told us, Trey's jaw went tight, his eyes bright with pride and something more protective than I've ever seen in him. That's saying something. He hugged her so tight she squeaked, then promised he'd be at every graduation ceremony, pinning ceremony, and flight demonstration she ever had.

Now he's leaning against the doorframe, arms crossed, watching her open cards and gifts. There's a shine in his eyes that has nothing to do with the overhead lights.

I cross the room to him, sliding my arm around his waist. "You okay?"

"Proud," he says simply, voice low so only I can hear. "Scared too, but...mostly proud. She's got the same fire as Tommy had, the brains too."

"And your determination and heart," I add.

He nods, his eyes still on her. "I think Sarah and Tommy would be over the moon to see who she's become."

That gets me.

"She's going to be incredible," I tell him. "She already is."

The younger two—Jacob and Chloe—chose that moment to come thundering down the stairs in their pajamas, faces lit up like they'd just been handed cotton candy. Jacob's clutching a crayon drawing of a helicopter, and Chloe's holding a stuffed hawk that Adeline bought her for Christmas last year.

"For you," Chloe says, shoving the hawk into her big sister's arms. "So you won't forget us."

Adeline laughs, eyes glassy, and promises she never could.

Later, when the house is finally quiet and the dishwasher hums in the background, Trey and I step out onto the back porch, Trey sitting on the outdoor sofa, me taking a seat next to him and curling my legs up. He sets his arm over me, his thumb making gentle sweeps over my thigh as he stares out into the sky. The June air is warm for Seattle. And then he looks down over at me, and I get the same goosebumps he always gives me.

"Nine years," I say. "And somehow, you still look at me like I'm the runaway bride who jumped in your SUV."

"That's because you are," he says with a crooked grin. "The only difference is...now you're also the woman who gave me two more kids, made this house a home, and somehow still makes the best hot cocoa I've ever had."

"Even though you've tried to copy it a dozen times?"

"Even so," he says, brushing his thumb over my hand. "I think it's the magic."

We sit there until the stars come out, talking about the future—about visits to Adeline on base, about Jacob starting hockey next year, about Chloe in karate for balance and body self-awareness, as Trey always says.

I think about the girl I was nine years ago, running in the rain away from a life that didn't fit, straight into the arms of the man who would become my everything.

Some stories start with an escape.

Ours just never stopped being worth the chase.